IN THE WIND

A NATE VIGIL THRILLER

CONOR BLACK

GENRE MONK LLC

Published by Genre Monk LLC, Sacramento

ISBN ebook edition: 978-1-961205-01-7

ISBN paperback edition: 978-1-961205-02-4

ISBN hardback edition: 978-1-961205-03-1

Publisher's Cataloging-in-Publication data

Names: Black, Conor, author.

Title: In the wind / by Conor Black.

Series: The Nate Vigil Thrillers

Description: Sacramento, CA: Genre Monk, LLC.

Identifiers: LCCN: 2023914609 | ISBN: 978-1-961205-03-1 (hardcover) | 978-1-961205-02-4 (paperback) | 978-1-961205-01-7 (ebook)

Subjects: LCSH United States marshals--Fiction. | Witnesses--Protection--Fiction. | Mafia--Fiction. | Murder--Fiction. | Texas--Fiction. | Thrillers (Fiction) | Mystery fiction. | BISAC FICTION / Thrillers / Crime | FICTION / Action & Adventure | FICTION / Mystery & Detective / Amateur Sleuth

Classification: LCC PS3602 .L33 I6 2023 | DDC 813.6--dc23

IN THIS ADVENTURE

A stray bullet kills a wind farm worker and the Sheriff says it's an accident. "Wrong place, wrong time," according to the locals. But to Nate Vigil, it looks like murder.

There are secrets buried beneath the wind generators in Carlin, Texas. Worth billions to an evil man if he can keep them hidden. The only problem? He didn't count on Vigil showing up.

They never do.

FROM THE PUBLISHER

Meet Nate Vigil

BADASS BY BIRTH
DRIFTER BY CHOICE
VIGILANTE BECAUSE JUSTICE REQUIRES IT

Trained since childhood to survive the societal collapse his ex-Special Forces father believed was imminent, Nate Vigil wanders across America to see for himself the state of the nation and the character of those who call it home.

But a man with a code inevitably crosses paths with conmen, criminals, and the corrupt . . .

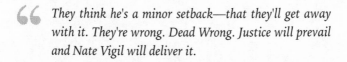 *They think he's a minor setback—that they'll get away with it. They're wrong. Dead Wrong. Justice will prevail and Nate Vigil will deliver it.*

WHAT'S IN A NAME?

The father of this book's protagonist has an interesting name. It contains an anagram: *Lance Vigil → Vigilance*. As to whether or not this was accidental on the part of his parents, records are scant.

Our hero, Nate Vigil, also has an anagrammatic name: *Nate Vigil → Vigilante*.

I am quite certain this was intentional.

~ Conor Black

CHAPTER
ONE

"**D**amn, dude. You're fuckin' *jacked*."

Vigil looked up from the paperback he'd been reading. He was leaning against the wall outside a 7-11 (not standing in the locker room of an NFL football team, or beside a dumbbell rack) so he was fairly certain the jacked dude in question was him.

Statistically speaking.

And sometimes his imposing physique actually worked in his favor.

The guy who gave him the compliment was holding a latte and standing beside a red Tesla over by the ice machine. He was about 5-foot 8-inches and tan. He wore slacks with a short-sleeve dress shirt; both tailored. A stainless steel Tag Heuer watch encircled his wrist. On his feet were shiny black shoes that would be far too slippery in a physical altercation. He looked reasonably fit. In a Tom Cruise sort of way. Trim. A little more muscle in his biceps than was useful, and a little less in the hips than serious labor would require. Big smile, like a salesman. Unnaturally white teeth.

Vigil said, "Thanks. Nice car, by the way—you mind if I

have a look? I've never seen one up close." Which was true. Vigil didn't know if it was a trait common to Tesla owners, or the fact it remained a relatively rare car, but he'd never been offered a ride from someone driving an electric vehicle.

The guy beamed. Probably a new purchase, and he hadn't yet tired of showing it off. "By all means. Let me give you the tour."

They talked cars for a while. Vigil mostly listened, because how much did a guy with no driver's license really have to say to an obvious car enthusiast? But also, people loved talking about themselves. Ironically, the more you let them talk, the better they liked you. And if they liked you, it was easier to hitch a ride. This wasn't Vigil's primary motivation for being a decent human being, but it was a nice side effect.

The guy spoke fast, but Vigil managed to interject and introduced himself. They shook hands. His name was Franky Bloom. He was a sales rep for a gym equipment manufacturer (which put his earlier compliment in context) and he was eager to make up for the hit he'd taken during the pandemic.

After touching on the Tesla's 0-60 times, and range, and recharging, Franky gave him an in. "What do you drive?—wait, let me guess:" He pointed to a black Dodge Ram 3500 that had been lifted a few inches. There were enough stickers on the back glass to fill a cork board at a country convenience store. Fox and ARB and Magnaflow and K&N Performance and a dozen other performance parts manufacturers Vigil hadn't heard of. He shook his head.

"No?" He scanned the lot for other possibilities, but the only vehicle remaining was a Nissan Leaf. "Surely not the Nissan," he said mockingly. "A tough guy like you?"

"I'm more of a boot guy," Vigil said, and nudged his pack with the side of his black leather tactical boot for emphasis.

"Oh . . ." Franky said, taken off guard, and not the kind of guy who talked to vagrants. Though—to be fair—Vigil didn't look like any kind of a bum. "Are you local?" he asked, recovering. "Or are you on your way somewhere?"

"I'm headed to Austin. Joe Rogan's new comedy club opens soon. I could use a good laugh."

Franky said, "I have appointments in Dallas—would that help you out?"

"Close enough for government work," Vigil said. "If you're offering."

"I don't usually . . ." Franky paused in a way that said *never* (Tesla owner, after all). "But what the hell—let's roll."

FRANKY BLOOM WAS THE KIND OF GUY WHO MADE everyone feel like they'd grown up next door to him. Best of all, he didn't ask Vigil about his childhood. They talked business and fitness. Hunting and sports. Vices and women.

Franky had gotten his start in San Diego as a personal trainer. Tired of helping gold digger divorcees slim down to woo their next ~~unsuspecting victim~~ wealthy beau, he became a GNC franchisee. Opened his first store in Ocean Beach and quickly expanded to Pacific Beach, Clairemont, and Del Mar, California. "The thing about supplements though? On the retail end of it? Pretty fuckin' low margin." So after a trip to the Arnold Classic six years ago, he cashed out and made the move to gym equipment. High end stuff. Huge margins. And having worked out all his life, he knew exactly how to win over gym owners. Besides, he hated all the headaches of running a business. And dealing with inventory? Fuck that, in particular. He stuck with sales and hadn't looked back.

Vigil told him about leading hunting expeditions in

Montana with dot-com billionaires. About spearing wahoo in the Florida Keys and fighting off a couple tiger sharks that had tried to steal his kill. Said absolutely nothing about doing bad things to bad men for good reasons. When asked what his obviously effective workouts were like, he shocked Franky with his calisthenics-centered routine, and his reliance on elk and bear meat over creatine or exogenous hormones.

"You're really natty?" He asked incredulously.

"I mean, I'll carry small boulders or logs up a mountain now and then."

Franky shook his head. "They need a disclaimer on The Declaration of Independence," he said. "All men are created equal—*my ass.*"

Vigil wondered if he'd upset him.

Franky changed the subject, "So are you just taking a break before your next big thing? Or have you gone full nomad?"

Vigil shrugged. "I like to wander."

They rode in silence for a while—true silence, because his Model S sure as shit didn't make any noise. It was like a sensory deprivation chamber on wheels. Like floating through the vacuum of space, or surfing a kaleidoscope of butterflies.

There wasn't a lot to see in that particular stretch of West Texas—unless you had an infatuation with scrub brush and a penchant for dust—so Vigil took a nap. He liked naps. He was good at them and could fall asleep pretty much anywhere. No eye mask, no ear plugs, no pills required.

It was the stench that woke him, and because of it, Vigil didn't even need to open his eyes to know they'd already taken I-20 at the split and veered northeast into oil country. It was a sulfur smell. Laced with benzene and notes of diesel exhaust, with undertones of cancer. It made his eyes water, and a mockery of the Tesla's famed "Bioweapon Defense

Mode" air filtration. As far as the eye could see in all directions were oil wells, their resident "thirsty bird" pumps swilling crude from deep within the Permian Basin. But it was the flaring pipes that accompanied the wells that generated the noxious fumes. Apparently, it was cheaper to burn the natural gas byproduct than it was to capture it.

"Geezus. Smells like New Jersey lit a fart around here," Franky said.

Vigil said, "I'm surprised this shit's even legal."

"Right? Good thing nobody lives out here."

"No one over seventy. That's for damn sure."

"I'm not gonna lie," Franky said. "I didn't buy this thing because I'm tryin' to save the planet. I bought it because it smokes Porsches off the line and humbles Ferraris in the quarter mile. That said, I'm glad it's helping us get off fossil fuels. I think if more people saw how the sausage is made, demand for greener alternatives would grow in a big way."

Vigil nodded. It definitely seemed like there should be a cleaner way to power cars. But for all he knew, the fancy batteries they put in electric vehicles polluted in their own ways. He wasn't a scientist. "You ever come through here at night?"

Franky shook his head.

"I did once. It was surprisingly beautiful. Like a desert of flaming cactuses."

"Speaking of go-juice, we'll have to stop at the Super Charger in Midland."

"Deep in enemy territory," Vigil said jokingly.

Which turned out to be prophetic.

THE TESLA CHARGING STATION WAS IN THE LOT OF a popular extended stay hotel chain, adjacent to a Love's truck stop. Eight parking spaces with eight charging kiosks. The kiosks vaguely resembled standard gasoline pumps at a fuel island, but were more futuristic, as if they'd been designed by the artists at Pixar who worked on the WALL-E movie. It was a practical setup. Convenient—were it not for the three Super Duty pickups parked end-to-end blocking access to the chargers.

"Fucking pricks," Franky said.

"Oil men." Vigil said. Not that it needed to be said. All three trucks had auxiliary diesel tanks in the bed and cell phone signal extenders mounted to the cab. Hallmarks of oilfield trucks. The bumper sticker slogans were simply redundant, probably intended to rile up white-collar coastal elites passing through on the interstate:

AMERICAN OIL FROM AMERICAN SOIL.

THIS TRUCK DOESN'T RUN ON PIXIE DUST AND UNICORN PISS.

DRILL BABY, DRILL.

Franky said, "We've only got another fifty miles of range. That's not enough to make it to the next charging station."

Vigil undid his seatbelt. "I'll take care of it."

He got out. The trucks' owners were nowhere to be found. Maybe they were in the hotel, peeking through the curtains and giggling like children. Maybe they were pounding hotdogs inside the truck stop. Or maybe they were laying down in the seats of their trucks, waiting to start some shit with an angry Tesla driver. *One can hope.* He approached the white truck at the front of the blockade. The one parked over the handicap spot, and therefore, the one most deserving of Vigil's wrath. He peered in the window to check

14

for someone hiding inside. If there was, he'd drag them out first—for their own safety.

By their hair.

But the big Ford was empty. Vigil strode around the hood to the curb. Turned away from the truck and faced the charging kiosk. Then he crouched slightly and leaned his weight into the vehicle, midway between the front and rear axles. Got some bend in his knees, allowing the slight convex shape of the body panel to rest in the arch of his lower back. Next, he straightened his legs, squatting against the truck like a strongman or a powerlifter. The Ford rocked sideways on its suspension. Not much—not at first—but after Vigil piston-ed into it a few more times, it was really rocking. He kept at it. Timing his thrusts to coincide with the helping hand of gravity and momentum. The truck was seesawing now. Aggressively. Like a sumo wrestler was shagging a Biggest Loser contestant in the backseat. Soon, the passenger-side tires inched off the ground. Soon after that they were bouncing. Vigil gave it one final, forceful shove and the Texas-sized truck toppled over on its side. What music it made! The wind chime *clink* of broken glass on pavement. The snap-crackle-pop of splintering plastic. And the metallic crumple of sheet metal never meant to bear a load. It was the sound of satisfaction.

He called over to Franky, who'd remained in the car, said, "It's a little tight, but you should be able to skirt around and plug in."

All Franky said was, "Dude." Then he maneuvered the Model S into position.

By now a small crowd of people from the Love's had congregated. Some of the onlookers were clapping. Others rooted for Vigil to dole out the same justice on the other two trucks. And he would have, save for two developments:

First off, his quads were on fire—not solely from tipping

the truck, but also from the residual fatigue of his morning workout. Second, six pissed-off oil men had stormed out of the hotel lobby, and they were trotting at an impressive clip for bow-legged roughnecks wearing cowboy boots. Two of them were brandishing handguns. This was Texas after all.

He told Franky to stay in the car and lock the doors.

"Fuck that, bro. I got your back. And a black-belt in Taekwondo."

Vigil shrugged. *It's the thought that counts.* He held up a hand like a traffic cop, said, "Put your guns away, boys. You ain't gonna use 'em."

All six oil men skidded to a stop. They were panting from their short sprint.

"I wouldn't bet yer life on that, asshole. Who the fuck do you think you are, messin' with a man's truck?" The guy thumbed the hammer back on his .357 Colt like an exclamation point conveyed in shit-kicker sign language. He wore a white straw cowboy hat and was shirtless underneath. "Don't Tread On Me" was tattooed on his right pec under a coiled rattlesnake. On his left pec was a Confederate flag. Completing the redneck trifecta was Japanese Kanji inked across his potbelly—loose translation: "Please don't let me impregnate you." Vigil had seen captive chimps draw with a steadier hand.

Crimes against artistry aside, the real sin was the amount of force applied to the trigger by the oil man's grease-stained finger. If the guy had been holding a Smith & Wesson of the same caliber, Vigil might not have been able to force a smile. S&W's tended to have a much lighter trigger pull from the factory.

Bad Tat stepped closer, but remained out of reach. "Somethin' funny about gettin' shot in the face?"

"In broad daylight?" Vigil nodded his head toward the

onlookers. "That many witnesses? I mean, you look pretty stupid, but there's no sense in winning a prize for it."

The guy's face flushed red. He didn't lower the Colt, but the big gun wavered a little.

"What's the matter?" Vigil said. "Your arm gettin' tired? I'd save your strength if I were you."

"Why's that?"

Vigil said, "You're obviously too weak to roll the truck upright by yourself. But if all six of you Dallas Cowboy cheerleaders lean into it, you might have a shot. Who knows? Resting your arm could be the difference."

The roughneck lowered his gun.

"Of course you'll have to wait until my friend's finished charging. Unless you wanna push it further this way?"

The six oilmen exchanged bewildered looks. In no universe did they imagine their prank turning out like this. It had to be humiliating. Six blue collar laborers—two of them armed—dressed down by a couple dudes riding in a damned Tesla. And to add insult to injury, three of the spectators were filming it on their smartphones. The whole sad scene would go viral. They'd never live it down.

Vigil gave them a moment to mull over their quandary: Walk away and get laughed outta Texas? Or retaliate and go to jail? While they bumbled their way to the obvious conclusion, he worked out how to thwart the only chance this might go south for him and Franky.

The other oilman with a gun—a Glock 19—was a wiry cat with a mustache he shouldn't have bothered trying to grow. He said, "You're real tough with all these people recordin'. But what happens when we follow you faggots outta here to somewhere more secluded?"

Franky spoke up before Vigil could answer. "You get a glimpse of our taillights for about ten seconds before we disappear over the horizon—and those piles of garbage you call 'trucks' redline and blow a seal."

Vigil was impressed. Outrunning them was a lot smarter than the plan he'd come up with. That said, he wanted to teach these dipsticks a lesson. Because even though they undoubtedly enjoyed their "free-dumb" enough to stay out of prison, their pride wouldn't let this go forever. *And what about the next electric car driver who comes through?*

Dirt Lip with the Glock said, "Ya think so, pretty boy? 'Cause you know what's faster than your little plastic toy there, don't ya?"

Vigil knew (even if Franky didn't), and it was all the encouragement he required. These shit-birds needed humbling.

"What's that?" Franky said, teeing him up.

Dirt Lip sneered. "The high velocity rounds comin' out the barrel of my deer rifle. So unless yer Tesla can teleport, I'd say we can keep up just fine."

"*Except . . .*" Vigil said with an almost weary calm.

"Except what, asshole?"

"I'm taking your keys. Then you're walking back inside the hotel, locking yourself in your rooms, and praying I don't decide to kick in the door and give you a permanent disability. While you're in there, cowering like the pussies you are, I'll park your trucks over in the Love's lot. Out of the way. Maybe I'll deflate the tires with the valve stem. Maybe I'll slash the sidewalls with my pocket knife. Depends how sincerely you apologize for wasting our time."

Dirt Lip tucked the nine-millimeter into his jeans. Bad Tat had already decocked and stashed his revolver; he crossed his arms and a genuine look of confusion came over him. The other four roughnecks puffed up their chests and grinned like the idiots they were. The one wearing a Bud Light ball cap said, "It's six-on-two. Not so good at math, are ya?"

"You'd be surprised," he said. "Take subtraction—"

Vigil lunged forward and fired a straight right hand into Dirt Lip's pointy chin. His head jerked down and back and his tiny brain bounced against the inside of his skull. Then he crumpled, one arm spazzing out zombie-style, which Vigil used to hold him up as he grabbed the Glock from his waistband. He let him fall, releasing the pistol's magazine before pulling back the slide and clearing the round from the chamber. Gun empty, Vigil pivoted and flung the composite weapon like a frisbee into Bad Tat's face. His nasal cavity cratered with a sound even more pleasing than the Ford rollover—like someone stepped on a tortilla chip in a racquetball court. Blood volcano-ed from his ruined nose, splattering from his forehead to his man boobs. His knees buckled and he toppled over right on top of Dirt Lip. Vigil relieved him of the Colt, released the cylinder, and extracted the rounds. Then he three-pointed the weapon into a nearby dumpster.

"Six minus two equals four. I've mastered that operation. You guys wanna watch me multiply now? Find the lowest common denominator?"

The Bud Light advert held up his hands, said, "Nah man. We're good. Come on boys, let's go back to the room."

Franky said, "You're forgetting something."

"W-w-what's that?"

"An apology."

"*W-w-we're s-sorry,*" they stuttered in unison.

"And your keys," Vigil reminded.

They handed over two sets and fished out Bad Tat's from the pocket of his Wranglers.

"Your IDs, too."

They didn't argue.

"I'll be monitoring the local paper. I read anything about blocked charging stations or vandalized electric vehicles, I'll

19

show up on your doorstep and fuck you up in front of your wife. We clear?"

The oilmen still capable of answering nodded their heads.

"And pick up your trash," Vigil said, gesturing to the magazine and the .357 rounds and their unconscious friends. "I hate litter."

CHAPTER
TWO

YESTERDAY IN CARLIN, TEXAS

J ustin Lackey ended the call and cursed under his breath. Betsy cocked a ragged ear and whined like old dogs stirred from sleep are wont to do, then nodded off again on her bed at the end of the couch. Hank Bondurant's father had stroked out last night and Hank wouldn't be coming in to work today—or the rest of the week, for that matter. He was already at DFW, waiting to board his flight to Kansas City (Missouri, not Kansas, though Hank always pronounced it "Misery," which seemed likely because it wasn't Texas).

He brought up the contacts app on his phone and stared for a good long while at the only initials in the list. Part of him thought he was clever that he hadn't spelled out LG's name, but that was just cheesy spy movie bullshit, and Justin knew it. Everyone around here, especially in his line of work, knew who LG stood for. The man's name was on half the buildings in Carlin for chrissake (the new ones, at any rate).

LG paid Hank under the table every month, same as Justin. Hence the trouble: Hank's sub wasn't in on the scheme. Worse, it was the new kid. Fresh out of college. None of the other wind jockeys in Justin's twelve man crew had much more than a high school diploma and maybe a little trade school. Will? An Electrical Engineering degree. *Waaayyy* overqualified for wind farm maintenance tech, but he was the son of some suit way up the food chain at Innova-Gen, destined for big things, and learning the company from the proverbial janitor's closet all the way up to the board-room. Hell, you had to respect it. And Will Prosser was a good egg, too. Interned for the past three summers and took all their abuse with nuthin' but a smile and the occasional eye roll at their incessant hazing.

The problem was the work order. An inevitability, Justin knew, but the timing was shit. Yesterday evening, before he rolled out, he'd watched over Velma Kline's shoulder in the control room as she typed the order into the Trello board. "Investigate Inefficiencies - Possible Drain" she'd titled it.

Oh, it's more than possible. It's a goddamned absolute fuckin' certainty.

At the time of its construction in 2009, the Carlin Wind Project was the world's largest wind farm. Thirteen years later, it was now the second largest, but still the most profitable. This despite suffering more than its fair share of output anomalies, which by no coincidence, spiked in 2012 after LG launched his side hustle.

Justin and Hank had become experts at "diagnosing" these irregularities and assigning blame to all the usual suspects: fiberglass debonding on the blades, worn gears, corroded instrumentation and electronics, etcetera. They'd "fix" the issue by performing the specified maintenance, and then—most importantly—let LG know which tower field to reduce his draw from temporarily. Except now, with Hank out for a while, Will would be eager to showoff his schooling.

Justin finally tapped LG in the contact list and nearly

pressed the blue call icon, too. Again, he balked. It was six o'clock in the mornin'. LG was a cold sunnuva bitch. Justin would rather call his ex to inform her of a late child support payment than this. But if he didn't call, and Will stumbled into LG's thing, it would be *his* ass. Hank's, too, when he got back from the funeral.

He set the phone down on the falling-apart flea market coffee table and stood and tried to think of another way. He didn't get very far—because really—what was there to think about? His little shit-box doublewide had a leaky roof, three cracked windows, and a mold problem. Lone Star lager stained the carpets; the beagle had, too (though it was never her fault), and he was pretty sure a possum had breached the skirting and given up the ghost in one of his walls. All the same, Justin was keen on occupying the residence until he could upgrade to one of those shipping container kit homes the YouTube algorithm kept serving him videos about. And without LG's monthly contributions, new digs were nothing more than a wild-ass fantasy.

He put the call through.

LG picked up on the second ring. "Shoot."

"Hank's out for the week."

"And?"

"The college kid will have to fill in . . . the one with the Electrical Engineering degree."

"Is he gonna be a problem?"

"Ordinarily, no. But we got a work order queued up concerning an errant draw." Justin didn't need to tell him that, this time, the usual culprits would be ruled out quickly (assuming Will had actually paid attention in class).

"Youse guys still using channel seven?"

"Six."

"I'll be listening," LG said. "He starts poking around where he shouldn't, give me a heads-up. I'll be close by."

"He's a pretty smart kid but I'll do my best to distract him."

"Good. You did the right thing callin' me. And Justin—"

"Yeah?"

"Maybe don't stand too close to him today."

IT TOOK THREE TRIPS BACK AND FORTH FROM THE equipment shed to load all the gear: Heavy things, like the hydraulic torque wrenches and tensioners, and lighter stuff, too, like the extra diagnostic equipment Justin barely ever used. Will was channeling his inner comedian the entire time.

"Lackey," he called out from the other side of the cage as Justin initialed the checkout log.

"Quit being so fuckin' chipper. Ain't even had my second cup of coffee yet."

Unfazed, Will launched right into another joke. "So an old bull and a young bull were hangin' out together one morning on a hill, and the young bull says to the old bull: 'Let's run down to the pasture and fuck a cow!' The old bull just snorts, says to the young bull: 'Nah. Let's *walk* down to the pasture and fuck *all* the cows.'"

Justin chuckled. He'd heard that one before—from his granddad—but today he'd decided to laugh at all of Will's jokes, even if they weren't that funny, and that one wasn't bad.

They double-checked the two canvas tool bags in the bed of the Chevy. The more distant towers were miles away and having to backtrack for a forgotten screwdriver was frowned upon, not to mention annoying.

"We good, partner?" Justin knew they had everything, but

part of breaking in a new technician was getting him confident, starting with the simple daily routines.

"Affirmative. Can I drive?"

"Fuck no, rookie." They got in the cab. Justin smelled something nasty wafting out from Will's cooler and asked him what he packed for lunch.

"Your ol' lady made me sardine sandwiches before I kicked her out this morning."

Justin whistled like he'd seen a large buck, said, "You let that mean ol' sow sleep next to you after rollin' off, you're a braver man than me."

They turned onto FM-608 (in Texas, the FM stood for "farm to market") and Justin pegged the accelerator. It was the only paved road along their route until they got to Highway 84. Smooth and straight as a ruler snake. The Silverado hit ninety before he slowed for a stop sign. They'd start in field 307b, eighteen miles north and west of the town of Carlin, otherwise known as Schnell's Farm, because Schnell, a cotton farmer, leased Innova-Gen the land. Schnell leased LG a little piece, too. Unofficially.

Will said, "You hear about the train derailment in China that killed a hundred people?"

"Nope."

"Well, since China's a communist dictatorship, all their trains are run by the government, right?"

"Right."

"A big tragedy like that happens? They can't take the blame. So they hold the train conductor responsible. Sham trial. Death penalty. The conductor goes to their version of death row. But get this: Dude survives *three rounds* in the electric chair. Three fuckin' jolts so strong it dimmed the lights in Shanghai."

"No shit?"

"I shit you not. And you wanna know why?"

Justin was fairly certain Texas had switched to lethal injection. *But just in case:* "Do tell."

"He was a bad conductor," Will said solemnly.

Justin rolled his eyes. "Christ, Prosser. Sure you don't have any bastard kids running around somewhere? 'Cause your dad joke game is strong. Now spare me the knee-slappers until we get there, I'm tryin' to drink this coffee without spraypainting the dash with it."

Schnell's modest farm house was at the southeast corner of the property on FM-4134. Justin turned left well before they got to it, onto FM-4133 which formed its western boundary. There were five turbines on Schnell's two hundred and forty acres. Three towers on the B-Line, and two on A. He pulled off onto the access road. No gate to mess with because cotton farmers didn't run cattle. Will already had the laptop open.

Justin put the Chevy in park, said, "Slam on the brakes."

Will clicked a button and the nacelle—the big box mounted to the top of the tower—spun clockwise until the rotor was no longer facing into the wind. Aerodynamically hobbled, the hub brakes engaged and it only took a minute to nix all rotation of the turbine's three massive fiberglass blades.

"Will, why don't you do a radio check on the GMRS before we get harnessed. Tell them we shut down 307b-005."

"The Control Center knows where we're at. They can see it on SCADA." SCADA stood for Supervisory Control and Data Acquisition, and was a software package wind farms used for sensor monitoring, remote control of the turbines, and maintenance schedules.

"We've been having issues with one of the signal repeaters," Justin said. "I just wanna make sure Nelson fixed it like he said he did. The lazy fuck."

"You shouldn't be so hard on him. Afghanistan, remember? PTSD."

"Shut the fuck up, frat boy. He was the best man at my wedding. You should hear what I call you when you're not around."

Will powered up the radio, turned the knob to Channel 6, and broadcast their status and location. A tinny, static-filled approximation of Velma's voice answered in the little speaker, "Copy that, Nepo."

"What's 'Nepo' mean?" Will asked.

"It's short for 'nepotism.' Now you know what I call you."

They buddy-checked each other's climbing harness from carabiner to strap stitching and then made their way to the base of the tower. Justin let Will take the lead, scanning neighboring farms for LG's Ford King Ranch pickup while Will wasn't looking, and watching for glints of sun or subtle movement that might reveal the man himself. He saw nothing and no one, though LG could have been camouflaged pretty well in the smattering of trees that ran along a creek bed to the east of the field.

"You remember the code?" Justin asked.

Will called out each digit as he punched them into the security panel: "1-8-7-2-4-3-1-1." It was a long code because it provided access to every single one of the Carlin Wind Project's six hundred twenty-seven turbines. The lock clicked and he pulled open the man door and they entered the giant tube to begin their climb.

"Don't forget to—" but Justin saved his breath because Will had already placed the lock on the emergency shutoff lever. Even though they'd already taken the turbine offline, the lock prevented another tech from turning it back on accidentally while they were working. Justin turned his attention to the logbook. Wrote: "Routine maintenance / investigate possible drain," for the description. Referencing the number from the work order in the appropriate column, he dated and initialed it. "I'll let you climb up and lower the crane."

"Gee, thanks," Will said.

Justin watched him clip onto the climb-assist cable that ran parallel to the first of three ladders. It would take Will a few minutes to climb the eighty-odd meters to the nacelle and lower the hook. He safety-checked the attachment and then walked back out to the truck.

He scanned for LG again. The surrounding cotton fields were flatter than his Junior prom date's chest and he could see all the way to the ice wall that surrounded this flat Earth (thinking of Nelson again, who *wasn't* lazy, but *was* crazy, and truly believed that kind of conspiracy theory nonsense). *There he is.* On the roof of Schnell's barn, a man was leaning up against the weather vane. Half a mile away. Far enough that Justin wouldn't have seen him if he hadn't been actively searching.

Had to be LG.

Who else would be glassing him through a rifle scope?

THEY WERE EATING LUNCH ON THE TAILGATE WHEN Will said, "I don't think the drain's on our end."

Justin sat downwind from him so he didn't have to smell the oily reek of those goddamned fish. "We still have two more turbines to check. My experience? It's always the last place you look."

Will nodded. He had that earnest, yet somewhat skeptical expression Justin had come to read as: *'I hear what you're saying, but my four-year degree taught me things your trade school only whispered about in hushed tones.'*

And he's not wrong, Justin thought. "Well let's hear it. You obviously have a theory."

Will swallowed the last of his sandwich and licked mayonnaise off the tip of his finger with entirely too much eye contact. "Absolutely we ought to eliminate those two on the B-Line," he said. "Just to be sure. But based on what we found in the first three—diddly squat—I doubt they'll be any worse for wear."

Didn't take an engineer to arrive at that conclusion. They'd measured for excess vibration in the gearbox. Examined the integrity of rotor insulation. Serviced hydraulics systems. Ensured the blowers on the cooling units weren't obstructed. Checked the blades for delamination. Three times over, all of it, methodically working their way down the checklists. Nothing had stood out.

"Probably not," Justin agreed. "By the way, after you've climbed the ranks to a lofty corner office in Hamburg, don't forget the plight of the American workingman. No pay cuts. Just sayin'."

"Yeah, yeah. I'd be more worried about a robot taking your job."

"But who repairs the robots? Tell me, Mister Prosser, who repairs the fuckin' robots?"

Despite this attempt, Will hadn't gotten sidetracked. "Even if we find something—a whole nest of flying squirrels in a transformer, or your missing cock ring shorting out the stator—it still won't explain the phantom draw."

"Sound pretty sure of yourself."

"I ran a report in SCADA. There's no indication of any inefficiencies from this field. No voltage drops. No resistance in the line. *Nada.*"

Justin played stupid, said, "So it's either bad sensors or a software bug." He knew better, of course, because before he'd watched Velma type in the work order, he'd listened to her take the call from the utility company.

Will shook his head. "If it was sensors or software, the

data would be bogus. Everything was in range. My money's on a parasitic draw somewhere between the connection to the trunk and the substation."

"The grid's not our problem," Justin said. "Thank God. The shit's cobbled together with coat hangers and baling wire. Lucky it didn't go dark during the ice storm last winter. It's an embarrassment. I want nothin' to do with that mess." He hoped that would be the end of Will's probing.

No such luck.

"It's not our problem, but if the utility thinks we're charging them for electricity they're not getting, bet your ass they'll make it Innova-Gen's problem . . . and then it becomes our problem."

Spoken like a future suit, but Justin kept that thought to himself. "Let's get back to work. Two more towers 'til beer-thirty."

CHAPTER
THREE

Will Prosser felt bad about Hank losing his father, but he'd also enjoyed this rare day in the sun. Even if it had been a snipe hunt.

He snaked the braided steel cable through the straps on the tool sack, secured the hook, and yelled, "Incoming!" down at Justin Lackey, who waited below next to the truck. Justin gave him a thumbs up and Will lowered the equipment.

When they were done packing up, he closed the bomb bay doors (wind jockey slang for the crane hatch) and clipped-in before descending from the nacelle. He made it down to the middle platform when a lightbulb went off. It was the transmission line that gave him the idea. The thick wire ran parallel to the ladder, and when innervated, carried as much as three thousand volts. Nowhere near the hundreds of thousands of volts it would be stepped-up to at the substation, but nothing you'd want your nervous system competing with, either. Hence, its thick polymer insulation which would be very hard to cut. *Though not impossible.* Could Schnell have accidentally nicked a buried cable with a farm implement?—

not enough to sever it, but—enough to expose some copper and reduce its carrying capacity?

By the time he'd removed the key from the emergency shutoff and locked up the tower, Will convinced himself it was a theory worth testing. He shrugged out of his climbing harness and tossed it in the bed of the already idling truck. Justin was at the wheel enjoying the AC; it had hit eighty-eight degrees by late afternoon and they'd left the windows rolled up on account of the dust.

Will cracked open the passenger door. "Gotta piss. Be right back."

He hustled over to the side of the access road, unzipped, and relieved himself into the shallow drainage ditch. A little extra irrigation wouldn't hurt the cause. He shook it off and wrangled the most impressive tool he'd handled that day back through the fly of his coveralls, then stood there a minute surveying the arid soil in the surrounding fields. Schnell wouldn't be planting any cotton until mid April, but he could have tilled fertilizer, or trenched in some drip line, or whatever the fuck cotton farmers did to their fields the three months between harvest and planting. A lot of the modern tractors had glass cockpits and high end stereo systems. Schnell could've damaged a cable without even knowing. *Then again, weren't the transmission lines buried beside the access road?* Will wasn't sure—hadn't really thought about it until just then—but that would make more sense than digging up a farmer's field unnecessarily.

Justin honked the horn at him, no doubt eager to pop the cap off his first of many longnecks. Will could hold his own with Lackey, though he was more of a weed guy. Tonight, in fact, he planned to get higher than giraffe pussy with Miley Castro, a fellow sativa connoisseur he'd met last weekend at the Diamondback. Ostrich boots below a flowy sundress . . . *good Lord.* This shit could definitely wait 'til tomorrow.

Except, at that very moment, he spotted something out in the field, sixty, maybe seventy yards distant. A rectangular patch of soil the size of a livestock trailer. Slightly darker than the surrounding dirt.

Justin laid on the horn again. Will flipped him the bird—didn't even turn around—keeping his eyes fixed on what could've been a shallow depression. He hopped the ditch and strode toward the disturbed earth. Now Justin was rapping on the horn like the little drummer boy at Christmas.

Relax, you fuckin' lush. You ain't gonna miss happy—

The bullet struck him in the forehead, tunneled through his brain, and made a big hole in the base of his skull. Will fell. No light shone.

B y the time Vigil pushed the roughnecks' pickup trucks out of the way, and deflated their tires, Franky Bloom had charged his Tesla Model S to eighty percent. It was lunchtime, but they both agreed to hold out for cleaner air before getting a bite to eat. It wouldn't be too long—not with Franky's lead foot. He rocketed them east out of Midland, Texas like they'd just robbed a pawn shop.

"*Bro.* That was the most badass shit I've ever seen!"

Franky was excited. The guy sold gym equipment for a living. And to be fair, it had taken Vigil years of training and dozens upon dozens of altercations before the comedown from a violent encounter was anything shy of drug-like.

He shrugged. "Just another Tuesday."

"It's Wednesday, my man."

"Is it?"

Franky laughed. "Must be nice."

"What's that?"

"Not being beholden to the calendar. Living carefree."

"I can appreciate why you'd think that. But at the end of the day?" he said, pausing for effect, "it's *much* nicer."

Franky's wry grin could've rivaled Bruce Willis in Die Hard. "Hey—I know it's a weird thing to ask, but you mind if I touch your wrist? For science."

"I guess not." Vigil rotated his arm on the center console to give him a better angle.

Franky rested two fingers just below the meaty part of his palm and counted under his breath. "It's official: You're an alien. Forty-five beats per minute while my heart's still thumpin' like a jackrabbit on viagra—and I didn't even hit anybody!"

"But you had my back and I appreciate it," Vigil said.

"Don't B.S. a professional bullshitter. I could've switched sides and it wouldn't have changed the equation any."

"It might've."

"Yeah? How?"

Vigil said, "I would've dropped you first. None of those guys had ever seen the inside of a dojo. 'Always start with the biggest threat.'"

Franky sat up taller in his seat, like he'd taken this as a compliment (which it was). "Sun Tzu? Miyamoto Musashi?"

"My Dad. Commander Lance Vigil."

Franky didn't probe.

Vigil noticed a three-digit number appear on the Tesla's instrument cluster, with the abbreviation *mph* below it. "You might wanna watch your speed." By no means did he feel unsafe, he just preferred to avoid unnecessary interactions with law enforcement.

"Shit. Still not used to how this thing just floats down the highway." Franky eased the car down to ten over the limit.

They remained in the thick of oil country, and Vigil's eyes had begun watering from all the filth in the air. He could taste soot at the back of his throat. It was getting to be a problem. Franky, meanwhile, seemed unaffected. Maybe he'd grown up around industry. Maybe his parents had smoked. "I don't mean to be rude," Vigil said, "but I gotta rid myself of some poison." He coughed and spat out the window.

Franky offered him a piece of gum.

"Thanks."

"Music?"

"Sure."

Bloom brought up his playlists on the giant infotainment screen and selected one called "Wake Up!" Led Zeppelin, AC/DC, Pantera, System of a Down, and Five Finger Death Punch kept them very alert all the way to Colorado City.

"Lunch?"

"A little further."

And it was the right decision. The number of oil wells had already fallen off dramatically, and in the distance Vigil could see their towering replacements.

"Damn. Look at all those windmills," Franky said.

They were wind *turbines*, not windmills, but Vigil didn't correct him. Everybody called them that. He'd always been fascinated by them. Found them beautiful—majestic even. Giant kinetic sculptures put to practical use. He liked sailboats for the same reason.

Franky said, "I've heard the blades kill a lot of birds."

"Compared to what?" Vigil said.

"Good question. I never thought to ask."

"I'm not a wildlife biologist, but my guess? Tall buildings are easier to fly into than a moving target. Especially since the windows reflect the sky like a mirror sometimes. Far more buildings than wind turbines, too."

"Right," Franky said. "And vehicles. I'm plucking feathers from the grill at least once a week. Multiply by a couple hundred million cars . . . 'Lotta dead birds."

"And don't forget cats. Those fucking savages murder billions of birds every year."

"Billions? That's some serious fowl play."

Vigil didn't acknowledge the pun. Might encourage him. "Like I said, I'm not a wildlife biologist."

"Hey, Siri. How many birds do cats kill every year?" Franky spoke as if he were addressing a precocious child from a faraway land.

An enthusiastic female voice with a British accent replied, "Here's an answer I found from the Orlando Sentinel: 'Each year, feral cats kill more than 2.4 billion birds.'"

Vigil decided—right then and there—if he ever found himself talking to a computer, he would immediately reverse course until he was back in nature, listening to the wind whisper through pine trees, watching the sun set behind a mountain.

Franky slapped the steering wheel. "*Geezus!* It appears the dire threat to our feathered friends from windmills is fake news."

At the next exit there was a mom and pop truck stop advertising "BBQ. BREAKFAST, LUNCH, AND DINNER" in red letters painted on a white sign. "You alright with meat smoked over a fire? I'm buying."

Vigil said he was. There were entire weeks he consumed nothing but meat.

Franky slowed onto the frontage road. There was a construction crew repaving the lot, with all kinds of plastic tape and orange cones and striped barrels to navigate. Upon closer inspection, it wasn't clear whether the establishment was even open for business. Part of the facade was torn from the building, as if a small tornado had touched down nearby. The damage looked like it had happened a while ago. Months, if not years. If it took the proprietors that long to repair, what did that say about the food? Vigil wouldn't turn his nose up at a free meal, but he was glad when Franky drew his attention to the billboard on the other side of the highway: "Eat at The Lumberyard. Voted Best Food in Carlin, Texas. Only 2 Miles."

They turned left and drove under the overpass. Followed the two-lane blacktop past a cattle ranch, a hayfield, and a giant expanse of dirt dotted here and there with white tufts of cotton. There were no actual plants to speak of, only the pale wisps shed from last fall's harvest.

"Almost looks like leftover snow," Franky said, "except it's pushing eighty degrees out here."

As they got closer to town, there were small houses with ragtag yards and stunted trees and propane tanks shaped like giant Tic Tacs. Rural living on cheap land; much of it remained empty. What homes there were, sat next to weed-choked lots full of rusting farm equipment. There was an RV park that had seen better days, with fifth-wheel trailers on cracked concrete pads. A tractor repair shop and a feed store. But mostly, it was hard-packed field waiting for spring planting—and wind turbines everywhere you looked.

Up close, they were enormous. Taller than the Statue of Liberty. By a lot. The blades must've swept through whole acres of airspace. Few things made Vigil feel small, but he felt tiny next to these pillars of human potential. They were para-doxical: Undeniably modern, yet possessing an air of ancient-ness; obviously man-made, yet seemingly spawned from the land.

He thought: *I wonder if they offer tours?*

CHAPTER
FIVE

LAST NIGHT, AFTER PROSSER'S MURDER

Justin Lackey popped the cap on a Lone Star and sank into the recliner with Betsy the beagle napping in his lap. The TV wasn't on, but he stared at it anyway as Will Prosser's brains JFK-ed out the back of his fact-filled head—over and over and over again, a gray-matter generated gif on repeat—until his forgotten beer was piss-hot and flat. He only remembered the bottle when Betsy nudged it with her snout and some of the beer sloshed out onto his crotch. He would've scratched her ears but in his other hand was a pistol. It was also warm. He'd been holding it for a long time.

He was shook. Straight up.

And he was scared.

Scared of LG.

He knew—fuckin' *knew*—that he shouldn't have gotten mixed up with the man. He'd heard the rumors. And a good thing he had, because the fear of that horrendous shit happening to him had helped Justin tell the Sheriff the only thing that might keep him alive:

Not a damn fuckin' thing.

You didn't see anyone?

No sir.

No unfamiliar vehicles in the area?

No sir.

Did you hear the shot?

Yes sir.

And where were you when you heard it?

I was in the truck messing around on my phone while Will went to take a piss.

So you didn't see him get hit?

No sir.

Justin figured that wouldn't be the last time he was questioned, but if he didn't see anything, it would be easy to keep his facts straight the next time, even under interrogation.

The real miracle was how he'd kept his shit together enough to make the story credible. He'd watched LG climb down from the barn and disappear into Schnell's house for a few minutes. Heard a second shot, which he didn't know what to make of, and then saw LG come back out before speeding away in a Ford King Ranch. He knew the roads LG would take and he made himself sit there for a solid ten minutes, breathing like a machine had taken over for his diaphragm, marveling at the way his fingers tingled from too much adrenaline. Only *then* had he called 9-11. That way, no first responders would see LG's truck fleeing the scene.

Much harder, was forcing himself to run over to Will's body. Justin knew he was dead before he hit the ground, but he also realized it would look weird if he hadn't gone to check on him—if his footprints didn't appear in the field beside Will's. Only a man who knew what had happened would have stayed in the truck. To fully sell it, though, Justin had to roll him over. He'd tried not to look, but couldn't resist the morbid curiosity. Will Prosser was dead and gone . .

. but his eyes? They were a ghost of guilt that would haunt Justin the remainder of his truncated life.

He eased Betsy off his lap and poured the beer in the sink. Through the window, he could see down the length of his driveway all the way to the dirt road. Suddenly, headlight beams lit up his mailbox like a stage actor. Then a late model Lincoln Navigator pulled up beside it, double-checking the address. Justin flicked off the pistol's safety and tried not to shit himself. The luxury SUV had tinted windows, but that didn't matter because he knew who it belonged to. And he knew there'd be more than one man inside, each packing way more firepower than his cheap little Ruger EC9 subcompact.

The driver's side window slid down and a gloved hand swung open the hatch on the mailbox and tossed something inside. No one got out, thank God, and the big SUV turned around and drove back toward Carlin. Justin let out the breath he'd been holding, flicked the safety back on, and went to retrieve the package.

CHAPTER
SIX

CITY LIMIT
CARLIN
POP. 1246

Just past this road sign was another one, far less utilitarian. It hadn't been mandated by the county, nor had taxpayer funds been spent on its construction. On top of a berm decorated with artfully arranged boulders and ornamental grass, the second sign read: "Welcome to Carlin, Texas. Proud home of the Carlin Wind Project, the world's largest wind farm."

The little spur they'd taken off the exit changed names from I-20 Business Loop to Broadway and the road itself became noticeably smoother the closer they got to town.

"A lot nicer than I expected," Franky said.

Vigil was surprised, too. So many of these aging communities in west Texas resembled ghost towns: Cracked sidewalks, boarded-up buildings, and abandoned storefronts, or worse—post-apocalyptic wastelands of discarded drilling equipment and leaky chemical tanks, with pill-addicted burnouts shuffling around like zombies.

But not Carlin. Carlin was downright prosperous by comparison. It wasn't Aspen, Colorado (hell, it wasn't even Branson, Missouri) but it was clean and tidy and tended to in a way that most towns this small simply weren't. Vigil figured their embrace of renewable energy must've boosted the local economy.

The way it was laid out, he could tell this particular dot on the map had been around long before the Interstate came through. Instead of being built up adjacent to the highway, or surrounding a big courthouse in a more typical "town square" setup, the heart of Carlin bordered train tracks on its northern edge. Mercantile interests—a bank, a barbershop, a dry goods store, a few bars and restaurants—ran two blocks deep along Broadway and Front Street. Then residential streets took over, extending south to I-20 in a more or less rectangular grid. A railroad town, originally.

They found the place they were looking for, but surprisingly, it was in even worse shape than the barbecue joint. "What's a man gotta do to get a meal around here?" Franky muttered. Apparently, The Lumberyard burned down, so they'd have to settle for no better than the second-best food in Carlin. "If they rebuild, they should change the name to The Waterworks. No sense tempting fate." Fortunately, The Diamondback Bar & Grille was just across the street, and the smell of sizzling hamburger bode well for their growling stomachs.

Vigil held the door for Franky, a thick slab of a thing made from repurposed timbers salvaged from an old barn. A door like that? The food had to be passable. Inside was a big open space with brick walls and a stamped tin ceiling that looked antique. There were tall booths along the wall to their right and a dozen or so tables in the middle. On the left, a long bar ran most of the length of the room; it was fashioned of dark, polished wood, with brass foot rails and intricately carved molding all around the perimeter to keep drinks from sliding off. There was a row of flatscreen TVs mounted above the liquor display, and a pool table in the rear by the bathrooms.

They stood patiently in front of a podium that had menus, but no host or hostess. The bartender took pains to ignore them entirely, buffing the bar top to such a sheen, Vigil wondered if he was gearing up to trim his beard in the reflection.

The place wasn't busy, but it wasn't dead either. There were eight other customers. Two at the bar dressed like office workers, a couple guys who looked like mechanics sitting at a booth, and four farmers hunched over one of the tables—though to be fair, bib overalls and boots don't necessarily constitute a uniform in Texas; they might've been financial advisors, or surveyors, or soil analysts, or attorneys.

None of the patrons were talking to one another. There was no music playing in the background (unlike every other bar and grille Vigil had ever eaten at), and although the TVs were on, the volume was turned all the way down (probably for the best, given the cable "news" talking head who was busy polarizing folks with the narrative of the day).

Finally, a waitress appeared from the kitchen carrying a tray of food, but even she didn't make eye contact. She brought the order to the men at the booth, set it down wordlessly, and then disappeared again, head bowed as if no one in Carlin ever tipped. Vigil updated his assessment. The place wasn't *empty*, but it was most certainly dead. Nobody had a pulse. He and Franky exchanged a look but said nothing.

They killed a few minutes perusing the menu: Standard American fare—burgers, steak, fries—classed up with sautéed shiitake mushrooms, raspberry-chipotle garnishes, and pepper-infused goat cheese. There was also a seasonal trout. It was that kinda place.

Still no service.

Nobody looked at them. Not directly. And no one spoke. You could hear the guy and the gal at the bar swallowing their beers. It was that quiet. No conversation whatsoever. Not even at the farmer's table, who by nature should've been jawing about the weather, or ranting about a politician (Vigil had decided they were legit ag men based on the faded Kubota tractor cap one of them wore).

Franky said, "Should we leave?"

One of the farmers nodded almost imperceptibly. About as much movement as a spring-loaded horse at a playground would make, if a sparrow landed on its saddle to take a shit. Maybe less than that.

But Vigil noticed.

He got the message loud and clear.

"No," he said. "We'll seat ourselves. I'm sure the waitress just has her hands full with such a rowdy crowd."

She must've heard him, because the kitchen doors swung open and she tried to usher them to a table next to the bathrooms. Vigil shook his head. "No thanks. We'd rather sit in front, by the window."

"Sure. Whatever."

They got situated and she asked them if they knew what they wanted and they said they did and they told her. She left and then returned with their drinks and an appetizer and then left them alone. Vigil noticed a jukebox back by the pool table. "My turn to play deejay." On his way past the farmer's table, he noticed that none of them were eating. No beverages, either. Not even water. Which was strange. They didn't even look up to acknowledge him, just stared at the table as if the cure for cancer was printed on the napkins. In contrast, the two guys in the booth were eyeing Vigil pretty hard now. Almost like they were waiting to see if the farmers might say something to him. When it was obvious they weren't, they nodded gruffly, like reasonable facsimiles of a human being. Vigil nodded back.

The jukebox had been modernized with a credit card reader and a little plastic square with an Apple Pay logo that was equally useless to someone with no bank account. Fortunately, it also had an old-fashioned coin slot. He deposited an hour's worth of quarters and made his selections. All blues numbers. Given the atmosphere, anything else seemed too aggressive.

When he got back to the table, their food was waiting. Franky hadn't started yet. "Please," Vigil said. "Too late in the day for etiquette."

They made quick work of a basket of fries and big dents in two cheeseburgers that were better than they had any right to be, and they listened to Stevie Ray Vaughan shred Texas Flood—just as good as his deal with the devil had entitled him.

With the music playing, it felt natural to talk again. Franky said, "When we walked in here, I thought *we* were the turds in the teapot. Now I think it was already brewing. I mean—look at those sourpuss hayseeds—I can't tell if they're angry? sad? or just slow?"

Vigil thought they looked paranoid, but wasn't ready to share his assessment. "Something's going on. That's clear. We should ask the waitress when she comes back."

"You think she'll talk to us?"

"Sure. Now that there's some background noise, she won't feel like she's broadcasting to the whole planet."

Franky signed his name in the air to get her attention and the waitress came over with the bill. She dropped it on the table and turned to walk away, but then Franky asked her her name.

"It's Carla. Like it says on the name tag."

Vigil couldn't speak for Franky, but he'd consciously

avoided reading it for the sake of decorum. The print was very small, her "decorative berms" were not.

"Carla, mind if I ask you a question?"

"Would it matter if I did? And how would I know until you ask it?"

"Well alrighty, then. Look, we're just curious: Why is everyone so morose around here?"

The way her face hardened, Vigil could tell she wasn't going to answer. But then Franky made a show of removing a half-inch thick wad of hundreds from his wallet, thumbing through the bills like a bank teller as he examined the total.

The waitress looked away, feigning disinterest (and probably noticing the expensive Tesla parked across the street). Then she must've remembered she liked money. She leaned in surreptitiously, whispered, "Those two guys in the booth over there? They're wind farm techs. Yesterday their friend got shot. He's dead now." She paused as the current song ended and waited for the next one to begin. "Guess who shot him?"

Franky shrugged. "No idea."

The waitress cocked her head at the table behind her. "A cotton farmer."

"Oh, shit."

Vigil said, "Murder?"

"So far they're saying it was an accident."

"They?"

"The sheriff. And the Schnells of course. It happened on their land. The old coot said he was shooting at a feral hog. Claims he didn't see the workers. Wrong place, wrong time kinda thing."

Vigil said, "Do you believe him?"

"I believe the owner of this fine establishment—*who signs my checks*—has far too many dealings for me to have an opinion on the matter."

Vigil nodded like he understood.

Franky scrunched up his face like maybe they'd been over-charged.

Carla got the hint. "But what I will say is this: The Diamondback caters to wind industry folks. Farmers don't come in here much. 'Specially after Innova renegotiated their lease deal."

"Innova?"

"Innova-Gen. German outfit. They're the ones that own all the turbines." The waitress straightened back up to her full height, which was pretty tall for a woman. "Take your time with those burgers, and if there's nothing else I can get for you boys, safe travels."

Franky trapped a hundred-dollar bill under his glass and made sure she saw him do it.

"Change?"

He waved her off.

"God bless you."

Vigil raised his glass and thanked Franky for his generosity.

"My pleasure. After what you did in Midland? Least I could do."

They finished eating. Said not a damn thing as Gary Clark Junior made his six-string moan. Out of respect.

The farmers never moved. Neither did the wind farm techs, except to sip their beers. Likewise for the office workers at the bar. Someone should have left by now, but no one did. As if they were all waiting for something.

Franky said, "You think it was really an accident?"

"Maybe. Feral hogs are a big problem in Texas. Incredibly destructive." As he said this, he noticed the farmers had grown very interested in their conversation. They pretended not to be, but their eyes had narrowed, an involuntary tell nearly everyone exhibits when they're straining to hear. Vigil obliged them. "Of course I'd wanna see the lay of the land where he was shot," he said, raising his voice, "and where the bullet struck him, before I jumped to any conclusions."

Franky frowned like he didn't quite follow Vigil's logic.

He walked him through it. "Awful flat around here. Pigs are short animals. The guy's dead, so most likely he took it in the chest. Maybe even the head. The gunman would have to be a pretty piss-poor shot to miss so high."

"Good point."

"He'd also have to be criminally irresponsible not to consider what was behind his target."

"That's like a fundamental rule of gun safety," Franky agreed.

"You'd think a country boy—from Texas of all places—would know better."

"You would, wouldn't you."

"Of course, it's none of *my* business," Vigil said in a tone that conveyed the exact opposite. "I'm *sure* the sheriff will get to the bottom of it." He mean-mugged the farmers as he said this last bit to see how they'd respond, but they remained poker-faced.

Franky stood quickly, as if he were nervous. "Ready? I need to get my happy ass to Dallas."

Vigil said he was, but not with any kind of conviction.

"THANKS AGAIN FOR LUNCH," VIGIL SAID WHEN they got back to Franky's Tesla. "And for the ride."

"You say that like you're staying behind. You're not going back in there to flirt with the waitress, are you?"

"Not my type."

"You like 'em more petite?"

"I like them more pretty."

49

"What about Austin?"

"It's not going anywhere," Vigil said. "I'm curious about the wind farm. Thought I'd get a tour." Which was the truth, but maybe not all of it.

Franky shot him a tight-lipped smile like he knew better, said, "Well then, pleasure getting to know you."

"Likewise."

"And if you're ever in Phoenix and wanna grab a beer—" Franky handed him a business card.

"Will do," he said. He put the card in his pocket and fetched his pack.

Franky got in the Model S and backed away from the curb. Then he stopped and buzzed down the window and Vigil leaned in to see if he'd left something. He said, "I forgot to tell you: When you were standing at the jukebox? As soon as your back was turned, the bartender dropped his towel and started texting. Two-thumbed and furious like it was urgent. Then, the second you looked up from your selections, he tossed his phone under the counter and got busy polishing imaginary smudges from a shot glass. It's probably nothing, but . . . be careful."

Vigil smiled, but mostly on the inside. He was tempted to remind Franky of what he'd said earlier about the way he lived—point out that "careful" and "carefree" can't coexist. Ultimately, he didn't say it. A wolf and a Jack Russell Terrier were both dogs, but the latter had no business hunting elk. "Thanks, Franky. Drive safe."

CHAPTER
SEVEN

The first text was worth paying attention to, but only because of who Will Prosser's father was, and the fact the strangers had arrived in a Tesla. Will's father, Jim Prosser, undoubtedly drove a Tesla, because Leonard had never met a single Innova-Gen executive who didn't.

Maybe Jim wasn't satisfied with the Medical Examiner's preliminary report? Maybe he spoke with the Sheriff and correctly concluded, *this stupid fuckin' hick law dog is too sure of himself.* Maybe Jim wanted to look these men in the eye before he could accept their version of the truth?

Except, from the bartender's description, neither man was Jim Prosser. The short guy had dark hair, the taller guy was too muscular.

But that didn't mean they hadn't been *sent* by Prosser.

The Tesla could've been a show of solidarity by someone Prosser hired to investigate his son's death. Good ol' fashioned brown-nosing.

Or . . .

It could've been a coincidence. Maybe they were nobody. Just a couple jerk-offs from outta state, pretending they were having an authentic Texan cultural experience. Whoever they were, Leonard didn't like the timing. He texted back and said to keep an eye on them.

The second text was two things: Strange and alarming. Strange, because the dark-haired guy drove away without the big guy, and the big guy was carrying a backpack. Alarming, because while they were still inside, the little guy pumped Carla for information on the shooting, and the big guy taunted a table full of cotton farmers with details he didn't seem to think added up to an accident.

The second text demanded immediate action.

CHAPTER
EIGHT

Vigil only had two-and-a-half hours of daylight left, so touring a wind farm would have to wait until tomorrow. He didn't mind waiting because he was rarely in a hurry. He'd explore Carlin's commercial district for a while and then find a room for the night. He pictured a two-story inn with wood siding and green shutters, not far from the railroad tracks. A humble refuge for weary travelers, family-owned since the days of the steam engine. Or maybe a former boarding house that a gay couple had spruced up and converted to a bed-and-breakfast. In Vigil's experience, towns like Carlin would have at least one such establishment.

He struck out east along Broadway. No particular reason other than he'd already seen what lay west on his way into town. It was good to walk after eating such a heavy meal. And nothing beat walking when it came to getting to know a place. It was the only mode of travel where the pace of discovery mirrored the senses' innate bandwidth. Drive down any country lane and they all look the same. Walk, and you notice the fence posts were cedar, not oak, and you remember what kind of cows were grazing in the pastures, and from which direction the wind blew.

He strolled past an ice cream parlor and an insurance office, both built with red brick; most of the buildings on Broadway were. He took inventory outside a gift shop trafficking in stationary and candles and corn-pone wisdom etched onto painted plywood:

"If mama ain't happy, ain't nobody happy."

"No man was ever shot while doing dishes."

"Home is where the heart is."

And where the junk accumulates. Vigil had never understood the compulsion to cover every available surface of an abode with knickknacks (admittedly, he rarely felt *compelled*). He supposed it wasn't enough simply to own a house; people had to fill it with furniture and appliances and electronics and bedding and all manner of landfill-bound ephemera so it didn't feel empty—so *they* didn't feel empty. He noticed the woman at the cash register had set down her romance novel to appraise him; she was surrounded by so-called novelty items, but Vigil was the real McCoy. He moved on.

On the next block, there was a dentist's office and a dress shop. An empty lot where there used to be something old and brick, followed by a patch of gravel in front of a square, squat cinder block building with no windows and a neon sign outside that said "liquor." Vigil wondered if this was the farmer's preferred hangout. He walked on, past Main Street, the only cross street not named after a type of tree. It seemed to have a different feel; he'd have a look after he looped back around.

So far, he hadn't seen many cars out-and-about. Parked or otherwise. Unsurprising in such a small town, and Carlin was small even by those standards. What vehicles he did see (less than a dozen) were pickups. Those in transit all slowed as they passed him to get a better look. *Behold, the mysterious stranger.* A charitable bit of telepathy, because over the years Vigil had heard enough folks yell out the window what they really thought about him: *Bum. Loser. Animal.* Whatever flavor of "other" fit their regional prejudices. Here in Carlin, they kept it to hard stares. He paid them no mind. It's what people do in cars in rural America. Face-to-face, the same folks were often all smiles and handshakes. Especially with Vigil.

He continued down Broadway until the businesses became increasingly agricultural and more spread out. Turned left on Mesquite and then left again on Front Street and headed back the way he and Franky had come into town. The proximity of the tracks determined much of what he found. Most prominent was a grain elevator that appeared operational, but wasn't long for the world. The only giveaway that it hadn't been condemned was the readout for the scale that heavy trucks used to weigh their loads; it showed five pixelated zeroes in bright red. There were businesses on the other side of the tracks, too, most of them cotton-related in some way. Big sheds where bales were stored before being loaded onto a train car. Equipment supply yards. That kind of thing.

It didn't take him long to get back to Main Street. Vigil turned left and followed it south past Broadway. Aging brick buildings gave way to structures made with Texas limestone mined down in hill country. None of these looked very old. The largest was the city hall building, which shared space with the police station, the jail, and a courtroom. Across the street was the library, also built within the last ten years, and also constructed with limestone. Vigil had no idea how such a minuscule tax base could support such lavish architecture.

There were more surprises beside the library, starting with an unbelievably well-manicured park that took up the rest of the block. It was practically a botanical garden and must've cost a fortune to maintain in this climate. There were bronze statues and ornate benches. Weeping willows and rose gardens and at least five different species of bamboo. There were even coy ponds, right out in the open. None of it made sense in a town of barely a thousand residents. And neither did the medical office he walked by a block further south. Embossed on a brass nameplate were the words: *Carlin Cosmetic Surgery | Dr. Anahita Ahmadi, MD.* What would he find next? A Maserati dealership?

What Vigil didn't find, in any of the places he expected to find it, was lodging. Not the end of the world. In his pack, he had a tarp and a sleeping bag to fall back on. Still, not ideal. The surrounding farmland was, by definition, "private property." A very contentious term, even among those who defended the concept, and Vigil himself had mixed feelings about it. Philosophically, he could argue both sides (growing up under his parents' roof had seen to that). On a more practical level—when it came to trespassing—he took the *If a tree falls in the woods, does it make a sound?* approach, and sidestepped the issue altogether. Even a man with a code has to contend with gray areas. That said, with so few trees to not make sounds behind—or hills, or boulders, or natural obstructions of any kind—it would be a hassle to go undetected. Plus, Vigil was well aware of Texas's shoot-first-ask-questions-later interpretation of the Stand Your Ground law.

He considered returning to the Diamondback. Anyone in there could point him to the nearest motel. But then, so could any local he bumped into anywhere in Carlin. Vigil decided to check a few of the cross streets he'd skipped, and if he still didn't find anywhere suitable to lay his head, he'd ask the first person who'd talk to him.

What's the point of antagonizing people already in a bad mood?

A rhetorical question. Yet an answer came. A smoke signal sent by the part of him that *did* feel compelled on occasion—the part of him that persuaded litterbugs to adopt a highway, and convinced assholes to take up loving-kindness meditation. One word . . . but this time Vigil ignored it.

Let the sheriff do his job.

Accident or not, no one had asked for his help. And anyway, he was supposed to be enjoying himself. He walked a little further south along Main to put some distance between him and temptation.

CHAPTER
NINE

Here at the very edge of Carlin's commercial district, he found yet another limestone building, pale gold in the glow of the soon setting sun. It wasn't as large as the library or city hall, but it shared the same architect and builder. That was clear. A plaque outside identified it as *The Carlin, Texas Museum of History & Wind Energy,* and then in smaller print below: *Made possible by a generous grant from Leonard Grainger.* Vigil made his way inside and a cowbell above the door jangled to alert the staff. He was greeted by an old woman sitting on a tall stool behind a glass display case. The docent, presumably, but she'd also qualify as the oldest artifact in the entire museum.

"Welcome, stranger. We close in thirty minutes, but feel free to look around 'til then. If you have any questions, my name's Delores. Happy to help."

"Thank you, ma'am."

The case was stocked with t-shirts, fidget-spinners shaped like turbine blades, and coffee table books written by a local author. On top of the case, there was the obligatory tablet computer connected to a credit card reader for purchasing souvenirs. Aside from this idle tribute to commerce, the place impressed him. It had vaulted ceilings held up with distressed oak timbers. Generous skylights and deer antler chandeliers. An overall "rustic charm" meets "modern gallery" vibe, with the walls contributing most of the feel with their partially exposed limestone and interspersed panels of gray slate against cream-colored plaster.

The exhibits themselves were equally well crafted. An annotated mural wound clockwise around the room, telling the story of the town from the days of bison hunters and early settlers surviving Comanche raids, to the arrival of the railroad in 1881, and concluding with the launch of the Carlin Wind Project in 2009. In the center of the room, two enormous scale models expanded on this most recent point of pride. The first, which stood nearly as tall as Vigil's shoulder, was a completely functional wind turbine tower, with the artificial breeze provided by a large fan. From neatly labeled acrylic plates, he learned several interesting bits of trivia:

- The 627 towers in Carlin's wind farms are all taller than a football field is long—the shortest standing at 315 feet, and the tallest at 450 feet.
- The electricity produced by each unit (up to 2 megawatts) isn't stored in batteries; it flows directly to the power grid through a network of underground cables.
- To remain upright against the incredible force of the wind, towers are held in place by 144 eight-foot long bolts, each anchored into a reinforced concrete base that's sixty feet in diameter and extends eleven feet below ground—that's over 300 yards of concrete per tower!

The second scale model featured a cutaway view of a "nacelle," the box at the top of the towers that the turbine blades are mounted to, and that houses the generator and related equipment. Inside the miniature nacelle, a continuous loop of alternating spotlights shone on the major components, each in turn, like a three-dimensional slideshow. A video panel complimented the exhibit with CAD drawings and motion graphics to help visualize the mechanical processes involved. There were hubs and gearboxes and transformers and hydraulic systems and cooling units and all sorts of other equipment Vigil hadn't realized was essential to wind energy.

Learning so much about how they functioned only stoked his desire to tour an actual wind turbine in the wild. He asked Delores if there was a way to schedule one, ideally for tomorrow.

"I'm sorry, young man. They don't give tours. Too dangerous. Not sure what you'd discover anyhow, that our replicas don't capture. They're awful well done, don't you agree?"

"Yes ma'am. First-rate." Vigil was disappointed, but he wasn't surprised. Good luck underwriting such a massive investment if the public had access. Too many Billy Base Jumpers. Too many Karens. Too many lawyers.

Waaayyyyy too many lawyers.

He decided to chat up Delores for a few minutes. Walking was the best way to familiarize yourself with an area, but talking to a local was pretty good, too. Especially an elder.

"Have you always lived in Carlin?"

Delores's eyes lit up as if few visitors ever bothered to inquire about her life. "Born in 1930 and called it home ever since," she said. "I'm ninety-two years young, if you can believe it."

Vigil *could* believe it. She looked ancient. Like a relic from the past. Her wrinkles had wrinkles. Skin so thin you could almost see the hairline cracks propagating through her brittle skeleton. And yet, Delores still had a lot of life in her. That was clear. She radiated vigor like a woman half her age. Vigil didn't see a walker nearby, either, which meant—not only could she still get around just fine—she'd managed to climb up on that stool unassisted, too. All four-foot-eleven of her. Damn impressive.

He said, "Carlin must share an aquifer with the fountain of youth."

"Well now yer just flirtin'. You shouldn't get an old lady's hopes up. Reminds me of my husband, God rest his soul."

"Your husband must've been a handsome fellow."

"Aren't you a rakish devil? 'Course, you'll have to be more specific . . . "

Vigil frowned, not understanding what Delores was getting at.

Without missing a beat she said, "Three of 'em were uglier than rocks."

"Have things changed a lot in Carlin since you were a girl?"

"Hand me that glass of water, would ya?"

Vigil did and wondered if he was in for a long yarn.

Delores took a sip and cleared her throat. "Yes. I reckon it has changed some. There's always been farming, of course. But when my parents were still alive, it was a lot less commercial and more about self-sufficiency. Back then, everyone ran at least a dozen head of cattle. A farm had chickens and pigs and a vegetable garden. Not to sell, but to feed your family and barter with the neighbors. No one got rich, but everyone had enough. Even during the Great Depression, mind you, which I was born into.

"Now it's gone corporate and mono-crop. Almost exclusively cotton, 'cause pretty much any other kind of crop grows better somewhere else. Farmers bale it up and ship it all over by train and truck. Buy what else they need at the store like city folk.

"A lot a farmers 'round here did purdy well for themselves. For a time . . . "

Vigil listened patiently as Delores gave him a firsthand account of the decline of the American family farm: Advancements in technology. Specialization. Higher yields. Commoditization. Market forces. Buyouts. Consolidation. And so forth, and so on, as the beast that is capitalism fed on tradition and shat out profit.

At least that's where Vigil assumed Delores was headed.

". . . But the families who were able to hold on? The very same wind they cursed after church on Sundays turned out to be their salvation."

"The wind farms," Vigil said, stating the obvious.

"That's right. They already had the wind and the land. They just needed the technology to catch up. Now they grow electricity, too."

Vigil figured this was the perfect time to test the intel he'd heard from the waitress at the Diamondback. "The farmers don't actually own the generators, do they?" he asked, feigning ignorance. *Just can't help yourself, can you?* He wanted to kick himself the second the words were out of his mouth.

"No. They lease their land to the wind energy company."

"How's that working out for them?"

"Purdy well, I'd say. Could they have survived without? Likely they could. Just like they always have." She pointed at the beginning of the mural. "Texans are tough people. Have to be to make a go of it in such an unforgiving land. But whereas before the wind project, the farmers were barely scraping by, now they're able to afford some of the finer things in life. You should see the houses some of 'em built."

Vigil wondered how many of these newly prosperous farmers there were? Enough to fund the new city hall? The library? The garden of Eden they'd somehow cultivated in this 110-degree summer overflow section of Hell? Seemed unlikely. And the farms probably weren't in the city limits anyway. They would be on county land. Could the tax revenue they generated even be used by the city? He didn't know.

As to whether the farmer's lease deal had been renegotiated recently, his question hadn't prompted Delores to speak on it. This didn't surprise him; discussing other people's finances in anything but the most general terms was considered impolite throughout the south. For the same reason, he decided to hold off asking how much a farmer collected for each tower on their land. For now, at least.

"Is there oil drilling around here?" Vigil figured that oil companies must pump plenty of cash into the communities where they operated. Probably a line item on their Annual Report: *Pay people to look the other way.*

"Sure. There were wildcatters come in here. But only for a brief window of time. They made a few strikes. You'll even find a pump-jack here and there, rustin' away in somebody's field. But the last well went dry back in the '70s. All the oil you hear about in Texas is further west. There's talk of shale deposits, and I hear there's ways they could get the oil out with fracking, but at this point, I hope they stick to wind power." Delores held up her water in salute, said, "After all, we gotta keep the fountain of youth potable."

Vigil remembered the plaque outside the museum, and the word 'grant,' and the name of the man who'd coughed up the money. Maybe his name was on other buildings in Carlin, too. "Leonard Grainger—is he a cotton farmer?"

"Our generous benefactor? No, he's a businessman. But he knows all the farmers on a first name basis. They love him. If it wasn't for Grainger, they probably would have lost their bid for the wind project to Roby or Sterling City."

"I couldn't help but notice the library and the city hall

building bear a striking resemblance to this museum. Did Grainger have a hand in those, too?"

Delores nodded emphatically. "Sure he did. And the park. And the new high school and elementary. And probably a stake in half the new buildings in Carlin, besides."

"Wow. That's impressive. So what kind of business is Mister Grainger into that's enabled such generosity?"

"Too many to list at this point. But I believe he got his start in concrete. Fairly humble beginnings, if I recall. But after he won the contract for the wind farm? The rest, as they say, is history."

It seemed plausible. Vigil had spent time around construction sites. He'd known concrete workers. Based on the "300 yards of concrete" figure provided by the exhibit, he did the math in his head and estimated the foundation for a single tower might run to $250,000 dollars. Multiply by 617 towers, and that's roughly $154 million and change. Plenty to get your name on some buildings in a small town like Carlin.

"What else can you tell me about Grainger?"

"Aside from what I've already told you? Not much. He didn't grow up around here. He's from the northeast, I believe. Has a bit of an accent. New York, maybe."

"When did he move to town?"

"'94? '95? Around then. I was already a senior citizen by that point, but I can remember being disappointed that he wasn't closer to me in age. He was probably about fifty. Very handsome—still is. And a fine dresser. You should see his darling wife. Mexican girl. Twenty years too young for him, but what a stunner!"

Vigil noticed the clock on the wall and saw it was almost closing time. "Delores, it's been a pleasure talking with you. Thank you so much for your time."

She nodded graciously, said, "You don't have to leave if

you still have questions. I'm rather enjoying your company. What was your name, by the way? I should've asked sooner."

"I go by my last name: Vigil."

"A strong name. Suits you. You sure there's nothing else I can do you for?"

"There is something, now that you mention it: Where's a good place to stay the night in Carlin?"

"Nearest hotel would be in Sweetwater. About ten miles east on the interstate. Next exit you come to."

"Nothing here in Carlin? I don't mind a motel, or a bed-and-breakfast."

"Sorry, youngin. Last place you could get a room folded decades ago, not long after the train stopped comin' here. Really no reason for travelers to stop in Carlin—not with a proper city so close by. There's a Best Western, a La Quinta, a Micro-Somethin'-Or-Other—right off the exits. Sweetwater's got you covered."

"Well thanks for the recommendation. Can I see you home?"

"I'm pleased to see chivalry hasn't completely died out. But I only live a mile away and my walks are sacred. Just me and my thoughts."

And that's a big reason you're still so spry, Vigil thought. He bid Delores farewell and went back outside to weigh his options.

CHAPTER
TEN

The package in Justin Lackey's mailbox had turned out to contain a burner phone with a yellow sticky note:

1. Speak to absolutely no one.

2. When the phone rings answer it.

3. Burn this note immediately.

He pocketed the burner, went back inside, and used the stovetop to torch the note. *Done. Done. And done.* For the first time since Will's murder, he stopped fearing for his life.

The adrenaline abated, and on its heels, a post-crash wave of exhaustion. He set the Ruger down on the coffee table and passed out in the recliner a minute before midnight.

Five hours later, the burner phone startled him awake.

"Hello?"

"You did good, kid. Real good. But I need you to *keep* doing good. Understand?"

"Yes."

"How you handled the Sheriff was perfect. You didn't say nuthin'. But given who was shot, that might not be the last time he questions you."

"I figured as—"

"Shush when I'm talkin' to you. Listen: Good chance it won't only be the Sheriff who wants to talk, either. And you didn't see anything, right?"

Justin said nothing, afraid he'd interrupt again.

"So now that I'm askin' you a question, you should answer me. It's okay. Relax. I know you're nervous. We're just havin' a conversation here. Like men. Let's try again: You didn't see anything, right?"

"Right."

"That's good. That's real good. You're a smart kid. But here's the thing: We never talked beforehand about what you would or wouldn't see. You follow me?"

"I follow you."

"And so the next time the Sheriff questions you—or the FBI, or Bondurant, or Osama fuckin' Bin Laden who faked his death—*whoever* you talk to—I need you to remember a couple details you must've forgot in the stress of the moment. Understand?"

"Yes."

"Good. Turns out farmer Schnell shot the Prosser kid. But you wouldn't know that, right? 'Cause you didn't see anything. 'Cause you're a smart kid. But now that you've had some time to think about it, you *do* remember seeing some feral pigs rooting around in Schnell's field not long before the terrible accident. You remember those pigs, don't you, Justin?"

"Absolutely."

"And how many pigs do you remember seeing?"

"Uhhh . . . I don't know."

"That's right. Because I haven't told you how many pigs you saw yet. You're doing so good, kid. Here's how many pigs you saw: You saw *six* pigs. How many pigs did you see, Justin?"

"I saw six pigs."

"Perfect. And did you see anyone with a rifle up on the barn roof?"

"No. I was messing with my phone."

"That's right. Because farmer Schnell is missing a leg. No way would he be up on the roof of his barn. But you wouldn't know that anyway because you didn't see anything—except for those pigs."

"I remember seeing some pigs. That's it."

"How many pigs did you see, Justin?"

"Six pigs."

"You're a standup guy, Justin. Take the day off today. Your whole crew. Tell them they have the rest of the week to mourn Will Prosser."

"I'll let 'em know."

"And one more thing: I want you to stash the phone you're talking on someplace you have access to, but where no one else will find it. I'm not telling you this because I think you're stupid—you're a smart kid—we both know that. You've proved it. But I bet if I hadn't said anything, that burner would stay in your pocket. Because you're loyal. You're loyal to me, aren't you Justin?"

"I am."

"And so you'd want to keep that phone handy in case I needed to talk to you again. Right?"

"Right."

"And then the next time the Sheriff or the Feds questioned you, they'd find it, and it would look suspicious, and you wouldn't know what to say to them about it, would you?"

"Uhhh . . . I wouldn't say—"

"*Shhh*. It's okay. I know you're loyal. But I also know investigators. They're fuckin' relentless. *You have no idea*—and why would you, Justin? You're a good kid. A smart kid. But more loyal than smart, right?"

"Right."

"How many pigs were there, Justin?"

"Six pigs."

LG ended the call.

Justin Lackey feared for his life again.

CHAPTER
ELEVEN

Vigil walked north again on Main toward Broadway. Further south was all residential. When folks got home from work and saw a big guy roaming around with a backpack, it would look nothing but suspicious. He decided the city park was as good a destination as any to plan his next move.

On the way over, he had a closer look at the city hall building and the library to satisfy his curiosity. Both had the name *Leonard Grainger* etched into the cornerstone below their dates of completion in 2010. Likewise in the park, where the name graced a brass plaque at the base of a fountain.

He found a bench, set his pack down on the ground beside it, and got comfortable. There was still a little daylight left, but he'd be walking in the dark whether he made the ten-mile trek to Sweetwater, or risked camping in somebody's field, instead. As a rule, he preferred having his sleeping arrangements sorted out well before nightfall. But it wasn't always possible. In theory, he could embrace his inner bum and crash right where he sat on the proverbial park bench. In practice, there were several issues that made it impractical: One, there was a surplus of ornate lamps throughout the park that looked like they'd been smuggled out of Paris or maybe somewhere in Italy; far too bright to get a good night's sleep, even for him. Two, the park was too close to the police station; Vigil had seen no signs of a homeless population in Carlin, and in today's America, that meant the cops didn't tolerate vagrants. Three, the bench was nowhere near wide enough to accommodate his frame.

What else?

The bamboo groves might work. The tall plants (technically grasses) were plenty thick to conceal him. But then he recalled the scourge that God must've afflicted Texas with as some kind of punishment: Fire ants. A terrible plague upon the land most would consider gratuitous, though Vigil could think of several worthy offenses perpetrated by the great state. A couple involving Presidents. (Texas was also home to a trailer park that had become a city, just so its residents could have a liquor store onsite . . . on second thought, maybe that should be celebrated.) Either way, the stinging, biting insects could be a problem anywhere he slept outside. Which sounded like the *opposite* of enjoying himself.

Ultimately, it wasn't that hard of a decision: No wind farm tours. No rooms. Demonic ants. Therefore, no reason to stay in Carlin.

VIGIL CLOSED HIS EYES AND RECALLED THE touchscreen in Franky's Model S. Specifically, the zoomed-out map view on display when they'd cruised into Carlin's commercial district. He had nothing like a "photographic" memory, but he did possess a knack for recalling maps, and it often came in handy.

To get to Sweetwater, he had two options: He could backtrack to I-20. Or he could stay on Broadway and follow it due east as it paralleled the interstate. Quiet country blacktop versus the roar of passing semis was no kind of dilemma. He slid on his pack, splashed a handful of water onto his face from the fountain, and then set out for a long, leisurely stroll on gentle ground.

But he'd gone no further than the corner of Main and Broadway when he froze.

There it is.

That magnetic pull, deep down in his gut, urging him to turn left instead of right.

Away from a hotel in Sweetwater.

Toward the Diamondback Bar & Grille.

And with the pull, the word, riding shotgun for a second time today. No mere smoke signal, now—big letters on a billboard in bold type—three syllables, all caps, impossible to ignore; his was a moral compass that worked on intuition and pointed to *INJUSTICE*. He wasn't the only one with such an instrument, but what made Vigil rare was his tendency to head in the direction the arrow was pointing. Most people went the other way, toward safety and comfort and a ripe old age.

This uncommon wiring necessitated certain Rules of Engagement. Otherwise, he'd be fighting all the time. Entire ecosystems could be disrupted. No way to live. Thus:

Rule #1
Don't go looking for trouble.

Rule #2
If no one's asking for help, mind your own business.

Rule #3
If law enforcement's involved, let them handle it.

Or to quote Jim Jeffries (another of his favorite comedians): "We're not animals! We live in a society!" The punchline earned its laughs through exaggerated irony—earnestly proclaiming truths we all agree to believe in, but on a more primal level, know to be bullshit. Although Vigil could accept that mankind might also be something more, he never deluded himself; *we are animals,* at our core. On this point, he and his father were in complete agreement, and it remained one of the most important lessons Dad had ever taught him. As for society? The construct had sparked long and heated debates between them—too many and too nuanced to trouble himself with now.

Which was still a lot of deliberation over whether to turn left or right, he thought. But so what? Unhurried contemplation ranked high among the joys of solitary wandering.

And all rules have exceptions:

The Asshole Exception

Notoriously, there's no law against being an asshole; therefore, whenever you encounter an asshole, it is your sacred duty to provide the ass-kicking said asshole has somehow managed to ass-scape until now.

The Crooked / Stupid Cop Exception

Is law enforcement too corrupt or too inept to do their job? Then step up to the plate.

The latter could very well apply to the Sheriff's handling of the wind farm tech shooting, though it remained to be seen and would be hard to prove.

Vigil shrugged. Turned right toward Sweetwater.

There was one more exception. But he had to be careful with that one. It was habit-forming. He left it on the top shelf of his mind like a prized bourbon.

CHAPTER
TWELVE

"What's the word, Vin?"

Vin was short for Vinny, so as not to be confused with "Lenny," which the older guys in his crew still called their boss, even today. Leonard would've called him Vin regardless, a tribute to his friend's former life as a car thief. It was Vin who taught Leonard how to file a VIN number all those years ago in Bensonhurst.

Vin said, "He spent a little time in the museum. Then he went to the park and rinsed off in the fountain like a fuckin' pigeon. I think he might be a bum or somethin'. Maybe crazy, too, or schitzo or whatever. He was standin' on the corner just staring at the sidewalk like a momo."

"Where is he now?"

"Walkin' east on Broadway. Outta town looks like. We pulled up short before it switches to the county road. Didn't want him noticin' the tail."

Leonard was quiet for a moment. "The Sheriff Department's down that road."

"Yeah. There's that. What do you want us to do, Boss?"

"Ask where he's headed. Then offer him a ride."

"And if he's on the way to see the Sheriff?"

"Convince him that would be a bad idea."

CHAPTER
THIRTEEN

On the edge of town, Vigil passed an electrical substation surrounded by a tall chain-link fence. Two bundles of high-voltage lines hung over the road, humming the chord of civilization. The air felt charged. To his left were the railroad tracks, and some distance beyond, through the indeterminate dusk, he could just make out the pinwheel silhouettes of wind generators, looming below their pulsing red lights, which warned yet soothed.

He walked by an empty American Legion post advertising $2 Miller Lite on Tuesday nights and the ruins of a decommissioned gas station. The night smelled of hay and rust and moisture that might condense to fog by morning but hadn't yet. A black cat carrying a dead rat in its mouth spotted him and fled up the concrete slope of the Highway 84 overpass, appraising Vigil from its cave-like perch between two girders as he crossed its path. It occurred to him that black cats are a great way to judge how dark it is outside, because if you can see one, it can definitely see you—and so can everybody else. He nodded at the cat and kept walking.

The county had taken over road maintenance, though there was no sign announcing the fact. Only a change in texture. The road had also narrowed considerably and there was no breakdown lane. When there were no vehicles behind him, Vigil stayed on the asphalt. When he could see his shadow from approaching headlights, he angled off into the grass. This had only been necessary once so far; an old Dodge pickup slowed to do the staring thing. The stink eye was minimal, but the man's gaze lingered, as though Vigil was some long-extinct primate escaped from a lab, out claiming territory. Then the pickup sped off and he watched it until the brake lights came on and it turned and bounced down a lengthy track toward a farmhouse. Vigil reached the driveway fifteen minutes later, the last sign of human occupation along this stretch of no-man's-land between Carlin and the more populated city ahead. He found an easy rhythm of forward motion, the steady snare beat of grit beneath boot heel, and the low rasp of distant traffic on I-20 carrying him along in a no-thought linearity over the land.

He was surprised when another pair of headlights appeared behind him. Anyone traveling further east should have taken the Interstate. Especially at night. The speed of approach also surprised him—or rather, the lack thereof. The road was narrow, true, but whoever it was crept along. Like maybe they were searching for something.

Or someone.

Vigil didn't look back. He wanted to preserve his night vision. The way the headlight beams lit up the surroundings told him plenty. For starters, the vehicle wasn't that old. These were the blindingly bright LED lasers that had become popular over the last decade or so, distinguished not only by their intensity but also by their purplish tinge. That, and whoever was driving was an exceptional asshole, because they hadn't dimmed their high beams.

It was *possible* they hadn't seen him. Technically. Certainly no one would expect to see a backpack-toting pedestrian this far out in the country. At night, no less. Except there was a reflective safety strip stitched into the seam of the pack (same as most running shoes), and it would've lit up like the eyes of a nocturnal predator the instant the headlight beam flitted across it. So Vigil was confident the driver *had* seen him, though he gave no indication that he was aware of the approaching vehicle.

He wasn't about to ask for a ride.

Still a hundred yards back, the vehicle slowed from a creep to a crawl, and another full minute passed before it caught up to him. A Lincoln Navigator, so new it could've been next year's model. A massive SUV. Sleek and black and luxurious. Real metal bolted to the same steel frame Ford used for Expeditions and F-150 pickups. Three rows of seating. Room for eight passengers. Not that Vigil cared. He trudged forward through the rough grass like a migrating wildebeest. Then the SUV stopped and a tinted window came down and a deep voice called out to him from the passenger seat.

Vigil was silent.

The driver tapped on the accelerator and the Lincoln lurched back alongside him.

"Hey! I'm talkin' to you." The guy took a drag from his cigarette and blew out the smoke in an angry cloud.

Now that the headlights were in front of him, Vigil finally turned his head to acknowledge the voice. "I heard you," he said, and kept walking.

The big SUV inched forward, matching his pace.

"You look like you could use a ride."

He noted the accent. Definitely not Texan. Boston maybe. Or New York. He wasn't sure. He hadn't been to the Northeast in a while. He preferred to stay west of the Appalachians.

"Do I?"

"Yeah. You do. The next town is miles away."

Vigil was silent. Kept walking.

"Where you headed?"

He considered lying. Briefly. But he didn't like lying, and he rarely did.

"Sweetwater," he said. "They have hotels there."

The guy in the passenger seat turned to confer with the driver, and maybe someone in the backseat, too. Hard to tell, because Vigil refused to look at them.

"And after Sweetwater—where to then?"

"What's it matter to you?"

"Suppose it doesn't matter. Suppose we were simply showin' you some southern hospitality and preparin' to offer you a ride."

"I'm content to walk." The seven or eight miles in front of him was nothing. Vigil liked walking. Especially after so many miles cooped up in a car earlier in the day.

"I get that. Walking is good exercise. But suppose we don't actually care where you're headed, or how you plan to get there. Suppose we saw you bumming around our quaint little community today, up to no good, and we wanted to make sure you didn't plan on coming back. What could you tell us that would convince us we'd never see you again?"

Vigil shrugged. "Fuck off, maybe? That would pretty much guarantee it." *Pretty much,* because their desire to oust him from their "quaint little" (murderous) community had rekindled Vigil's interest in rules and exceptions. It didn't take much.

He stubbed his smoke out on the roof and flicked the butt in Vigil's direction. "Geezus—the balls on this guy."

"Giant balls," someone concurred from the backseat. The voice was muffled by extensive sound dampening but still audible through the open window, yankee twang and all.

The first guy turned back to Vigil, said, "Try again. This time, with less death-wish."

Vigil stopped walking and smiled. Now he remembered what Delores had told him at the museum about Leonard Grainger's accent. Were these associates of his? He approached the SUV to get a better look at these sure-as-shit-not-Texans.

"I didn't threaten your life. 'Fuck off' means scram, get lost, beat it, and/or vacate the premises. In other words, if you leave me in peace, your odds of dying in a violent encounter go way down." Calculated bravado. Something for these not-so-good samaritans to pay attention to while he collected relevant details.

How many? *Three.*

Armed? *Probably* (he couldn't see their hands).

How old? *Hard to tell . . . something weird about their faces.* Also their ages were all over the map. The guy in the passenger seat was probably mid forties. The driver was much older—could've been sixty, could've been seventy-five. The guy in the backseat was closer to Vigil's age.

"You're a punk, but you're funny," said the guy riding shotgun. "Especially for a big guy. Big guys aren't that funny, usually. No reason to be. Everyone laughs at their jokes. Little guys, on the other hand, they're almost always hilarious. They have to use humor to defuse situations. Us regular-sized people, though? We use guns." He rested the barrel of an unusually large caliber pistol on the door frame. A Glock 20, chambered for 10mm rounds. Probably the least popular handgun in the Glock family, but definitely the most powerful. Pointed right at Vigil's chest.

Not ideal.

This did, however, all but confirm his intuition that the wind tech's killing had been no accident. Only something as heavy as covering up a murder would warrant this level of intimidation. *Because this isn't exactly random, is it?* Vigil had poked holes in farmer Schnell's account of the shooting while he and Franky ate lunch at the Diamondback—loud enough the whole bar and grille could hear him. These fellas got word. Apparently.

"What's the matter, big man? No more jokes?"

Vigil was silent. Barely heard the guy. He was remembering something else Delores had told him: *". . . he knows all the farmers on a first name basis . . . if it wasn't for Grainger, they probably would have lost their bid for the wind project . . ."* He was also recalling what Carla had confided at the Diamondback: *". . . I believe the owner of this fine establishment—who signs my checks—has far too many dealings for me to have an opinion on the matter."*

I bet I know who signs Carla's checks, Vigil thought: Leonard Grainger, the charitable contractor, the savior of farms—he had to be involved. Simple profiling suggested as much. Even one New York accent was unusual in a Texas town as small as Carlin. But four? In the same vehicle? It was absurd.

There were more dots to connect, but evidently the guy in the passenger seat wasn't good with uncomfortable silences. He tapped Vigil in the chest with the barrel of his Glock. "Come on. Tell us another joke, you fuckin' clown."

Not ideal at all.

For the guy in the passenger seat.

Because Vigil really, *really* didn't like being poked in the chest. Especially not with the barrel of a loaded weapon. On any other day of this moron's waste of a life, Vigil would have ended it. Effortlessly. Because the arrogant prick had nullified one of the primary tactical advantages of a handgun: Its ability to destroy the target, before said target could close the distance to engage. Military tacticians called this "maintaining stand-off". Or simply, "reaction time" in Vigil's shorthand—a calculation he performed automatically when he encountered a threat. As natural as breathing.

"Alright. I've got one for you."

"Let's hear it."

"Knock, knock—"

"Who's there?"

"—knockin' on Heaven's door," Vigil said, and relieved the fool of his pistol with a maneuver no soccer mom had ever practiced in a bullshit Krav Maga class. He stepped back out of Lucky-To-Be-Alive's reach and the arc of the Lincoln's door—still point-blank range by any measure. And since it was a Gen 3 with a Loaded Chamber Indicator, Vigil didn't need to waste time racking a round. The gun was ready to fire.

Everyone in the Navigator raised their hands.

"Why aren't you laughing? That one always kills."

The driver spoke for the first time, said, "You're dead. You know that, right?" Same accent as the other two guys, only thicker.

"Only on the inside," Vigil said.

He was no kind of cold-blooded psychopath, but they didn't know that. And in situations like these, it was best if he kept them guessing about his sanity.

"Listen carefully," he said. "Turn off the vehicle and toss the keys outside."

The septuagenarian with the unnaturally taut skin did as he was told.

"Good. Now sit on your right hand. All of you."

They did.

"With your left hand, retrieve your weapons, barrel first, then drop them outside. Don't forget your spares, either. Now's not the time to tempt fate."

The driver dropped a .38 revolver onto the road. The guy in the backseat disposed of two guns, a double action /

single action Sig, and a .22 small enough to tuck in a sock. The guy in the passenger seat had already surrendered his sidearm.

"Good. Now put both hands back in the air where I can see them."

Thirty manicured fingernails, six wrists, and three gold watches hovered below the headliner.

That a grave injustice had been committed in Carlin was crystal clear now. But Vigil's rules were still providing the friction they were designed to, and the first two exceptions weren't much help. Not only were murder and criminal conspiracies well outside the intended scope of the Asshole clause, he lacked knowledge of the Sheriff's competence and character. Which left only the third exception to consider— his nod to the arbitrary nature of all rules, whether voted into law, or self-imposed:

Nothing Is Written In Stone.

One could argue this caveat was a little too convenient— that it rendered the entire notion of "rules" obsolete. And admittedly, the potential for abuse was high. Like an Indian casino next door to a degenerate gambler. But as long as he could secure proof more solid than the circumstantial evidence he had so far, he was willing to risk it.

After all, a *Vigil* is going to *ante*.

The challenge was getting these guys to talk. "We could play twenty questions," he said, "but I doubt you'll tell me shit. Who wants to be a rat, right? Tough to live down."

He paused. He wanted them to worry: *If this guy isn't asking questions, what's that leave?*

"Leonard Grainger sent you. Let's start there."

The younger guy in the back seat was blinking like he'd just been slapped hard in the face. The driver chewed the inside of his lower lip. And the guy in the passenger seat twitched his pinky finger.

Encouraged by these tells, Vigil continued, "The wind farm tech was murdered and you're helping Grainger cover it up. You came looking for me, because someone at the Diamondback gave you my description. Probably Caleb, the bartender. How am I doin' so far?"

To their credit, the three men stared straight ahead and kept their mouths shut. Vigil figured he was pretty warm, though; they were sweating like the SUV was a sauna.

"The question is, why? Why would silk shirt clad, Rolex-sporting maggots from the Big Apple help a cotton farmer from Nowhere, Texas? I get Schnell's motive: The wind farm company screwed them on the lease payments—yeah, I know about that, too. But Grainger got rich pouring concrete for Innova-Gen . . . why would he take the farmer's side?"

The old man at the wheel said, "Too bad you'll never find out."

Vigil said, "Challenge accepted."

Then he noticed the headlights approaching from the east, anything but slow.

Red and blue lights flashed above them.

Warning, not soothing.

CHAPTER
FOURTEEN

H e didn't wait to find out if the patrol car was coming for him, or for the goons in the Lincoln Navigator. He preferred to avoid unnecessary interactions with law enforcement.

The Sig Sauer the guy in the backseat had dropped was a P220 Legion, also chambered in 10mm, a heavy steel weapon which Vigil favored over the composite Glock. He knelt down and snapped it up, then took his own advice and fucked the hell off.

Across the road the cover was sparse, but still better than a barren field, so he sprinted in that direction and hustled through a ditch choked with alder and sumac. The stunted, bush-like trees lashed at his arms as he ran, while the dried stalks of last year's noxious weeds rattled and snapped against his chest. A dozen yards beyond the ditch, railroad tracks lay at the top of a tall gravel embankment. Vigil powered his way up the slope and then flattened himself out on the opposite side. He considered putting more distance between himself and the road, but this was much better concealment than he'd hoped for, and he could peek over the rails without being seen. He stayed put and watched to see how the guys in the Lincoln would handle the officer.

By the time he looked back, they'd retrieved their two remaining weapons and the keys and pulled the Navigator off the road to give the patrol car room to pass. To Vigil, this seemed optimistic. The farmer driving the Dodge pickup must've called in a suspicious individual snooping around his fields as soon as he arrived home. Which put the Lincoln and its occupants in the vicinity shortly thereafter, and therefore, worth questioning.

Sure enough, the Crown Vic came to a stop two car-lengths away from the Lincoln. It was from the Sheriff's Department of Nolan County. Said so right on the door. There was no "K-9 Unit" verbiage stenciled anywhere, fortunately, and no sign of a dog inside the vehicle. Vigil was fleet of foot for his size, but no match for a police-trained German Shepherd or Belgian Malinois.

The deputy—or maybe the Sheriff himself—switched on his high beams and then added a spotlight to the equation. Standard procedure (and also karma, as far as Vigil was concerned). The old guy at the wheel turned off the Lincoln's headlights, signaling cooperation. The officer remained in his vehicle for a minute, running their plates. Presumably there were no open warrants, and having identified the registered owner, the officer got out and approached the vehicle with the swagger that comes from wearing a badge. He didn't rest his hand on the butt of his weapon, but his right arm wasn't exactly loose at his side, either. Vigil could just make out the word DEPUTY printed on his uniform beside his last name, which read MANION. He watched him make his way over to the passenger side to avoid blinding himself with the spotlight. The window was already down.

"'Evenin' fellas. I'm looking for a tall white male, east-bound on foot, carrying a backpack. Seen anyone who fits that description?" The deputy spoke loud and clear in that artificial tone of presumed compliance.

No sirs, all around.

There were few insects and no wind, so Vigil didn't need to strain to hear the exchange.

"Nobody? Huh. Not like Jacob Boyce to waste time with nonsense."

The goons in the Lincoln continued to play stupid.

They didn't want the deputy to find Vigil.

That was clear.

Because they don't want me talking to him about the shooting. Who knew what their relationship with the Carlin police was like? But at least with the county law enforcement, it didn't seem suspiciously friendly.

The deputy nodded, a resigned expression on his face, said, "Mind tellin' me why you were stopped out here in the middle of the road?"

The driver said, "I thought I had to piss."

"*Thought?*"

"False alarm."

Manion cocked his head a little to the side and frowned.

"Prostate. I'm fuckin' old."

The deputy smiled and patted the Lincoln's roof and bid them all goodnight. Then he got back in his cruiser and killed the spotlight before speeding off further west. He'd pull into the Boyce's driveway and make sure there were no suspicious men with backpacks loitering around his property. Maybe he'd even do a safety check at the house, on account of everyone being on edge after yesterday's shooting. Vigil would have, if he were an officer of the law. And he would've pressed the goons in the Lincoln a lot harder, too. Asked them where they were going tonight. Asked them if their AC was broken since they were sweating so profusely. It wasn't outright incompetence by the deputy, but it wasn't exemplary police work, either.

The Lincoln didn't move for a long minute. Vigil watched the old guy hammer-fist the steering wheel and bicker with the two other goons about what they should do next. In the end, they kept driving toward Sweetwater. That way, they could at least claim due diligence. They weren't about to play *The Most Dangerous Game* with him, that was for damn sure.

He memorized the plate as they drove away at a normal speed. They couldn't afford to crawl again or the deputy would catch up to them on his way back to the station and ask more questions. Vigil stayed off the road for the same reason.

He still needed a place to sleep for the night, and it was still too dark to check for fire ants. He followed the railroad tracks east and thought of two more things he'd have an easier time finding in Sweetwater. Both would come in handy when he returned to Carlin, and bug spray wasn't one of them.

CHAPTER
FIFTEEN

L eonard Grainger was sitting in the hot tub on the back deck, dick still hard because he'd taken too much viagra. If he didn't let the jets work their magic after making love, the arthritis in his hips would ache like a bastard tomorrow morning, and no amount of Tylenol would touch it. Jacuzzi + half a Vicodin + wine—*that's* how a seventy-six-year-old man gives Father Time the finger; Joe Biden could learn a thing or two. He took another sip of the 2013 Stag's Leap Cabernet. Five-hundo a bottle. He'd come from Sicilian stock, but get outta here with that dirt-flavored Chianti bullshit. It was vino from Napa Valley, or go fuck your mutha.

The sprawling ranch style home sat on a hill overlooking the largest expanse of wind farm south of Carlin, and from his low perch he could see all the way to the lake. The red bulbs at the top of the turbines blinked on and off like broken stop lights. Combined with the intoxicants, they were hypnotizing. He felt something like gratitude: For beautiful Mariana, already asleep. For Raymond, their twenty-seven-year-old autistic son who'd never left the nest (down in the basement as usual, stealing nuclear codes from China or whatever). Leonard used to resent the kid—especially all the time he spent in the dark playin' on his computer. But not anymore.

"Say hello to my little friend!" The ringtone for Vin jerked him out of his reverie.

"What's the word?"

He knows it was a murder.

He got away.

We don't know where he is.

That was the gist of Vin's bad news, even though the fuckin' guap drew it out with meek apologies and bitch-ass excuses.

"He mentioned me by name?"

"Well . . . yeah."

Vin's hesitation meant Leonard's current name, not the one he'd grown up with. Which was a good thing. An enemy from the old neighborhood would be an entirely different kind of situation.

"Tell me again what he knows."

"Said he knows Prosser was murdered, and that you're coverin' it up. Buys that Schnell was good for it, but questions his motive. Yours, too, for what it's worth."

"A couple hours he's in town—who is this bum? Sherlock Homeless?"

"He ain't the regular kind of homeless, that's for sure. We think he might be ex-military. He had the boots, the build, the buzz cut . . . a lot of vets come back with like, PTSD, or whatever—might explain his situation. But a momo, he ain't. Before, I said he might be, but he's definitely not slow. Anthony, on the other hand . . ."

"Now's not the time to be bustin' balls, Vin."

"Sorry, Boss."

"You're sure he didn't stop by to see the Sheriff?"

"We watched the front door for a couple hours after he ran. Never saw him."

"And you checked all the hotels in Sweetwater?"

"We don't have his name yet, but yeah, we asked around."

This sounded like bullshit. But when had Vin ever lied to him? "Anything else you wanna tell me?"

Vin breathed out heavily, said, "He's packing heat, for sure. Took Bruno's Sig. Anthony's Glock."

"Christ. Are they clean?"

"Of course, Boss. We ain't exactly amateurs."

You ain't exactly hittin' on all eight cylinders anymore, either, he thought, but Leonard bit his tongue and managed not to say anything he'd later regret. It helped that his balls were empty and his body was numb. It helped a lot more, that soon—very soon—he'd be a billionaire.

"Boss? You there?"

"Yeah. Just countin' to ten."

"You want," Vin said, "We'll come over and keep watch outside your gate. This guy's no joke."

Leonard said, "Is he a wizard?"

"No."

"A ghost?"

"No, Boss."

"Then he ain't gettin' to me here." Leonard turned his head away from the mouthpiece. "Ruskie—Irish: *Bed!*" The two Dobermans trotted obediently to their respective bear skin rugs at either side of the French doors. The dogs would kill to protect him. No doubt. But they weren't shit compared to the home security systems Raymond had obsessed over (as only a kid on the spectrum could). Not to mention, he had more guns than a cartel pig roast.

"I'm sorry, Lenny. We dropped the ball on this one."

He was about to tell Vin to get some rest, in case this asshole came back tomorrow, but then he thought of something. "You wanna feel useful? Take a van from the yard and strip everything from the box in Schnell's field. Bare metal. Before morning—just in case it all goes sideways."

"On it."

Leonard smiled. His crew would assume this was simply to hide evidence—which it was—but it was also just the beginning. Tomorrow night, they'd use excavators. In different fields, the Sheriff wasn't investigating.

It was time to cash out. Past time, in truth. Shooting Prosser had finally forced him to pull the trigger. Literally and figuratively.

He dialed a number from memory. It went to voicemail, which wasn't ideal, but now that they were in the endgame there was no time for playing phone tag. He left a message, "I need you in Carlin. ASAP."

Because what good was cashing out, if he couldn't cover his tracks?

CHAPTER
SIXTEEN

Vigil used his fake South Dakota ID to check into a Microtel off the interstate where Delores had pointed him.

When he got to his room, he scrubbed down the clothes he was wearing and showered—one lather, one rinse—and then had BBQ delivered. He ate ribs, watched a show about outlaw drag racers in Oklahoma, and went to sleep. He dreamt of fist fights and gun battles and beautiful women he couldn't remember the names of.

CHAPTER
SEVENTEEN

Officer Tyler Hunt of the Carlin Police Department only made it to *Qué tengas buenas noches* in his Spanish lesson before he muttered *no mas*. He wasn't having a good night—in any mongrel language—and no amount of getting paid to learn wetback would change that. He'd never make detective anyway. Not even in this bumfuck backwater. So why keep kissing ass?

Not to mention the monumental waste of time this was— over a mishap that everybody with two eyes could see was an accident. Schnell had hobbled out with the goddamned rifle before Prosser was even cold. Shook the Sheriff's hand and pointed at the tracks left by the hogs he'd been shootin' at. Case closed, right there. Everything else was theater. *Christ.* If Baker wanted to burn taxpayer money, shouldn't one of his deputies be losing sleep? Schnell's place was way outside the city limits. This wasn't Carlin PD's problem.

Hunt poured another coffee. His third of the night. At the rate he was going, the thermos would be empty long before dawn. Not that the burnt dishwater that passed for coffee at the station was helping. Every sip he took just pissed him off a little more.

"Choke on a dick, Chief."

Ramirez had acted like it was merely Hunt's "turn" for a graveyard shift, but he knew this was punishment. No two ways about it. A slap on the wrist for notching his second brutality complaint in as many months (not the worst rap in these parts, except the complainants had been female).

He dumped the rest of the coffee (decaf—had to be) and took a leak in the culvert. The lights at the Schnell house had been off since nine-thirty, like any self-respecting farmer's would be, and the closest neighbor was three whole miles away. Obviously, no one was coming to screw with Baker's precious crime scene.

Fuck it. Nap time.

Hunt started up his patrol car and idled a little further down the access road toward the wind turbines. Even if some night owl cruised by on the farm road, they wouldn't get a good look at him.

Inside of five minutes, he was snoring. He dreamed of a Mexican wrestler with a gold *Lucha Libre* mask, demanding Hunt give him a blowjob. It was a good dream. Until the knock on his window startled him awake. The youngest and most imposing member of the Grainger Goon Squad, Bruno Nash, stared down at him. Guy couldn't walk by a cow without lifting it. Hunt buzzed his window down.

"You scared the bejeezus outta me. What the hell you doin' out here?" He checked the rearview. There was a long wheelbase Ford Econoline on his bumper. A Lincoln Navigator parked behind it.

"We'd like to do some stargazing. Sip hot chocolate."

"You can see that yellow tape, can't you? Why the hell you think I'm out here? For shits and giggles?"

"Don't need to mess with the crime scene," Bruno said. "We'll stay in the field."

"I don't know, man. I've been fuckin' up lately."

"Lately?"

Hunt ignored him, said, "Someone sees you . . . calls it in . . . Ramirez might shit-can me this time."

"Are you retarded, Officer Cunt? Why do you think he sent your sorry ass out here? Because of your stellar crime-fighting ability?"

Hunt finally caught on, said, "How much we talkin'?"

"You're the one on the take. You tell me."

"How long you need?"

"Three, four hours."

Hunt sighed. "Five hundred." *I'll never make detective, but at least I'm makin' bank.*

Nash opened an envelope and pocketed half of what was inside it before handing over the rest. "Thanks for wettin' my beak, you fuckin' putz."

CHAPTER
EIGHTEEN

Vigil woke at six-thirty the next morning without an alarm and felt invincible. Like most days. He repped three hundred crunches and a few dozen handstand presses and felt even better when he was done.

In the nightstand between the two queen beds he found a phonebook and thumbed through it for the name of the local newspaper: The Sweetwater Reporter. Carlin was too small to have a paper of its own. He also looked up the address of the nearest gun shop. As of September 1, 2001, you no longer needed a license to carry a handgun in Texas, concealed or otherwise. To be legal, though, you did need a holster.

It was a five mile round trip to and from Sidewinder Tactical so he called a taxi. The cabby was an amiable Middle Eastern guy named Ahmed, who seemed eager for repeat business. Vigil tipped him and took his card.

At gun store he sold the Glock at a hefty discount. This earned him a stark indifference as to the weapon's origins and kept his real name off the Bill of Sale. Then he picked out an inside-the-waistband style holster for the Sig. When it came to carrying concealed, Vigil favored the appendix carry over the strong side or hip. His preference stemmed primarily from ease of access and speed of draw, but there were also aesthetic reasons: Even a gun as large as the P220 wouldn't bulge beneath the untucked western-style denim work shirts he wore. Clothing manufacturers knew their market—standard-issue, fat-ass American—so any collared button-up that fit over Vigil's wide shoulders also billowed around his narrow waist like a maternity blouse. He threw in a couple spare magazines, and fifty rounds of 10mm Winchester 175-grain Silvertips to complete the purchase. The bullet was lead, of course, not silver, but it sounded cool and it was all they had. He thanked the proprietor for her help and paid for everything in cash.

A few blocks south he found a cafe. Ordered a coffee—black, no room for cream, in a ceramic mug like a gentleman. He asked the barista if they subscribed to the Sweetwater Reporter and she pointed to a copy another customer had left behind on one of the tables. He sat down and saw what he was looking for right on the front page:

LOCAL COTTON FARMER SHOOTS AND KILLS CARLIN, TX WIND FARM WORKER

Vigil sipped his coffee and read the story, committing relevant details to memory. The article filled in a lot of blanks:

- The victim's name was Will Prosser. Notably, the son of Jim Prosser, a high-level executive at Innova-Gen.
- Maintenance Foreman, Justin Lackey, was with Prosser during the shooting, and was unharmed.
- The alleged shooter, Oswald Schnell, was a cotton farmer who leased his field to Innova-Gen. Schnell volunteered himself to authorities at the scene shortly after Sheriff Baker arrived to investigate.

- Emergency responders determined the victim had expired prior to their arrival, and this was confirmed by the Medical Examiner who pronounced Prosser dead shortly thereafter.
- The Examiner's preliminary report listed the cause of death as "Homicide," though sources in the Nolan County Sheriff's department were quick to point out the term is neutral and does not imply criminal intent. In Texas, all purported "hunting accidents" are required by law to be listed as a homicide on the Death Certificate; whether charges are eventually filed is left to the discretion of investigators and the District Attorney.
- Schnell claimed he was attempting to shoot at feral hogs which were damaging his fields, and that he did not see the wind farm technicians working behind the animals.
- Texas law requires that all hunting accidents are fully investigated to rule out foul play. Sheriff Baker confirmed this, and added that his department will carefully review all the evidence in this ongoing investigation.
- Off the record, however, anonymous sources within the Sheriff's Department are mostly convinced that the shooting was a terrible accident, with charges unlikely to be filed.

Vigil set the paper down and gulped the remaining coffee. Went back to the register and ordered a refill and a blueberry muffin with real butter. None of that margarine crap.

He took the muffin back to the table. Actually tasted the coffee this time and worked out his next move. He didn't waste energy on whether or not to get involved (*"double jeopardy applies double when it comes to decisions,"* as Dad used to say), and focused instead on how he could empirically verify what his gut already knew. Unlike his Rules of Engagement, his desire for physical evidence wasn't a self-imposed sanity check, or a guardrail of good intentions. It was a test: Was the Sheriff's Department misled? Incompetent? Or in on the coverup?

Deputy Manion hadn't greeted the goons from last night with any good-ol'-boy familiarity that Vigil could see, so for now he'd give the investigators the benefit of the doubt. Do his own detective work. Share what he found. What happened after that was up to them. Arrest → trial → verdict → sentence? Or Vigil's more expedient and primal form of justice?

He was eager to get started, and the paper had provided names and photos of two people he'd like to question: Justin Lackey, the eyewitness. Oswald Schnell, the shooter. He was sure they wouldn't be as eager to chat, but Vigil could be persuasive. And there was also Leonard Grainger. A rich man, and therefore, a powerful man. A big fish who would know everything that went down in the small pond of Carlin and have a hand in most of it—in covering up Prosser's murder, for damn sure.

Ironically, if Grainger hadn't sent the thugs in the Lincoln, Vigil would have been halfway to Austin by now.

He wanted Grainger to know that.

Vigil wanted to tell him to his face.

He should reach out to Will's father, too. Express his condolences and urge him to be skeptical of the official narrative. In cases involving a possible homicide, the law required an autopsy. Results would be public record and available by request. Five days, max—maybe the next day in a rural area that didn't see a lot of murders. But if the Sheriff had been compromised, then the Medical Examiner might also be bent, and their final report wouldn't be worth the cheap Windows

PC it was typed with. Family members could order an independent autopsy.

He brushed the crumbs off his shirt and had the barista call Ahmed the cab driver. There was too much to do to waste time walking. He waited outside and thought more about motive. Why Grainger would help Schnell with a coverup was a question with no obvious answer. The concrete contractor had gotten very rich from the same company whose employee the farmer had killed. And by that same logic, why would a cotton farmer who received regular checks from Innova-Gen bite the hand that feeds him? *Because they reduced the payments, remember? Soured the deal.* But by how much? Something was still better than nothing. Would the other farmers with lease deals go on a killing spree? Seemed unlikely. Or was Schnell simply a hot-head?

Ahmed's twenty-year-old silver BMW pulled up and Vigil tossed his pack in the backseat and got in. The Sig was comfortable even with his knees bunched up in the rear of the coupe. The holster was performing admirably.

"Where to my friend?"

"Carlin. The Diamondback Bar & Grille."

"Wow. It is off beaten path."

"Sorry you won't find a fare back to Sweetwater."

"Is okay my friend. For you, is no problem."

He remembered the tip, no doubt, and lucky for Ahmed, Vigil still had a thick enough stack to repeat it. "I might need a ride out, later. Can I count on you?"

"My friend. Is God not great? Is Ahmed not cab driver? You call me, I will take."

CHAPTER
NINETEEN

Leonard Grainger woke up in a spare bedroom because Mariana wouldn't let him sleep in the master anymore on account of his snoring. He checked his phone and read the update from Vin.

> Done. Van in the yard. Lemme know where to junk everything.

Good question.

Now, even small decisions, like this one, took on an outsized importance. Vin was smart enough to realize this, and Leonard was glad he could count on him because there was no room for even the slightest mistake.

Definitely not the local landfill, he thought. A shipping container's worth of electronics would stand out among the old refrigerators, broken microwaves, and busted furniture that ordinary folks dumped at the public drop-off. It would draw attention. A worker might remember who brought it in. Plus, what his crew had stripped from the box in Schnell's field was peanuts. There were a hundred more containers full of gear. Mountains of aluminum and solder and plastic and wire. And there were ordinances to consider. A household might get away with tossing an old TV or computer tower into a dumpster, but e-waste was a regulated commodity. Best if he got rid of everything the right way. There are murderers rotting in prison who only got caught because they didn't pay a parking ticket. Given his former life, the irony of this waste management challenge wasn't lost on him.

The good news was, there was money in electronics recycling. Not the kind of scratch that got Leonard out of bed in the morning, but enough that there were plenty of providers to choose from. Couldn't be a mom-and-pop, though. He needed industrial scale. Again, not local. Dallas would have one. But Houston might be better. A facility in Houston would probably put the crap on a boat and ship it to China. Let the chinks handle it. Hell, the slant eyed bastards manufactured most of the shit, anyway—circle of life and all that.

Destination sorted, Leonard focused on getting everything from point A to point B. Even with excavators plucking entire containers from the fields, this was a big job. Especially the transport. The best option entailed securing the steel boxes to a flatbed trailer. There was one at the yard, and a semi to pull it, but with only one truck and one driver it would take weeks. *Days* is what he wanted. Plus a few layers of middlemen between Grainger Concrete Co. and all that potential evidence.

So he'd call a freight broker. A Russian or Ukrainian who answered to someone overseas, accent so thick they *couldn't* ask too many questions. Plenty of those to choose from, too, but a lot of the Eastern Bloc brokers were Landstar agents, and Leonard wanted to deal with honest crooks for this job, not institutionalized thievery. He scrolled through his business contacts and found Pyotr Petrov. An independent broker.

He'd used him many times for loads of rebar. Never a problem.

The Ukrainian picked up on the second ring. "Petrov Freight. How may I be of service?"

Leonard described the job: Carlin, Texas to Houston. The loads would pickup in the middle of the night. Fifteen, twenty thousand pounds, max—light. 48-foot loose containers, already loaded. Old electronics. Non-hazmat. Flatbed or step deck, chains or straps required. No big carriers, no rookies. Owner-operators only, with fifteen-plus years experience and a good safety rating. He'd pay a premium. "And if you'll sign as the consignor on the bills of lading," he added, "I'll sweeten the pot."

"How many you need moved?"

"A hundred. Need 'em gone by the end of the week."

Petrov named his price and Leonard didn't haggle.

He texted Vin back:

> Good. We'll talk later about disposal. For now, lineup some excavators. Night shifts. Friends only. As many as you can get. Tonight we dig.

Vin would know exactly what "friends only" meant. And what the excavators implied, he'd quickly piece together. Given his promised cut, he'd be happy Leonard was shutting it all down. Vin had never been sold on the idea in the first place. He was old school: Gambling. Garbage. Construction. Prostitution. Every other day he was grumbling, *This tech shit's for the birds.* And hell, for most of his life, Leonard felt the same way. It wasn't until his electric bill quadrupled back in 2012, and he'd asked Raymond if his new computers were to blame, that Leonard finally appreciated the extraordinary opportunities in hi-tech.

And speaking of his adopted quant, the creepy fuck was

staring at him from the bedroom doorway like a psychopath. Leonard was still lying beneath the silk sheets in bed. Fortunately, the viagra had worn off in the night and there wasn't a pup-tent.

"307 is down, Leonard. 307 is down. This is very unexpected."

"Relax, kid. We disassembled it last night. I should've given you a heads-up, but it was late and I didn't wanna wake you."

"Oh. Okay. Disassembled . . . permanently?"

Leonard could see the disappointment taking hold. Monitoring the fields was Raymond's second favorite pastime. "We're cashing out, Raymond. Just like we talked about, remember? So we don't get in trouble?"

Raymond didn't respond at first. Leonard hoped he hadn't triggered another fit. Once, Raymond stripped off his shirt in a crowded McDonald's and proceeded to slap himself in the chest like a faggot gorilla. The welts were tremendous.

"Oh. Okay," Raymond said finally. "Do I get to go to The Wizarding World of Harry Potter now?"

"Once I finalize some things, you can buy the whole theme park," Leonard said.

"Uh, unlikely. At today's exchange rate we will only be worth two billion, three hundred seventeen million, six hundred nine thousand, forty-eight dollars, and three cents. The owners of the Harry Potter IP would likely demand a premium on their $3.4 billion dollar asset, therefore—"

Leonard held up a hand, stifling a laugh. *Only?* He said, "I was exaggerating, Raymond. You know how I do." It wasn't like his step-savant was going to see a penny of the proceeds anyway. He'd be staying here in Carlin with his mother. Comfortable. Taken care of, but not to the extent Elon Musk's exes enjoyed.

Raymond said, "Oh. Okay. Now I will need to play more

games to occupy my time now. Leonard, you won't get mad at me, will you Leonard? You used to get very mad at me for playing video games, you did."

"You can play all the games you want, Raymond. I won't get mad. Promise. Not even a little."

"Oh. Okay." He nodded his head three times (always three), seemingly placated.

Leonard shooed him away. Put on a wife-beater and some sweats and went over to his eight-car garage where he'd built a commercial-grade gym. He did StairMaster and a few crunches, then went outside for some shooting practice on his private range. Two hundred rounds through an AR-15. There were worse ways to start the day.

CHAPTER
TWENTY

There were three times as many people in the Diamondback as there had been the day before, and it wasn't even lunchtime.

Eight pissed-off looking wind farm workers in booths.

Thirteen cotton farmers at the tables daring them to say something.

The bearded bartender.

Carla, the waitress.

Plus a woman roughly the same age as Vigil, a lot easier on the eyes, and the only person in the place who hadn't regarded him with confusion, open hostility, or outright fear. She smiled at him from the bar.

Vigil smiled back. A confident expression he wore easily. For half a heartbeat, he forgot all about poor Will Prosser and righting wrongs. Enjoyed an entirely different kind of pull than the one that had brought him back here. Then she looked away and it was like a million years of evolution never happened; a mirage between frames of fleeting memory. By the time the door closed behind him he was indifferent again.

Vigil inhaled sharply and nodded to the two wind farm

techs he recognized from yesterday. Winked at the farmers to plant a seed. *First I will sow, then I will reap.*

There were plenty of empty seats at the bar. The woman was leaning over her pale beer and he sat down three stools away from her. A two-stool gap would've been presumptuous. Four, aloof. The bartender wouldn't look at him. He was clearly terrified.

Vigil tried to put him at ease, said, "No hard feelings— they came, they saw, I conquered."

Which had the opposite effect. The guy visibly trembled. His first kiss was probably on Snapchat.

"Seriously. We're good. Bring me a beer and I'll toast to your health. Coors, if you have it."

Tending to a familiar routine seemed to comfort him. "Light?"

"Banquet. I'm not an animal."

The bartender brought him a mug, which he waved off, and a brown bottle with a gold and blue label from the cooler.

"What's your name?"

"Caleb."

Vigil made eye contact with the woman, then with the bartender, and raised his beer. "To Caleb, may he forever thrive and prosper." The woman grinned approvingly and raised her mug, and the two of them drank a healthy pull. Caleb relaxed some, but looked distracted, like maybe his phone was calling out to him from below the counter.

Carla paid no attention to any of this. She was leaning against the far end of the bar, arms folded, flustered as a guard goose. He was tempted to buy her a beer. Or a shot. She wasn't having a good day. That was clear. If she'd worked a day in her life in the service industry, Vigil thought, it was undercover. She didn't budge. Just shook her head at him, incredulous, holding up a menu like a protest sign until he shook his head back at her.

His beautiful bar mate raised an eyebrow, and Vigil's stoic indifference faltered, if only for an instant. Then he got back to the serious business of pretending he wasn't attracted to her. Back to actual serious business.

Vigil preferred not to have his back to a crowd, but behind the bar, between the shelves of liquor, there were mirrors, and so he was okay with it. He used the reflection to scan the room. Read faces. Tested assumptions. He figured the wind techs in attendance had been given the day off to mourn. No one was in any kind of uniform. No mechanic's coveralls like the two from yesterday had been wearing. He recalled the picture from the paper; Justin Lackey wasn't among them. Vigil didn't know what, if anything, to make of his absence.

For what it was worth, Oswald Schnell wasn't with the cotton farmers, either.

"The Diamondback caters to wind industry folks. Farmers don't come in here much." And yet there were three times as many of them as the day before. Obviously trying to send some kind of a message to the wind techs: *We believe Schnell.* Or: *Y'all best accept it was an accident.* Or: *If y'all ain't careful, you might be next.* Something along those lines, Vigil was sure of it.

But both his gut and plain ol' common sense told him there was more to it than this show of solidarity / subtle-not-so-subtle threat. Namely, Leonard Grainger, who—like Lackey, like Schnell—wasn't here either. But then, he didn't need to be. He owned the place. And in a way, he owned the farmers, too. He remembered Delores saying, *". . . before the wind project the farmers were barely scraping by, now they're able to afford some of the finer things in life. You should see the houses some of them built."* There was a rabbit of insight fleeing down this trail, but for the moment, it escaped him.

As he'd been reading the room, the woman had been reading him. She was discrete about it, like most women are. But not so discrete he didn't notice. Probably on purpose. He smelled faint traces of vanilla and lavender and musk from her perfume and made peace with the fact she was going to be a problem. Best to face it head-on.

He leaned over and offered his hand. "Vigil. Nice to meet you."

"Mira." She had an unexpectedly firm grip. Not callused, but familiar with a pull-up bar. She said, "I'm sorry for staring. I was trying to make sense of you."

Vigil was silent. He was trying to make sense of her.

She gestured to the stool next to him. "You mind?"

He didn't. Not one bit. She scooted over.

"Come to any conclusions?" he asked.

"I'm still mulling it over."

He said, "How was your flight?"

The corner of her mouth levered up like someone peeking through a blind. "My rental car. Not bad."

Vigil shrugged. "I might not have noticed if we weren't in pickup country. A Prius stands out." He sipped his Coors, said, "Your turn."

Mira lowered her voice, said, "Why does half the room hate you, and the other half is hoping you're on their side?"

"That's not how this works," he chided playfully. "You have to puzzle it out."

She nodded like this was the only acceptable response.

Vigil hoped she wouldn't rush her deductions. He was taking her in, liking what he saw. Her dark brown hair was cut reasonably short and hung just above her shoulders with a wavy nonchalance made for a stiff breeze. She had bangs, possibly to mask a very faint scar that ran diagonally from her brow to her hairline. Makeup could've easily rendered it invisible, but Mira displayed very little; a hint of gray-green eyeliner, a whisper of gloss. She wore a textured off-white cotton top with a blue blazer cut somewhere between bohemian and business casual. Jeans. Tight with some stretch to them. He looked away momentarily and imagined two sloths playing chess before the holstered Sig got uncomfortable.

"I'm ready," she said.

"Let's hear it."

"First of all, you're built like an NFL linebacker. Except you're early thirties, so probably a smidge too old to still be playing. Plus, a former pro baller would be wearing designer denim, not Levis (no offense).

"Then there's the accent. It's all over the map. Midwest mostly, a little southwest, but definitely not Texas. You're not from around here.

"You're also carrying a backpack, and you're real tan, like you spend time in the sun. Not a homeless guy—not in the usual sense—because you're too clean-cut and you smell like you've showered recently. This feels like a lifestyle choice, not a tragedy.

"The boots scream military, and so does the haircut, but I just can't see you taking orders—something about the way you carry yourself—the 'fuck you' twinkle in your eyes. I wouldn't rule it out, though. Ex-Special Forces? *Maybe*—if you got booted for insubordination.

"Also telling: The scars on your knuckles . . . I suppose you could be a fighter—except you don't look like you get hit enough. A really good fighter possibly. I'll go with part-time bodyguard for rich VIPs.

"And so, in a room of blue collar, salt-of-the earth Texans, I'd say you must've come by yesterday and insulted Willie Nelson. And now you've come back to tell them that Walker, Texas Ranger is a terrible disgrace to television."

Vigil grinned. "That's your conclusion?"

Mira laughed, said, "No—yes—I have no idea! This is harder than I thought. I feel like an extra on the set of a Tarantino movie."

"Hate to break it to you, but you'd be a lot higher up in the credits than extra. Uma Thurman saw you coming and retired. Margot Robbie would have to settle for sidekick."

Mira batted her eyelashes at him. "Are you hitting on me, Mister Vigil?"

"Possibly. They say hindsight is 20/20."

Mira played coy and changed the subject. "Going by your last name—that's a military thing, too. So are you?—in the military?"

"I'm more of a one-man army," he said matter-of-factly. "You can call me Nate if you want to, but no one does."

"No. I like Vigil. It sounds protective somehow."

He nodded, "It's from the Latin: *The act of keeping awake, especially at night.*"

"*Hmmm,*" Mira said, smirking mischievously. Then, like she hadn't: "You know Latin?"

"Almost none."

They finished their beers. Vigil ordered them another round. In the mirror, he could see four of the more formidable farmers discussing him. Maybe they were working up the courage to throw him out. He considered sending over some whiskey—liquid courage—but didn't want them misinterpreting it as a peace offering.

Mira said, "So why *are* you here?"

Vigil shook his head. "First I get another turn."

"This should be good," she said. Sarcastic, but not really.

He said, "I have an advantage. I arrived in Carlin yesterday. I also explored a little. Aside from a nice park, and a little museum I didn't see advertised on any billboards, there's absolutely nothing worth seeing. So you're not a tourist.

"There was a shooting the day before I got here. The guy who was murdered—his family lives out of town. So, you're not here for the funeral, because it'll be somewhere else.

"You could be visiting relatives, but like me, your accent isn't Texan. And if you were visiting a friend, they'd be with you. Therefore, no local ties.

"Which leaves some kind of a business trip. Almost certainly wind industry related, since that's the only thing here besides cotton, and cotton doesn't require a lot of outside consulting.

"Except that blazer doesn't fit as loose as you'd like, and you're leaning forward a lot . . . to help conceal the shoulder rig for your service weapon. You couldn't carry it on the plane, so you didn't realize the fit would be a problem until you landed. Unfortunately, you didn't pack any of your regular, more conservative blazers because they would scream 'Fed.'

"But if you *were* a Fed, you wouldn't mind people knowing. As a woman in an unfamiliar and potentially hostile environment, you'd want them to know. So I'll back off a little and go with *former* FBI, turned private investigator.

"My guess? The Prossers had a hefty policy on their son. The claims department at the insurance company doesn't wanna take the Sheriff's word for it, and they sent you to find out if there was foul play. If so, they delay the payout, and you tell them who to sue.

"How'd I do?"

Mira's cheeks flushed. "On a scale of 'in-the-ballpark' to 'nailed-it'?"

Vigil grinned, trying to hide his disappointment in her career trajectory. "That close?"

"Frankly it's a little disturbing." Mira's eyes narrowed. "Was I way off? Are you a criminal profiler or something?"

"Not in the way you mean. And you were actually pretty warm for a cold read."

"Which part?"

Vigil saw the bartender dusting bottles, Definitely Not Eavesdropping™. But he wasn't concerned about Caleb—what could Vigil say now that the goons in the Lincoln hadn't already shared with Grainger. It was Mira who gave him pause, because:

Fuck insurance companies.

In all the holes.

He'd never paid a premium in his life, but who didn't know at least one family who'd gone bankrupt when their provider refused to pay for a hospital bill? Everyone had to make a living, but as far as Vigil was concerned, Mira was one step away from taking blood money. If he answered truthfully, she might view his background and his expertise as an asset. Not ideal. Alternatively, she might conclude his interest in the case was suspicious and his capabilities made him a suspect. Even worse.

Mira looked at him expectantly. Made the *And-then-what-happened?* spiraling gesture with her hand.

The enemy of my enemy is my friend, probably applied here. Cliche because it was so often true. That said, he didn't know this woman. Vigil breathed in slowly, said, "I never served, but I have a deep respect and familiarity with the military. My father was a SEAL. Instead of tossing a ball around, we used to run drills together."

"So why didn't you follow in his footsteps?"

He wanted to say: *Because that would be impossible.* Commander Lance Vigil had been a war hero. Four tours in Vietnam. One of only seven Navy SEALs ever awarded the Medal of Honor. So renowned, he'd been invited to join the very first Delta Force—which he politely declined—only to become a founding member of SEAL Team Six, instead. Not to mention all the things he did after getting out of the military.

Vigil shrugged. "Guess I fell in love with the road. That, and you were spot-on about me not taking orders." A couple *attaboys* to keep the conversation rolling, but nothing much more specific than what she'd already guessed.

Mira was nodding her head like he finally made sense to her. She said, "I think you're holding back a little."

Vigil was silent. He was holding back a lot.

She said, "You used the word 'murder' to describe the shooting . . . are you a friend of the Prosser family? The P.I. they hired because they don't trust the Sheriff?"

You just gave me the perfect cover. But Vigil didn't like lying, and he rarely did. He said, "I don't know the victim's family. I'm more of a hobbyist."

"You investigate murders . . . for fun?"

Vigil frowned. "That came out wrong."

"How so?"

"The investigating part is a necessary evil. I need to be *sure* before I commit."

"Before you commit to what?"

"Righting wrongs." He could see the way Mira was looking at him, like maybe he was a crazy person with a Batman complex. But he could also tell she was intrigued. He attempted to clarify, said, "I try to let the system do its thing, but when it's failing, someone needs to take responsibility. It's not about 'fun.' It's about what needs doing. Most people aren't willing to step up and even fewer are capable. I'm that rare motherfucker who's both."

Mira said, "So you're a vigilante."

Vigil shrugged. "You say that like a pejorative."

"What about the legal consequences?"

"If you were still a Fed, I might've kept that last part to myself."

Mira said, "Maybe we can help each other?"

The way she posed it made Vigil wonder if leaving the Bureau hadn't been up to Mira. He said, "I'm not sure you'd want my help. And if I'm honest, I'm not sure I wanna help you."

"But I agree with you. I don't think the shooting was accidental, either."

"Yeah, well, Oxymoron Mutual Life Insurance—or whoever you work for—would love if you proved it, so they don't have to pay. I'm not into robbing the bereaved."

"But the family gets a check regardless. There will be a civil suit. Usually the judgment exceeds what's in the policy."

Vigil shook his head. "Two things wrong with that logic: First, you're assuming whoever's guilty has the money. Second, that they live long enough to pay it." This earned him a stern look in the mirror from the table of farmers closest to the bar.

Mira put her hand on his knee, balancing as she leaned closer to whisper in his ear. "What if I told you that I'm that rare boss bitch who's willing to do the right thing—even when it's not in my employer's best interest?"

He assumed Mira had whispered this last part for a reason. He brought his mouth close to her ear, said quietly, "If that was true, you'd never work for an insurance company." Vigil heard metal chair legs grinding on concrete and checked the mirror again. Four cornfed cotton farmers were standing up from their table.

Mira kept her hand on Vigil's knee and rested her other hand on the nape of his neck. "I'm a contractor—they're just one client—but I get where you're coming from," she whispered. "And if you give me a chance, I'll prove it."

In the mirror, he saw one of the farmers make a fist. Gearing up for a sucker punch.

She said, "When I stop kissing you—*duck*."

Vigil didn't want a kiss, the same way an obedient Labrador doesn't want a squirrel. Then her lips were on his, and then her tongue, and he felt exactly like a million years of evolution would dictate.

CHAPTER TWENTY-ONE

Q ueue the Metallica soundtrack. Tweak the lyrics:

Kiss with one eye open, gripping her pistol tight
Duck the right
Enter fight
Broke his hand
The farmers make a foolish stand

MIRA'S TACTICAL GIFT WAS BOLD AND EFFECTIVE. After scissoring forward at the waist to dodge the incoming blow, Vigil heard the guy scream as the bones in his wrist shattered against the bar top. He tried to sit back up, but Mira had leverage and held his head down. She drew her weapon and used it to clothesline the whimpering farmer on the bridge of his nose. He timbered backward like a felled tree, out cold before the floor could spark him.

She took her hand off Vigil's neck and stood up from her stool as the next farmer shuffled forward to try his luck. Vigil got his feet under him, grabbed hold of the now empty seat by two wooden legs, and swung hard. The stool was heavy and well made. So was Vigil. It caught the second farmer on both sides of the knee—high calf, low thigh—and the joint hinged sideways in a manner not described in the owner's manual. The now crippled farmer yelped and then toppled over into a vicious uppercut, thrown by Vigil as he raised himself to full height. The guy's jaw broke upon impact, a sound like a sledgehammer hitting a coconut, and his concussed friend cushioned his fall.

The third farmer—by far the biggest—took a tentative step forward, hands up like a boxer protecting his face. He was so enormous it didn't make sense. Three hundred pounds. Easy. Maybe three-fifty. A rodeo bull in size-15 boots and bib overalls. The guy won tractor pulls at the county fair without a tractor—just a wheelbarrow and spite.

Vigil said, "Take your best shot, big man. I'm no kind of a bully."

Which had the intended effect.

The behemoth trudged forward and threw a looping over-hand right that came at Vigil's head as big and slow and obvious as a 747 gliding in for a landing. He easily side-stepped the punch, and the momentum from the miss sent the farmer stumbling toward the bar.

Toward Mira.

She didn't move a muscle. Just stood there. Like a bull-fighter. Then, right before the clumsy side of beef would've slammed into her, she soccer-kicked him so hard in the balls that his great-great granddad doubled over in his grave. Even the wind techs watching from the booths groaned; a few of them had to look away. The colossus-turned-castrato clutched his ruined nuts, dropped to his knees, and cried falsetto. That's when the ten remaining farmers stood up and drew an impressive array of handguns.

'Cause Texas.

Vigil left the Sig in the holster, covered by his shirt. He didn't think the farmers would fire on him with Mira, the waitress, and the bartender so close behind. Plus, if they didn't realize he was carrying, he could surprise them later. He raised his hands. Slowly. Started to stay something smart, at which point the terrible, beautiful *schlack-clack* of a pump-action shotgun registered from behind the bar.

'Cause Carla.

She said, "I've got four rounds of 12-gauge triple-aught for anyone who doesn't put their gun away, and a deep-seated resentment for y'all no-tippin' puffball peddlers.

"And Caleb—put that fuckin' phone down! We ain't callin' the police over obvious self defense. I got a useless husband and mouths to feed."

The cotton farmers put their guns away. Mira had already re-holstered her weapon. Vigil lowered his hands.

Carla said, "All y'all farmers, listen up: Drag your buddies outta here and go lick your wounds. You come back—and I don't advise it—best order somethin' and tip like yer lookin' for a new wife."

The guy with the broken hand and the busted nose woke up. "I'm pressin' charges!" His voice sounded like he'd choked on a kazoo.

"The fuck you are, Petersen," Carla said. "That camera over the bar works just fine and will show you throwin' the first punch. Same as I'd tell the respondin' officer."

One of the farmers Vigil recognized from yesterday said, "What about you, Caleb? You forget who butters yer bread?"

"Look man. The video won't lie. Just get outta here. Please."

The guy narrowed his eyes at Carla. "Alright. Since Caleb asked nicely." Then he looked at Vigil. "I'd march yer bum ass on down the road, I was you."

"If you were me, you'd know that's not happening."

"That a fact? Well then, I guess we'll be seein' you." He glanced at Mira and opened his mouth to speak, but then thought better of it. Maybe threatening a woman was frowned upon in Texas. Or maybe he wanted *none* of that smoke.

While the farmers were tending to No Nuts and Needs Crutches, Mira whispered, "We should get out of here before they do. They catch you on the road, they'll kill you."

"They'll try."

"Okay bad boy. But they have home-field advantage and they outnumber you. There's a hundred or more hicks they can call for backup, too. Not to mention, they're farmers. Plenty of land to bury a body."

She was right, and Vigil knew it. "Alright. But from now on, keep those sweet lips to yourself. You and me are strictly business."

"So now you're a professional? I thought this was a hobby."

"Like I said, it came out wrong. I don't play."

He put three tens on the bar. One for Caleb, two for Carla. Resisted the urge to maim another farmer on their way out. As he held the door for Mira he pointed to the wind techs, said, "Anyone wants to talk, find me." Then he addressed the farmers. "You, I'll find myself."

CHAPTER
TWENTY-TWO

Mira's rental was parked across the street and she used the key fob to open the hatchback. She took off her jacket. Vigil tossed his backpack inside, closed the hatch, and hopped in the Prius's passenger seat. They were underway before a single farmer had exited the Diamondback. Presumably, farmers don't carry smelling salts, so it might've taken them a while to revive their friends.

Mira backed away from the curb in a hurry. Chirped the tires.

"Drive normal," Vigil said. "We're not running."

"We kinda are."

"No, we're regrouping. Big difference."

Mira glanced over at him, then focused on the road. She was nodding her head, but Vigil didn't know what to make of her expression. Approval he didn't need? Agreement he didn't care about? Or filing away some private grievance he'd have to deal with later? Hard to tell.

"So where to?"

"Turn on Main Street," he said. "I haven't seen the residential parts of Carlin yet, and the farmers will stick to the edges of town or stay out in the country. They need to regroup, too."

They drove by the city complex, which was home to the courthouse, the police department, and the jail. Across the street was an impressive library, bordering a beautiful park. The buildings' limestone walls soaked in the late morning sun and cast a sepia glow over the street that reminded Vigil of a spaghetti Western. As they passed the cosmetic surgery office and the wind energy museum he searched Mira's face for some kind of reaction. She seemed oblivious.

"Notice anything unusual?" he asked.

"Awful nice park for Podunk, Texas."

Vigil nodded. He supposed a cosmetic surgeon wouldn't even register on Mira's radar. She wouldn't be in the market for a boob job or a facelift, that was for damn sure. In an ad, she would be the *After* photo. He said, "By the way, you did good in there."

"For a woman, you mean."

"I'm not a fan of sliding scales. You did good. Period."

"You too."

Vigil nodded. He'd done as expected. Untrained men had no business throwing down with someone like him. Neither did trained men, for that matter. He said, "The kiss was brilliant . . . tactically speaking."

Mira gave him a look somewhere between curious and miffed. "*Tactically?*"

"You short-circuited their Boyd loop."

"OODA: Observe → Orient → Decide → Act. Yeah, well, it's not just for fighter pilots."

Vigil was impressed. Named after Air Force Colonel John Boyd, the behavioral model systematized a process whereby agility can trump superior strength or numbers. "They teach that at Quantico?"

"Sure." Mira changed the subject, said, "So what's the

plan? Or do you need to *observe* more of this peaceful neighborhood before you feel *oriented* enough to *decide* how you're going to *act*?"

Vigil grunted. *Fair play*, as the British would say. Nonetheless, he *did* want to orient himself more fully. He wasn't sure how long he'd be in Carlin. "Let's make a loop." Exploring by car wasn't the best for noticing detail, but for efficiency, it beat walking.

'Peaceful' turned out to be an apt descriptor: It was an all-American neighborhood with tire swings suspended from oak branches, big front porches with wicker furniture, house cats napping on window sills, and ol' glory hanging proud at every other house. Lawns were mowed. Junk kept to a minimum. There were swing sets and trampolines and barbecue grills. The occasional bass boat in a driveway. A Baptist church and a Lutheran church within a stone's throw of one another. Nine blocks of this nothing-special and they were to the Interstate.

Mira turned on the frontage road and headed west and then turned north on Hickory Street, tracing a horseshoe on the map if they'd been consulting one. They passed Carlin Collegiate High School, home of the Fighting Farmers. Not so much, Vigil thought, though the track and the football field were nice enough to host a pro team. Even for Texas, where football was a religion, the astroturf and the massive LCD scoreboard were a tad over-the-top. They even had box seats. Then he noted "Grainger Field" stenciled in big purple letters across the gable of the field house, and it made more sense.

He said, "Can I borrow your phone?"

"Why?"

"To make a call."

"What's wrong with yours?"

"Don't have one."

Mira appraised him with bemusement bordering on contempt.

"I travel light."

"The average smartphone fits in a pocket," she said. "You travel *Luddite*."

"It's more of a privacy thing. What's the point of going anywhere you want, if someone always knows where you're at?"

She made a show of rolling her eyes, said, "What? You think there's an NSA agent assigned to you? Watching your every move?"

"I'm practical, not paranoid. There's three hundred and fifty million people in this country. The personnel cost would be prohibitive."

"So why forsake the convenience of carrying a phone?"

He said, "I prefer to avoid unnecessary interactions with law enforcement."

"Committing crimes much?"

Vigil answered with a question of his own. "Do you think everybody in prison is guilty? Or were at least some of the inmates wrongfully convicted?"

"The system's not perfect. But locked up and totally innocent? Four, five percent. Max. Still too many—obviously—but it could be a helluva lot worse."

That last bit sounded like Mira was defending her resume, but that wasn't the point Vigil was making. He said, "Let's say you're in a city, sitting at a table in front of a cafe, enjoying a coffee. You have your phone out, killing time doom-scrolling social media. A half-block away, on the other side of the street, some pervert snatches a kid walking to school. Takes them into an alley and does bad things to them. Leaves them for dead. You didn't see a thing, of course. You were staring at Twitter or whatever. You go about your day."

Mira sighed, said, "I see where you're going with this.

Obviously, I'd get a call at some point from the lead investigator, wanting to know if I'd noticed anyone suspicious in the area, or—"

"If you could come down to the station and answer some questions," Vigil said, cutting her off.

"Why would you assume I'd be a suspect?" Mira fired back.

Touchy, Vigil thought. Before he could clarify that he'd meant the generic "you" (as in everybody, not Mira in particular), she went on.

"There would be people in the cafe who saw me sitting there, eating a muffin and drinking coffee or whatever. Probably cameras behind the register, too. Not to mention, *dozens* if not *hundreds* of other people nearby, who would show up on the cell tower's logs. By your logic, that would make everyone in the area with a cellphone, a suspect."

"Not everyone. A good detective would prioritize. They'd cross reference against a list of registered sex offenders. If there were no hits, they'd match against ex-cons who lived in the area. Only when none of the parolees checked out would they get around to interviewing John Q. Public types . . . then there'd be a gang of new recruits hitting the phone banks, inquiring about job status, that day's itinerary, alibis, etcetera.

"Of course, the actual baby-raper might be smart enough to leave their phone at home. So now the detective's got no leads. What to do?

"Well, imagine that it wasn't *you* sipping coffee at the cafe, but *me*—an unemployed vagrant with no I.D. and no real reason to be wandering around. If I have a phone, and they triangulate it, and it puts me near that alley—bet your ass I'm a prime suspect. I'm innocent, but that doesn't keep them from putting me in a cage until they can verify my story. Which takes a while. Been there, done that, got the t-shirt. I've got better things to do."

"Well I have a job," Mira said. "And I need my smart-phone to do it."

"So are you going to let me borrow it, or not?"

"No."

"Why?"

"Would you trust a former Fed stupid enough to hand you their smartphone?"

"Point taken." And Vigil knew better than to protest with the naive *"If you've got nothing to hide . . ."* argument—especially after asserting his own desire for privacy. Mira could have all sorts of perfectly legitimate items on her phone she wouldn't want him to see: Addresses, browser history, family photos, naked selfies . . .

Or she could, in fact, be hiding something.

"Maybe helping each other isn't going to work out so well." When it came to playing nice with others, Vigil was out of practice.

Mira took it in stride. "Or maybe I can take you to a convenience store and you can buy a burner," she said. "Who do you need to call, anyway?"

"The victim's father."

"Reason enough not to let you use my phone. I suppose you'll convince him to request an independent autopsy."

"Yep."

"No need. The insurance company already ordered one."

"I should still get a burner. At least until we get to the bottom of this. That way, if we split up, you can still reach me."

"Burners still talk to cell towers. You know that, right?"

Vigil said, "Of course. But I don't have to buy a plan and sign my name to paperwork to get a burner. And you're going to buy it for me. I'll reimburse you."

Mira said, "Are you in a hurry?"

"Rarely. We can grab one tonight on the way back to Sweetwater."

"Sweetwater?"

"They have hotels there."

Mira nodded, said, "I think we should talk to Justin Lackey first."

"Agreed," he said, "Then we pay a visit to Oswald Schnell and—"

"Take a look at the crime scene," she finished.

"I was gonna say, 'and compare their stories,' but that, too. Should've asked Caleb for directions before we left."

"No need. I can look it up on my phone."

"I didn't think private investigators had access to the DMV database."

"Depends on the state, but it doesn't matter. I'll use property records. They're public. Most County Clerk offices have a searchable database online. I'm tellin' you, Vigil, a smartphone is indispensable in this line of work. That, and a laptop."

She wasn't wrong, but what Vigil said was, "Pretty soon I'd need to rent an apartment just to keep all my gadgets charged. Buy furniture and bedding, and pots and pans. Hang pictures on the walls. Neighbors would want me to feed their cat when they went on vacation. I'd have to sort through junk mail. Wash the pots and pans. Dust the pictures. Make the bed. Next thing you know I'm working at the local factory so I can pay for a maid. Lots of overtime so I can buy a car to get back and forth from the factory. I'd drink too much and exercise too little. Eventually I'd need to talk to a therapist—who only became a therapist because they were going crazy on the same damn hamster wheel and wanted to improve their self-talk. They'd tell me, 'but there's a pill for that.' Write me a scrip. There'd be lots of 'working for the weekend' and binge watching TV series about guys who live like I do now."

"I bet you're a fun date," she said.

Vigil remembered saying, *". . . strictly business,"* and kept his mouth shut.

Mira took a right on 7th Street and pulled into an overflow lot across from the high school auditorium. It was limestone, too. Same builder as Grainger's other namesakes. While she tapped and swiped and typed and clicked, he looked out the window and noted how all the lawns adjacent to the school had diagonal dirt paths worn into them like livestock trails. He supposed they were. *Sheep in training.*

"Found it. He's off a gravel road fifteen miles north of town."

"What took you so long?" Vigil teased, thinking: *That's a long walk with no car.*

"Lackey doesn't own property. I had to dig a little."

Vigil frowned. "Interesting."

"What?"

"You'd think a foreman for the world's second largest wind farm would get paid enough to afford a house, no?"

"Depends. Maybe he's waiting for the housing bubble to burst. Have you seen prices lately?" Mira propped the iPhone up in the cupholder so she could see the map and then answered her own question. "Of course you haven't."

F M-608 took them north of Carlin for much of the short drive. At first, it ran arrow-straight, through flat dirt fields dotted with remnants of last harvest's cotton and wind turbine towers standing like sentries. Then the road wiggled up into low, brush-covered hills with switchgrass and buffalograss chewed ragged by longhorn cattle. The last mile on County Road 443 was gravel-on-red-clay.

Vigil said, "Given your experience, I'll let you ask most of the questions."

Mira nodded. "No shit."

Good, he thought. *Keep thinking I'm all brawn and no brains.* "Game plan?"

"Kid gloves," she said. "We only need details the sheriff didn't get out of him. Something to contradict Schnell's story when we talk to him."

Vigil was silent.

"He's probably in shock. But I've got ways to open him up: Nurturing mother. The hot girl he wants to impress. Compassionate therapist."

"He might get down on one knee," Vigil said.

"What we don't want," Mira continued, "is to fall into the Good Cop / Bad Cop stereotype. We do that, he'll clam up." Mira slowed before a black mailbox with peeling silver stencils. Checked the street number and nodded, then pulled into the rutted driveway. "Looks like he's home."

Stunted mesquite and scrub oak covered most of the property, but a large enough swath had been cleared that Lackey's trailer house was visible from the road. It had aluminum siding, hanging off in places where the wind had torn it loose from the rivets, uniformly dented by decades of hail on the southwest side. The exterior was mostly a mildew-mottled white, with sun-bleached brown accents that had turned a shade of pink Vigil associated with uncooked bacon. There were holes in the flimsy skirting (meant to hide the concrete blocks the manufactured home was strapped down to), and burrows dug underneath the corrugated fiberglass by foxes or rabbits seeking shelter in the redneck basement. In other words, your base model white-trash domicile —more common to Arkansas or southern Missouri than Texas, but Vigil had seen plenty throughout the country.

Nosed-up to the "deck" (which must've been built by a one-armed carpenter with vertigo) was a Ford Bronco with a comically raised suspension. Centered on the back glass was a bumper sticker featuring Calvin, from the Calvin and Hobbes comic strip, gleefully pissing on a Chevy badge, asscrack showing as big as his smirk. In the dust beside it someone had written:

FUCK FORD

A footpath led to a rusted steel drum at the edge of the yard, still smoldering from recently burned trash. Next to it was a shallow pit where the scorched refuse would be (theoretically) buried at some point, but it was piled so high with ash-dusted beer bottles and aluminum cans it would require a backhoe to tame. Vigil saw no sign of one.

He let Mira lead the way. Figured she'd have ID she could show Lackey if he asked to see it. No one bothered asking the sidekick to show their ID. Didn't film well, and most people dealt with cops like movies and TV had taught them to. Plus, Mira was the kind of woman you'd invite inside. Purely for aesthetic reasons. If Vigil approached alone, or in front of Mira, Lackey might pretend to be in the shower or on a long walk or in a coma.

They went up three sagging steps to a ramshackle porch. She knocked on the flimsy screen door which clung to the frame with hinges forged from recycled hubcaps and hope. Vigil heard muffled footsteps and squeaking boards and then the door opened.

"Justin Lackey?"

"You're talkin' to him." He was tan and tall and blonde. Reasonably clean-cut. Lean in the way of men who drink most of their calories from a twelve-ounce bottle and work it off lifting heavy shit in the sun all day. The inevitable paunch had yet to rise, bread-like, above his waistband, but it was only a matter of time. He wore a black Whiskey Myers t-shirt and a pair of denim shorts over flip-flops. A bottle of Lone Star in one hand, a compact Ruger pistol in the other. "Who are you?" he said. His breath was like a keg party, but he wasn't slurring, which was surprising.

"Mira Getty. This is my partner, Nate Vigil. You mind if we come in?"

Partner. Nice touch.

Lackey looked nervously at Vigil, said, "This's about Will, ain't it?"

Mira nodded. "Yes. We just have a few questions."

"I already talked to the Sheriff. And I know Carlin's finest on a first name basis—y'all Feds or sumthin'?"

"Private investigator," Mira said. "I work for Innova-Gen's insurance company."

Lackey squinted like such a thing had never occurred to him. "If you promise he's not goin' to arm wrestle me," he said, pointing at Vigil with his longneck, "I guess that'd be alright." He held the door and gestured to a brown plaid couch dating back to the Reagan era. "'Scuse the mess. I've been batching it for a while now. And don't mind Betsy. She don't bite."

Mira sat down on the edge of the cushions a respectful distance from the beagle, and Lackey got comfortable in a faux-leather recliner. Vigil stood in the doorway.

"Close that, would ya? The AC's leakin' out."

Vigil closed the cheap hollow-core door, thought: *Either he's awful trusting, or he's not alone.*

"Can I grab you guys a beer or somethin'?"

"You can put the pistol down," Mira said.

"Oh. Sorry. Forgot I was even holdin' it." Lackey set it down on a low coffee table. Looked up at Vigil. "You?"

Vigil shook his head. "I'm good, thanks."

"Whaddya wanna know?" Lackey asked, unprompted.

Vigil was silent. He was very interested in what Lackey had to say, to be sure, but he was just as eager to see how Mira handled herself. Did she still lean on those good investigative habits they taught her at Quantico? Or had she gotten rusty freelancing?

Mira reached over and put a comforting hand on his arm, said, "Slow down. We'll get there. Why don't you tell us a little about yourself?" Her smile was warm like homemade taffy.

Lackey took a deep breath and let it out. "Okay. You want me to start with my childhood? or . . ."

"Wherever you'd like," Mira said.

She was establishing rapport. Standard operating procedure for an initial interview. They listened as Lackey gave them a rambling account of his lackluster bio:

Born and raised in Carlin. Town kid. Parents didn't inherit land they could farm; both of them commuted to office jobs in Sweetwater—school secretary / manager at a rent-to-own furniture store. He played second base on the baseball team. Pretty good, too, but Coach booted him for getting his wife's sister's daughter drunk after homecoming his junior year— the start of a pattern: "Me and beer," he said, raising his bottle and waving it around at his surroundings like it explained everything, "get along." He tried to clean up by joining the Marines, but blew his knee out in bootcamp and decided the military wasn't for him. Came home and moved back in with his parents. They died in a car accident soon after, left him the house. He knocked up a stripper, got married, became a father. Finally decided to get his shit together. Went to trade school and became a wind jockey. Kept his head down, promoted to foreman. Everything was great . . . not so fast. Got divorced; half of almost nothing. Alimony. Child support. Life sucks—get a helmet. Made a deal with himself that as long as he kept it to beer, and never let a hangover keep him from working, he could drink as much as he wanted. "And here I am. Livin' the dream."

Mira thanked him for sharing, said, "Before we dive into what happened, please accept my condolences."

"Thanks. We weren't super close, but Will was a good egg. I liked him."

"So what brought you and Will to farmer Schnell's field? Let's start there."

Will. Not Prosser. She's not terrible, Vigil thought.

Lackey's face scrunched up a little. Like a cranky two-year-old threw a tantrum and caught his cheek with a flailing arm. A micro-gesture but Vigil noticed. Surprise, maybe. Or panic.

"Funny," he said, "Sheriff Baker never asked me that. 'Course there was no need. We were in our coveralls and covered in grease. Obviously doin' maintenance. All five towers on the 307 A and B lines."

"And was this standard, scheduled maintenance you performed that day?" Mira asked.

Lackey seemed confused for a moment, said, "Yeah. I mean, we followed procedure. There's troubleshooting checklists we adhere to."

Vigil cut in, said, "What she's asking is, were you performing routine maintenance? or was there something wrong with one of the turbines in Schnell's field that prompted the trip?"

Mira looked up at him, face blank. A little too blank. Like, *You wanna know how angry I get when you mansplain?—fill in the blank*. Vigil looked down at his boots sheepishly in lieu of an apology. He wasn't sorry.

Lackey paused, as if perplexed by the question, but to Vigil he looked like he was buying time. "Oh, right. Routine maintenance." Lackey's eyes darted back and forth between them like bad poker players do when they're bluffing. He also glanced at the Ruger. Vigil noted that, too.

Mira continued, "The paper said that Schnell was shooting at wild pigs, missed, and hit Will. Did you notice any pigs in the area when you were working?"

'The paper said . . .'—what the hell, Mira? Comforting was one thing, but in Vigil's experience, it was always better if you didn't remind someone what they'd already said on the record. Stories often change when you're under pressure and covering lies.

"Sure. Counted six of 'em. They were rooting around in Schnell's field not long before we packed it up for the day. I paid them no mind. Hogs are everywhere 'round here. Farmers hate 'em. They do a ton of damage."

Mira said, "How far away is Schnell's house from where you and Prosser were working?"

"Half a mile. Give or take."

"Close enough to see someone standing," she said, "but far enough away you might not recognize them?"

"I guess. But if it was someone I expected to see there, I'd know if it was them or not."

"And did you see Schnell that day? Holding a rifle?"

"No."

"Did you see anyone else on Schnell's property holding a rifle?"

"No. Like I told the sheriff, Will was takin' a piss, and I was lookin' down at my phone. I didn't see anyone. Just heard the shot, looked up, and saw Will facedown in the dirt."

"Could you tell from which direction the shot came?"

"Not really. I was in the pickup. Idling with the AC on high."

"So when you heard the shot, and you saw Will lying on the ground, what did you do next?"

"I got out and ran over to him."

"Did you know he'd been shot?"

Good question, Vigil thought.

"I assumed he had. Why else would he be layin' there after somebody fired a gun?"

Mira said, "What did you do when you got to him?"

"I rolled him over on his back. Checked if he was still breathin'." Lackey sighed. Started to tear up. He took a moment to gather himself. "I'll never forget his eyes," he said. "They were like . . . bottomless wells."

Mira patted his shoulder. "Must've been hard seeing him like that."

"It was."

Vigil said, "Getty. We need a moment."

Mira's expression wasn't quite so blank this time. "Okay. Please excuse us, Justin."

They went outside on the porch and Vigil closed the door behind them. The AC unit was roaring along but he still spoke softly. "Are you going to keep lobbing him softballs?"

"I told you: Kid gloves. We're not law enforcement. He doesn't have to talk to us. We press him too hard, he'll realize that. And we might need to follow up with him after we talk to Schnell. The only way that happens is if we're easier to talk to than the authorities . . . or keeping quiet."

You say that, because you don't think he could be complicit. Vigil didn't tell her this because he might've been making assumptions of his own. He said, "When we go back in there, let me have a go at him. So far he's just regurgitating what he told the sheriff. He needs to know we won't settle for that."

"But he's not a suspect! We're just trying to—"

Vigil held up a hand and cut her off. "Trust me. I assumed you already knew some things you obviously don't. I'll catch you up when we leave."

He could tell that Mira wanted to protest, but Vigil had already opened the door.

"Everything alright?" Lackey asked.

He ignored the question. Launched right in. "Where was he shot?"

"Here comes the Bad Cop," Lackey quipped.

He was trying to play it cool, but Vigil could tell he was nervous. "I'm not a cop."

"Right. You work for an insurance company." His tone was suitably dismissive.

Vigil smiled. Tried to make himself look like a teddy bear. *Let him think whatever he wants. For now.*

"He was shot in the forehead," Lackey said.

"You said he was lying facedown—did you see an exit wound when you approached him?"

"Yeah. Base of his skull. I mean, I knew he was gone right away, but . . . you hope—ya know?"

Now we're getting somewhere. Lackey might not have realized it, but he just proved the shooter wasn't aiming at hogs. The trajectory was all wrong. He glanced at Mira, but if she understood where he was going with this, she gave no indication. She nodded sympathetically at Lackey, then looked up at Vigil like she'd heard enough. But Vigil was just warming up.

"You ever go deer hunting?" he said.

"Sure. I've killed a buck before."

"Rifle?"

"Yup."

"Scope?"

"Of course."

"How far out was he? The buck?"

"A hundred yards. Maybe less."

"Easy shot, right?"

"Sure. I hit him clean."

"Would you have taken the shot if the deer was two hundred yards away?"

"Probably. I'm no high-level marksman by any stretch, but with a scope and a good rifle, that's still an easy shot."

"What about five hundred yards?"

"Me? I'd wanna be closer. But there are plenty of good ol' boys 'round here who'd take that shot. Hell, a buddy of mine dropped an elk in Arizona at thirteen hundred yards."

Vigil said, "I don't doubt it. Especially if the elk was standing still. An elk is a big animal. A pig, on the other hand? They're pretty small. Compared to an elk. Furtive, too. Shifty little things. An elk stands, what? Five feet tall at the shoulder? A thousand pounds or more? Large animal. Good meat. How tall would you say a wild hog is, Justin?"

Mira was looking like she could use a cigarette, and Vigil

was pretty sure she didn't smoke. If she did, though, she could've used that stare to light one.

"I don't know. Two, three feet, tops?"

"Pretty small animal compared to a deer or an elk," Vigil said. "Would you shoot at a pig from eight hundred yards away?"

Lackey was white-knuckling his half-empty Lone Star and digging his fingers into the recliner's armrest. "Probably not."

"Why? They're an invasive species. They do a ton of damage."

"You know damn well why. I just told you I'd pass up shooting a buck at five hundred."

"And yet, Schnell shot at a hog from eight hundred yards away . . . " Vigil trailed off to let the implication sink in.

Lackey said, "Might've been a fuckin' sniper for all I know. I think he fought in the first Gulf War. Maybe eight hundred yards is no big deal for him."

Vigil shrugged as if Lackey had a point. Then let him know he wasn't buying it. "A sniper wouldn't have missed . . . oh, wait . . . he didn't miss, did he?"

Lackey stared at the matted shag carpet, gears grinding like a faulty transmission.

Now he'd proven the shot was deliberate. Vigil kept up the pressure. There was one more hole to punch in his story. "How tall was Prosser?"

"An inch or so taller than me. Six-three, thereabouts."

"And those six feral hogs you saw rooting around in Schnell's field—were they closer to Schnell's compound than Prosser was when he went to take a piss?"

Lackey nodded. "'Course they were. Else he'd have seen Will."

Vigil said, "When you heard the shot, you must've looked around for the shooter, right? I mean, you saw Prosser lying there—you could've been next. You'd have wanted to make sure there wasn't a gunman waiting for you to step out of the pickup."

Lackey said nothing at first. He looked like a guy who'd blown a tire, but figured he could make the next exit without bending the rim. Mira, meanwhile, looked like a cat contemplating a cold bath.

"In the heat of the moment," he said, "my safety wasn't a concern."

Vigil was tempted to tell him he was a goddamned hero, but figured that would be too much for Mira to keep holding her tongue. He said, "Are there any houses or other structures visible from Schnell's field?"

"Wind turbines, obviously. Other than that, just Schnell's place, his barn, and a couple out-buildings. Maybe a chicken coup."

"So naturally, you would've looked in that direction for the shooter."

"Sure. I guess. But like I said, I didn't see anyone."

"But if Schnell was eight hundred yards away, you should've seen him there with a rifle. You said it yourself, that's close enough you might have recognized him. So why didn't you see Schnell holding a rifle?"

Lackey downed the rest of his beer, searching for something to fill the hole in his story in the same place he searched for everything else he lacked in life. His brow was an oil slick, despite the AC being set so low. Mira's arms, in contrast, were covered in gooseflesh. He put the beer down on the coffee table, said, "I think he must've fired from inside his house. Through an open window or sumthin'. That's why I didn't see him."

"You ever shoot a hunting rifle inside a house?" Vigil asked.

Lackey shook his head. "No."

"Me either. Because they're really, *really* loud. We're talking permanent hearing loss for anyone inside. I wonder why Schnell would be willing to damage his family's hearing over a damn pig?"

"Maybe because the old man has an artificial leg. Got his foot caught in a harvester blade or sumthin' like that. I don't remember the details. But I know he's got a terrible limp."

"Interesting," Vigil said. "Probably not up for climbing ladders, then."

Lackey stood up and walked over to the fridge. Helped himself to another bottle. "You know what?" he said. "I think I've answered enough of your questions."

Vigil said, "You most certainly have."

CHAPTER
TWENTY-FOUR

L eonard was thinking about lunch when a text arrived from Caleb, the bartender.

> Big guy came back. Nate Vigil. Met w/ woman, Mira—not from here—strangers? He made threats. She kissed him. Left together after sending three farmers to the hospital. Scary fuckin dude! / 1 bad bitch—carrying! Carla wouldn't let me call the police.

HIS FIRST THOUGHT WAS: *This fuckin' guy.* HIS NEXT thought was: *I should give Carla a raise.* It wouldn't have mattered if Caleb called the Carlin police (unlike the Nolan County Sheriff's Department, the city pigs were on the payroll)—it was the principle of the thing. Carla was good people. Reminded Leonard of his ex. *Especially that rack.* He might try to bang her before he disappeared. From behind, so he could hold on to those big floppers.

As for this Nate Vigil character?

He'd get handled.

The motherfucker *had no idea* who he was dealin' with.

Leonard just had to be patient before green-lighting the hit. So far, the sheriff was buying Schnell's stray bullet bullshit. But if Leonard dropped another body so soon after Prosser, Baker might decide to take a closer look. A problem, because ol' Schnell didn't exactly have a leg to stand on.

Well, just the one.

Leonard chuckled, checked his phone. Like he was psychic, it started ringing. The caller ID read Maynard Hickman, the only cotton farmer with permission (and the balls) to call Leonard's private number. No one he was in the mood to talk to. He cut him off before he could speak, said, "Yeah, I know about him already. And I know you fuckin' pussies took a beatin' at the bar. Youse oughta be embarrassed."

"You know about the woman he was with?"

"I'm not worried about the chick."

"You should be."

"What the fuck did you say to me?" This came out more harshly than he'd intended, but Leonard was already annoyed at the farmers for the drama the Diamondback. Naturally, he understood their show of force. They were backing their people. And unless Schnell wanted to die by running his mouth, the other farmers weren't even aware of who really pulled the trigger. Even so, their ignorance and friends-in-low-places loyalty had aroused suspicion, and Leonard was none too happy about that.

Hickman kept his mouth shut.

"That's right. Remember who you're talkin' to. Now listen: I'm actually glad you called. There will be some digging on your land. Starting tonight—all of youse. Don't worry about it."

Hickman said nothing, but Leonard could hear him breathing heavily, stifling a complaint. He knew what his monthly contributions meant to the farmers' bottom lines.

"You gotta problem with that?"

"No. It's just . . . "

"Just what?"

"A lot of us are depending on—"

"I said don't worry about it—the money either. Just don't forget what else it buys."

"Yeah, well, for some reason, the big guy doesn't think it was an accident. He was sittin' there at the bar, right next to us, threatenin' to kill Schnell like it was just another errand on his To-Do list. We ain't gonna let that happen."

"I'm okay with that. But I need you to wait until I find out who he is. If he's undercover, we all go to jail. Just hang tight until I give you the word."

"What about Schnell?"

"He'll be fine. I'll put my guys on protection detail. We clear?"

"Crystal."

"Good. Go spread the gospel."

Mariana had a meatball sub waiting for him in the kitchen and they ate together out on the deck. She complimented him on last night's performance. Hinted she might be open to an encore after dinner. Truth be told, he was in the mood for things too unsavory for his wife. Kinky shit he saved for his sidepiece, or a local slut who needed money. How many kids in Carlin got what they wanted for Christmas, 'cause mama was shameless? He winked at her. "We'll see."

Belly full, Leonard nailed down the e-waste recycler in Houston and coordinated with the freight broker. It took longer than expected, and by the time everything was lined up, he was ready for a nap.

He was nodding off in the backyard hammock when his phone rang. No caller ID this time, but Leonard recognized the number. It was the burner he'd given Justin Lackey.

CHAPTER
TWENTY-FIVE

Mira stormed to the Prius.

Vigil took his time. He didn't want Lackey thinking he was in a hurry. Hurry reeks of desperation. What Vigil wanted Lackey to appreciate was:

1) *this guy knows I'm a liar,*

2) *he won't stop until he gets to the bottom of this,* and

3) *getting on his bad side would be even worse than crossing the people I'm covering for.*

And if it wasn't for Mira, Vigil would've told him exactly that on his way out. But Mira was acting strange.

She already had the Prius in gear when he got in. She whipped them around and then punched the accelerator, pelting the undercarriage with loose gravel. He held the grab handle to steady himself as the little hybrid raced down Lackey's driveway and drifted onto the dirt road like a rally car. If she was trying to get a reaction by driving reckless, it was a lost cause. Vigil had been hitchhiking since Johnny Cash came back from the dead. He believed in a driver's instinct for self-preservation. Trusted seatbelts and airbags and crumple zones.

He leaned back and got comfortable. Considered taking a

nap. He liked naps. He was good at them and could fall asleep pretty much anywhere.

"You did the *exact* thing I told you *not* to do." Mira over-enunciated like she was talking to tech support in an Indian call center.

Vigil didn't take the bait. Arguing with an angry woman merely fueled her rage. Every retort, another shovelful of coal into the fiery furnaces of hell, where demon chemists brewed scorn in cauldrons of boiling sugar and spice. Better if you didn't feed the flames. Let the heat dissipate.

He closed his eyes. Got comfortable.

"Great. The strong-and-silent treatment." Much of the venom had drained from her voice, replaced by the flirtatious tone she'd led with at the bar.

"No need to respond," he said. "I pressed Lackey harder than you wanted me to. But it worked. So if you're looking for an apology? Not gonna happen."

"Well if you're waiting for a pat on the back, you'll be waiting a long time."

"I don't need a treat," Vigil said. "I'm just surprised getting the result we came for doesn't trump your bruised ego." He should've remained silent.

"Excuse me?"

"You heard me."

They were on paved roads now, and Mira was doing at least eighty. "The only 'result' you achieved is ensuring that Lackey never cooperates with us again."

"If I need him to talk, he'll talk. Believe that."

"I'm sure you can be very persuasive."

"Yep."

"So you just—what?—start yanking fingernails?"

The accusation offended him. He didn't believe in torture. "Doesn't matter anyway."

"It *might*—if I need a sworn deposition when this goes to trial."

"I thought you said you were that 'rare boss-bitch willing to do the right thing?' But there you go talking about trials."

"And you said you don't get involved until the system's failing . . . you *don't know* if it's failing or not."

"I know 'anonymous sources within the Sheriff's Department are mostly convinced the shooting was a terrible accident, with charges unlikely to be filed,'" he countered, quoting the article from the Sweetwater Reporter.

"Because you can *always* trust anonymous sources in law enforcement—and 'journalists,' for that matter."

She has a point.

"Don't you think," she said, "if we uncover enough evidence, the Sheriff's Department will have to keep investigating? The way I see it, that's still doing the right thing."

Vigil had to concede this point, too. The anonymous source suggested the investigators might be inept, but so far he had no reason to believe they were corrupt. He tried to put himself in the Sheriff's shoes: *What would you conclude, if you've got a body in a field, and the owner of the field walks up to you with a smoking gun and confesses that his shot—intended for a hog—went wide?* Admittedly (assuming he found pig tracks), Vigil might've arrived at the same conclusion as Sheriff Baker. After all, Baker hadn't been privy to the cotton farmers' shady conduct at the Diamondback. Nor had he loudly announced his skepticism of Schnell's story, only to have three thugs with a New York accent attempt to run him out of Carlin.

"Fair enough," he said.

"What does that mean?"

"It means I'm willing to give the Sheriff a second chance to get it right." This sounded a little *too* agreeable, even to him.

Mira must've sensed there was more beneath it. *"But . . ."* she prompted.

"But before we hand over the evidence, we figure out what really happened. And *why* it happened. We idiot-proof the case—leave Baker no alternative except to do his damn job. If he still doesn't see the light—"

"We do what needs doing," she said, finishing his thought.

Now it was Mira who sounded a little too accommodating. Like maybe *she* was the one playing Good Cop / Bad Cop —*both roles*. Her motives for this low-key manipulation were unclear. But for sure it meant she didn't trust him yet. Which was fair, because he didn't trust her yet either.

Not entirely.

They were leaving the hills and the scrub brush and re-entering the flat land of cotton fields and wind farms. Mira let her foot off the gas and decelerated to a more pedestrian sixty-five. "Before you took over with Lackey, you said you'd catch me up on some things . . ."

Vigil took another deep breath. It would look suspicious if he held back now. And if they were to continue helping each other, Mira needed to know the full extent of the fuckery going on in Carlin.

He said, "Ever hear of a concrete contractor named Leonard Grainger?"

She shook her head. "No."

He gave her the condensed version, starting with what he and Franky Bloom had learned at the Diamondback. Brought her up to speed on the cotton farmers' debt to Grainger for helping them win the Innova-Gen project. Finished with the thugs sporting New York accents attempting to run him out of town last night. "Obviously Grainger's involved in Prosser's murder—the coverup at a minimum."

Mira cleared her throat. "Pretty—*ahem*—circumstantial,

you ask me." Her voice was cracking, probably dried out from the recycled air on her flight and Lackey's AC. She took a sip from an open water sitting in the console, said, "I wouldn't say it's obvious."

"Depends on how you feel about coincidences," he said.

"How do you feel about them?"

"They happen all the time. *Except* when someone's been murdered nearby. Then there's no such thing."

They reached the first long, straight stretch of asphalt on FM-608. "Agreed," she said. Now her tone was grim, almost wistful. Vigil waited for her to add some kind of sarcastic wisdom to her remark, but then, and out of nowhere, Mira slammed on the brakes and brought the Prius to a standstill.

"Get out."

He said nothing. Just sat there for a long moment and looked at her.

She wouldn't meet his eyes.

Vigil gave her a silent standing eight count, then shrugged. Used the lever to raise the seat back, opened the door, and exited the vehicle. Then he walked to the rear, expecting her to pop the hatch for him so he could grab his bag.

Mira gunned the Toyota and left him standing there empty-handed.

He raised his arms to shoulder-height, spreading his fingers and turning his palms up in the universally translatable gesture for, *What the fuck?* Then he shrugged again, over it before she'd driven a quarter mile. It wouldn't cost much to replace the totality of his worldly possessions. A few hundred bucks, maybe? If that. He still had a roll of cash in his pocket, his knife, and the Sig. Ballin' out of control by his standards.

A half mile down the road, the Prius's brake lights came on and it slowed to a stop. Mira got out. Too far away to close the gap in any reasonable amount of time, so Vigil just stood there on the blacktop and spectated. He watched her open the hatchback and remove his bag, then set it down on the asphalt and unzip it. She removed most everything—change of clothes, jacket, tarp, sleeping bag, and canteen—examining each item carefully. The boxes of ammunition for the Sig were at the bottom of the bag; she left them alone, but spread the zippered opening wide to let some light in, presumably so she could read the packaging. Satisfied, she shoved everything back in the pack and tossed it in the ditch.

And drove off again.

"Probed my bag a lot deeper than Lackey's bundle of bull-shit," Vigil said to no one in particular. Two more profound points like that one, he mused, and he could draw a triangle.

He started walking. By the time he retrieved his pack, Mira and the Prius were out of sight.

"Talk."

"I think I fucked up."

Leonard listened to the shit-faced wind tech recount the visit from Nate Vigil and Mira Getty. He stopped him a few times to have Lackey repeat the exact words he'd used, or to ask him how his interrogators had responded to certain pieces of information, but mostly, Leonard let him blather.

"I'm s-sorry, Mister Grainger. I told him there were six pigs—that I didn't see anything—but . . . he j-j-just w-wasn't havin' it. And I tried to make him see how Schnell could— you know?—so you didn't get in trouble, and—"

"Shhh. It's okay Justin. Sit tight. You didn't fuck up half as bad as you think."

Half wasn't nothing, but since Lackey had been straight with him, Leonard would tell his guys to make it quick.

CHAPTER TWENTY-SEVEN

Mira had abandoned him about five miles north of Carlin. The terrain was smooth and level, and his pack, though full, was no major impediment. A standard military quick time march at 120 steps per minute would get him back to town in an hour and a half, give or take. A little quicker was the so-called Ranger Standard: 140 steps per minute—four miles per hour, versus three-point-four. As far as he knew, there was no SEAL Standard for marching, or his father would've mentioned it. Even without an official term, he knew it would be faster than whatever the Army considered elite, and Vigil proceeded accordingly.

Soon he found his rhythm and broke a sweat. Adjusted his breathing to sync to the demands of his pace. Scanning, always scanning, but there wasn't a lot to see. It was the offseason as far as cotton farming was concerned. That was clear. The only thing growing in the fields was electricity. Tall white tubes, sprouting from gray concrete pads, buried in beige dirt; row upon row of three-bladed propellers spinning slowly in the mild west wind. Interesting and beautiful in its way, but by this point, familiar scenery.

On the one hand, this was a delay he could do without (and a prime example of why people carried smartphones, though he'd never admit it). On the other hand, Vigil tended to focus on opportunities, not setbacks, and nothing beat a long hike for calm and clarity.

Monks and Californian "life coaches" might disagree with him about the effectiveness of roaming on two feet, pointing to meditation as the superior technique for clearing the mind. But most of them had never stared death in the eye, so what would they know about living?

Meditation was simply his default mode. He'd read the definitive books on the practice, but wasn't convinced he should make it a separate habit. The vast majority of his nomadic life was *already* steeped in the supposedly elusive, rarified states touted by the authors—ways of being that were nothing new to him. By age ten, it was second nature to breathe in the sun and the breeze and all that's good in the world . . . to exhale the fear, frustration, and other bullshit your body clings to like burdock on a pant leg. The mountains and forests of Idaho had been his teacher. No "guru" required. Crossing his legs and sitting on a cushion while repeating a made-up mantra? Nope. Vigil was a *man*—no *tra* (la-la) required.

He in no way disrespected Eastern Philosophies (which had given rise to meditation). In fact, his mother had made them a pillar of his childhood studies, and their wisdom had influenced his way of navigating the world nearly as much as his father's instruction in combat and survival. But for him, the Eastern perspective felt incomplete. Though Taoism (and later, Zen Buddhism) emphasized expanding one's Awareness (an aim he embraced wholeheartedly), Eastern sages offered Acceptance—no judgment / no attachment / no expectation—as the be-all, end-all for coping with life's suffering. Beyond that, they had little to say.

While Vigil agreed with judging your past and your fellow man less harshly—with letting go of things you can't control, and not predicting the future in a vain attempt to force reality into a delusional mold—stopping there and calling it "enlightenment" was bullshit.

Because there are things one shouldn't accept.

Because *purpose* is important, and to realize a higher calling, *struggle is required:*

Lance Vigil refusing to "accept" that mankind might go extinct if civilization collapsed, for example, and striving to raise a son who could survive the fall. Vigil himself—refusing to "accept" the collapse of civilization in the first place— endeavoring to stay strong enough and deadly enough to battle injustice, which he saw as society's biggest threat.

Maybe that was why so many "enlightened beings" ended up in Himalayan caves, or sweeping the floors of remote monasteries? Because in isolation they weren't forced to acknowledge the evil in the world, or to admit that calling it "karma" was a copout, no matter how single-mindedly you chant down your inner bitch.

Such were the paths tread by his mind as he trekked along.

No wonder then, that a quarter mile closer to Carlin, Vigil was so zen about the minor setback Mira had caused him. Would her assistance have been nice? Sure. In some ways. As a former FBI agent, she would be smart, fit, and calm under pressure. Reasonably good with a gun. She had reliable transportation, and access to a phone and the internet. A very nice ass—*ahem*—*asset*, in that her good looks might cause certain people to underestimate her.

But can I trust her?

A moot point, because Mira didn't trust him.

Vigil didn't take it personally (or if he did, he made sure no one would have been able to tell—himself included). Nor did he particularly care that she'd decided to part ways. He was more than capable of handling things on his own. Usually did. Almost always preferred to.

But still, it wouldn't hurt to consider what had upset her so much.

Certainly not the kiss in the Diamondback. That was her idea, and while it may have been initiated on the pretense of diversion, it felt like the real deal, in all the ways you can't fake. Him taking over Lackey's interview a sore spot, no doubt. But after venting her frustration Mira seemed to have calmed down. They'd even reached a compromise of sorts, each making concessions, and ultimately, agreeing to bring those responsible for Prosser's murder to justice. Together, presumably.

Until I mentioned "coincidences."

Which must've been what spooked her. Because up to that point, they were a nascent, yet functional team. Two investigators (more or less), with a common goal and complementary skill sets.

Now, Mira seemed to be viewing *him* as a suspect. He'd told her at the bar that he'd arrived in Carlin yesterday, and that Prosser had been murdered the day before—but maybe she doubted his timeline . . . maybe his *no-coincidences-when-it-comes-to-murder* quip caused her to view their chance meeting in a more sinister light? After all, Vigil hadn't divulged much about himself, and what he had shared was purposely vague. Perhaps Mira was realizing just how evasive he'd been?

Except it didn't make sense. None of it did. Because if she was worried that he was one of the bad guys, then why leave him the ammunition? And if she trusted him enough to ensure he could reload his weapon, why not put the car in reverse after searching his things and invite him back in?

Vigil couldn't quite make the pieces fit, but it seemed like Mira's impression of him was currently in some kind of limbo. Not an enemy, but not an ally, either. In her mind, somewhere between *threat* and . . . what, exactly? The word that came to him was, *mistake.* Which stung a little, even though he'd never—

What's that?

He cocked his head in an attempt to hone in on the sound. The ground was flat overall, but it rose slightly between him and the horizon, and therefore he heard it before he saw it: A gruff keen of rubber on rough pavement. Whoever it was, they were headed toward him from Carlin in a real big hurry. The county hadn't bothered painting dividing lines and the road was very narrow—practically a sidewalk. Vigil got out of the way.

Seconds later, a familiar vehicle came into view.

Not a Prius.

THE BLACK LINCOLN NAVIGATOR WITH THE TINTED windows flew down the farm road toward him like a bat out of a Wuhan lab, big V-8 engine roaring at the top of its rated RPMs. The nearest structure capable of stopping a bullet was the wind turbine tower, several hundred yards away. Nowhere to hide. Not even if Vigil was the hiding type.

Which he wasn't.

He drew the 10mm Sig and crouched down in the shallow ditch to present less of a target.

They're headed for Justin Lackey's. Had to be.

He pictured the inebriated wind tech foreman calling Grainger to provide an update as soon as they left. It showed his loyalty, but Grainger wouldn't have liked what Lackey let slip; he would send his crew to silence Justin before his big mouth and small brain did any more damage. Choices have consequences, Vigil thought. That said, he wasn't thrilled his interrogation put Lackey in more danger.

Grainger's goons must've seen him by now. He was hard to miss. They would be making their own calculations: *Do we shoot him? Stop and try to outflank him? Or just blow past and stay focused on the job at hand?* It was difficult to predict which of these options would seem most attractive to three men who'd already proven themselves tactically inept. But so far, they weren't slowing down. A half mile away and closing. Vigil had fifteen seconds—tops—to decide how he was going to handle this. The timer in his head began counting down.

Fourteen seconds.

He took off his pack and lied prone behind it, using its bulk like a tripod to steady his aim. He canted his left knee outward and crossed the ankle over the calf of his outstretched right leg. This classic "rollover" position took the weight off his diaphragm to ensure his breathing wouldn't interfere with accuracy. Should it come to that.

Ten seconds.

Three options:

1. Kill them immediately.
2. Disable the vehicle—then kill them.
3. Allow them to pass—and let them silence / torture / kill Justin Lackey.

Nine seconds.

Option one entailed taking out the driver well before the Lincoln reached him. Then he'd deal with the second two combatants after the SUV careened off the road and into a field. There was always a chance the passenger would grab the wheel and keep the vehicle on the pavement, but to do that, he'd have to keep his head exposed in order to see. Most people in that situation would duck, dive on the brake, and take their chances. Vigil liked this option. But there were two things wrong with it: First, the Navigator's windshield might've been replaced with bulletproof glass. A popular upgrade in states that bordered Mexico. A favorite among cartel members. Second, if he did kill them, he'd have to leave Carlin for good, and those responsible for Prosser's murder would likely get away with it. *Not happening.*

The problem with option two was similar. If he shot out the tires while the Navigator was traveling at such a high speed, they would explode catastrophically; the SUV would veer into the ditch, skid sideways, and then roll. The occupants *might* survive the crash. But then again, they might not —forcing Vigil to leave town, same as Option One. Again, no justice for Prosser.

Which left Option Three: Let them pass unimpeded. This had the advantage of not having to kill anyone (yet). Which meant no unnecessary interactions with law enforcement or jail time. Favorable outcomes in Vigil's opinion. And if he wasn't a fugitive, he could stick around Carlin and hold Prosser's murderer accountable. The only downside? The New York transplants' bad intentions for the wind tech.

Seven seconds.

The question was, did *silencing* Lackey necessarily mean *killing* him? Grainger's goons were simply following orders. Vigil tried to put himself in the shot-caller's shoes: *If I was covering up a murder, what would I do to an eyewitness who contradicted an earlier statement?* Much would depend on *why* Grainger was covering up Prosser's murder. But Vigil didn't know that yet. So he began by assuming Grainger was smart —risky logic when you're dealing with a criminal. But say Grainger was at least of average intelligence? Vigil figured what the thugs would or wouldn't do to Lackey was all about supporting the existing narrative, which meant giving the

Sheriff nothing that would arouse suspicion. Mixed news for Lackey, bottom line.

If an eyewitness to a murder turned up *dead*—while said murder was still being investigated—that would look very suspicious indeed. Alternatively, if the eyewitness *disappeared* (but there wasn't a body)—it would still look suspicious, but —the authorities would need to investigate further to determine whether there was foul play. Which could take a while. Thus giving Grainger more time to put out fires.

Intimidating the witness was another possibility: Scare the shit out of the wind jockey. Remind him of the consequences of saying the wrong thing. But leave him unharmed. This was probably the smartest way Grainger could handle Lackey's loose lips; tell him what to say when investigators follow up with him, and give him a new script for controlling any damage the previous slip-up might've caused.

Three seconds.

Ultimately, Vigil let go of all this rational analysis and went with his gut: As long as all the windows stayed closed, he wouldn't fire.

Two seconds.

What he hadn't considered, however, was getting turned into roadkill—which is exactly what the driver of the speeding Lincoln Navigator had in mind all along.

No more seconds.

VIGIL'S LIFE DIDN'T "FLASH BEFORE HIS EYES," AND he felt oddly disappointed. As if he'd been lied to by countless subpar storytellers. Except, he *didn't* die—managed, in fact, to spring out of the way of the swerving Lincoln like a startled leopard.

Exactly how he'd avoided getting hit, he couldn't say. The

monkey stenographer in his mind, responsible for recording memories, must've covered its eyes and braced for impact. He was left only with the *whoosh* of the air displaced by the SUV as the vehicle careened past, way too close. They were lucky they hadn't lost control when they swerved, but the ditch where he'd flattened out wasn't quite deep enough to launch the Navigator's frontend. Vigil took a few deep breaths in and out to burn off the 'bout-died adrenaline. Brushed himself off and foreshadowed the death of Grainger's men with the look he gave them.

Then he holstered the Sig, slid his pack over his shoulder, and walked on toward Carlin.

Five minutes later, he spotted another familiar vehicle.

Not a Tesla.

CHAPTER
TWENTY-EIGHT

Mira stopped in the road beside him, said, "Get in."

Vigil was silent. Just stood there for a long moment and stared at her.

She didn't look away this time. "For fuck's sake, get in the car."

He didn't move. Considered the dimensions and the angles and thought: *For that, you should've rented a Land Cruiser.*

"Are you waiting for an apology? Come on, let's roll!"

He ran his tongue over his teeth for a moment, then shrugged. Walked around to the passenger side, opened the back door, and threw his bag on the backseat. Within reach— just in case. Then he plopped down in front.

Mira floored it and the Prius advanced at a medium pace.

He smelled cigarette smoke and it surprised him because there were no wrinkles around her lips. Still too young, he thought. Though her fingertips weren't stained, either. Maybe the nicotine was just an occasional indulgence. For focus, or to relieve stress.

"Why did you leave me on the side of the road?"

She ignored the question. "They're going to kill Lackey. We have to stop them."

"Yeah, they might. Especially since you gave them a head start. But here's why they probably won't." Vigil explained how the smart move was to merely intimidate Lackey, and thus avoid throwing more heat on the Prosser investigation.

"I hope you're right," she said, "but I'm not waiting for the post-game show to find out."

Which Vigil respected. "Good. In the meantime, I'll ask you again: Why did you kick me out?"

"I had a change of heart."

"No shit. But that's not what I asked. I wanna know why you doubted me in the first place?"

"Look," she said, "now's not the time. First let's keep Lackey alive. Then I'll tell you some things I hope I won't end up regretting."

He said, "You need to do better than that, or just let me out."

"You don't care about Justin?"

He knew what she was doing. And vagabond or not, Vigil wasn't interested in guilt-trips. "Whatever happens to Lackey, he brought it on himself. Answer the question." He also knew he wasn't getting out, because he *did* care about Lackey (his ability to testify, at any rate)—but no chance was he letting Mira dodge the question.

She sighed. "I'll give you the short version. But you gotta trust—"

"*Trust you?*" Vigil chuffed. "That's earned, not given."

Mira rolled her eyes and bit down on the corner of her lip. "I get that you're not good at that, but yes, *trust me.* I just need more than ten minutes to explain everything. And a stiff drink."

Vigil did a rough calculation and figured that Grainger's crew was already at Lackey's trailer house. He and Mira weren't even to the hills and scrub brush yet, and with his added bulk, the Prius was stuck in the double-digits as it strained up the incline. "Alright," he said. "In a nutshell, then."

She took a deep breath, held it for a second, and then let it out like a punctured tire. "At first I wasn't sure if I'd over-estimated you, or vastly underestimated—but the way you finessed Lackey? *Christ.* It was better than most professionals. Subtle. Sly as hell. I started to wonder, *Is this guy ATF? or DHS? or what?* I got worried."

"I don't do well with authority, remember? But just to play devil's advocate, why would it concern you if I was from a three-letter agency?"

"That part will make sense later. Let me finish."

Vigil was silent.

"Anyway, I kept telling myself that you're nothing like a Fed—that you look like who you say you are. More or less. But then I thought: *Who the fuck is that, exactly?* And the way you mentioned 'coincidences' . . . I guess I got spooked."

Which lined up with what he'd already guessed. More or less. "You went through my bag—learn anything?"

"That you're either afraid of bears or compensating."

Now wasn't the time to get into a pissing match over properly spec'd EDCs (short for everyday carry). And Vigil didn't need to defend his manhood. "Only Grizzlies," he said. "I will ride a black bear like a pony."

Mira tried so hard not to laugh it made her blush.

"I do like Sigs, though. And arming myself with the bad guys' weapons—I'm frugal . . . but you changed the subject again. Do I look the part?"

"Yes—I mean, no—I don't know. You're like half Rambo, half Caine from Kung Fu. Except—"

"More handsome?"

"I was going to say, 'bigger.'"

He almost said *same difference,* but he'd already been too flirtatious for someone who didn't want to mix business with pleasure. It hasn't been *that* long, he thought. *A couple months?* But Mira wasn't simply beautiful, she was also . . . Vigil didn't quite know how to articulate it. She drew him in, like the part of a song you can only hear with good headphones. Or a red door in a white room. He'd need to be more careful.

They were on the dirt road now. Mira said, "So what's the plan?"

"They don't know your car, so at least they won't know we're coming."

"Three-on-two, though."

"Or four, if Lackey decides to shore up his loyalty."

Mira said, "He did have a pistol."

"The problem is, the crunch of the gravel will alert them."

"If they're still in there."

"Well if they're not, we'll see them on their way out," Vigil said. "Lackey will either be with them, or he won't."

"If he is with them, do we try to take them down?"

Vigil looked at the instrument panel. "No. We follow them. They'll need to stop for gas before we do."

She said, "But then what if they force the issue?"

"Then it's self defense, and we've got a witness."

An eighth of a mile from Lackey's driveway, Mira slowed to a stop.

"Not again."

"I have an idea," she said. "They know you from last night, and from what you told me, you didn't make a good impression. So why don't you get out and sneak through the woods and flank them. I'll act like a Jehovah's Witness—take 'em by surprise."

Vigil pointed out the obvious: "But Lackey knows what you look like."

"True, but he might be happy to see me, depending on how the guys in the Navigator are treating him."

He thought through how it might go down. It was risky. Three armed men, possibly four, with cover and concealment. She would be totally exposed. No body armor. It would all depend on how cautious they were when Mira approached. If they didn't consider her a serious threat, Vigil liked her chances. Even if she'd gotten a little rusty in her new life as a private investigator, what he'd seen from her in the bar suggested she still remembered the basics from her time in the Bureau.

"Let's do it," he said. "But go slow the rest of the way. I need a couple minutes to get into position. I'll set up to the south. Clear line of sight to the front and rear doors."

Mira nodded, said, "One whistle means I need help. Two means it's all over. Shots fired and no whistle . . . well, you know what that means."

"Copy that."

Vigil reached behind him and into his bag. Removed the two extra magazines. Each one held eight rounds of bear-stopping 10mm bullets. Humans—even the three percent Cro-Mags from New York—wouldn't be a problem. He got out and disappeared into the brush.

CHAPTER TWENTY-NINE

Vigil found cover behind the remains of a collapsed chicken coop, rough-hewn wood rotted and silver with age. Its crumpled tin roof was destroyed. Wrapped around the trunk of a nearby tree. Another hail-beaten casualty of a Texas thunderstorm.

Mira timed her approach perfectly. He heard the Prius's tires crunching over gravel at the end of the driveway right as Lackey's trailer came into view. He waited. Calm, alert, in the zone. The front porch was visible through a tangle of low limbs, but thick clumps of weeds at the edge of the clearing prevented Vigil from seeing the driveway at all.

He listened: The Prius accelerated suddenly. There was no high-pitched whine from the transmission like there would've been if it was in reverse, so Vigil figured that everything was still okay on Mira's end.

He heard her get out and she came into view at the foot of the porch, wearing her jacket for concealment. She walked up the warped treads, loose nails squeaking beneath her weight. She knocked lightly on the screen door. No answer. "Justin? Are you there?" No answer. Mira drew her weapon. She eased open the screen door, slowly turned the door handle, and then burst inside with a two-handed grip on her Glock, which was raised to eye-level. Very professional.

Vigil scanned his approach. The limbs were no big deal, but he could see chunks of half-buried boards and rusting pipe here and there in the undergrowth, as if an old homestead had once stood here. A rusty nail would ruin his afternoon.

Mira was taking what felt like forever, but Vigil knew this was just the dilation of time that occurs when you're fully in the moment. She'd clear rooms; hopefully not find any bodies.

He waited, crouched down on one knee, the heavy Legion Full-Size trained at the front door.

Mira emerged from the trailer, gun holstered. She whistled: Two sharp chirps. "All clear."

He remained alert, the Sig extended in front of him as he walked, using his free hand to divert branches of copse wood from his path. He relaxed some when he saw that it was only the Toyota parked in the patch of hard clay in front of the trailer.

No black Lincoln Navigator with dark-tinted windows.

No Ford Bronco, either.

"Lackey's gone," she said.

"What about the dog?" Vigil asked.

"Shit—I forgot about the beagle. I didn't see her but she could be hiding."

"I'll go check." Vigil went inside and poked around in all the places a medium-sized canine could hide. Found nothing but bottle caps and cobwebs. He went back outside, said, "Must've taken her with him."

"That's good news, right? It means Justin left before they showed up."

Vigil shrugged. "Could be. I didn't notice any blood or other signs of a struggle. But I still think they took him. They just wouldn't want Justin to go missing with an abandoned pet and his vehicle sitting in the driveway."

"Yeah. Guess that would look pretty suspicious."

"Exactly. This way, it looks like he just needed to get away for a while."

She said, "But why didn't we see them on the way out?"

"The dirt road keeps going past his driveway. They must know another route."

Mira took out her phone. "Only one bar, but maybe I can download enough to see where it leads."

Vigil shrugged. He'd explored enough rural farmland to know that dirt roads crisscrossed the region like a plaid shirt. More forks than a Waffle House.

"Well that wasn't helpful," she said. "They could've made it to three different highways. Should we try to get lucky?"

Vigil shook his head. "They're long gone. Let's go talk to Schnell."

Mira said, "I don't like how fast they got here. Were they already on their way? Or do you think Justin called Grainger to give him an update after we left?"

"The latter. Lackey realized he screwed up. He wanted to get out ahead of it—show his loyalty by telling Grainger what went down. It was probably the right call. If Grainger heard it secondhand, it would look like Lackey had ratted him out. That said, I'm sure he wasn't pleased with his report, and so he sent his crew over for damage control. No doubt about it."

"Won't Grainger be worried about Schnell, too?"

"Maybe. But right now his guys are busy with Lackey. They can't be two places at once. That's why we need to go see Schnell like an hour ago—before *he* takes a vacation."

She seemed to grasp what he was implying. "You wanna drive?"

"Nope. No drivers license."

Mira frowned and shook her head. "Of course not."

CHAPTER
THIRTY

Despite his objection, Vigil ended up driving from the passenger seat, holding the steering wheel while Mira found Oswald Schnell's address on her phone.

"Fifteen miles north and west if we stay on back roads. Twenty-six if we take Highway 84."

"As the crow flies," Vigil said. "Maybe we'll get lucky and kill two birds with one stone."

Mira raised an eyebrow. "The crow?"

"Grainger's crew. Unlikely, but stranger things have happened. Fun fact: A group of crows is called a *murder*."

"Yes, and a group of ravens is called a *conspiracy*," Mira added.

He nodded. "Or sometimes, an *unkindness*."

"Do you know what a group of murderers is called?"

"Nope."

She lowered her voice and whispered, *"No one does."*

Vigil grinned. "Good one."

They drove for a while, not saying anything. He was curious about Mira's big reveal, but figured she'd give him the same excuse as last time so he didn't press her. Actions speak louder than words, anyway. They were on the same page, hunting down those responsible for Prosser's murder. That's what counted. He was okay waiting until dinner.

Mira turned west onto a dirt road, said, "I don't wanna get blindsided this time. Let's talk through how this goes down with Schnell."

"Alright."

"What are you hoping to learn that Lackey hasn't already told us?"

"Schnell's connection to Leonard Grainger, obviously."

"I'm not saying there isn't a connection, but explain to me again why you're so sure."

Vigil laid out his reasoning one more time, most of which he'd already shared before she'd dumped him on the side of the road. "And then—right after Lackey cracks and contradicts what he told Sheriff Baker—*boom!* Grainger's goons show up to silence him. I forgot to tell you: They tried to run me over."

"I'm surprised you didn't shoot them."

"It crossed my mind."

"It is a few too many coincidences," Mira conceded. "But still . . . "

"Still what?"

"Pretty circumstantial."

"True. But if we can get Schnell to talk—"

"Pretty big 'if'," she interrupted. "You said it yourself: He's a cotton farmer getting paid for wind turbines on his land—wind turbines *that wouldn't be there*, if it wasn't for Grainger." Mira slowed down as they came to a concrete-lined creek bed.

Vigil said, "Did I mention that Innova-Gen renegotiated the lease payments?"

"No."

"So maybe that doesn't earn Grainger as much loyalty as

it once did. 'What have you done for me lately?' as the saying goes."

"Wait—you think Schnell killed Prosser to send a message to the wind company? But I thought—"

"No. But I bet it gave Grainger more peace of mind, knowing he could use that to frame the farmer if need be. Keep in mind, I'm ninety-nine percent positive Schnell didn't pull the trigger."

"Right," she said, nodding her head. "Because of the angle of the shot and—"

"Schnell's bum leg."

"So who's your shooter . . . Grainger?"

"Him or one of his men."

"But why? What's so important that an already wealthy man has to murder Prosser over it?"

"Something big," Vigil said. "That's for damn sure. And it must involve the wind farm."

"But not the lowered lease payments?" Mira said skeptically. "Explain."

"Lackey's not lying solely because he's afraid of Grainger. That's part of it—sure—but he's also in on the larger scheme. Because if he wasn't dirty, they'd have killed him, too. Which means Prosser must've seen something he wasn't supposed to see. And why were they at Schnell's farm in the first place? They're maintenance techs. Had to be wind generator related. I'd bet a lot of money—"

"You have a lot of money?" she teased.

"—that Lackey and Grainger were in contact the day of, or the days leading up to Prosser's murder."

Mira said, "If so, the Sheriff should be able to check the phone records."

Vigil was quiet for a minute, watching turbine blades throw shadows over the furrowed fields like falling dominoes. Then he reiterated his hunch, as much for himself as for Mira. "The wind farm is the only thing that ties them all together. Take that away, and the cotton farmers and Grainger have no connection. Likewise, no wind farm, and Grainger has no use for Lackey."

Mira turned onto a paved road. "Almost there."

"Keep in mind, too," he continued, "Schnell's not the only one with skin in the game. The farmers who confronted us at the Diamondback? I bet every one of them has towers in their fields, and that every one of them has dealings with Grainger."

She stopped once Schnell's spread came into view. A short driveway (if you could call it that) led onto a small rectangular homestead notched into the southwest corner of a much larger field. As yet unplanted, it contained five wind generators arranged diagonally in two separate lines. The closest tower stood at about the midpoint of the property. The farthest, near the northwest corner. Maybe two hundred acres for the entire operation.

She said, "I appreciate you being patient with me. I know I've got some explaining to do, and I want you to know you won't have to drag it out of me, okay? When we're done here, let's find a place with good food and strong drinks and I'll tell you everything."

Vigil was silent.

"As for how we handle Schnell—your reasoning's sound. But how do we use it to get more out of him?"

"Let me worry about that," he said.

CHAPTER
THIRTY-ONE

M ira parked between a beat-up Dodge Ram pickup and a Chevy panel van with a handicap sticker on the plate.

For rural farm living, it was roughly what Vigil expected. A tall barn in back, plus two smaller supply sheds along the perimeter, all three clad in corrugated steel. Old irrigation pipes, fertilizer tanks, and other ag-related hardware lying about. Everything baking on a layer of crushed limestone spread over smooth clay. Most of it looked functional, none of it looked modern. A "make-it-last-as-long-as-possible" venture.

The house was a one-story ranch with a tin roof and vinyl siding, surrounded by an oval of patchy, yellowing lawn which only covered about a third of the lot. There was a flower bed / litter box for strays, ruled by a garden gnome bleached whiter than bone. Three oak trees provided not near enough shade. An old-school satellite dish with a hornet's nest hanging from the receiver stood at the edge of the yard, next to an empty dog house obscured by nettles. That was it for amenities. Zero fucking quaint.

"Ready?"

Mira nodded.

In lieu of a porch, a wooden wheelchair ramp led to the front door. The house's foundation was minimal, and therefore the ramp was short. Vigil knocked like he meant it, wrapping his knuckles hard against a No Solicitors sign. Mira shuffled sideways a half step so the farmer could see her.

The curtains parted through the living room window. A moment later Oswald Schnell answered the door. Vigil recognized him from his picture in the paper. He had a reasonably full head of white hair combed back over a pink face mottled with liver spots. Deep frown lines weathered his forehead and creased the corners of his eyes. He was old, but the nursing home was still a ways off. Stocky, but not fat. He wore pinstripe overalls and a sweat-stained undershirt.

"Whatever y'all are sellin', I ain't interested."

"We're here to talk."

"Ain't interested in talkin', neither."

Vigil smiled. "About the murder of Will Prosser? I think you might be."

Schnell's demeanor went from merely aggravated to belligerent. He stepped back and proceeded to shut the door.

Or tried to, at any rate.

Vigil blocked it with his foot.

"Son, this is private property and you're officially trespassin'. Get the hell outta my house and get yer ass off my land—or I'll call the Sheriff."

"You're assuming I'd *let you*," Vigil said.

Schnell didn't know what to say to that. What color there was drained from his face and he seemed to have forgotten how to breathe. Vigil patted him on the shoulder and then squeezed down on the meat above his clavicle—half as hard as he could've, because he wasn't trying to do any damage.

The cotton farmer winced.

"Fortunately, I'm still in a good mood—so go ahead—call

Baker. When he gets here, I'll pass along what Justin Lackey just shared with us . . . little different tune than he sang the first time. I imagine he'll wanna take a closer look at the ballistics." Vigil paused to let that sink in, then thwacked the hard plastic shin of Schnell's artificial leg with the toe of his boot. "Hell—he might have you climb up a ladder while carrying a rifle. Oughta be pretty entertaining."

The old farmer's cheeks twitched as he mouthed his dentures. He must've known he was screwed, but didn't yet know how bad, or if there was anyway out of his predicament. The uncertainty paralyzed him.

Mira gave him an assist, said, "This is where you invite us inside and offer us some iced tea."

Her soothing voice seemed to snap him out of it. Schnell stepped back and opened the door wide for them to pass. He directed them past a formal sitting room with overstuffed furniture covered in clear plastic, and they settled in a den in the rear of the house opposite the kitchen. There were thick drapes covering the windows and underpowered sconces shaped like a candle. Built into a bookcase was an old television tuned to FOX News. It did little to brighten the room. The air smelled like an attic cluttered with old computers and broken electronics. And there was a sound coming from a room on the far side of the house. A slow metronomic hiss, muffled but unmistakable.

"Ventilator," Schnell said.

"Sick wife?"

Schnell nodded blankly. "Cancer. Doctor said it coulda been from the pesticides we used to spray before we got better ones—but hell—Pamela smoked a pack of menthols every day, most of her damn life, so . . . Doesn't matter. She don't have long."

"Please accept our condolences."

"I don't even know you," Schnell said.

"My name is Vigil."

"Mira Getty."

No one shook hands.

"And by what authority are you here makin' accusations and threatenin' an old man?"

"Moral authority," Vigil said.

"Is that right?"

"As rain."

Schnell searched his eyes a long minute then looked away. "I've known men like you . . . "

Vigil doubted it, but let the farmer talk.

"Men who had a firm grasp on right and wrong and wouldn't let go of it no matter what. Maybe I was one of them, once upon a time. Now? I've slipped some. Won't deny it. But I ain't no murderer."

"No. You're a liar."

"Fuck you. I've got a lien on my farm, a double mortgage on a home passed down from my father and his father before him, and I'm about to lose the only woman I've ever loved. Call it what you want, but I'm just tryin' to keep my life from fallin' apart, and failin' somethin' fierce.

"What happened to Prosser was terrible. Just terrible. But wasn't nuthin' I or anyone else coulda done that woulda saved him. This way—what Sheriff Baker believes went down —no one else has to die."

"You mean *you* don't have to die," Vigil said.

"Son, it ain't dyin' I'm worried about."

Mira started to cut in but Vigil held up his hand to silence her. "You're afraid of what Leonard Grainger will do to you. *Before* you die."

Schnell swallowed and his throat made sticky noises in the stale air. His face hardened. He brought his voice down to a low rasp, said, "I'd appreciate it you don't mention his name in my home again."

"We know he's the one responsible," Vigil said. "Tell us what he's protecting and we'll make sure he doesn't hurt you."

"So Justin Lackey didn't tell you that part, huh?" The old farmer smiled as if he'd seized some kind of victory, and maybe he had. "Lemme save you a little time—and probably yer lives, if you're smart enough to listen: I'm stickin' to my story. Prosser's dead either way."

Mira was practically squirming next to him and Vigil nodded for her to jump in. "Doesn't his family deserve justice?" she said.

"God will provide it. In the end. And when my time comes, He'll understand what I had to do."

"And what if Lackey recants and tells the Sheriff what he told us?" Mira countered. "You'll spend the rest of your life in prison for a crime you didn't commit."

"If it comes to that, I'm willin' to take the fall. Hell, I'll tell Baker it was to punish Innova-Gen for screwin' us on the lease payments. Means, motive, confession . . . you think he'll dig too deep?"

Mira said, "But it doesn't have to come to that. If Lackey tells the truth, and you testify against Grainger, then *he* answers for his crimes."

"That easy? And in this utopian paradise you speak of— rich men never get away with murder? Potential witnesses never turn up in barrels at the bottoms of lakes?"

He's not wrong, Vigil thought. He said, "You were right about me not letting go of this. It's not in my nature. Prosser's family deserves justice and I'll see that it's served. By any means necessary."

"That a fact?"

"Thing is, I like to sleep at night. And I do. Like a baby. Because I always make *sure* the people I punish deserve it . . . and that *everyone* who deserves it gets punished. So with or without you, I'll figure out why Grainger had Prosser killed. Eventually. And then I'll end him.

"But you need to understand something: If you keep covering for him? Then I'll have to end you, too. Because how would I know you're not just as culpable as he is? Right now, I don't think you had much to do with it. But I could be wrong about that. So I need you to help me out. Doesn't have to be much. Just a little somethin' to show me your heart's in the right place."

Schnell slowly nodded his head and looked Vigil in the eye. "Like I said, I've known men like you, Vigil. But make no mistake, there are other kinds of men."

"I'm aware. I've killed my fair share of them. Now, if you'll excuse me, I'll be outside examining the crime scene. If you're lucky I'll find something helpful and give you credit for it."

"Knock yerself out."

"Mira, make sure he doesn't confuse me for a pig."

CHAPTER
THIRTY-TWO

Vigil went out the backdoor. The sun was behind him, as high in the sky as it would get this time of year, casting shadows toward the crime scene.

He began his search by examining the ground along the south wall of the barn and quickly found two parallel depressions indicating a ladder had been placed there. *Right where I thought*. He found the shooter's footprints, too, though they were too indistinct for purposes of identification.

Vigil walked clockwise to the north side of the structure and stood for a moment facing the fields. In the distance, faint yellow strips fluttered in the breeze. The cordoned-off perimeter of police tape. Beyond was an access road that led from the farm road on the west edge of Schnell's property. He checked for a police presence but there was no one there.

Two sets of fresh footprints led into the surrounding field: Schnell on his way to make a false confession, and his shameful hobble back to the house. He knew they were Schnell's prints because they were made by a man with a limp wearing two different sized shoes. Vigil followed them toward the police tape and the access road and the three closest wind towers.

He didn't know what he was looking for and he accepted the possibility he might not find anything. Schnell seemed too laid-back about him searching his property. Like he knew Vigil would strike out.

Along the way he cataloged animal tracks, of which there were no shortage: Birds and deer and mice and rabbits had all left their mark. As had a coyote, a possum, and a veritable herd of feral hogs. At least six of them. But not all the tracks in Schnell's field were left by animals. Running from the edge of the access road and continuing well past the perimeter of police tape were tire tracks.

Not the kind a tractor would make.

They'd been left by the same vehicle. A long-wheelbase truck or van. Two sets: One from the access road, and one leading back to it after a wide-arcing U-turn. Vigil veered away from the trail Schnell had left and aimed for the turn's apex.

Interesting.

Perpendicular to the tire tracks was a short path that terminated at the edge of a large rectangle of recently disturbed earth. To Vigil, it looked like someone had filled in a hole roughly the size of a school bus. And it was fresh, the soil a shade darker than the rest of the field.

He shuffled around the edges of the anomaly, using his boot to push and probe and sweep. Then he felt something. Hard, but with some give to it. Clearly manmade. It was a chain, and it was attached to an object hidden in the damp topsoil. Vigil grabbed hold of the loose end and pulled. As he yanked it taught, the earth at his feet began to lift. He tugged harder and some of the dirt fell away, revealing a giant piece of thin sheet metal. The edges of the sheet flexed up a few inches. Vigil knelt down, holding the chain tight over his head to get a better look at what lay beneath: More steel—

smooth and painted a dull orange. Almost certainly the top of a shipping container. He used the sides of his boots to clear away enough dirt to slide the makeshift trapdoor out of the way.

And there it was:

The Pandora's Box that got Prosser killed.

A SQUARE HATCH HAD BEEN CUT CRUDELY INTO THE roof of the shipping container with a blowtorch. He leaned over and looked inside. Couldn't see much. Only the narrow section of bare floor lit by the sunlight shining through the hatch. He would need to go in to be sure.

Vigil wasn't especially claustrophobic, but the idea of being trapped Down In A Hole didn't appeal to him (no matter how good the song was). Then again, short of someone setting off a stick of dynamite nearby, he supposed there was little risk.

The jagged opening was about the width of a manhole cover. Narrow for someone with Vigil's shoulders, but he managed. There were no stairs, nor had a ladder been welded to the mouth of the entry. No big deal, since the drop was only a little over head-height. He placed his hands on either side of the hatch and lowered himself as far as he could, then let go and landed on both feet.

I'm the man in the box, Vigil thought, and was pleased with himself for referencing two songs by the almighty Alice In Chains in less than a minute.

He let his eyes adjust to the gloom.

The box was empty.

Stripped.

Bare.

He knelt down and scoured the metal floor. The container's previous occupants must've tracked in dirt and Vigil hoped to find footprints.

No dice.

What little sediment remained had been thoroughly swept.

He turned his attention to the corners of the container where small bits of debris would be hard to dislodge with a broom and would tend to accumulate. *Bingo.* Traces of black plastic and several minuscule strands of copper. Both materials cut by a sharp blade.

Wire, he thought.

He'd seen similar scraps on the floorboards of cars when hitchhiking; in every instance, the driver had recently installed a new stereo, backup camera, or alarm system.

And where there's wire, there's electricity . . .

As for what kind of equipment the electricity might've powered?—Vigil could only guess.

But he did have a pretty good idea where the electricity had come *from.*

MIRA HAD HER GLOCK OUT WHEN VIGIL RETURNED to Oswald Schnell's den. The old farmer was squinting at the television, reading the closed captioning with the volume all the way down. A panel of talking heads was pontificating about the Russian invasion of Ukraine.

"You wanna tell me what was in the box?"

Schnell ignored him.

Vigil picked up the TV remote from the end table and pressed the power button. Repeated the question. Which he hated doing.

Schnell stopped rocking in his recliner. "What box?"

"The shipping container buried in your field."

"Oh, that one. It's a storm shelter. I ain't gotta basement or a cellar, and we're in the middle of tornado alley. Seemed prudent."

"Bullshit. Too far from the house. Even if your lame ass could get to it in time, there's no door. A twister would suck you right out."

"Good point. I should move it closer. Hire a welder to fabricate some kind of a hatch."

Vigil cracked his knuckles, one by one. Breathed in, deep and slow, expelling irritation on the exhale. "I understand you're afraid of Grainger. Lackey was too . . . did you hear about what happened to him? They disappeared him already. Came by his trailer shortly after he talked to us and collected him." Vigil didn't specify whom he meant by 'they' because he was pretty sure Schnell knew exactly who he was talking about.

"Well then," Schnell said, looking awful pleased with himself, "I guess he won't be able to contradict what I told the Sheriff, will he?"

"That's one way to look at it," Vigil said. "Someone more cynical might wonder if you're next in line."

Schnell said nothing. He looked scared, but also hopeless.

Vigil was silent for a long minute. He wanted the farmer to sit with his fear—to stew in the deep well of despair he'd fallen into, and realize the only way he wouldn't drown, was to grab the lifeline they were dangling in front of him. Finally he said, "Look. I know Grainger was stealing electricity from the wind generators. I saw the cable. Just tell me what it was powering. Then we'll leave you alone and I'll pretend I figured it out all by myself."

"Congratulations. Ya got me," Schnell said. "See, a little while before Pamela got sick, I was preparin' for if shit ever hit the fan. Seemed like a distinct possibility, what with

Obama in office. So I started buildin' a bunker. Coulda used a diesel generator, like most folks would, but you run outta fuel, and then what? Ain't like—"

"Save it," Vigil said, rising to his feet. "And remember: I tried to help you do the right thing."

CHAPTER
THIRTY-THREE

They decided on a steakhouse for dinner, owing to the reputation of such establishments for serving top-shelf whiskey, bourbon, and wine, which—in Vigil's opinion—covered all the bases when it came to consuming alcohol (tequila notwithstanding).

They decided on Sweetwater, owing to the superior selection, and more importantly, common fucking sense.

Mira launched the Yelp app on her phone, typed in the appropriate search terms, and clicked on the icon of a place she said looked promising. "It's actually forty-five miles east of Sweetwater, but that might be a good thing. We've made enemies around here."

"Dress code?"

"Not from what people were wearing in the pictures," she said. "Your denim shirt will fit right in."

"Good. I didn't pack a suit."

"*Although* . . . " Mira said, drawing out the word as she gave his soaked armpits the side-eye, "it looks like a nice place. Maybe we should clean up first."

"Agreed. Someone thought I needed to march a few miles today."

185

She ignored the jab. "Where are you staying?"

"I rented a room in the Microtel, right off the Interstate. You?"

"I booked an Airbnb in Carlin but I think I'll cancel it."

"What's Airbnb?"

"You can't be serious."

"Is it an app?"

"Yes, it's an app. You can stay in private homes."

"You need a credit card to use it?"

"Or PayPal."

"Well there you go."

Mira said she'd prefer the Hampton Inn a couple exits down, which was fine with him. He rarely stayed in the same place two nights in a row. She went to check in while he waited in the Prius. He'd get his own room, and Vigil could see no benefit to being recorded together on the hotel's security cameras. They exchanged room numbers in the elevator.

AN HOUR LATER THEY WERE SHOWERED, DRESSED in fresh clothes, and driving to the steakhouse. Vigil wore basically the same outfit: The gray denim western shirt he'd washed in the shower last night, in place of the blue one now hanging to dry on the shower rod. Black jeans. Black boots. Concealed Sig.

Mira, by contrast, had leaned into her femininity. She wore a merlot-colored floral-print dress which fit snug from the waist up and hung in loose pleats almost to the knee. A hint of cleavage showed above the wide V-cut and thin straps hung over bare shoulders. Vigil supposed these were to keep the dress from sliding down, but he was no kind of women's fashion expert; if the straps were indeed functional and not simply decorative, they were redundant. That was abundantly clear. As for makeup, only slightly more than before—similar gray-green shades but with a pinch more sparkle. Lipstick in place of the gloss, amplifying the natural rouge of her lips. And she smelled fantastic: Essences of vanilla and lavender, with notes of cinnamon and black tea in place of the musky undertones he'd detected in the bar.

He said, "You still carrying?"

Mira slid up her dress just enough to show the barrel-end of a composite thigh holster. "Always."

Vigil looked away and imagined another tedious game contested by boring creatures—tortoises playing bridge this time. Which mostly worked, but he was still glad he'd left his shirt untucked.

They talked very little. He could tell Mira was nervous about whatever she had to tell him. And to be fair, he wasn't always the greatest conversationalist. He was comfortable with silence. Some would say too comfortable. A useful trait considering the amount of time he spent alone, but in the company of others, he understood how it might be off-putting. He just didn't care.

Fortunately Mira didn't seem bothered by it. He let her rehearse how best to explain her earlier behavior, while he mulled over what kind of equipment was worth killing Prosser to keep secret.

Fifteen years ago it could've been a meth lab. Maybe. But these days the manufacturing had moved to Mexico where cartels paid legit chemists to cook the stuff at industrial scale. Plus, men with their names on buildings don't murder someone over a little meth. That was biker-gang-level bull-shit. So Vigil let his imagination drift into darker spheres of criminality: *An underground studio for shooting snuff films?* A disgusting possibility. But with smartphones and modern handheld video cameras, he knew battery power would suffice for something like that, and tapping into the electrical grid would be overkill. *Human trafficking cells?* No. There had been no ventilation pipes installed in the container. Even with the open hatch, with a layer of soil covering the sheet metal panel, fresh air couldn't get in. Vigil considered a few more unsatisfactory options and then set the puzzle aside. They passed a road sign for Abilene and he asked where in Gaia's green Earth Mira was taking him.

"The place is called Perini Ranch. On the outskirts of Buffalo Gap. We're close."

They turned south off the highway and followed a narrow farm road for another fifteen minutes. The terrain was similar to the low hills where Lackey lived, except there were fewer cedar and mesquite trees, and a lot more oak. Here, it was all about the cattle. Plenty of ranches, not many cotton farms, and no wind turbines whatsoever. Based on the health of the animals he saw grazing on clover and alfalfa in the lush fields, the chef would have something to work with. His mouth watered.

M ira found the sign and turned onto a gravel drive. They followed it under a thin canopy of post oak until it curved around to a parking lot lined with old railroad ties and piles of stone. True to its name, the grounds had once been a ranch. Or still was. There were longhorn cattle drinking from troughs in a corral, though Vigil suspected these were for show.

On their way inside, they passed an armadillo the size of a fuel tanker. "Neat," Mira said. "But I'd like it better without the name tag." She was referring to the "Barbadilla" necklace hanging from the creature's rust-brown neck.

Vigil nodded. "The sculptor needs their artistic license revoked."

The restaurant itself, however, hit exactly the right tone. It had started life as a hay barn—or a wealthy rancher's updated version of one, at any rate. Eschewing a more traditional log cabin design, it was fashioned from raw timbers arranged vertically like a fort. *Pièce sur pièce* was the French name for the construction technique, which Vigil only knew because there'd been a cabin built that way near his childhood stomping grounds in Idaho. Michel Beauregard, an old hermit originally from Montreal, had built one by hand; he'd also taught a teenaged Vigil the proper way to drink wine.

He held the door for Mira and nodded at all the turned heads. Not aggressively—more of a matter-of-fact acknowledgment that said, *Your eyes are working properly.*

"Old frontier meets rustic chic," Mira said of the interior, which Vigil thought was apt.

There were exposed wooden beams supporting the underside of the tin roof. Cow and bison skulls mounted on the walls, slick with varnish, alongside painted wood planks advertising cold beer. A brick fireplace dominated one end of the dining room, with an oil painting of a Comanche hunting party above the mantle. Opposite was the bar, and if you squinted, you could see Tommy Lee Jones holding court with the ghost of John Wayne.

"A gentleman cowboy retires and refurbishes a saloon," Vigil said, doing his best Sam Elliot impression (which wasn't all that good). Mira rewarded the effort with a grin and a raised eyebrow, and Vigil smiled. He shrugged, said, "I was playing along. Best I could come up with." He let his eyes linger on hers for a beat, added, "You look beautiful, by the way."

"Why thank you, gunslinger."

They got seated. Mira asked for a beer and a shot of their best mezcal. Vigil also went with beer, but paired it with Woodford Reserve Double Oaked, served neat. They perused

189

the menu. The waitress came back with their drinks and took their order.

"For the lady?"

"The filet. Medium."

"And I'll have the ribeye. Medium rare." He raised his shot glass. "*Salud.*"

"*Salud.*"

They clinked glasses, drained them, and chased the high-proof with cold lager. Vigil wasn't a big drinker by any stretch, but his size lent him a respectable tolerance. He decided he'd stop at no more than a mild buzz, in case Mira liked to go hard and he needed to drive back to the hotel. Driving without a license beat a DWI every day of the week.

She asked him if he knew Spanish and he admitted to speaking *muy poco* and they kept it to small talk until the food arrived. He was glad because he sensed Mira might need a couple more shots before broaching what she'd promised to tell him. Plus he was hungry, and didn't want anything she might say to ruin what was bound to be a delicious meal.

CHAPTER
THIRTY-FOUR

Turned out she needed three more shots, and the steaks far exceeded their expectations. The waitress cleared their plates and asked if they'd like to move out to the patio and enjoy the fire pit. They would, thank you very much, and they took their beers and sat across from each other in rocking chairs. It was a few clicks north of the true heart of Texas, granted. But the stars that night were damn-sure bright.

Mira said, "So how 'bout those Astros . . . "

Vigil rolled his eyes. He could tell she was messing with him. "I've been patient," he said. "But we're in the bottom of the ninth, here."

She smiled in a way he hadn't seen from her thus far, simultaneously sly and rueful. "At the Diamondback—when you guessed I was a former Fed?"

"Yeah?"

"I went along with it. What's the saying? 'Close enough for government work?'"

"Close enough to keep the cigar?" He was enjoying the banter, but it seemed a little forced. His gut said, *Get ready to be blindsided.*

"I wasn't a Fed," Mira said flatly. "I *am* a Fed. Present tense."

Vigil nodded slowly. On the outside, he was sure he looked as stoic and unfazed as ever. But on the inside, a private compilation of greatest *hits* streamed past his mind's eye, unbidden. Fortunately, suppressing emotional cues was as natural to him as compartmentalizing. *Master the internal and the external takes care of itself,* to quote his father. There was no escaping the fact that he'd done a lot of things over the years a federal agent would be very interested in should past deeds be brought to light, and Vigil had to reassure himself there was no way Mira knew about any of it before he felt ready to reply.

"Can't say I'm too surprised," he said, maintaining an air of calm. "The skills I've seen from you so far seem pretty sharp. I'm just glad you don't work for an insurance company. I like you a lot more now."

"That might be premature," she said.

Vigil was silent. He found himself wondering if she had handcuffs looped around her leg, opposite the holstered Glock.

She added, "You were also wrong about the agency. I'm not FBI."

Which, given the roaming nature of his vigilantism, was *probably* a good thing? "Well that only leaves twenty-three other possibilities, not counting officers for the various Inspector Generals. You want me to guess?" Truth was, he was afraid he already knew.

"I'm a U.S. Marshal."

Dammit.

"You look disappointed."

"I'm not sure yet," Vigil said. "Marshals are known for two things: Apprehending fugitives . . . and running the Witness Protection program."

"You missed a few. Notably asset forfeiture, protecting judges, and prisoner transport. But yeah, you nailed the sexy stuff."

"Just tell me you're not in town for Witness Protection." This wasn't reverse psychology on Vigil's part; he wasn't a fugitive. Whatever laws he'd broken putting his thumb on the scales of justice, he'd never been convicted of a crime. Never escaped from prison.

"Not . . . *entirely*."

"What do you mean, 'entirely?'"

Mira finished her beer then set the bottle down and sighed. "One of the most infamous cooperating witnesses in U.S. history was placed into WITSEC and relocated to Carlin, Texas."

"Lemme guess: Leonard Grainger."

She nodded somberly. "AKA, Lenny 'The Lion' Grabasso."

It rang a bell, but it was an old memory, maybe from childhood. A name he'd heard listening to the evening news with his father, or a character in some movie. Somebody dangerous . . . a killer. Then it clicked: "The mobster?"

"Not just any mobster. The underboss who testified against Vito Molinari back in the '90s. Molinari, you might recall, was the so-called 'Boss of Bosses' in La Cosa Nostra. His conviction ranks as the single biggest success in the war against organized crime—before or since—and it led to the near-total collapse of the Italian mafia in the United States. All made possible by Grabasso turning State's witness. It was a big fucking deal."

Vigil drained his beer and wished it was straight bourbon.

"So are you?—disappointed?"

"I don't know what I am right now," he said.

He excused himself and went to find the restroom. He didn't need to piss all that bad, but while he was at it he could splash some water on his face and cool down. Make sure he wasn't still back in Harley's Kenworth dreaming all of this.

He found a urinal and took a moment to assess the emotions battling it out inside him after Mira's bombshell: The sting of being lied to. The relief that she'd finally come clean. The dread that her professional obligations would interfere with his mission. The dubious hope her authority and connections might help him deliver justice all the more swiftly. And most of all, the anger—the scalding ember of rage fueled by the hypocrisy festering inside *each and every* fucking system and institution he wanted to believe in, but inevitably couldn't.

Not 'entirely.'

Because beneath the so-called Rule of Law, there were always bureaucrats willing to bend the law in order to tout a pyrrhic victory. Sure, he understood the need to protect innocent citizens brave enough to go on the witness stand and testify against evil, dangerous men. But how the State could absolve *equally* evil and dangerous men—and then *reward* them with a fresh start in a peaceful town—*shield* them from ever having to take responsibility for their heinous crimes? That was something Vigil could never abide by.

And it's Mira's job.

When he got back to the fire pit, she wasn't there. He was glad. It gave him more time to compose himself. He flagged down a waitress and had her bring two coffees.

Mira returned with another shot of mezcal. She looked at the coffee and made a little face like, *Look who's a lightweight,* then knocked back the double-distilled agave. "I'm sorry for lying," she said. "Especially after you were honest with me."

"You ran a background check." It wasn't a question, because of course an active U.S. Marshal would want to know exactly who she was dealing with.

"I did. One of the stranger reports I've seen, but it

confirmed what you told me at the bar: Nate Vigil. Son of Commander Lance Vigil, Navy, Retired."

"What was strange about it?" Vigil was pretty sure he knew, but couldn't pass up the opportunity to verify how little the government had on him.

"You mean aside from the complete lack of official documentation identifying you as a citizen? I don't know—that that's *all* there was?—just those two details and in parentheses: 'verified by sworn affidavit from former neighbor.' I pulled up your father to see if there was anything more about you in his file—sorry about what happened to him, by the way—but most of his was redacted. To be honest, I'm not even sure why you showed up in the system in the first place. No Social Security Number? No Birth Certificate? We've got more on Bigfoot."

"What about the arrest record?"

Mira frowned like she wasn't expecting the question. "I didn't see one."

Vigil shrugged. "I was never charged. They must've expunged it."

"Dare I ask?"

"Possession of an unregistered firearm. Turns out they're pretty lenient on that sort of thing in Montana. I was only detained because I had no way of verifying my identity. The magistrate locked me up for two weeks while an investigator went to Idaho to find someone who could vouch for me. Then I was released."

"You do realize they kept your prints, right?"

Vigil acknowledged her insinuation with a quick nod and then got back to what he really cared about. "So Grainger—Grabasso—he kills Prosser, and you're here to make sure he doesn't dox himself . . . another pat on the back from Uncle Sam. Is that it?" He sounded indignant, and he supposed he was.

Mira shook her head as if he'd insulted her. "No," she said. "That's not it at all."

"Please enlighten me."

"Keep in mind, I was seven when Grabasso entered WITSEC. He was way before my time. But people retire. Or they get promoted. Like my boss. Grabasso was his witness, originally. But he offloaded all the grunt work to me shortly after I got my badge in '09. Probably because Grabasso had been in the program for so long, and there'd never been any issues with him. He was what we call 'well assimilated' into the local community. Easy work for a rookie.

"I might've been green, but I was also ambitious. I studied everything that went right with Grabasso's new life, figuring I could apply the lessons to future program participants. Unfortunately, a lot of what I learned wasn't replicable.

"A fair portion of Grabasso's success comes from expertise he developed in the mafia. Turns out that working with concrete is quite the transferable skill—especially if you're from the East Coast. New Yorkers are just *better* than the tradesmen here in Texas. They work on more kinds of projects, do bigger jobs—skyscrapers in Grabasso's case—and they're used to a more cutthroat business environment.

"But mostly? It's Grabasso's charisma. He has it in spades: The looks, the accent, the confidence of a shot-caller. Plus the wry sense of humor to make it all endearing. In a part of the country not exactly known for embracing strangers—especially yankees—he won over the locals through sheer charm and perspicacity.

"To be honest, I became a bit enamored. I devoured his old files—practically memorized them. It was like binging a reality TV show and getting paid to watch.

"Most witnesses struggle in their new lives. They barely scrape by. But not Grabasso—even before he won the wind farm contract, he was killing it with his concrete business. He poured pools for the country club crowd. Became the preferred supplier for all the best housing developers. Put in a state-of-the-art sewer and drainage system for the City of Carlin. The guy was raking in the dough and making it look easy.

"We had meetings to discuss whether he'd become too powerful and needed to be moved. Ultimately, it was decided he would stay—for fear the local economy might collapse. He was getting up in age, anyway. Why not let nature take its course?

"Fast forward to late 2013. That's when I started hearing rumors. Nothing specific, just . . . *grumblings* about Grainger's negotiation tactics. I poked around a little. Turns out that the son of a rival contractor disappeared under mysterious circumstances just prior to the Innova-Gen bid. There was talk that Grainger had something to do with it. That he tortured the guy. But no one would go on record.

"I told my boss we have a problem—that Grabasso might be committing crimes again. He wasn't interested. In fact, he assigned his file to another Marshal, and threatened to transfer me to Judicial Security if I didn't get over my, quote: 'unhealthy obsession'."

Vigil said, "And yet you're here, in Grabasso's backyard."

She held up her empty shot glass to the waitress, said, "Yeah, I'm getting to that. Let me finish."

He let her talk.

"So I followed orders . . . at the office. But off the clock? I doubled down. In hindsight, it *was* a little creepy. Definitely dangerous. But I knew something shady was taking place, and I was determined to shine some light on it."

The waitress came back with Mira's shot and she gulped it down.

"Don't worry," she said, "I'm Irish as fuck. Besides, if I

wasn't this many drinks in, I wouldn't have the nerve to share the rest."

Vigil was silent.

"Everything is logged, so I couldn't use my credentials to monitor Grabasso's file without alerting my boss. Instead, I was able to 'obtain' the other marshal's password. Still, I had to be careful and limit the number of login attempts to avoid suspicion. Rely more on local contacts.

"Eventually my patience paid off. I found a note in Grabasso's file about three new associates. Names that were familiar to me. Two of them were *made guys*. Former members of Grabasso's Bensonhurst crew. The third guy was younger, but well known in the neighborhood for being a straight-up killer.

"Here's where it gets crazy: These associates? *They're also in Witness Protection* . . . and all three of them were recently transferred to—"

"Carlin, Texas," Vigil interjected.

"New names, new ID, plastic surgery—the whole calzone."

Vigil said, "I'm guessing that's not standard operating procedure."

"Fuck no. That should *never* happen. Which brings me to why I'm here: I think the U.S. Marshals Service—my boss, at a minimum—has been compromised."

"Compromised how?"

"Either Grabasso is paying him a lot of money, or he's got some dirt on him."

"So you're not here in any official capacity?"

"No. I'm undercover."

"Who else knows?"

Mira filled her lungs with cool night air. As she exhaled, Vigil witnessed what revealing a secret you've guarded for eight long years looks like. For a moment, everything in her body went slack, like an exhausted fighter splayed out on their stool between rounds. The relief was short-lived, however. Her shoulders drew up the very next breath. She was a marionette pulled by strings of stress and paranoia.

"Only you."

Their eyes met. Mira's teetering between shame and longing, before finally betraying her altogether—posing the question she was too afraid to ask, and didn't need to: *Can I trust you with what I've shared? Or do I continue down this dark path alone, freshly wounded?*

The intimacy of her unburdening surprised him, and Vigil felt some of his resentment morph into resolve. Now he knew why he'd spooked her after they questioned Lackey—why the possibility of him being a Fed from a different agency was such a threat. Whatever Grainger / Grabasso was up to, Mira didn't want another agent (who might be investigating the ex-mobster independently) to think she was involved. Nor could she risk her crooked boss finding out that she was scheming against him as a freelancer.

"We'll figure it out," he said. He sipped his coffee and found it was cold. "We have to assume everyone in the Diamondback reports to Grabasso—not to mention Lackey and Schnell—he must know you're here."

Mira shook her head. "We've never met in person. There were a few phone calls over the years, but my voice was electronically altered to sound like a man's."

Vigil thought about this for a moment. He supposed the Marshals had all sorts of hi-tech gadgetry at their disposal. "What about the security cameras behind the bar? He could send the footage to your boss."

She shrugged. "Maybe. But why would he? I'm sure Caleb overheard me saying I'm a private investigator from an insurance company. Same as Lackey. I doubt he considers me a threat. You're the one he oughta be worried about."

He sensed the alcohol was getting to her finally. Her lids seemed heavier. Her speech was slower and slightly slurred.

"My impression of Grabasso over the years," Mira continued, "is that he's a master delegator. He's using the Marshals for what we're good at: Relocation and flawless IDs. Besides, I wouldn't be surprised if those cameras are just for show. You've watched Forensics Files, haven't you? Even if they are operational, the footage will be too pixelated to ID anyone. Hell, they probably used VHS tapes."

She was probably right, but Vigil didn't like it. He shrugged, said, "What's done is done," and changed the subject. "So do you already know who murdered Prosser? I assume that's what brought you here . . . the timing and all." He posed the question with as casual a tone as he could muster, but he cared a lot how she would respond.

"No—I mean—if I didn't at least *suspect* Grabasso was behind it, I'd have stayed in Arlington. But whether he pulled the trigger? I don't know yet."

Vigil wasn't a hundred percent satisfied with her answer, but it was a helluva lot better than if she'd had proof Grabasso was the killer and had kept it from him. "You played dumb when I first brought up Grainger. You were still testing me." Not a question. A statement of fact.

"Yeah. Your story checked out, and you're exceptionally capable, but . . . I wasn't sure if you would ever trust me enough to assist my investigation."

He didn't view it as *her* investigation (or strictly an investigation for that matter), but he let it slide. "What sealed it for you?"

"When we raced back to Lackey's trailer and you let me take the lead. Which also convinced me you don't let testosterone come before tactics."

I'm still working on that, Vigil thought, but there was no reason to correct her.

She said, "And when you had me cover Schnell for you—that was huge, too."

"So going forward . . . where does that leave us?"

"The night is young," she winked.

Which wasn't what Vigil meant, and started to say so, but Mira was already raising her empty shot glass and calling for the waitress. Serious conversation was on hold for the night. That was for damn sure.

He said, "I'm not sure that's a good idea."

And it wasn't.

CHAPTER
THIRTY-FIVE

Mira's fighting Irish absorbed an impressive number of shots from the mezcal in the early rounds, but as so often happens in boxing, the Mexican fighter refused to quit, and eventually put her on her ass with a shot to the liver.

To her credit, she managed to walk out of the restaurant under her own power, but by the time they crossed paths with Barbadilla, Vigil was carrying her to the Prius. Light work, because she only weighed about a buck-twenty, tops. He eased her into the passenger seat and made sure she was buckled in.

"Thanks for driving," she said, and then hiccuped, high-pitched like a dog's squeak toy. "Oh, my."

Vigil got behind the wheel. "Lemme know if you're gonna be sick."

"I'm fffffiiiiiiiinnnnne. Not to drive, obviously. But I'm in full control of my ffffuck-you-tees—I mean—*faculties.*"

She giggled at this Freudian slip (if that's what it was), and Vigil couldn't help but grin, even though he didn't want to encourage her.

"Clearly," he said.

Mira said, "It wasn't exactly a date or whatever, but I really enjoyed myself."

"Me too."

"I know you're just gonna tell me I'm drunk," she said, "and to be clear, I'm *vvveeeerrrrry* drunk—but you wanna know something?"

He was surprised she was still conscious. "What's that?"

"You're very nice to look at."

"I suppose both things can be true at the same time," he said.

Mira slugged him playfully on the shoulder. "You're supposed to say I'm nice to look at, too."

"I already told you what I think on that front."

"Oh, right. You said I look beautiful. But maybe you were just bein' polite?"

"I'm no kind of a sweet talker. I give you a compliment, that's how I feel."

"Do you still think I'm beautiful?"

It could have been his imagination, but her dress seemed to be revealing a little more cleavage than he remembered, and showing off a little more thigh, too, which Vigil knew shouldn't be possible—not both things at the same time— because physics.

"How much could you possibly have aged in one night?" he said.

"Ha, ha. Guess that's what I get fishing for compliments."

She was quiet for a while and Vigil concentrated on driving between the lines and staying under the speed limit. He thought she might've fallen asleep finally, but shortly after he accelerated onto the interstate, Mira leaned over and rested her face against his shoulder. This didn't seem like the most comfortable position. Not with the console in the way, grinding into her ribs. Not with his granite delts. But during his time as a bouncer he'd seen drunk people sprawled out on bathroom floors, facedown on bar tops, spread-eagled in alleys, cuddling against curbs, and even snoring in bathroom stalls with their pants down around their ankles. She could do a lot worse for a pillow, he conceded.

He listened carefully. Her breathing was barely audible over the road noise, but it seemed to have slowed. Then he felt her jaw go slack and her mouth part and he knew she was out for the count. He still wanted Mira to purchase a burner phone for him, but decided it could wait until morning. Better to let her sleep.

BY THE TIME THEY GOT BACK TO THE HOTEL, a warm, wet crescent of drool had soaked through Vigil's shirtsleeve.

He parked and then eased Mira into an upright position in the passenger seat. She barely stirred, chin on her chest, practically sedated. He came around to the passenger side and softly whispered her name. "Mira? We're back."

She didn't respond, but in the glow from the dome light, he could see her eyes darting back and forth behind closed lids, lost in a dream. He considered shaking her awake. But with a startled and paranoid U.S. Marshal packing a loaded 9mm, it wasn't an experiment he wanted to run. He bent down and plucked her from the Prius and cradled her in his arms. Inside, he nodded at the front desk clerk working graveyard shift and got her to the elevators. At a certain point Vigil knew he'd have to wake her, because he had no idea where she'd stashed her room key. No purse. No pockets in sight.

The doors slid open and he pressed the button for the fifth floor. Her body was on fire against his in the enclosed space. He could smell her: The alcohol evaporating from her pores, sweetened by the subtle spice of her perfume and suffused with the lemony zest of her sweat. The sensation of being carried must've penetrated her; she draped an arm around his neck for support and snuggled her face into his chest.

It felt good. Too good.

Snails playing solitaire. Cows playing cricket. Rhinos—shit.

The doors opened and he carried her the rest of the way to 517. He was in 424. "Mira," he said, keeping his voice low so as not to disturb the other guests, "I need your room key."

She didn't open her eyes, but a tipsy smile coalesced on her lips as she reached down the front of her dress and retrieved a magnetized card from her bra. If pressed, he would've liked to report that he looked away. But Vigil didn't like lying, and he rarely did. Mira slid the hard plastic into the slot and a little green light came on. She tugged on the handle and the door cracked open.

Vigil carried her across the threshold, shuffling sideways into the room. A floor lamp was turned on in the corner and he carried Mira to a large King bed and gently laid her down on one edge. Then he peeled back the top-sheet and comforter, leaning across and lifting her just enough to scoot her over to the now bare fitted sheet.

Her dress caught on the pile of bedding and clung tightly to the curve of her hips. Vigil grabbed hold of the blankets, but as he began to ease them back into place, Mira tensed, perhaps getting more comfortable before drifting off again. He hesitated. Her hand rose absently from her side then came to rest on the slope of her breasts. For the briefest moment he imagined it was *his* hand, then pulled the blankets up to tuck her in. He turned off the lamp and walked toward the door. Mira called out to him as he passed the foot of her bed.

"You can stay if you want to."

And Vigil *did* want to. Who wouldn't?

But the invitation could've been the alcohol talking.

"Thing is . . . " he said, trailing off because he felt conflicted.

Mira looked at him expectantly.

Desire, chivalry, and propensities Vigil wasn't terribly proud of grappled in his gut with no clear victor, pulling him in three different directions all at once.

He cleared his throat and composed himself. Laid a hand on Mira's leg through the comforter. Said the right thing, in the wrong way, for a dumb reason. "The thing is, I prefer to avoid unnecessary interactions with law enforcement."

CHAPTER
THIRTY-SIX

S leep eluded him. One does not give the finger to millions of years of evolutionary programming without repercussions.

The insomnia sucked, but mostly Vigil felt bad about being so blunt. And for what? Why did he have to be such a dick about it? He could've said simply, *"Sweet dreams, Mira,"* and went on his merry way—not exactly content, but—secure in the knowledge he'd been a gentleman. Instead, he'd come off as an asshole. A grudge holder. Petty. Even though she'd apologized for her earlier deception, he couldn't quite let it go. More self-reflection was undoubtedly warranted, but when was the last time he'd indulged in that? *Probably the last time you spoke to your mom.*

Instead of jerking off to fall asleep like a standard-issue adult, Vigil decided to let his frustration fuel an all-nighter. He got dressed and went downstairs to the lobby. There was a conference room he remembered from earlier, with guest computers and a printer. Mira had accused him of being a Luddite, but he wasn't actually opposed to technology. He just wasn't addicted to it. Or enamored by it. Or willing to let it track him like a radio-collared wolf. Smartphones /

computers / the Internet—they were simply tools. Tools Vigil could wield competently enough when the need arose. As his father used to say (adding a critical distinction to the quote attributed to Francis Bacon): *Knowledge is power—but only _superior_ knowledge.* Bottom line, when he had the opportunity to study his enemy, Vigil took it.

He sat down in front of a Windows PC and searched for "Lenny Grabasso." The Wikipedia entry was the first result that came up and he read the article and memorized relevant details:

- Born Leonardo Salvatore Grabasso on March 13, 1945 in Brooklyn, New York to Sicilian immigrants (age 77).
- Former underboss who testified against Vito Molinari, head of the Mangano crime family.
- Associates call him "Lenny." Earned his nickname "The Lion" after several made-men witnessed him fighting three older kids over a stolen watch.
- After joining La Costra Nostra, excelled in the construction business. Ran a powerful concrete company. Involved in union corruption and racketeering.
- Grandiose. Absurdly vain. Notorious womanizer. Alleged rapist.
- A reputation for cold-hearted brutality and extreme violence.
- Confessed to 19 murders. Suspected of many more.
- Previously known for his unwavering loyalty to the mob.
- Served a minimal prison sentence before entering the Witness Protection Program in 1991.
- Universally reviled as the biggest rat ever to betray the Italian mafia.

In sum, a total piece of shit.

And at least nineteen more reasons to take him down.

Unfortunately, the article provided no clues as to why Grabasso would steal electricity from a wind farm, or for what purpose. And Vigil was no closer to an answer than he was before dinner.

But does it really matter?

Grabasso had made a mockery of the system. The families of all the people he'd murdered had never gotten closure. It was a matter of public record. So as far as Vigil was concerned, he was no longer obligated to solve the mystery behind Prosser's murder. Killing Grabasso would be a guilt-free favor to society—even before his crimes in Carlin.

It was Mira's involvement that made things messy. Though they'd forged some kind of an alliance, her intentions weren't clear. She was in a precarious position. Undercover, but unsanctioned. Risking—not only her career, but—her life. And she was also active duty law enforcement who had a pretty good idea of what Vigil was capable of. Consequently, before taking out Grabasso, he wanted to make sure she was okay with bringing the ex-mobster to justice—his way.

At least until morning then, he'd put on his investigator hat and keep puzzling out why Grabasso was leeching electricity from the wind farm.

He wondered if he'd dismissed the possibility of a drug operation too quickly? Maybe it wasn't a meth lab, but some kind of new designer drug that demanded a premium on the street? Except that didn't feel right, either. Most addicts (most Americans, for that matter) weren't exactly rolling in dough; they relied on the cheap fix. The few who could afford a better high still favored cocaine, which took a lot more space to refine than a shipping container (and as with meth, could be produced much less expensively south of the border).

Vigil felt like he was beating his head against the wall. But then suddenly, the sheer repetition of arriving at the same dead end over and over again sparked an idea:

There was probably *nothing* so profitable Grabasso could manufacture—*in a single shipping container*—that he'd have killed Prosser over it.

But what if there were *more* containers?

Buried in more farmers' fields?

Stealing *a lot* more electricity?

Well you're not knockin' boots, so you might as well put 'em on the ground and find out.

I t had been a long day. Productive, but the problems he'd yet to solve were playing Ring Around the Rosy in his skull. On top of that (in a misguided effort to stay sharp) Leonard skipped the wine and the Vicodin before going to bed. Predictably, this backfired, so when Vin texted him at three in the morning with an update on the container extraction, he was still wide-fucking awake, cursing sheep.

> Thirty-one down, sixty-nine to go. Should knock out twice that tomorrow night. Probably finish early.

Leonard typed a quick reply:

> Good. And the other thing?

Vin:

> Took care of itself.

Even better.
Now he was down to only the one problem again. A very

big problem. Liable to keep him awake the rest of the night. That was the Catch-22 of problems: You were supposed to sleep on them, but they wouldn't let you. Fortunately, the devil created Xanax for just such occasions (he was the Angel of Darkness, after all). Leonard swallowed a 3 mg tab and slept like the dead.

CHAPTER
THIRTY-EIGHT

Vigil got lucky after all.

Before he logged off the hotel's guest computer, he brought up a map of the entire 100,000 acre Carlin Wind Project. It was incomprehensibly immense, sprawling across four *counties*. He'd have to drive hundreds of miles to visit every field. Search acres upon acres at each stop to find where a shipping container *might* or might not be buried.

While trespassing.

At night.

In rural Texas—with cotton farmers already looking for an excuse to shoot him.

Not the best plan I've ever had. But it was late, he was agitated, and he wanted to make some kind of progress. Vigil's drug of choice was forward motion.

He took the same exit that Franky Bloom had taken on their way into Carlin, but on the north side of the highway. As he slowed at the bottom of the ramp, something caught his eye over at the mom-'n-pop truck stop.

They'd finished the repaving project. That was clear. And the lot was full of semi trucks. Parked hood-out and packed in like sardines. A handful of the rigs were pulling flatbeds, and three of these had shipping containers strapped down to their trailers, partially covered with tarps cinched down with black rubber bungees. The containers were dirty. Coated with a layer of dried mud and clods of dirt clinging to the sides. Like they'd been buried and then dug up.

Recently.

Vigil decided to take a closer look.

He parked by the front entrance of the truck stop and went inside and bought a small flashlight. Figured, what the hell, and purchased a burner, too. He paid cash for both. Took the items back out to the Prius and drove over to the far side of the gas pumps where there was overnight parking for RVs and camp trailers and the like. He backed in between a Sprinter van and a decommissioned school bus repurposed by hippies with more imagination than craft.

He pocketed the flashlight and got out. Padded around back to the side of the lot reserved for commercial vehicles. It was 3:30 in the morning, and most of the truckers would be asleep in their bunks. Vigil stood beside a dumpster and looked for the flatbed that was the farthest away from any overhead lights. The one in the southeast corner would do, and he made his approach.

The tricky bit would be getting inside to examine the load without waking the driver. Cargo theft was a real problem. Most of the truckers who'd given him rides over the years had stories of stolen freight, and all of them were very attuned to the signature rocking and jostling a trailer undergoes when someone is moving around on it. Gusts of wind could fool them sometimes. Or heavy loads idling past on a loose slab. But the night was calm, and there were no other trucks searching for an empty spot at this hour.

Fortunately, his target was a long-nose Peterbilt with a pre-emissions diesel. A Caterpillar. No DEF system, which meant it could idle all night without damaging the engine. The low growl and vibration would provide Vigil some cover. Better still, it was parked between two refrigerated units, and one of them had a loose belt that squealed like pigs in a slaughterhouse.

He shuffled sideways into the alley of dark formed between the trailers and emerged behind his target in a trash-strewn patch of weeds. The vast majority of shipping containers had swing doors with locking mechanisms at the rear for loading and unloading. As did this container. But like the one buried in Schnell's field, the doors had been welded shut. To keep out moisture, Vigil figured. He bet he'd find another open hatch cut into the roof for access; no need for the tarp otherwise.

Ideally, he'd use the rear bumper as a step and then pull himself up, Alex-Honnold-style. Easy enough considering Vigil could rep-out at least fifty chins in one go . . . except now he had to move very, very slowly. Any sudden movement would rock the trailer and risk waking the driver. One of those rare times his two hundred fifty pound frame worked against him.

The easy maneuver would've looked like a fast pull-up, using momentum to carry his torso all the way over the edge of the roof and into an arms-locked muscle-up position. But since momentum was the enemy, Vigil moved like ivy scaling an ivory tower. With only his nose clearing the container, he flexed his trunk and sideways-flag-poled his legs vertically until he could get a knee up on the roof. This accomplished, he let his lower body do most of the work, gripping the slick steel with the rubber sole of his boot, while simultaneously walking one hand forward like an inch worm fucked a spider.

Slow and low, that is the tempo.

It took him five agonizing, lactic-acid soaked minutes before he was lying fully prone on the roof of the container.

He laid there for a while, just breathing. Listening while he let his heart rate slow. The chrome stacks purred. The reefers thrummed. The loose belt screamed bloody murder.

He stashed the Sig against a butt cheek so it wouldn't grind against the metal. Then Vigil slid onward. Inch by inch. The dried mud and grit like sandpaper against his jeans and shirt.

Once he got to the tarp, progress was smoother, but of course the thick, rubberized fabric also blocked access to the interior of the container. He felt around with his palm and located one corner of the jagged hatch. Then he used the point of his pocketknife to puncture the tarp—*slash*—and again on the opposite corner—*slash*—cutting a giant 'X' in the compromised material. He peeled back the four resulting flaps. The tarp could be patched, but he felt bad about the damage. Tarps were expensive. Diesel was five-bucks a gallon. But it couldn't be helped.

Vigil had been prepared to lower himself inside to examine the contents, but it turned out there was no need. Flashlight in hand, his perch provided ample visibility of the internals: Electronics of some kind. That was clear. Two floor-to-ceiling shelves of tech mounted to the walls of the container, end-to-end, with a narrow aisle of bare floor between. Everywhere there were power strips and extension cords and ethernet cables. Dozens upon dozens of brushed aluminum cases with shiny circular grills protecting many-bladed plastic fans. Vigil's only point of comparison was the "server racks in a data center" shot, a popular trope in the techno-thriller movies he'd seen. This stuff looked similar. Not anything you'd set on a desk and connect to a keyboard and monitor, but vaguely computer-like. Mira would probably know right away what he was looking at. Another instance when a camera-equipped smartphone would've come in handy.

But Vigil didn't have a smartphone. Or a camera. Or a smartphone with a camera. He had eyes, and a brain, and he knew how to read. He noticed that many of the components had words embossed into their cases. Brand names, presumably. Or model numbers. Two in particular were as ubiquitous as classified documents in Mar-a-Lago: "Bitmain AntMiner" and "Nvidia". The made-up words meant nothing to Vigil, but he could pass them along to Mira—or better yet —just google them when he got back to the hotel.

He rolled off the roof on the Peterbilt's passenger side and landed hard on the fresh blacktop. Predictably, the sudden movement rocked the trailer, and the trailer rocked the cab, but by this point Vigil didn't care. If he woke the driver, he'd be long gone by the time the guy got dressed and came outside to investigate. He left five Ben Franklin's under the windshield wiper for a new tarp and strode back to the Prius in a somewhat better mood.

CHAPTER THIRTY-NINE

After going down a deep rabbit hole on the hotel's guest computer, Vigil went to his room for some shuteye.

Less than he'd have liked.

Right before the good part of a dream, the phone rang. "I need greasy hash browns, runny eggs, and a pot of strong coffee. Join me?"

The clock on the nightstand read 7:35 AM. "Ten minutes. I'll meet you in the lobby." He rinsed off, packed his bag, and headed down. He liked being able to leave a place on a whim. Unlike Mira, he wouldn't have to come back to his room for a toiletry bag, a suitcase, a laptop, or five extra pairs of underwear.

Speaking of the devil, she'd seen better days. Probably most of them were better.

"Ready?"

"Always."

They walked to the Prius and got in. Mira scooted the seat forward and adjusted the mirrors. Vigil was surprised she wanted to drive with such a brutal hangover.

"Hey," she said, "about last night . . . "

"What about it?"

"Thanks for being a gentleman."

Vigil nodded.

"To be honest, I don't remember anything after the seventh shot of mezcal. But when I woke up this morning it was clear that—you know—we didn't . . ."

"Not my style."

The closest thing resembling a diner was at the TA truck stop, a couple exits closer to Carlin. He'd have preferred an IHOP or a Denny's or even a recently fumigated Waffle House, but figured it was hard to fuck up an omelet. On their way inside he scanned the truck lot for more flatbeds hauling dug-up shipping containers. Didn't see any.

They sat at a booth, ordered food, and drank coffee in silence until their meals arrived. Mira wasn't what you would call a morning person, but once she had a little caffeine and carbohydrate in her, she looked ready to hear about his discoveries.

"After I tucked you in, I went exploring."

"Find anything?"

He said, "What do you know about bitcoin?"

VIGIL HIMSELF, KNEW VERY LITTLE. AND A FEW hours ago, even less.

He recognized the word, but wasn't sure if he'd actually heard it spoken aloud before. It was some kind of digital currency. One more "modern convenience" on a long list of things he was perfectly content not having to ship / register / assemble / charge / secure / configure / insure / program / tweak / optimize / diagnose / dust / store / maintain / upgrade / obtain dongles for / delete data from / sell /

recycle / or dispose of in an environmentally sustainable manner. In other words:

Not for him.

Writing checks wasn't for him.

What use did he have for a "crypto wallet?" (one of many pieces of jargon he'd had to decipher after googling "Bitmain AntMiner" and "Nvidia").

Dubious utility aside, Vigil didn't have the patience to master such a tedious technology. Once, on a Greyhound bus traveling from St. Louis to Denver, he'd found himself with nothing to read. The only diversion available was watching an old woman knit a sleeve onto a beige sweater. Compared to researching bitcoin and cryptocurrencies? The monotonous yarn craft had been spellbinding.

He blamed the techies for making crypto such a yawn-fest. Their godlike ability to render an otherwise fascinating topic lifeless and dull was unrivaled. And unfortunate. Because on a purely philosophical level, Vigil found the core principles of blockchain-based currencies pretty intriguing. *Dad would have, too.*

He could picture them at the dinner table, debating the merits of a fiat-less currency with a decentralized public ledger . . . the ability to conduct business while remaining anonymous. In many ways, the technology aligned with some of his father's anarchistic beliefs. Granted, not having much faith in the long-term viability of civilization (or the electrical grid, for that matter), Dad still would've argued against any means of exchange that required networked computers to operate. And as a practical matter, Vigil tended to agree.

Lenny 'The Lion' Grabasso, on the other hand? He was a true believer when it came to bitcoin. But then, a number with nine zeros after it buys a lot of faith.

It turned out that the dozens of devices embossed with "Bitmain AntMiner" in his shipping containers were a brand of cryptocurrency mining equipment—specialized computers that perform difficult, CPU-intensive calculations in order to verify and process financial transactions. In the process, these mining "rigs" create new bitcoins—a portion of which they get to keep. Similarly, the components stamped with "Nvidia" were GPUs—"graphics processing units"—which, in addition to their applications in gaming and artificial intelligence research, can also be used for mining bitcoins . . . $2.5 billion dollars' worth, if Vigil's rough calculations were anywhere in the ballpark.

He'd found a web-based crypto mining profitability calculator to help with the math. Doing it by hand would've required him to grok hashrates, network difficulty, block subsidies, and a boatload of other dork-speak he had no intention of understanding. All Vigil wanted to know was: *Is mining bitcoin so lucrative that Lenny 'The Lion' would murder Will Prosser to protect his operation?*

Yup.

Especially since he'd eliminated the cost of electricity—by far the most expensive line item in crypto mining. And *especially* if the price of bitcoin rose from $13 bucks a coin in 2012, to more than $64,000 dollars per coin at its peak in late 2021.

Which it had.

Depending on exactly how many rigs Grabasso had buried, Vigil's estimate might've actually been low. And for that kind of money? A guy like Grabasso would do a lot worse than kill a nosy wind tech.

"I KNOW ABOUT AS MUCH ABOUT BITCOIN AS I KNOW about brain surgery," Mira said.

"Same. Until I spent the last three hours reading up on

it." While she finished eating, he briefed her on what he'd found in the shipping container last night, and what he'd learned while cramming all things bitcoin this morning.

"Hells bells, that's a lot of money."

Vigil nodded. Made quick work of his neglected bacon.

"I see it now," Mira said. "It's the perfect crime: Free electricity. Justin Lackey there to run interference if Innova-Gen notices the phantom draw. And cotton farmers with access to the wind turbines—totally dependent on Grabasso paying them under the table if they wanna stay afloat."

"But it's only the perfect crime if he gets away with it," Vigil said. "He still has to cash out."

"If he's making as much as you think he is, why would he? Too much heat after killing Prosser?"

"Probably. But also, how much money do you need? Grabasso's an old man—he can't take it to the grave. Doesn't strike me as the type of guy who'd set up a charitable trust to benefit future generations, either."

"Yeah, not so much," Mira said.

"I think Prosser was a wake-up call. And Grabasso's gotta be kicking himself for not cashing out sooner. However much bitcoin he has now, it's *halved* in value since late last year."

Mira was staring deep into her mug like it was some kind of an oracle. "But what you just said about him being old—he is—seventy-six this March. How many guys from his generation know anything about mining bitcoin?"

"I hear you," he said. "But I'm sure he can afford advisors."

"Lots of them."

"But going back to him cashing out . . ."

"Sorry, I sidetracked you."

"We know he's done, because he's removing the mining rigs from the fields. But that also means he's planning to get the hell outta Dodge."

"You think?"

"Absolutely. Funny thing about bitcoin: It was designed so that the owner of a digital wallet can buy and sell goods one hundred percent anonymously. And mostly, it works . . . unless you try to move massive amounts of it while engaging in illegal activity—or you mine an insanely large amount and then attempt to convert it to cash. Do either of those things, law enforcement takes an interest. And apparently they have ways of unmasking a wallet's owner, so long as the amount justifies the man hours necessary. $2-$3-$4 billion worth of bitcoin? That's worth recovering. And don't forget, there's a bunch of cotton farmers involved—and even *one* is too many —after the FBI or the Secret Service starts poking around. They'll fold like a pair of deuces once he runs away with all the chips."

"Right." Mira was nodding her head now. "Of course— that's why Grabasso needs a U.S. Marshal in his pocket: He has to start over again. And he needs a new identity to do it. Official and flawless. Straight from the source. Then it won't matter when the farmers start talking, because it'll be too late to catch him. Can't extradite someone who doesn't exist."

THE WAITRESS BROUGHT MORE COFFEE AND VIGIL asked her to leave the pot. He said, "We still had a lot to discuss last night before you—"

"Went offline."

"That's one way of putting it."

"So let's talk."

He thought for a moment about how he might keep this tactful, but Vigil didn't like sugarcoating, and he rarely did. "For what it's worth, I don't usually do this."

"Eat breakfast?"

"Run things by people."

Mira nodded warily and sipped her coffee.

He continued, "Before I left the hotel last night, I read up on Grabasso's background. Nineteen murders. That he admitted to. Probably a lot more we don't know about—and that's just the killing. Then there's the extortion. The racketeering. Rape allegations. Torture.

"And for all that, he serves—what?—two-and-a-half years? There are people rotting in a cage for piss-ant drug convictions. Grabasso, meanwhile, gets a pat on the back from Uncle Sam and a clean slate. Keeps committing crimes. Keeps stacking cash. Keeps killing people.

"Bottom line: It's time he pays for what he's done."

"You're preaching to the choir, Vigil."

He frowned. "Am I? The U.S. Marshals made his latest fucking crime spree possible."

"No. Our justice system made it possible. We just followed orders."

"Grabasso's orders, apparently."

Mira crumpled her napkin and dropped it on her plate into a congealing film of egg yolk. "That's why I'm here, remember? And not *only* to hold Grabasso accountable, but also, to fix what's broken in the Marshals Service."

"I hope you're sincere."

"You think I'm risking my career for shits and giggles?"

Fair point. He said, "When I say it's time Grabasso pays— you understand what I mean, right?"

"Yes. If it comes to that. But I still want to give Sheriff Baker another crack—especially now that you uncovered the motive. *Like we agreed.*"

"But when I agreed to that, it was before Grabasso's thugs abducted Lackey. Now he won't be able to amend his earlier statement. And Schnell? You were there. He's not changing his tune, either. He's terrified."

"So what then? You just show up and assassinate him? Vigilante style?"

He shrugged. "More or less."

"But if you do that, you know what happens to my boss and any other corrupt marshals, right? Jack. *Shit*. They get away with it. Probably do it again. The only way they get punished is if Grabasso goes down for Prosser's murder, and then agrees to testify against them."

"To reduce his sentence," Vigil said, not even trying to suppress his sarcasm. "*Again.*"

Mira set her mug down hard on the table, rattling the silverware. "He's seventy-six years old. He'll die in prison. Best case, he negotiates a few perks—TV, tobacco, maybe an extra pair of socks."

Vigil was silent.

"We do this my way, I can get back to fighting the good fight without the weight of corruption around my neck every day. You kill him, the rot remains."

There was a bitter taste in his throat and a soreness at the hinge of his jaw from grinding his teeth. He swallowed more coffee but it only made it worse. *Fuck.* Only a moment ago, he'd ranted against the hypocrisy of plea deals, and now he found himself agreeing to a similar compromise. *Because like it or not, she's right.*

"Fine," he said. "But I have conditions. One—when you coordinate with prosecutors, you make sure Grabasso gets charged separately for this bitcoin scheme. I want his earnings seized and distributed among victims' families. Two—if Baker refuses to see the light, then I'm free to put this piece of shit in the ground. And three—you turn a blind eye."

Mira used her fingers to roll the paper wrapper from her straw into a tight little ball while staring into her coffee for more guidance. "Deal," she said finally, "*if* you agree to *my* conditions."

"I'd expect nothing less from you."

"First, I need you to go to the Sheriff. Nobody official can know I'm here. Not yet. If my boss catches wind . . . that would be bad." She paused, a mischievous grin slowly forming. "Second, I'm technically on vacation. So you and me? We're no longer 'strictly business.'"

Vigil frowned but stopped short of shutting her down. "I'll talk to Baker. But there's one more thing I need you to agree to, and it applies no matter which road we go down with Grabasso."

"Name it."

"When this is all over, you don't work Witness Protection anymore. You're better than that."

Mira stiffened in her seat, tilting her head to one side, incredulous. "You want me to quit the Marshals?"

"No. Just WITSEC. Transfer to the fugitive division, or asset forfeiture, or whatever."

Now she looked angry. "You realize there's a lot of innocent people we protect, right?"

"And a lot more scumbags. Be honest: Percentage wise, what's the proportion of witnesses who make a deal to avoid taking responsibility for their crimes?"

"I don't know the exact number."

"Ninety percent. I googled it last night after reading up on Grabasso. *Ninety. Fucking. Percent.*"

"Maybe so, but—"

"Not 'maybe,'" he said, cutting her off. "That's from Gerald Shur. The guy who created the program."

"But even criminals have families. Wives. Sons. Daughters." She looked away, her eyes prismatic with morning sun and held-back tears. "We protect them, too."

Nothing he could say to that. She'd confronted him with

reality—tangled and frayed and full of tradeoffs. He'd been so focused on his moral compass, he'd stopped listening to his heart. Covering her hand with his, he proposed a compromise, "What about this: Next time somebody like Grabasso enters the program . . . if they don't stay on the straight and narrow—get in touch with me. Fair?"

"(A)—Grabasso's one of a kind. (B)—there's this thing called the Rule of Law. I took an oath, Vigil."

"And I didn't need to."

He let go of her hand and flagged down the waitress for the check.

CHAPTER FORTY

B ack inside the car he said, "Take me to the Sheriff's
department."

"Right now?" She sounded perplexed.

"Best to get it over with."

"I thought you'd want more evidence first. 'Idiot-proof'
the case—isn't that what you said? So Baker has no alternative but to keep the investigation open?"

"Any idiot can already see Schnell didn't pull the trigger."

"Don't take this the wrong way, but you're smarter than
you look, Vigil. It's possible the Sheriff didn't even notice
Schnell has a prosthetic leg. Plenty of people who limp can
still climb a ladder."

"Then it'll be a teachable moment."

"Shame you didn't grab one of those mining rigs off the
flatbed last night."

"I didn't have tools. Hard enough getting a peek without
waking the driver."

"So shouldn't we get pictures of a buried shipping
container first? Something you can show Baker to help paint
the picture?"

Vigil shook his head. "For all we know, Grabasso's men

dug them up already. And even if they haven't, we don't know where to look."

"We could drive around. Big yellow excavators and semi trucks are pretty easy to spot."

"They won't be working in broad daylight for that very reason. And if Baker needs corroborating evidence, he can go check the empty container at Schnell's. The buried power line's still running to it. I sincerely hope he doesn't waste the time, though. Clock's ticking."

"What clock?"

"What do you mean, 'what clock?' As soon as Grabasso converts his bitcoin to cash, he's in the wind."

"How long do you think it'll take him to cash out?"

"I'm kinda surprised he hasn't already. But then again, Grabasso was probably mining bitcoin right up until he killed Prosser—and it's not until he starts converting it to dollars that he risks his anonymity."

Mira said, "I thought the whole point of bitcoin was that it was anonymous. Isn't that why criminals like it so much?"

"It's more accurate to call it 'pseudonymous.' Anonymous, in that there's no personally identifiable information attached to a digital wallet—but also traceable."

"Traceable, how?"

"By leveraging the blockchain."

Mira looked at him like he was speaking alien.

"It's a data structure where all the transactions are stored," he said. "Fully decentralized, *and public*.

"Think of it as a digital ledger everyone has access to. For some types of criminal activity, that's a reasonable tradeoff. Say you're shopping for a personal amount of MDMA from a seller in Denmark? They accept bitcoin, you send it to their wallet anonymously, and they mail you the drugs. As long as your contraband doesn't get intercepted, everyone's happy. Nobody knows what you're buying, and the amount's so insignificant, no one in law enforcement would waste time looking into it.

"But when you move *billions* worth of crypto?—that's a different thing entirely."

"How so?"

"Typically, you'd rely on an exchange to turn bitcoin into regular money. The conversion constitutes a transaction and it gets recorded on the blockchain the same as any other. It's an anonymous transaction, sure. But like I said in the diner, if the amounts are large enough, they're also conspicuous."

"So the owners of the exchange have to comply with a subpoena?"

"Yeah—when it gets to that point. It's not that the exchange goes out of its way to expose the bitcoin holder's identity," Vigil clarified, "it's that the large volume of transactions coming from a single wallet, combined with the 'know your customer' requirements that legit exchanges now have to abide by, ensure a would-be money launderer leaves tracks. Then it's simply a matter of good ol' fashioned police work plus software. The digital breadcrumbs eventually lead back to the wallet owner.

"That said, methods exist for criminals to cover their tracks. But these take time. How much or how little time? I have no idea. But with a billion dollars at stake, it's of the fucking essence. That's for damn sure."

"Good to know."

A quarter mile from the Sheriff's headquarters, Mira pulled over.

"You really think I need more exercise?"

She rolled her eyes, said, "Cameras in the lot. Maybe even license plate scanners."

He nodded. Tilted the seat all the way back and unholstered the Sig. "I'll leave this with you. It's legal, but I don't need any extra hassles if they wanna see ID I don't have." He took the burner out of his pack. "What's your number?" She recited it and he punched it in and then called her to make sure the burner was functional.

Mira's phone vibrated in the console and she dismissed the call. "You think Baker will take you seriously?"

"He might." Though Vigil found himself hoping he wouldn't.

CHAPTER
FORTY-ONE

The Nolan County Sheriff's Department was on the same road Vigil used to walk out of Carlin the night before last. He didn't recognize the building because he'd been on the railroad tracks avoiding unnecessary interactions with law enforcement.

Up close, it appeared to be relatively new construction. The exterior walls were an irregular grid of limestone blocks, capped with beige-painted concrete the final five or six feet under the roofline. The stone work wasn't uniform. In size or color. As if the builders had tried to save money by using excess material from previous projects. There was a metal roof and windows with aluminum frames. A couple of immature oak trees in front, grown at a nursery and planted after the turf had been rolled out. Not one of "Grainger's" buildings, Vigil thought. Too functional, too modern, too generic. More, school-administration-building-in-the-suburbs, than a place Texas lawmen reported to.

Inside, it was like the waiting room of a prosperous dental group. The only difference being that the receptionist was a uniformed duty officer with a badge, and that the counter she sat behind was separated from the lobby by bulletproof glass. There was a recessed slot to facilitate the exchange of forms and other small items, and an inset speaker with a perforated aluminum grille for communication. Vigil doubted the speaker would stop a bullet, though he was impressed by the sound quality when the woman gestured to a clipboard and asked him to print his name, the date, and his reason for visiting.

"How may I help you?" she droned without looking at what he'd written. Had she looked, she wouldn't have needed to ask.

"I'd like to speak with Sheriff Baker. Would that be alright, Deputy Strayed?" He made a point of reading her name off the patch affixed to her shirt. Best to lead by example.

"Regarding?"

"The murder of Will Prosser."

She had a pretty good poker face. But the way she locked eyes with him a moment too long, and her newfound interest in the guest log, told him that Prosser's name was still fresh in her mind, and that 'murder' didn't match up with the departmental narrative.

"Do you have an appointment?"

She knew, of course, that he did not. Asking questions they already know the answer to is standard operating procedure for law enforcement. It weighs heavily in the selection criteria for new recruits. Annual refresher courses are scheduled. Daily "rhetorical question quotas," set.

"No Ma'am."

"Please have a seat. I'll see if he can fit you in."

He'd mentioned the magic word, so if Baker was there, he'd make time. The delay was so she could type Vigil's name into a computer and query all the databases our totally-free-

and-absolutely-not-one-bit-Orwellian country has to offer. It pleased him to know she wouldn't find much.

Aside from bureaucratic busy work, making him wait was about status. The same reason doctors and lawyers and all manner of suits take their time before gracing you with their presence, appointment or not: A little preemptive signaling to remind you their perch sits higher than yours on the social hierarchy. Vigil, of course, didn't give a shit about hierarchy or status. If you locked him in a cage with a dozen other bad motherfuckers, he'd emerge with nary a scratch and twelve phone numbers for next of kin. He didn't need society to tell him his worth or rank.

He also didn't feel like sitting, so he wandered over to a table where a selection of magazines had been arrayed and assessed his options. Elon Musk appeared on the cover of *TIME's* December 2021 issue, brooding about something. The December issue of *Car and Driver* featured the new Z06 Corvette (in yellow for some reason, because there's no accounting for taste). *Newsweek* was the most current with "THE FOREVER VIRUS" rendered in all-caps on the cover. Impossible to fact check, but Vigil figured this was a true statement. *Technically*. He'd never heard of a virus that simply ceased to exist. Certainly the common cold had been around a long time. And even smallpox, reportedly eradicated, must live on in a bioweapons lab—*somewhere*. He shrugged, reminded yet again why he preferred reading fiction.

After a few minutes a door buzzed open next to the bullpen, and Deputy Strayed invited him back to see Sheriff Baker. He followed her around a small nest of desks and cubicles to an office in the far corner with Baker's name on the door. She ushered him inside and left.

"Have a seat, son."

Vigil didn't like anyone referring to him by that particular diminutive except for his dad—and he was dead. But there was no sense in starting out on the wrong foot by censoring sobriquets. Besides, he tended to give his elders more leeway with their turns of phrase, and people in the South, a little extra on top of that. Baker might still prove himself a good public servant. He'd certainly been doing it a long time. Thirty years, give or take, based on the dates printed on various plaques on the walls.

He sat down on a faux leather swivel chair and reached over the Sheriff's oak desk to shake hands. "Nate Vigil."

Baker shook, but not what you would call enthusiastically. "I'm tempted to tell you to save your breath," he said, "but you look as earnest as a church goin' retard, and the week I've had, I could use some entertainment."

Vigil smiled, unsure if the vulgar joviality was just a part of his schtick, or something more calculated. "Well I hope it gets better—your week, I mean."

Baker grunted and leaned back in his chair. Even sitting down, he looked tall. Rangy. His sixty-odd years had slumped his wide shoulders forward some, and added a little girth to his waistline, but Vigil could imagine him bucking a few hay bales, or surprising an unruly kid with a hip-toss in a pinch. Overall, he'd aged well. Good skin. Enough hair left to hold a crease from the cowboy hat which hung on a rack behind him. Vigil could smell the man, but it wasn't offensive, thanks to the wet cedar halo of Old Spice cologne.

"Before you start yappin'—you read the article in the paper at least?"

"I did."

"Alright, good. That's good. Half of you fuckin' crackpots come in here can't even sing the alphabet." He looked tired. Brown uniform damp under the armpits. "Well go on then— tell me why it didn't happen just exactly the way two eyewitnesses said it did." Baker folded his arms and put his boots up on his desk like he was ready to watch a favorite episode of The Lone Ranger.

Given the icy reception, Vigil decided to abandon his usual slow and methodical approach he favored when bringing people up to speed, and skip right to the part the Sheriff had gotten wrong. He said, "When Oswald Schnell limped out across his field holding a rifle, he wasn't wearing shorts was he?"

"No, Sherlock. He's a cotton farmer, not a cross country coach. Probably doesn't even *own* a pair of shorts."

"Probably not. It's too bad, though. Because if he was wearing shorts, you might've noticed why he was limping."

"Artificial leg. I noticed."

Talk about getting off on the wrong foot. He tried to recover, said, "I assume you ran a ballistics report—saw the trajectory?"

"Sure did."

"And you don't find it hard to believe Schnell's able to climb a ladder while holding a rifle?"

Baker smirked. "Guess the ol' bull refused to accept what a lesser man would consider a limitation. But please, continue tellin' me about all the clues I missed."

Vigil took it on the chin. "I might've concluded the same thing. Given what you encountered."

"Damn right you would. But lemme guess: You're privy to information I'm not aware of—that's where you're goin' with this, right?"

He was beginning to feel like the butt of a joke. Like Baker was stringing him along and letting him flail, purely for his own amusement; indeed, he'd already said as much. The question was, could Vigil still win him over by explaining "Grainger's" bitcoin mining scheme, and the motive it gave the ex-gangster for killing Prosser?

Maybe.

Unless Baker was in on it.

Vigil considered getting up and walking out. But if he didn't honor Mira's conditions, she'd have every right not to honor his. There was also what he'd told Schnell:

Everyone who deserves it gets punished.

And this applied equally to the Sheriff.

He sat up in his chair and took inventory of the items on Baker's desk that could be used as weapons. Should it come to that, the rattlesnake head encased in a resin globe would do nicely. He said, "I do have some information. And I do hope you're not aware of it. Just give me five more minutes to lay out the facts, and I'll get out of your hair."

"Hell, I'll give you ten."

Vigil started with the paranoid farmers at the Diamondback and proceeded step-by-step like he'd originally planned: Grainger's goons trying to run him out of town, the bar fight with the farmers, Lackey's lies, the buried shipping container in Schnell's field, and the bitcoin mining rigs stealing electricity from the wind farm. The only thing he left out was Mira's involvement, and Grabasso's true identity for the same reason. "I realize Grainger's concrete business made him a millionaire," he said, "but this bitcoin he's been mining? That's worth at least a couple *billion*. Bottom line, he couldn't afford to let Prosser any further into that field."

Baker got his feet back under him and leaned forward in his chair, propping an elbow on the edge of his desk and massaging the loose skin at the point of his chin. "Energy theft. I'll be damned. Seems like somethin' we'll have to investigate at some point . . . if and when the wind farm operation wants to file a grievance, or one of the cotton farmers wants to come forward. 'Til then, it don't make a ton a sense to rile up folks I can depend on at the ballot box."

Fucking politicians. "So you won't even look into it?"

"No need."

Baker was a snake, alright. *But is he a snake in the Grabasso?* Vigil had to know. "You ever hear of Lenny 'The Lion?'"

The Sheriff frowned. Half annoyed, half confused. "Who?"

"Leonard Grabasso. Former mobster."

"Oh, right. Helped bring down Vito Molinari back in the day. What about him?"

Vigil was silent. His cold stare worked better than any polygraph.

Baker wasn't amused. "You forget to take your medication or somethin'?" The Sheriff snapped his fingers twice like he was dealing with a catatonic.

If he's acting, Vigil thought, he should retire and move to Hollywood. "Never mind." He stood to leave.

"Sit down, son. I'll tell you when we're done talkin'."

Vigil just stood there for a long moment. And when he finally sat, he took his time about it.

"If you woulda come by yesterday, I'd have been more receptive to your little conspiracy theory. But see, I know somethin' *you* aren't privy to. Ordinarily, I wouldn't share details of an ongoing investigation. But you're a man who's convinced himself he knows better than everybody else, and I'd like to disabuse you of that foolhardy notion:

"Oswald Schnell took his own life last night. His wife's too."

Didn't see that coming. But damned if he'd give the man the pleasure of witnessing his shock. "Lemme guess," he said flatly, as if Baker's revelation was so obvious it bored him to tears, "he left a note."

The Sheriff retrieved a pocket-sized notebook from his desk drawer and donned a pair of reading glasses. "As a matter of fact. Quote: 'I can endure hardship and pain, but not with the weight of this guilt. Taking Prosser's life is too much to bear. Forgive me, Pamela. We go now to a better place.'"

Vigil had heard enough, and didn't particularly care if Baker was finished talking. He stood, said, "Thank you, Sheriff . . . "

"Glad I could set you straight."

. . . *For giving me two more reasons.*

CHAPTER FORTY-TWO

L eonard woke up late, groggy from the benzos, and scrolled through headlines on his phone to clear the cobwebs. National coverage consisted of the usual Disease, War, and The-World-Is-Coming-To-An-End! clickbait:

PUBLIC HEALTH OFFICIALS SHOCKED! COVID KILLS MORE 99-YEAR-OLDS WITH AN AVERAGE OF 5 COMORBIDITIES.

RUSSIAN MILITARY TERRIBLE AT FIGHTING—INVADES UKRAINE ANYWAY. MILITARY INDUSTRIAL COMPLEX ANGERED BY SANCTIONS.

STARVING KIDS IN AFRICA SURVIVING INTO ADULTHOOD REIGNITES FEARS OF OVERPOPULATION. WILL RISING SEA LEVELS DROWN ENOUGH CLIMATE DENIERS TO MAKE A DIFFERENCE?

Etcetera.

He read a few of the articles—just in case there were actionable facts hidden between the party lines and propaganda—but there was little of interest. Nothing of concern out of Sweetwater, either. He supposed the Sheriff's Department hadn't told the paper about Schnell eating a bullet. Or maybe no one had called it in yet.

Regardless, still the one big problem.

And sleeping on it hadn't helped.

Fucking crypto.

GIVEN HOW RICH IT WAS ABOUT TO MAKE HIM, Leonard knew surprisingly little about cryptocurrency. More than he knew ten years ago, to be sure. And way more than Vin. But far, *far* less than Raymond, who could probably hold his own with Bitcoin's creator, Satoshi Nakamoto. Therefore, Leonard *didn't need* to know much about crypto, because Raymond knew everything, and Raymond did whatever Leonard told him to do (especially after that one time he didn't).

After the out-of-control electric bill incident, and listening to enough of the kid's explanation to realize: (A)—bitcoin was about getting rich, and (B)—the solution to its biggest profitability bottleneck was right in his backyard, Leonard went to work on (C)—how to get away with it (perhaps his greatest talent . . . just ask the Department of Justice).

The key was to study people who got caught, and learn from their mistakes. Before they even buried the first mining rig, he instructed Raymond to print out every news article available on the topic of crimes involving crypto, and to keep him current with weekly updates. In 2012, the binder of printouts was thin. Now, in 2022, he had three binders, each one fatter than Carla's tits. Leonard reviewed the articles so many times he could almost recite them word-for-word.

Aside from exposing personal information online (which Raymond assured him he would "never, never, never-ever let happen"), by far the most common reason crypto con men got caught was how they bungled cashing out. The basic challenge for all would-be money launderers was that transactions couldn't be too large, or too numerous. For digital currency, criminals developed techniques like "peel chaining" and "layering" and "coin joining" and "mixing" to stay under the radar of regulators, analogous to the shell corporations and private accounts in the Caymans cartels used back in the '90s to wash their money. As for the technical details underlying these methods? Leonard understood them about as well as Joe Biden rode a bicycle.

Didn't matter.

Because the methods didn't work.

If they *had* worked, the fuck-nuggets in the Secret Service and the FBI wouldn't have let reporters know how they were being fooled, and the stories never would've been written.

Yet, criminals were still using bitcoin. Which meant the Feds were still getting fooled now and then (somehow). And few things gave Lenny The Lion Grabasso more pleasure than fooling the Feds (just ask the U.S. Marshals). Why should this time be any different?

See, what the crypto dorks who'd gotten caught didn't seem to appreciate, was that—when it comes to ill-gotten gains—*cash is king*. Not this digital bullshit. U-S-fucking-D. Gold, silver, and legal goddamned tender.

You want anonymity? Cash is anonymous *and* untraceable.

You want an agreed upon medium of exchange? Cash is accepted by everybody.

You want decentralization? It doesn't get more decentralized than people's pockets.

Leonard understood bitcoin wasn't simply *money*—it was also an *asset*. A stupendously appreciating asset. Since he'd started mining in early 2012, the S&P 500 had only gone up 287% ("standard" and "poor" indeed—investing for peasants). Meanwhile, the value of bitcoin had gone up something like *8,700%* at its peak.

And the really nice thing about an asset that appreciates so much? Even if it's a toxic asset (which illegally mined bitcoin most certainly is), when it comes time to offload it, it makes for a great "distressed" asset. One you can sell at a steep discount, and still make *b-b-b-bank*. Like the contraband cartons of cigarettes that used to "fall off a truck" back in the day. Or stolen stereos hocked in a mall parking lot. Easy money. All you had to do was find the right buyer and offer them a deal. In Leonard's experience, half-price was pretty fuckin' hard to walk away from . . .

. . . *Except* when you're trying to offload a billion dollars' worth of bitcoin, apparently.

Two things he should've given a lot more weight to:

One, a buyer who had that kind of cash, probably didn't have it in *cash*-cash. It would be tied up in an account somewhere, with identifying details attached to it (see the twin banes of money laundering, above). Two, the kind of buyer who *did* have that much cash on hand—what the fuck would they need bitcoin for?—*even if* it was worth double?

This was the way-more-than-a-million dollar question.

It wasn't a problem at first. Because back in 2012, there was still plenty of time to find the answer. Leonard was confident he'd figure it out, sooner or later. Always had. And so he'd gone ahead with the operation, knowing that—as long as he didn't spend, transfer, or convert the bitcoin—he was safe, and more importantly, earning ridiculous returns.

But now his golden goose had come home to roost, and he'd yet to find a buyer for the goddamned eggs.

Now it's most definitely a fuckin' problem. (A goose that acts like a chicken is always a problem.) There weren't any more wind farm contracts in the pipeline, and Leonard couldn't afford to keep paying the cotton farmers indefinitely for fields that were no longer earning. And once he stopped the monthly payments? They'd rat him out quicker to the FBI than he'd squealed on Vito Molinari—*ain't karma a bitch.*

Every day he held the bitcoin wallet was another day it might be seized.

The clock was ticking.

CHAPTER FORTY-THREE

Vigil left Baker's office unescorted and walked to the road and stormed west toward Carlin, pissed off about the perverse incentives of a representative democracy.

He thought about how elected officials care more about winning the next election than doing what's right. How the will of the people only applies to those whose team is in power. How no one else gets a say. In this part of Nolan County, cotton farmers corrupted by Grabasso's hush money got a say. Locals who worked for Innova-Gen were outnumbered; Baker didn't give a shit about them.

He'd hiked nearly a mile before he could unclench his fists and find his way back to calm. The rage was still there, of course, smoldering at his core like a hot coal. But he didn't see it as a problem. Other people might, but he didn't consider outside opinions a problem, either. In fact, by the time he got around to calling Mira, Vigil felt pretty damn justified about what he had to do. He even managed a smile as she approached in the Prius.

"I take it the Sheriff wasn't receptive." She must've seen the gleam in his eye.

"He was not."

"*Damn.*" She put the Prius in gear and they accelerated at a medium pace to well under the speed limit.

"You know what's worse?" he asked.

"Give it to me."

"Schnell's dead. His wife too."

"Grabasso's guys?"

"Baker says suicide. There was a note."

"You think it was staged?"

"Not sure. Schnell said the guilt from killing Prosser was 'too much to bear.'"

"Convenient."

"Right? But ultimately it doesn't matter. He's dead and Grabasso killed him. Even if he didn't pull the trigger, the fear of him did. Immoral equivalency, the way I see it."

Mira said nothing. She was taking in short, sharp little breaths and chewing at the inside of her lips, probably realizing that any chance of a successful prosecution had slipped away. There were no eyewitnesses to Prosser's murder left to put on the stand.

"So now we do it my way."

Mira said nothing.

"I kept my end of the bargain. Gave Baker every opportunity—tried to let the system handle it. But he wasn't interested. The system failed."

Mira said nothing.

"I won't fail. Will that be a problem?"

"You don't have to remind me what I agreed to, Vigil. Believe me. And I'd like to point out something you seem to be forgetting—"

"You still tryin' to seduce me?"

"*Touché.* Maybe." Mira grinned momentarily and then her face hardened again. "You said that when Grabasso went to trial, you wanted to compensate the victims' families with the stolen bitcoin? If you kill him, I don't see how that happens."

"He'll give me the private key to his crypto wallet," Vigil said. "I'm very persuasive."

"You looked awful offended yesterday when I implied you tortured people—now you're willing to go there?"

"Don't put words in my mouth, Mira. Didn't you say Grabasso's a good businessman? I'll make him an offer—"

"'He can't refuse.' How poetic. In a cliched sort of way."

"Oh, he can refuse it all right. But he won't. All sales are final in my line of work."

"So he gives you the bitcoin. You let him live?"

Vigil shook his head. "He'll suffer some buyer's remorse."

"And then *you'll* be the one trying to move billions in bitcoin without alerting authorities."

Vigil was silent. She had a point (though he tended to classify such challenges as, Good Problems to Have).

She drove a little further, said, "Plan on taking a cut?"

"A cut of what?"

"The bitcoin, dummy."

Fair question. He paused a moment before answering because he hadn't considered it until she'd asked. "Maybe enough to cover a few meals and the hotel . . . a few supplies. No more than that."

She let out a little puff of air, said, "You're unbelievable. You know that, right?"

Vigil shrugged. Seemed like more of a rhetorical question.

"So what now?"

"Time to slay 'The Lion.'"

Mira eyeballed him like he wanted to pet a real one in the wild. "In broad daylight? Are you fucking mental? Not to mention, the last marshal who visited his compound said it's an absolute fortress: Cutting-edge security. Dogs. Booby traps. And more weapons than a Dallas pawn shop."

"Not right now. We need to do a little surveillance first. We'll head over tonight."

"And in the meantime?"

"I didn't get much sleep. Let's go back to the hotel. I'll nap and you can compile maps of his compound. Satellite, surveys, anything you can find. Architectural blueprints would be nice, too."

"A guy with a concrete business must've used a local builder. I'll ask around. Anything else?"

"This is your wheelhouse. Whatever you think would be helpful. After I wake up, we'll visit a few places in Sweetwater and buy gear."

Mira nodded absently like she was already planning. She was sharp. He looked forward to what she'd come up with.

Vigil said, "What about you? You want some of Grabasso's bitcoin?"

"You do appreciate the position you're putting me in, don't you? It's not like you kill him and that's the end. There'll be an investigation. Skimming would link me to his death. Can't do it. However tempting."

She turned into the Hampton Inn lot and parked. They got out and walked to the lobby.

"Maybe I should do it John Rain style?" Vigil proposed.

"Who's John Rain?"

"The protagonist in a series of novels by Barry Eisler. Rain is an assassin whose methods mimic natural causes."

"You can do that?"

Vigil shrugged. "I scared a guy to death once."

Mira rolled her eyes. "Boys."

"Road rage incident. Must've been 2008, 2009. Near Detroit Lakes, Minnesota. I was hitchhiking with this college kid on his way back to campus over Thanksgiving break. Some asshole in a GMC Suburban decides he's driving too slow in the passing lane. Whips around him. Slams on his brakes. This was a two-lane highway in morning traffic, so we had no choice but to come to a stop right there in the road. Anyway, the guy gets out and marches toward our vehicle with bad intentions. Then I get out. The guy freezes— falls down like a fainting goat. Paramedics said it was a heart attack. Odd, because he couldn't have been much older than thirty-five. And aside from some weird-looking moles on his face, he looked fairly healthy. Must've been fright. No other possible explanation."

"I guess it happens," she said. "But Grabasso did a lot of dark shit in the mafia. He won't scare so easily."

"We'll see." The elevator dinged and the doors opened to the fourth floor. "We'll talk more in a few hours."

CHAPTER
FORTY-FOUR

Leonard was still in bed ruminating when his phone buzzed. He silenced it. It was the Ukrainian freight broker. The poor guy was probably calling with some sob story about his overseas team getting lit-up by Russian cruise missiles, and how they might need more time to fulfill—

Stop the fuckin' presses.

He remembered the news article about the war in Ukraine . . . in particular, the heavy sanctions. It was increasingly difficult for Russia to buy weapons and supplies (not to mention antifreeze—to keep their soldiers' stone-cold hearts beating).

No one could do business with them.

Nobody would take their money (except Iran and China) because they were afraid of upsetting NATO.

But I bet they'd take bitcoin.

Leonard scrolled through his contacts, searching for a name that was very hard to spell. Someone he hadn't spoken to since the old days. A mobster, but not Cosa Nostra. Russian. Every wise guy in New York knew at least one member of the *Bratva*. Part of doing business.

There he is.

Alyosha Lebedev. Leonard could barely pronounce his name, but he remembered how the Ruskie had often bragged about his ties to the KGB and corrupt officials in Moscow. Old as the hills, but still alive-and-killing, according to recent news articles. Lebedev had moved up in the ranks since Grabasso had turned State's evidence. Authorities believed he'd orchestrated all manner of heinous shit, but they couldn't prove it—probably because there were very few rats in the Russian mob. Lots of mooks missing a foot. But very few rats.

Conversing with another powerful man while lying in bed felt too disrespectful, so Leonard went to the master suite and got dressed. He was in the closet, choosing between black Salvatore Ferragamo moccasins and the lighter Mario Bruni loafers in brushed calf skin, when the buzzer for the front gate sounded.

He glanced over his shoulder at a bank of security monitors and honed in on the screen that showed the access kiosk and the area surrounding the foot of the driveway.

"Well it's about goddamned time."

Lebedev could wait.

CHAPTER
FORTY-FIVE

H e'd read somewhere that sleep debt was repaid in REM—short for Rapid Eye Movement, a characteristic of dreaming. Vigil owed big. He stripped, set his pistol on the nightstand, and fell into darkness like a mirror dropped in tar.

Dreams of childhood—his training—his father.

Enduring another test. Learning a lesson only struggle can impart.

After, they debate what Nate will do with his developing skill set. Dad not understanding that a different path doesn't necessarily imply a different aim.

"Why son?"

"It's like you always say, Dad—"

But he couldn't remember the rest. Phantom memories lost in fog . . .

Because of the *knock-knock, knockety-knock-knock* on the door to his hotel room.

No longer asleep, but not yet fully awake, either, Vigil went to answer it.

"Time to get up," Mira's muffled voice announced from the hallway.

This was becoming an unfortunate pattern. He opened the door, forgetting he was still in his birthday suit.

Mira didn't seem to mind.

Not one bit.

She glanced down at his naked body. "Talk about 'rise and shine'," she said, pushing the door out of her way and stepping into him.

THERE WAS VERY LITTLE FOREPLAY. EXACTLY THE right amount. Two days of sexual tension—plus last night's impressive feat of restraint—rendered an elaborate warmup unnecessary. Novelty did the rest.

Vigil nudged the door closed with his toe. They were already kissing, lips parting just long enough to peel off her shirt. Her tongue was cinnamon, her hair, slightly damp from the shower, a fruit-flower bouquet. He reached behind her, unclasping her bra in one smooth motion. Mira stepped away and kicked off her sandals, wiggled out of her jeans and panties; she allowed him only a cursory glance before closing the gap once more. Not enough time to isolate all the variables, but plenty to solve for (se)'X': She was a balanced equation. That was for damn sure.

She pushed him backward and he let her, shuffling blindly to the bed where they fell in tandem. The sheets were still warm from his nap . . . though not as warm as her breath and her skin and the slick fire between her legs, pressing and slipping and yielding to his own locus of heat.

"I don't have a condom."

"I'm on the pill—fuck it."

Which was dumb. But then again, there's the smart thing, and there's the wrong-but-oh-so-right thing, and at that very moment Vigil cared more about the latter. He rolled on top of her. Mira reached down and adjusted the angle, raising her hips and pulling him closer even as he ensured they couldn't get more close.

It was first-time sex. A give-to-get dance choreographed with sighs and moans and fingernails and fervent nods of encouragement. And then, after a brief interlude, it was the second time. Slower and softer, faster and harder, as required. So nice that when they were finished Vigil asked her if she wanted the proverbial cigarette.

"I don't smoke," she said.

"Me either."

Which was good, because it was a non-smoking room, but mostly because round three demanded healthy lungs and heavy breathing.

WHEN THEY WERE FINISHED, THEY REVISITED landmarks their rapid ascents hadn't allowed them to linger on en route.

"Puma?" Mira mused, tracing her finger along the ridge of a thick scar that traversed his left pec from collarbone to sternum.

"A pimp in Spokane, Washington," he said. Which landed about like you'd expect.

She tensed. "A pimp?"

"He was roughing up a lady of the evening who preferred to stay independent. My father caught wind of it through an old SEAL buddy. Sent me to take care of him—a training exercise."

"Training exercise?"

"That's a pretty deep foxhole. Another time maybe."

"Okay. What about the pimp—you killed him?"

Vigil shrugged. "He killed himself when he started abusing women."

"How old were you?"

"Sixteen."

Mira said nothing.

"For some reason he was unarmed when I caught up to him—I wasn't. I carried a .45 auto Smith & Wesson 1911, and a Bowie knife by SOG. He ran into an alley. Dead end. Said something to the effect that I wouldn't be acting so tough without the weapons. I laid my pistol on the pavement and tossed him the knife. Quoted a line I stole from some action flick. Not the brightest thing I've ever done."

"The folly of youth."

Mira had scars of her own. The almost invisible one on her forehead, and a surgical scar three or four inches long that ran horizontally across her lower abdomen. From a c-section, he figured. "You're a mom?"

"Yes. I have a daughter."

"How old is she?"

Mira hesitated. "She's twenty."

Vigil was no kind of accountant, but basic arithmetic told him not many women Mira's age had twenty-year-old daughters. *Unless she's a lot older than I thought*. Which seemed even more unlikely—especially after the sex they just had.

In his experience.

Mira addressed it before he said something awkward. "I was raped when I was fourteen. A neighbor kid who lived down the block. He said he'd kill my mom if I told anyone, so I didn't . . . until, you know, I had to."

"I'm sorry that happened to you."

"Don't be. I love her more than anything."

"Of course."

"When my mom found out, we moved away, and when

Elise was born, she adopted her as her own. She wanted me to live a normal life. We told no one."

"Does Elise know?"

"She figured it out when she was fifteen. To this day, I don't know how. Anyway, we talked. She understood. Kept calling her grandmother 'momma,' and started calling me, 'mom-bee'—sarcastic little shit that she is sometimes."

"Like mother, like daughter," Vigil teased.

"Oh, she's way smarter than me. In her third year at Harvard. Double major: law and international finance."

"Well done."

"What about you? Any kids?"

He shook his head.

"Plan on settling down someday?"

"Never thought much about it."

"*In love with the road,*" she said in a poor imitation of his deep baritone.

"And wilderness. And solitude. And counting falling stars from the tops of boulders in the desert."

"Must be nice."

"It is."

"If only we could all live like that," she said wistfully.

Vigil was silent. Once upon a time you could, he thought. Today, people like him were a relic. Today there were too many people.

They were quiet for a while. The room was cool in the wake of their stillness. Mira pulled up the sheet. She said, "So tell me—why do you care about a society you're barely a part of?"

"I don't."

"*Please.*"

"It's true. I don't care about society. I care about the things it facilitates that hunters and gatherers never got around to: Books, primarily. Standup comedy. Good bourbon. The rest I could do without."

"You seem to care a lot about people . . . in your own way."

He thought: *A way that makes it impossible for them to care about me.* Said, "People exist independently of society. Me especially."

Mira frowned. "You could find a place to call home— rejoin the human race."

"I'm more useful outside of it."

"What about connection?"

Vigil was silent.

CHAPTER
FORTY-SIX

The clock ticks so slowly when you're waiting for someone. So quickly when it's counting down. And the truly fucked-up thing about it? It's the same damn clock.

Leonard had attempted to contact the Russian immediately after dismissing his visitor, but Lebedev hadn't picked up. Unsurprising, since the Bratva big shot wouldn't recognize the name "Leonard Grainger" on his caller ID. He left a message, making it clear who was actually calling, and thus guaranteeing the Russian would respond—eventually—if for no other reason than to ferret out the location of the world's most notorious rat. After all, Cosa Nostra still had a sizable contract on Grabasso's head. *Peanuts compared to the finder's fee he'd collect from the bitcoin, though.* Which nullified the risk.

Now, four hours had passed since he'd made the call, and Leonard's patience was wearing thin. He also felt like he was forgetting something important from the earlier meeting. That he'd missed a crucial detail. Fortunately, security cameras and hidden microphones had captured the entire conversation in perfect fidelity.

Although it was a poor substitute for his usual anti-anxiety go-to (a fat glass of Cabernet with a Valium chaser) reviewing the footage would distract him from watching the clock—and without slurring his speech—*For when the asshole finally gets around to returning my call.*

February 2, 2023. 13:05.
Camera 22 – Back Deck:

THEY SAT ON CUSHIONED WICKER CHAIRS overlooking the yard, wind turbine towers tick-marking the horizon like reticles in a rifle scope. The Dobermans crouched on their respective rugs, bookend-ing them.

Leonard said, "You've been in town—what—two days? Why'd you wait so long to pay me a visit?"

"I got sidetracked at the Diamondback. I'm sure Caleb told you all about it."

"Yes. Nate Vigil. I hear you've been spending time together."

"He seemed like too big of a coincidence. I had to make sure he wasn't a Fed."

"You think he's undercover?"

"Not anymore."

"Not anymore, as in, he used to be a Fed?"

"As in I'm now certain he's not, and that he never was."

"So nothing to worry about, then?"

She didn't answer right away. It was unnerving. "*Rrrrr-ight*, Mira? Geezus, between you and Lackey it's like I'm talkin' to a wooden Indian."

"Vigil's a problem, alright. Smart. Dangerous. Relentless. By far the biggest threat you've ever faced."

"Which is why you're going to kill him for me. He's not *my* problem. He's *your* problem."

"No."

"Excuse me, sugar tits—what did you just say?"

"He's too good for that. He has to believe I'm on his side. That's the only way we get his guard down. He follows me into a trap. You spring it."

"Does he trust you?"

"He will."

"*Will?*"

"We'll continue to bond," she said.

"Mira, you dirty little whore."

"Go fuck yourself."

"I'd fuck you if you were better looking. Sweet little Elise though? *Mmmmm*-ight have to. How's the Ivy League treatin' her? She keepin' her grades up? My guy says she's been partying too much this semester."

Mira said nothing. But then, what could she say? She'd keep doing exactly as she was told, or he would give the signal and his man in Boston would kill her pride and joy. Slowly. Same, if Leonard should die of anything except old age.

"See," he said, holding up his phone, "look how tired she looks in this picture."

Mira looked away, so close to crying it turned him on.

"Look at her, Mira. You need to remember what's at stake here."

"I know what's at stake."

"That's good. Real good. Because if Vigil becomes a problem? Not only will I tell my guy to have his way with her first, I'll have him livestream the whole thing. From fing—"

"*Enough!* He won't be a problem."

Ruskie raised his snout and sniffed the air. Irish growled ominously.

"*Shush!* Go make the rounds."

The sleek canines loped into the yard and began circling the fence line. They would continue to do so until Leonard gave them a different command. In this way, the dogs and Mira were quite similar.

"We're surveilling your compound tonight," she said. "Preparing for a hit."

Leonard twisted in his chair. "Well that doesn't inspire confidence, now does it?"

"Hear me out: Last time I was here, you bragged this place is more secure than the White House."

"Correct. Buttoned up tighter than Raggedy Ann's asshole."

"Perfect. We want Vigil to see the full extent of what he's up against. If it looks too easy, he'll know it's a trap. But he also needs to think you've overlooked something. We need to allow him to uncover an apparent vulnerability—a fatal flaw he can leverage to bypass all your security measures. That way, he feels like he's outsmarted you, and we can blindside him."

"I like where you're goin' with this," Leonard said. "I know just the—"

"Don't tell me where the breach will be yet," Mira interrupted. "If I know what to look for, Vigil will sense my anticipation. He's very perceptive."

Cunning little cunt, isn't she? Maybe too cunning.

"So how do we plan the ambush without going over the details beforehand?"

Mira didn't answer right away, but this time Leonard wasn't offended. She was obviously deep in problem-solving mode, nibbling on the inside of her upper lip, staring blankly at nothing in particular.

"I spoke too soon."

"I thought so," he said.

"I'll kill him."

But that wasn't at all what he thought she'd say. He smiled. "Tell me more."

"He wants the private key to your bitcoin wallet. He won't try to kill you until after you give it to him."

"Well that ain't gonna happen."

"Of course not. Because when he's interrogating you, what better time for me to shoot him in the back?"

Leonard couldn't think of one. It was exactly the kind of setup he'd used half a dozen times in the mob to whack associates who'd run afoul of a higher-ranking gangster. Plus, he'd get to see the look in Vigil's eyes—the sudden shock of betrayal when the fucking bum realized Mira had been playing him all along. Few moments were more intimate or intoxicating. Ever since he'd testified against Vito Molinari, these pained expressions in response to unveiled treachery had become something of a fetish. Sometimes he'd backhand one of his sidepieces right as she came so he could enjoy a similar effect.

"Perfect," he said. "But that's not a detail we wanna improvise on the fly, no? Shouldn't we go over the logistics?"

"No, and for the same reason: He'll sense it. The less I know in advance—the more Vigil susses out on his own—the more natural the operation appears. Just make it look like he caught you with your pants down, metaphorically speaking. You've got at least a day to plan that part. Tonight we're just looking for a way in."

"You sure about that?"

"Positive. He'll want to plan the actual hit in detail to minimize the risk of me getting hurt. Vigil's very protective, too. It's kinda cute."

"So how long before he comes for me?"

"He wants to take you down as soon as possible. Be ready by tomorrow night."

"And you'll be in touch before then to finalize everything?" His voice rose in pitch at the end of his question, and Leonard didn't like it. He sounded nervous.

To her credit, Mira didn't call him on it. "Yeah. We'll touch base. I don't expect there to be many surprises."

Leonard didn't either. Even so, he didn't survive to his seventh decade making assumptions, or thinking the first good idea somebody had was the best one (or even that good, once you started poking holes in it).

He said, "Hypothetically—what happens if I just stay home, lock the doors, and let this gorilla beat his head against the wall of my defenses?"

"I think you'd be underestimating him. And instead of knowing ahead of time, when, where, and how he'll find you —Vigil will have the advantage."

"Interesting . . . did you know that after Raymond gave me the thumbs-up, I hired a team of former Special Forces operators to run a penetration test on the new security system? I told them, 'Take me hostage, I'll pay you double.' They couldn't do it. Why are you so convinced Vigil can?"

Mira said, "I read his father's file. The parts that weren't redacted. Those operators you hired? Total badasses, no doubt. The elite of the elite, trained by the greatest military the world has ever known. The difference between them and Vigil? They started training at eighteen. He started at age five."

"Five? How's that even possible?"

"His father was Commander Lance Vigil. A Medal of Honor recipient. After he retired, he founded a wilderness survival school in Idaho. Some say it was a front for a paramilitary extremist group, but I couldn't substantiate those rumors. What I can tell you is that he had controversial views on the long-term viability of western civilization, and that he raised his son to thrive in the aftermath. He trained him to become the kind of human who could survive the disasters he thought were coming, taught him all the skills he'd acquired as a Special Forces operator—and where his own knowledge was lacking, brought in subject matter experts from around the world he'd met in the military.

"Vigil learned to track wild animals, made improvised explosives, and devoured volumes on the history of combat. By sixteen, he'd put full-grown men in the hospital. By seventeen, he could've staged a coup."

Leonard leaned back and folded his arms. Gooseflesh rose on his forearms and he tried to cover it with his palms. "Sounds like a badass," he said dismissively. "But I've known men like Vigil. The 'relentlessness' you see in him? That's just obstinance dressed up with dumb muscle and pride. Inevitably, it's their downfall."

Mira shrugged, said, "Don't say I didn't warn you."

"Alright," he said. "We'll go with it." Because if Vigil was as formidable as Mira claimed, at least the plan she'd put forward took prowess out of the equation.

"Something else to consider," she said. "On the off chance your defenses did hold up? If he gets frustrated, there's nothing keeping him from handing over what he's uncovered to the press."

Good point. Crypto crime was a hot topic. Some putz reporter could clue-in the Feds. Until he sold the bitcoin wallet, he was vulnerable. "Where is he now?"

"At the hotel taking a nap. He was up late examining one of the mining rigs you're disposing of. Found one at the truck stop."

Fuck. He'd explicitly told the freight broker, No stops for at least a hundred miles. "Put it all together, has he?"

"Most of it. By the way, I heard about Schnell. Did your crew kill him?"

"I gave the order. But he must've known it was coming after you and Vigil paid a visit. Hastened the inevitable. How did you hear? It wasn't in the news when I checked this mornin'."

"Vigil went to see the Sheriff."

Leonard sat up straight in his chair again. "You let him?"

"I *took* him. It would've looked suspicious if I tried to talk him out of it, and now we know Baker isn't a concern. Two birds, one stone."

"Ballsy," Leonard said. "What if he'd convinced Baker to keep digging?"

"Then I would have played the 'ongoing Federal investigation' card," she said. "What about Lackey?"

"Vin took your advice to heart. He's still breathin'. For now."

Mira nodded, gears turning. "After we take care of Vigil, there's a lot of people I'll need to interview. How much more time before you can cash out?"

"I'm workin' on it, but a helluva lot less than yesterday."

"That's good."

"Changed your mind about taking a cut, didn't you? I could afford to wet your beak."

Mira regarded him skeptically. "Why would you?"

"A better question would be: What does it buy me? You wanna suck my wrinkled dick before you hand over the new passport?"

Curled-lip, squinty-eyed disgust flashed across Mira's face, there and gone. She'd tried to hide it. But he saw. And it pissed him off. Sure, he was getting up in age. But since when did money and power stop being an aphrodisiac? He was tempted to make her blow him right then and there. And she would, too—anything to keep her daughter alive—but Leonard needed her sharp in the coming days, and he was afraid too much abuse might exhaust her. Plus Mariana would undoubtedly be watching them on one of the security feeds, paring knife in hand, daring this *gringa* bitch to touch her *apuesto esposo*. He didn't need that kind of drama.

"Let's stick to the deal," Mira said. "I only care about Elise."

"*Yeeaaahhhhh* . . . about the deal. I need to amend it slightly."

Mira leapt to her feet, hands on her hips, glaring down at him like an elementary school teacher who'd had just about enough of his clowning for the day. "Define *slightly*."

There was something hysterical about the way she was scolding him. Leonard put his hands up and tried not to laugh, said, "I agreed to sever the deadman's switch—"

"*And* provide me tangible—"

"—proof—"

"*Before*—"

"—my flight leaves U.S. airspace—now will you shut the fuck up and let me finish?"

Aside from snorting the tear-laden snot back into her nose, Mira was quiet again.

"I'm gonna need a little help from you on the other end. *Then* you can stop worrying about your daughter. Now sit down before you do something stupid."

Mira dropped down in her chair. "What kind of help?"

"With the cash drop. I'm dealing with fuckin' Russians. Need I say more?"

"And after I help you—how do I know you won't find another excuse to go back on your word?"

Leonard smirked. "Truth is? *You don't know*. And you never did.

"But think about it: Once I'm settled in, sitting atop a pile of money so high I could never spend it all—what would I need you for? Plus, you'll be the only person on the planet who could find me. That makes it an even better deal, sugar tits. I've sweetened the pot."

'Course, it'll also make you one helluva liability.

But Leonard assumed Mira's maternal instincts would blind her to that.

CHAPTER
FORTY-SEVEN

He lay there next to her, believing the silence was for his own benefit. But silence doesn't discriminate. It sneaks up on you. You can't hear it coming.

"I'm sorry," Mira said. "That was cruel of me."

It was true she'd exposed his wound, but there was no harm in letting it breathe. What mattered was her intent: Rub salt? Or apply a salve?

She said, "Hurt people—"

"Hurt people," Vigil finished. The sour, musky fragrance of their sex lingered in the air, anchoring the moment in memory. "But you weren't trying to hurt me. You were . . . *connecting*. Because I'm not so good at that. Apparently."

"No—I mean . . . I—" And then something shifted in her. Almost imperceptibly at first, like the stirring of a leaf in still air that reveals the praying mantis there all along. She rolled to her side and buried her face in his chest and sobbed. Initially, there was no voice to her pain. Only hot breath, winded spasms, and tears.

And it was fine. He didn't take it personally. There was nothing to fix. He held her. Sex was a release, after all.

Sometimes it was like a dam breaking. All your defenses get washed away in the deluge of intimacy and pleasure, and all the ugly things locked away in the hidden chambers of the heart break free. Sometimes people laugh, or cry, or tremble, or simply fall asleep. Vigil was fine with all of it. People are complicated. More so when not wearing a mask, not less.

He squeezed her tight, let her feel his strength.

Her tremors subsided. Aftershocks of some self-seismic event.

He glanced at the nightstand.

At his gun.

The silence is always there, screaming truth.

"Are you okay?" he said.

She rolled onto her back again. He handed her a tissue.

She shook her head. "I have a confession to make."

And then he finally understood what the silence had been saying. A realization so sudden, he couldn't help but blurt it out: "Lemme guess. You're the compromised Marshal."

Mira flinched. "Yes . . . but—but how did you know?"

"I didn't . . . until now." Then he thought about it for a moment, said, "It was the cigarette smoke. When you came back for me before the return trip to warn Lackey—you reeked of it. It wasn't there when you kicked me out. At the time, it confused me. You didn't strike me as a smoker. I figured it was something you only did when you were stressed. That you must've lit up after you drove away.

"But after you just fucked me—was that the second or the third time?—I teased you with a cigarette. Which you declined. *Because you don't smoke.*

"But you know who does smoke? Grabasso's goons. The night they tried to run me out of Carlin, they flicked a butt at me. You must've waved them down when you saw their SUV racing toward Lackey's. Filled them in on what he said during my interrogation. One of them blew smoke in your face.

"And now you fall apart. Tell me you need to confess—and *bam*—all the nagging details that looked like one thing, suddenly look like something else: The plastic surgeon's office—out of place in a small town like Carlin, but—handy for putting a fresh coat of paint on new identities. Not letting me use your phone, because I might've seen the recent call from Carlin, Texas in the log. The way you pitched softballs to Lackey and got upset when I tricked him into telling the truth. You pretending to come clean at the steakhouse, 'revealing' how Grabasso's crew were all in WITSEC. Even convincing me to see Sheriff Baker—you were really just buying time for Grabasso. You're a fucking mirage, Mira Getty. It's right in your name."

"Don't you want to know why?"

Vigil picked up the Sig off the nightstand. Out of an abundance of caution.

Mira looked at him, a crude portrait of incredulity, as if coarse swaths of hurt and shock and disbelief had been pallet-knifed into a convincing representation of her features. "That's it? Now you kill me?"

I might, he thought, said, "No sense tempting you."

"You think if I wanted you dead I'd be telling you this?"

Vigil was silent.

"Grabasso found out about Elise right after I was assigned to his case. I don't know how, and it doesn't really matter. What matters is, he has a hitman on retainer who follows her every move. I disobey, he makes a call and his guy tortures and kills her."

"I'd have put a bullet in his head for threatening my family," he said. "And served the time with a smile on my face."

"You think that wasn't my first impulse? It's not so simple. There's a deadman's switch."

Vigil was familiar with the term. It was named after the power cutoffs installed in early trams and steam engines, designed to trip in the event a conductor became incapacitated. A failsafe, originally. Or in evil hands, a fail-deadly. There were dozens of ways to set one up. Lawyers, safe deposit boxes, and escrow companies represented one common, low-tech possibility. Now there were probably services on the so-called "dark web." Or even something as simple as an email scheduled to send unless the (not yet) "dead man" is still alive, and can manually postpone delivery. Someone who knew his way around cryptocurrency like Grabasso would have no problem setting up a suitable method.

"If Grabasso dies of anything except old age," Mira continued, "his guy gets word and fulfills the contract. What was I supposed to do? What would you do?"

"First thing I'd do is make sure he wasn't bluffing."

"Which is exactly what I did. After he threatened me, I got on the next flight and went to visit her. Elise was seven at the time, living with my mom. The three of us went to the zoo. She had so much fun. She petted a donkey. Fed koi. Watched sea lions do tricks. The whole time, of course, I'm looking for tails. I'm trained to find them, after all. But *nada*. I don't spot anyone out of the ordinary.

"But when I got back to Arlington? There's an email waiting for me with a .zip file attached: I think the filename was 'death-wish-at-the-zoo.zip'—something like that. It was a compressed photo album filled with snapshots from our outing. Grabasso's hired killer had taken them. Today, with smartphones, they text me pictures of her. As 'a reminder.' Like I need one.

"After that, I was his bitch. Either do as I was told, or find my little girl starring in a snuff film on YouTube."

Vigil wedged a couple of pillows behind his back and sat

up against the headboard. "So why in the hell would you confess now? To me, of all people?" It was a cold question, even by his standards. The implication being: *Why risk your daughter's life, when you know I'll kill Grabasso anyway?* Which was true. Technically. But also, not exactly what he'd meant.

As expected, his icy matter-of-fact-ness had stunned Mira, and words temporarily escaped her. He took advantage and attempted to clarify. "This is where you ask me to walk away, right? So nothing happens to Elise. Is that my ticket back to humanity?"

Mira sat up and crossed her legs beneath her, clutching the sheet. "No. That's not what I'm asking. I know you can't stop until you get justice for Prosser."

She didn't say *'won't* stop,' he noted. She said, *'can't* stop.' *She'd make a great profiler.* "And for the families of everyone else he's murdered over the years," he added. "So what do you want from me?"

She didn't answer right away. "I went to see Grabasso when you were sleeping. We came up with a plan to kill you."

The pistol was warm in his hand. He smelled the tang of his sweat on the steel. The hydrolytic oxidation of polymers wafting up from the composite handgrip. "This oughta be good," he said.

Vigil listened as Mira went over their plot and everything that led up to it. He was impressed by her tactics. Her idea of using his confidence against him, in particular.

"Sounds like a decent plan—why abandon it?"

"Because I want your help. I have a lot more faith that you'll kill Grabasso than I do in a notorious snitch keeping his word."

Well there's a backhanded compliment.

Mira continued before it riled him. "It's more than that, though. What I said when we met in the Diamondback?

About wanting to do the right thing? I wasn't blowing smoke. Of course I'd do *anything* to save my sweet Elise—no hesitation. But if I can keep her from getting hurt *and* stay on the side of good? That's absolutely what I want to happen. I just didn't see a way . . . until I met you."

Vigil was pretty sure he understood the implication. Mira knew he wouldn't walk away—she'd just said as much—so she also knew that Grabasso was as good as dead . . . along with her daughter when the hitman caught wind of it. It was a classic Catch-22. And there was only one way to resolve it: She wanted him to kill Lenny 'The Lion' *after* the ex-mobster disabled the deadman's switch—*after* ensuring Elise would be safe.

I can be very persuasive, he'd responded earlier, when Mira had quizzed him on confiscating Grabasso's crypto wallet. At the time, he thought she was calling him a hypocrite—pointing out his aversion to torture as a guilt-trip aimed at keeping him within the confines of law and order. But now he realized that Mira had actually been testing his resolve. Elise's life was at stake. Therefore, Mira couldn't afford to doubt whether he'd follow through.

"Instead of negotiating for the bitcoin, you want me to offer Grabasso his life in exchange for eliminating the threat to your daughter."

"I was thinking, *in addition to,* his bitcoin—but yes. It's that, or Elise dies."

"So why wait until now to ask me for help? And why sneak over to meet with Grabasso in secret?"

"I think you already know the answer to the first question."

"You needed to hear me say I won't quit."

"Yes. And I was afraid if I'd told you any of this before I met with Grabasso, he'd sense the betrayal. All those years in the mob made him wise to deception."

Vigil had to admit, her plan was ingenious . . . devious as hell—but ingenious. He said, "So tonight then—rather than hang back and gather intel—we surprise him and go in early."

Mira shook her head. "No. I told him you wouldn't rush. Tonight he's merely showing you the opening. If you go off script, he'll know I double-crossed him."

"And?"

"*And,*" Mira said, "instead of meeting zero resistance, we'll find ourselves in a gun battle. Maybe worse—with a pretty good chance of him getting away."

"Thanks for the vote of confidence."

"I'm putting Elise's life in your hands. I don't get more confident."

He nodded solemnly. *Point taken.*

"Grabasso told me he hired an entire team of former Special Forces operatives to test his defenses, and even they couldn't penetrate them. Why make it harder than it needs to be?"

Vigil considered letting her in on a little secret concerning so-called "penetration testing" consultants: Because their clients didn't want property destroyed, it took many of the most effective tactics a real-life intruder might use, off the table. But he kept this to himself. She was right, after all. Like Dad always said: *Do the simplest thing that could possibly work.*

"Okay. We wait until tomorrow night. Waltz right through the chink in his armor you convinced him to expose."

Mira was nodding her head, obviously pleased with herself. "Exactly."

"It's brilliant."

"So you'll help me?"

CHAPTER
FORTY-EIGHT

Mariana had prepared her prized tamale recipe: Stewed pig's head meat from a pit-roasted boar, dough made with hominy in place of corn, and spices passed down from the Aztecs. She and Raymond waited patiently for Leonard to give the okay. He raised the first bite to his lips, breathed in the savory sweet aroma of tender pork, and opened his mouth.

It was at that exact moment the Russian finally returned his call.

Leonard was both relieved and annoyed. He excused himself, silencing Raymond before he could blurt how *"Leonard is breaking the rules, and rules are meant to be broken, because Leonard breaks them"*—or whatever Tourettes-infused, autistic-tard nonsense these deviations from routine inspired in the man-child. Irish and Ruskie followed him out to the back deck.

"Your arrogance knows no bound. This, I have always known. But today only, did I learn the fool you are. Years ago, when you had still your honor, I did not realize."

"Alyosha, my friend. Do you think I'd have risked calling you without an offer far in excess of that chickenshit mafia

275

contract?" Leonard's tone was upbeat. Jovial even. For as good a businessman as he was, he was an even better salesman.

"You are not friend. What you did for my nephew Boris—I do not forget such things. This has earned you warning. But now debt is repaid. And this is your warning. Make peace with God. Soon you will die."

"Okay, then—business. Does five million dollars buy me some consideration? Or are you more interested in your preferred currency—*power*? Because I can give you both."

Lebedev laughed dismissively. "Five million merely tells me you are desperate. And it tells me you are ignorant to my current fortune. As for 'power?' You were once powerful, true. Lenny 'The Lion' you were called. The 'King of the Concrete Jungle.' But now you have shown what you truly are. A filthy rat. King of sewer."

Leonard expected nothing less than this kind of abuse from Lebedev. It was worse when he liked you. "Eight million. And instead of rubbing elbows with low-level bureaucrats in some unremarkable backwater downstream from Chernobyl, let's upgrade you to the Kremlin. You'll be Putin's favorite new pet."

"You should be very careful throwing his name around, *mu-dak*. These are tense times. Ten million—and you die the slow death you deserve if this offer of power is as pathetic as what you have become."

Leonard sighed heavily, pausing a beat before answering. "Deal," he said, knowing full well the Bratva boss would want more by the end of the negotiation.

"So I hear the Russian army is having a hard time buying supplies . . . " And Leonard went on from there, summarizing how he'd obtained over $2.5 billion in bitcoin by stealing electricity from a wind farm, and how the time had come for him to cash out. The appeal of cryptocurrency during Putin's misguided war in Ukraine was obvious, as was the favor and influence brokering the deal would buy Lebedev. It took him all of five minutes to explain.

"I take your deal to my comrades in Russia—but fee is twenty million."

This was half of what Leonard had budgeted, but he managed to sound butt-hurt and insulted anyway. "You greedy fuckin' communist bastard. *Twenty?* Fifteen, and you'll be happy to get it."

"Twenty, or go fuck yourself, you rat piece of shit."

"Fine. Twenty."

Lebedev chuckled like he'd stolen a chocolate bar from a child. "And you must know, what you sell—this is not merely 'distressed asset,' as you say, but—very *toxic* asset. My comrades will no doubt demand steep discount. What is bottom dollar?"

"Let's start at one-point-five billion dollars. Cash. Delivered in person at a location of my choosing. Not in the U.S., for obvious reasons."

"This is exclusive offer, yes? No bidding war bullshit."

"Come on. Who the fuck you dealin' with, here?"

"Good. I recall my men. But if all is not as you say? You know well what happens to those who cross me."

CHAPTER FORTY-NINE

"**D**on't worry about Elise," he said. "Or Grabasso."

Mira leaned forward and kissed him on the cheek like a friend. "Thank you."

Vigil was silent.

They collected their clothes and got dressed and went out to the car. The sun was low in the sky and stores would close soon. As they pulled out of the hotel parking lot he said, "I don't suppose you procured the architectural prints I asked for?"

"Negative. I only had time to visit Grabasso."

"So what's he leaving open for us?"

"It should be obvious."

"Or you could just tell me."

"No idea. I had to walk a fine line between selling Grabasso and not arousing suspicion."

I bet.

"Unlike me," she continued, "he's skeptical of your capabilities. He'll leave an opening only a skilled operator would notice—or know how to exploit. If you can't spot it, then he'll assume you're not as good as I claimed and send in his crew to take care of you."

"And why aren't you more skeptical of my capabilities, Mira? What have I really shown you?"

"Aside from what just transpired in bed?"

"You know what I mean."

"You've shown me plenty. The way you finessed Lackey, how you handled those farmers without breaking a sweat . . . we've been over this."

Vigil sensed she was holding something back. By now he'd had a lot of practice. "There's more to it than that. What aren't you telling me?"

Mira breathed out heavily. "Your father's file wasn't as redacted as I let on. There were links. To scanned documents."

"What kind of documents?"

"Handwritten journals. Thirteen years worth, at least. What stood out to me was the training exercises he put you through. I read enough to know you're one badass mother-fucker. No pun intended."

"Bullshit. He burned his journals before he committed suicide. I saw the ashes."

"Well, he must've scanned them, too. Like a backup."

"Dad wouldn't even turn on a computer. He didn't scan them."

"I'm just telling you what was in his file, Vigil. Obviously the journals existed."

They'd existed alright. Until they didn't.

VIGIL BLINKED AND HE WAS NINETEEN AGAIN, back, reluctantly, in his childhood home. Six months after Dad died. Only a week since he'd heard the news.

Potential keepsakes appeared throughout the cabin: Guns, timepieces, an antique oak desk, and so on. But none of these things were what brought him here. He wasn't sentimental.

Nate only cared about the journals.

One night—he must've been about ten-years-old—he'd asked Dad what he wrote in them. *"Everything that matters,"* he replied. Nate was still too young to know what mattered and he pestered his father until he read a few pages.

Lance recounted the training exercises he'd put Nate through and how his son had progressed; thoughts on the world and where it was headed; survival skills, combat tactics, and psychological warfare; ongoing preparations for the societal collapse he believed was imminent. Mistakes made. Lessons learned. *"One day, when I'm gone, you'll have a record."*

When his father filled the pages of a notebook, he'd store it inside the large chest at the foot of his bed with all the others. The chest was the first place Nate looked. He turned the metal latch, pausing before he raised the lid as he flashed back to the last time he'd seen his father—the night he'd left home.

They'd argued fiercely. It hadn't come to blows, but things were said that shouldn't have been. True things mutual respect had kept bottled up until that night. Nate loved his father. Was beyond grateful for all that he'd taught him. But he had to find his own path. His decision hurt the old man; he'd been clearing a path for Nate to walk since the day his son had been born, and now he wanted no part of it.

If there was some other reason Dad did what he did, it would be recorded in his draftsman-like print on those white, blue-lined pages.

But when Nate raised the lid, the chest was empty.

Sifting through a pile of ashes in the fireplace, poking at blackened spirals of wire and hardened lumps of melted plastic, Vigil wept into the burnt remains of his father's secrets. Any hope he might stop blaming himself had been lost.

Redacted by fire.

"ARE YOU ALRIGHT?"

No. But he answered, "When this is all over, I want access to those scans. I'm not asking."

"Absolutely."

She parked along the curb in front of Sidewinder Tactical. They went inside and picked out a pair of night vision binoculars and a deer rifle with a quality scope. Mira stocked up on more ammunition. Vigil added a sling for the rifle. He let her pay for everything on account of the generous law enforcement discount.

Walmart came next: Plastic zip ties, duct tape, headset com units, ski masks, batteries, and black clothing. They split the items into two separate carts and two different purchases, mixing in innocuous household supplies and groceries they didn't need. Mira wouldn't swear by it, but she was rightfully concerned the FBI had installed some kind of AI-powered early alert system into the barcode scanners, triggered when you gear up for an obvious kidnapping or bank heist.

Finished with the shopping, they drove back to the hotel. Vigil left the rifle in the Prius. Mira ordered a couple more things online she wanted for tomorrow night's assault and had them shipped overnight. When she was done with her laptop, he used it to study Google Maps to get a sense of Grabasso's compound. From the satellite imagery alone, he thought he might've spotted the weakness in The Lion's lair, though he didn't tell Mira.

"Can you show me how you look up property records?"

"Look at you. Maybe you're not such a Luddite after all."

"I'm just a monkey surrounded by a million keyboards," he said.

She pulled up an official Nolan county website (circa 1995, by the looks of it) and pointed to the field where he could input a query. He searched for a few different addresses, referencing the Google Maps tab between each result. The names of the various property owners that came back weren't much help, but it was the purchase dates that were of interest. Two of the dates didn't fit with his hunch, but one lined up nicely. Of course he'd keep an open mind until he got there. The map was never the territory.

Mira kicked him out of her room so she could nap, and Vigil was likewise happy to reclaim the hour of sleep she'd snatched from him.

A little before midnight, they reconvened and drove toward Carlin.

CHAPTER
FIFTY

After ending the call with Lebedev, Leonard rejoined Raymond and Mariana at the formal dining table where they'd been waiting patiently for his return. He nodded for them to start eating and then took his time savoring every morsel of the delicious meal. There was no hurry. Tonight required minimal preparation.

The "breach" in his security had always been there, if you knew where to look.

Certain places didn't need security cameras.

Certain places, you didn't *want* security cameras.

Maybe the drifter was smart enough to puzzle it out? Maybe not. Either way, Leonard would roll with it. He always did.

He finished eating and took a glass of wine out to the hot tub. No Xanax, regrettably. And just the one pour, not the whole bottle. He needed a clear head to plan the exchange. Even with home field advantage, large, in-person cash transactions were tricky. Doing it overseas with no network in place raised the level of difficulty considerably. Though having Mira with him would help. He'd also lucked out with the new country he'd chosen to reside in: Not only did

Georgia lack an extradition treaty with the United States, it bordered Russia, and Russians could visit without a visa.

Karma's a bitch, alright—but serendipity? She's a saint.

Sure, there were other challenges. Some obvious, some not so obvious. But these were old school concerns Leonard had been dealing with his whole life. After a half hour sipping wine, working the angles, and mulling over different possibilities, he'd come up with a pretty good plan.

His phone growled on the fiberglass ledge with another call from Lebedev. The Russian's ears must've been burning. Leonard turned off the jacuzzi jets so he could hear.

He said, "That was quick."

"Bad news travels fast."

Leonard felt a heavy fist close around his heart. If Putin's cronies weren't interested in his bitcoin, he was officially out of ideas. And time. "No buyer?"

"Not that bad. But as I warned, they will pay less than asking price: Two hundred million."

Christ. Two hundred million was good money—well over ten-times his current net worth.

But not good enough.

"Less than ten cents on the dollar? With all due respect, I think you're tryin' to rob me, Alyosha."

"Very well. I suppose King of Sewer still smells bullshit if stink is strong. They will pay five hundred million. But my cut is eighty."

"I admire the attempt. Respect. Seventy, and we have a deal."

"Do not test my patience, Grabasso. Eighty, or your name will be remembered—not for biggest rat—but for method we invent to torture you."

Leonard shivered in the 102° water. "Okay. Eighty. And another five for takin' my call."

They wrapped with him verifying he owned the crypto

wallet in question. A straightforward process on the blockchain, using transfers too small to attract attention from the Feds. Then Lebedev gave him a number to call and hung up.

Leonard turned the jets back on for a few minutes and cranked up the heater. He was used to being the one who was feared, not the other way around. Russians were a different kind of white people.

"Five hundred million," he mused once he'd finally gotten rid of the shakes. Minus Lebedev's finder's fee and the two million a piece he'd promised Vin, Anthony, and Bruno—what did that come to?—four hundred and change? *Fuck that.*

He was toweling off when his phone chimed with a new text. Now it was Vin's ears that must've been burning:

> The excavator crews got it handled tonight.
> Said they'd be done by morning.

Leonard thumb-typed a reply:

> Good news, b/c I want all 3 of youse over here watchin' the front gate. The big guy's pokin' around with Mira tonight. Let her handle him. Don't interfere. But be ready in case I change my mind.

The more Leonard thought about divvying up the loot, the more he liked the idea of testing Vigil with his crew. And if Mira was right about how dangerous he was? Then it was another six million to the good without lifting a finger.

> On our way.

CHAPTER
FIFTY-ONE

Mira accelerated down the on-ramp, westbound toward Carlin. Aside from the occasional semi truck, I-20 was deserted. A light fog glowed aura-like in the enveloping darkness, illuminated by the headlights. Great for stealth, but not ideal for long-range surveillance.

"I'm nervous," she said.

"Don't be."

"What if you can't find a way in?"

"I will."

"But what if—"

He cut her off, said, "I thought you had confidence in me."

"I do. It's just—"

"Then stop second-guessing yourself. I know what's at stake. And I promise you, I won't let Grabasso hurt your daughter. He's done hurting people. Believe it."

Mira took a slow breath through her nose, paused, and then topped off her lungs with another quick inhalation before slowly exhaling. "Aren't you nervous?"

"No."

"Do you ever get nervous?"

"When there's reason to."

"Don't you think there's a reason?"

"Tonight's just for show, remember?"

"Not entirely for show," Mira protested. "You have to find the breach."

Vigil turned. Appraised her sternly. "You're doing it again. Stop."

"Easy for you to say."

She wasn't wrong. *After all, it's not my daughter.* But Vigil knew that projecting confidence was the best way to keep Mira calm. Plus, he couldn't help it. The wiring was built in. A few more words of encouragement probably wouldn't hurt, though. "Look, your plan is solid. But on the off chance I can't find the opening? Doesn't matter. We'll revert to Plan B."

"What's Plan B?"

Vigil said, "Remember when you were telling me how secure his compound is? How you described it as a 'fortress?'"

"I remember."

"Well what do you call a fortress when it goes up in flames?"

Mira shrugged, said nothing.

"A furnace. If we can't find the way in, then we smoke him out. That's Plan B. The ex-Special Forces guys he hired didn't have that option—not if they wanted to get paid. They gave him a false sense of security."

Mira nodded slowly, seemingly appeased. "We'll be there in under ten minutes. How do you wanna do this?"

"Gimme a sec." Vigil closed his eyes and brought up his mental map of Grabasso's compound, gleaned from the satellite imagery Google Maps provided. The residence was a U-shaped McMansion, sitting dead-center on a five-acre lot.

Maybe five thousand square feet. Ten thousand if it was two stories. He said, "Grabasso's place—one or two floors?"

"Three," Mira said, "if you count the finished basement."

Fifteen thousand, then. And more evidence in favor of his hunch.

Vigil zoomed out a little in his mind's eye, somewhere between what a bird would see, and the view from the cockpit of a jetliner. The parcel was mostly lawn. Only a few trees, none of them big. Reclaimed cotton field surrounded by more of the same, now gone fallow. He figured Grabasso purchased a small farmhouse when he first entered Witness Protection, and later—after his concrete business took off—tore it down to build the larger home he now occupied. At the same time (or soon after) he probably bought all the surrounding acreage, so he didn't have to listen to tractors in the spring and harvesting equipment in late summer.

And I bet he didn't stop there . . .

Mira took the exit and turned left onto FM-608, which ran south of Carlin. Grabasso's place was only a few miles away, a stone's throw east from the turn onto FM-107. There were wind towers on this side of town, too. Red lights blinked far in the distant darkness. The fog had cleared and visibility was no longer an issue.

Vigil said, "About a mile before the turn there's a dirt track leading into some scrub. We'll park off the road and hike the rest of the way."

CHAPTER
FIFTY-TWO

Down in the basement, opposite the end that Raymond had claimed for himself, Leonard was sitting in his wheeled office chair in the room he liked to call his Command Center. Other people of means would probably call it a safe room.

It felt very safe indeed.

The walls were three feet thick: One foot of fireproof ceramic brick sandwiched between two layers of steel-reinforced concrete. The entire house could burn down around him and he'd survive to greet the fire department after they doused the smoking ruins. For entry, there was a massive circular steel hatch salvaged from a bank vault. He'd upgraded it by bolting a two-inch thick plate of kevlar-braided carbon fiber to the inside surface, making it impervious to not only blow torches, but the point-blank firing of munitions up to .50 caliber. Redundant air shafts ran hundreds of yards outside to let in fresh air from pipes concealed in the landscaping. The room had its own backup generator. A bathroom and a shower. Seven days' worth of food and water. He'd hired the world's foremost expert in doomsday bunker construction to build it; a former Department of Defense contractor, the guy knew his shit. As evidence of his expertise, he'd insisted that Leonard needed a lot *more* than a mere week's worth of rations. But then, the guy didn't know about the customizations Leonard would add himself after completion.

Just like in the closet of the master bedroom, flat panel security monitors provided coverage of every square-inch of his home, including the detached garage / gym, and the 5.25 acres surrounding. They took up an entire wall of the Command Center. Thirty-six in all. Much larger than the displays upstairs. Cradling his head, elbows propped on the top of his desk, Leonard focused his attention on just two of the screens. The two linked to cameras capturing footage far outside his fence line.

Both of the remote feeds came from solar-powered wireless trail cams. Both pointed at the road. The first was affixed to an oak fence post an eighth of a mile south of the Interstate on FM-608, camouflaged with discarded bailing twine draped over the plastic bits like a sniper's ghillie suit. The second camera was attached to the back of a "Posted: No Hunting" sign near the intersection with FM-107. Like all such signs in Texas, it was peppered with bullet holes and buckshot. The lens peered through one of the holes, while the camera itself was hidden from view behind the largely intact sign.

Thirty-six security feeds, streaming to thirty-six displays, added up to more screen real estate than one person could monitor. To make it less taxing, he had Raymond program the displays to automatically dim when there was no motion on the feed; conversely, when its assigned camera captured live action, the display would brighten. This made the setup much more functional. An unintentional bonus was that the sudden illumination of an active LCD would jar him awake if he dozed off late at night.

Which he had.

But then monitor 35 lit up. Streaming footage from FM-608.

It had been triggered by approaching headlights. Leonard fixated on it. Seconds later, a small Toyota hybrid came into view. Mira's rental.

Leonard noted the time. FM-608 was paved. Traveling at reasonable speeds, a vehicle destined to turn left onto his road would trip Camera 36 in about three minutes. Give or take.

Ten minutes later, however, the camera aimed at FM-107 still hadn't picked up the Prius. Which meant Mira and the meddling bum had pulled up short.

Leonard picked up his phone to text Vin. His crew had been guarding the front gate for well over three hours already, but now he had a better idea.

CHAPTER FIFTY-THREE

Gray brooms of sagebrush scraped at the Prius's undercarriage as they crept down the dusty track, while leafless branches of mesquite batted at the side mirrors. A few dozen yards later, they found themselves parked in a weed-choked glade, hidden from the road.

A dilapidated corral stood sagging in the middle of the clearing. Not many right angles remained in its construction. Boards hung loose from rusty nails. On top of an upright timber, someone had balanced the skull of a goat. The former livestock concern hadn't seen a live animal in a long time. That was clear. Now, the shabby glade was a place for shooting at bottles and dumping tires. For late night extracurricular pursuits on the bench seat of a battered pickup, or in the backseat of a teenager's car.

Mira performed a three-point turn so they were facing toward the road, and then she killed the engine. They got out and stretched. A mile southeast, on a dead-reckoned diagonal intersecting the two farm roads, was Grabasso's compound. They couldn't see it yet. Not through the intervening scrub and scraggly trees. But it was there, alright. And Vigil felt it tugging at him. As if its grotesque weight had warped the surrounding earth, forming a low spot in the land where an evil man had found his level.

He took the deer rifle out of the backseat and set it down on the hood of the Prius. The Winchester Model 70 was a capable weapon, and it worked pretty good for shooting humans, too. None other than Gunnery Sergeant Carlos Hathcock, famed Vietnam era Marine Corps sniper, had relied on a previous iteration for many of his 93 confirmed kills, including one through the scope of an enemy sniper known as The Cobra. If it was good enough for "White Feather" (the nickname Vigil's dad used when telling Hathcock's story), then it was good enough, period. This one shot thirty-aught-six Springfield ammunition. He opened the bolt and pressed three cartridges down into the internal magazine, one after the other, plus a final fourth cartridge that he pushed into the chamber. Closed the bolt and thumbed back the multistage safety all three clicks. Vigil had no intention of firing the rifle tonight. But just in case.

He used his pocketknife to cut slits in the ski masks to fit around their ears. The com units wouldn't slide that way. They didn't plan on splitting up, so the headsets were probably unnecessary. But better to have and not need, than to need and not have.

Meanwhile, Mira tested the night vision binoculars. Thermal imaging would have been better for aiming at warm bodies, but for recon under the light of a quarter moon, the military-spec glass by AGM was more than adequate. At thirty-five hundred bucks, they'd better be.

"Cover one of your eyes and count to two hundred," Vigil said. It was an old trick for all-natural night vision—pirate style (it's why they wore eyepatches). They had the binoculars, but shit happened. Two was one. One was none. A lesson he learned early in life.

They checked their weapons and set out into the dark.

CHAPTER
FIFTY-FOUR

Leonard didn't wanna talk to Vin—for obvious reasons he didn't dwell on and wouldn't acknowledge. But his eyesight wasn't what it used to be, and trying to text what he wanted done would be too cumbersome. He called instead.

His oldest, most loyal friend picked up on the first ring. "What's up Lenny?"

"Change of plans. Take the long way back to I-20, then loop around the normal way onto the farm road. Once you're off the interstate, drive slow. Turn off your headlights and creep along."

"Why the cloak-'n-daggers?"

"Just listen—you know the little turnout where kids go to smoke weed and fuck?"

"The old corral in the clearing?"

"Mira's Prius should be parked there. Her and the bum are hiking this way as we speak."

Vin said, "If we stay put we can intercept them."

"They'll be expecting that. I want you to ambush them when they get back to the car. Fill that motherfucker full of lead."

"I could leave Bruno behind to watch your place," he offered.

"No. They're not lookin' to get inside tonight. And if this guy's half as savvy as Mira says he is, you'll want all three of youse to make sure it gets done this time." It was hard for Leonard not to pile on Vin's last failure, but he managed to stop with just this light jab.

"What about Mira?"

"We still need her. She'll probably make a show of returning fire for Vigil's benefit, but don't worry about it. Her shots will go wide. Use that to your advantage."

CHAPTER
FIFTY-FIVE

Their eyes had mostly adjusted to the meager moonlight, but progress was halting at best. Prickly pear cacti, mesquite branches, and even the occasional thorny limb of a non-native mimosa tree demanded caution and a circuitous bearing.

Strange tracks (also non-native, some of them) made them wary as well. This being Texas, the abandoned ranch they were hoofing it through might have once been home to exotic animals rather than cattle. Private hunting preserves were big business throughout the region. Hunters could pay just a couple thousand bucks to a so-called "high fence" outfit and bag animals indigenous to Africa or Asia. Way cheaper than a safari. What happened to these animals when a big game business went belly-up was anyone's guess. Vigil had read somewhere that more tigers lived in the Lone Star State than all the wild tigers in the world combined.

"What the fuck is that?" Mira pointed to a large, oddly shaped print preserved in a patch of dry clay. "A chupacabra?"

Vigil knelt down on one knee to get a closer look. "That," he said, "is two different animals. The bottom print is an

American Bison. And the top print is the biggest damn cat in North America, which must've been stalking it."

"A mountain lion? Geezus."

He saw no real benefit in sharing his tiger statistic. "Yeah. Keep your eyes open. For snakes, too. Lots of rattlers out here at night."

There was a light breeze at their backs. Their scent would warn any nocturnal predators ahead of them of their approach. Possibly a good thing. Depended on how hungry the predator was. Mira removed her Glock from its holster and Vigil brought the rifle up to a low ready position. They pressed on.

"We'll come out of this brush at about the halfway point," he said. "Then we'll have a clear line of sight all the way to Grabasso's place."

"I know," Mira said. "I've been there, remember?"

"So tell me what I couldn't see in the satellite imagery."

"Closer in, there's a beautiful wrought-iron fence with lots of decorative flourishes. Ten, maybe twelve feet high. Surrounds the entire lot. The gaps between the bars are as narrow as a prison cell's. Not even a small child could squeeze through. You wouldn't wanna climb it, either—each bar is capped with a sharpened spear. Plus, I'm pretty sure it's electrified. I never saw a bird land on it. Like they knew better. It's really something. The steel alone must've cost a fortune, and it's all supported by massive brick columns every twenty-five yards or so—each with a concrete lion statue perched on top."

He could've done the math, but asked, "How many columns?"

Mira didn't answer right away, like she was counting. "Sixteen?"

"How big are the lions?"

"The statues? I don't know—life-sized? They look enormous up close."

"Seems excessive," Vigil said. "Even for a flamboyant prick like Grabasso. I bet they're not purely decorative."

"What do you mean?"

"You know about Tannerite, don't you?"

"Shit," she said. "I hadn't thought of that."

Tannerite was the brand name of a binary explosive composed of ammonium nitrate and powdered aluminum. In small quantities, people used it for target practice. Certain militia types were rumored to use much larger quantities to booby trap their driveways. *Dad had. Allegedly.* You could hit it as hard as you could with a sledge hammer, and nothing would happen. Same if you shot it with a pistol. But fire a high-velocity round into it with a large rifle? *Ba-boom!* That's gonna leave a dent. Half the explosive power of C4, but perfectly legal and easy to purchase in many states.

"I bet they're hollow and filled with the stuff. Thirty yard kill radius, easy."

Mira said, "Well there's that. Inside the fence, he's got Ruskie and Irish. Two professionally trained attack dogs. Dobermans."

"What about the house itself?"

"Brick. Modern, but with Gothic Revival and Tudor-esque influences."

Vigil looked at her blankly.

"I'm just messin' with you," Mira said. "He's got cameras everywhere. Bars on all the windows. And the front door looks like something from a medieval castle. Inside, more cameras. Motion sensors. An alarm system, obviously . . . what else? I mean, it's not like he ever gave me a tour. All I know is, his stepson, Raymond, is the stereotypical autistic techie. Whatever's cutting edge, they probably have it installed."

"Is there a guard house at the front gate?"

"No. There's a kiosk with a keypad. I don't know the code. The gate was open when I came by today. I just drove in."

Vigil nodded. They were almost out of the woods.

As they neared the flat expanse of unplowed fields, Mira cursed under her breath, said, "Coulda saved a few bucks on the night vision binocs."

Grabasso's entire compound was lit up brighter than a Monday Night football game, thanks to a bank of literal stadium lights. They looked identical to the ones installed at the high school sports complex bearing his new name.

"Never noticed those before," she said. "Never been here at night."

Vigil used the rifle scope to zoom in on the yard, the home, and the detached garage. Stadium lights notwithstanding, Mira's overall description of Grabasso's security measures had been pretty spot-on.

"You think he's planted any surprises for us in the field?" Mira said.

"Like what? Land mines?"

"Yeah. Like land mines."

"I doubt it," he said. "Too many deer. But also, why bother? Nobody's getting anywhere near that place. It's a goddamned fortress."

Mira hissed through her nose. "I told you. Now do you get why I was nervous?"

"No," he said. "Because there's another way in."

"'Plan B?' It sounded better in the car. Wouldn't smoking him out just draw attention? What happens when the fire department shows up? With the Sheriff in tow? They'll arrest us for arson."

"You're right. It was a terrible idea. I was just calming you down."

"So what do we do? Parachute in?"

"A little too Mission Impossible for my taste. Steep roof, too. The dogs might take offense if we flubbed it and had to land in the yard."

"Well what do you have in mind?" Mira said.

"Follow me."

Vigil reversed course a few dozen yards into the scrub and then led them almost due south, keeping parallel to the field. The going would have been easier out in the open, but it was better if they remained concealed. Choreographed or not, he knew if he did anything overtly stupid or bold on their recon mission, Grabasso would suspect Mira of double-crossing him.

They made it to FM-107 in short order, encountering no dangerous wildlife or booby traps along the way. The farm road was on the other side of a badly damaged chain-link fence. In the past the barrier would've been a formidable obstacle, but now there were gaping holes cut along its length at regular intervals.

They ducked through one such rift and approached the road and listened. The night was as hushed as the library at a mime academy. The glow from Grabasso's compound was visible to the east, but the structures themselves were obscured by the stand of trees they'd emerged from. There were no approaching headlights, no signs of activity of any kind. He shrugged, said, "I misjudged the angle a little but he won't be able to see us if we hug the ditch."

"Are we going back to the car?"

"Not yet."

They followed the road further west a short distance and then stood still again. Ahead, the slender moon was outshone by the spillover from a standard-issue, rural American light pole.

"Neighbor," Mira said. "They're probably asleep this time of night, but they might have dogs. Should we duck back into the woods?"

"No need," he said, and continued walking.

When he brought them to a stop they were in front of an unassuming one-story farmhouse. Wood siding with peeling white paint. An uninspired roof line. Weathered asphalt shingles the color of an armadillo slowly dying of emphysema. The curtains were drawn. There was a chimney on one end made from coarse rock, puzzle-pieced together by someone with more time on their hands than money or skill. On the other end of the house, a single-stall garage had been tacked on, not part of the original construction.

"Notice anything strange?" Vigil said. He didn't whisper.

"Not really. Looks like an old farmhouse. Probably rented for cheap to someone who couldn't afford something closer to town."

"Looks can be deceiving," he said. "Look closer."

Mira humored him, but it wasn't long before she gave up. "I don't know what I'm supposed to see."

"Nobody lives here," Vigil answered.

"What are you talking about? The electricity's on. Maybe they're vacationing."

"Folks poor enough to rent a dump like this work two minimum wage jobs because neither pays overtime. No sick days and definitely no vacations."

Mira said, "Says the guy with no address."

"Look at the driveway."

"It could use some work," she said. "I mean, it's gravel. What do you expect? Pretty typical out in the country."

"True, but look at the ruts. They're almost completely grown over with grass and weeds—from the garage, all the

301

way to the road. I've seen my fair share of gravel driveways. That doesn't happen unless nobody drives on it for a long time."

Mira said, "Maybe they don't have a car? Maybe they use the garage for storage like everyone else in America."

Vigil shook his head. "Out here? They'd starve to death. No way to get to the grocery store without a car."

"Says the guy without a driver's license. So what are we looking at? The worst Airbnb of all time?"

"Let's go inside and find out."

THEY BROKE IN THROUGH THE BACK DOOR. ONE swift kick near the frame, right below the handle. That was all it took.

No dogs barked.

No alarms went off.

Nobody stirred.

They didn't need their flashlights because many of the outlets had nightlights plugged into them. Dim yellow bulbs, but after traipsing around in the dark for the last hour, more than adequate illumination. They found themselves in a cramped kitchen that bled into a dining room. Cramped because it was small, not because there was much of anything in it. There were no appliances on the counters, and the cabinets were empty save for a few black plastic roach motels. No dishes. None in the sink, either. Inside the fridge there was only a bottle of ketchup. The expiration date read March 3, 2013. The freezer held an empty tray and a layer of frost thicker than the Antarctic ice shelf. There was no table to eat at. No chairs. Same in the living room: No couch. No recliner. No TV. No pictures on the walls or decorations of any kind. Only nightlights in the outlets. Every surface covered in dust—even the walls. The place smelled like old newspapers and neglect.

"See? Nobody lives here."

Mira nodded. "Let's check the bedrooms just to be sure."

They did. The rooms were full of nothing and no one. No beds, no dressers, nothing hanging in the closets. Inside the only bathroom, a cheap vinyl shower curtain powdered with long-dead mold, and a half roll of toilet paper nibbled to confetti by mice in search of insulation for their nests.

That left the garage.

It was behind an oak-paneled door centered on the wall between the dining room and the front of the house. Vigil tried the handle. It was locked—from the garage side, which was unusual.

"Stand back," he said.

He kicked the door in roughly the same spot as he'd kicked the back door, and with roughly the same amount of force. It held. It was a much newer door, not part of the original construction. He kicked it again. Harder this time, but still nowhere near full strength. This time the frame splintered as the deadbolt broke free of the jam on the opposite side. He nudged the door with the toe of his boot and it swung open on squeaky hinges.

Unlike the rest of the house, the garage *wasn't* empty.

CHAPTER
FIFTY-SIX

C ertain places don't need security cameras.

Certain places, you don't *want* security cameras.

Escape routes, for instance.

When someone is trying to kill you—someone skilled enough and determined enough to penetrate your considerable defenses—the last thing you want is to show them how you're getting away.

Or *where* you're getting away *to*.

So when it comes to escape routes, a simple indicator light is preferred. Triggered by an electronic tripwire. A straightforward heads-up in the unlikely event someone stumbles across your emergency exit.

Leonard leaned back in his chair in his Command Center and smiled ruefully to no one in particular.

The red LED indicator light mounted to his desk was on.

Vigil had found the breach.

CHAPTER
FIFTY-SEVEN

They stepped into the garage and the lights came on. Motion-activated switches—handy in a room where someone's hands would often be full carrying groceries, or small children, or tools. Disconcerting in a house where nobody lived.

"Nice car," Mira said.

Occupying the majority of the modestly sized stall was a 2021 Land Rover Defender. A capable luxury SUV, and a very nice car indeed. Pretty much the last vehicle you'd expect to find in the garage of a vacant farmhouse—except *this* farmhouse was just down the road from Grabasso's place—so Vigil wasn't surprised at all.

The black four-wheel drive British import looked sleek and modern, even beneath the thick layer of dust. Fast, too, in spite of its off-roading pedigree. The chrome 'V8' badge affixed to the bottom of the door panel flaunted the size of its super-charged power plant in a world of eco-friendly, six-cylinder hybrids.

The hood was open. A yellow extension cord snaked up from the receptacle on the far wall to a black metal box balanced on the engine cover. Two cables—one red, one black

—ran from the rear of the box and connected to the battery terminals with alligator clips. A battery tender. Necessary because the SUV wasn't driven frequently enough to keep it charged.

He tried the handle. Unlocked, like he knew it would be. Same as he knew the keys would be in the ignition (they were) and that there'd be a full tank of gas (there was).

He closed the door. Surveyed the rest of the crowded space. The garage wasn't wide, but like many garages that doubled as a utility room, it was longer than strictly necessary. A hot water heater supported by a plywood platform took up one corner, and in the other corner was a fiberglass sink, deep enough to fit a mop bucket. Between the two plumbed appliances were nine plastic storage bins, gray in color. They sat on top of a cheap rug, stacked three-high against the wall, covered in a layer of grimy disuse like everything else. Vigil didn't need to check to know the bins were empty. They'd been placed there for concealment purposes. As had the rug.

"Who stores a $150,000 dollar Land Rover in a shit-box like this?"

"One guess." Vigil said.

"Grabasso?"

"Who else."

"But why? His garage is massive—eight stalls I think."

"Getaway vehicle."

"You think?"

"I know."

Mira looked perplexed. He gave her a minute to puzzle things out.

She said, "His place is—what?—a third of a mile away? What does he gain by staging a vehicle here, as opposed to where he actually lives?"

"You can't see his compound," Vigil said. "It's shielded by the woods."

"Yeah, so? He would still have to get here. Anyone looking to nab him would have plenty of opportunity."

"Not if he walked," he said, his voice salted with irony.

Mira shook her head. "What are you talking about? He's in his seventies. If he walks over here, he's an even easier target."

Vigil cocked his head toward the bins.

Mira shifted her weight to one leg and put her hands on her hips. A wry look of *are-you-saying-what-I-think-you're-saying* slowly taking hold.

"Go ahead. Have a look."

She moved the empty storage bins off to one side. Used her foot to scoot the rug out of the way.

"I'll be damned," she said. "How'd you know?"

A R-15 at the ready, Leonard aimed dead-center at the $30,000 dollar Persian rug concealing the trapdoor in the floor of his Command Center.

He knew he was being silly. Because he knew how much Mira loved her daughter.

I die, Elise dies.

Which meant Mira would stick to the plan. Like she always had.

Nonetheless, he stood there ready to spray and pray in the event the blue LED lit up, warning him that someone was in the tunnel. The weapon felt good in his hands. Power-trippy; a non-fatal dose of an ill, lethal drug. It made his dick hard, just like the old days.

He imagined what it would be like tomorrow night, pretending to be caught off guard as his would-be assassin burst through the trapdoor with a sexy, two-faced fox at his heels. Then he thought: *What if I flipped the script? Shoot the fucker in the face as soon as he pokes his head out?* The problem, of course, was that he might accidentally put a round through Mira. He still needed her help for the exchange with the Russians.

But did he? Did he really *need* her help?

Or am I just angling to fuck her before I finally undo the dead-man's switch?

It was a legitimate question. Leonard realized how sadistic he could be . . . how tempting that curvy little milf ass of hers was. Urges which might cloud his judgment.

He should sleep on it.

But if the blue LED came on?—the one wired to the hatch?

All bets were off.

CHAPTER
FIFTY-NINE

"It wasn't any kind of a genius deduction," Vigil explained. "I was primed. First by the buried shipping containers—the guy likes to dig. And second, knowing Grabasso did commercial concrete in New York City —which told me he's familiar with tunnel construction."

"That's all it took?"

"No. But it pointed me in the right direction. When I was looking at the satellite layer on Google maps, I noticed how close this farmhouse was to his compound. Thought it was odd. Why would a rich guy choose to build such a lavish home just down the road from an eyesore? Not like there's a shortage of land around here. Then I noticed the grass had grown over the ruts in the driveway, which meant it wasn't seeing much action. Made me wonder who owned the place. That's why I checked the property records. Sure enough, Mariana Grainger appeared on the deed—I assume that's his wife?"

"Yes."

"Right, and so it occurred to me why Grabasso could brag that a team of ex-Special Forces operatives couldn't get to him: Because even if they'd been able to penetrate his security perimeter and get inside the house, he'd just scurry away underground like the rat he is."

Mira made a little grunting noise that sounded like admiration. "Primed or not, that's still impressive detective work."

Vigil shrugged.

She said, "Should we verify the tunnel leads to his place?"

"It doesn't lead to China. That's for damn sure. Unless you wanna go in early? Grabasso dead one day sooner seems like a win to me."

"We've been over this," Mira scolded. "We go in now, he knows I betrayed him. He'll be waiting at the other end with a submachine gun, ready to mow us down."

Vigil was silent. *No guarantee he won't get twitchy tomorrow night, either.*

He knelt down and used the barrel of his rifle to lever up the hatch.

CHAPTER
SIXTY

The blue LED on Leonard's desk lit up.

CHAPTER
SIXTY-ONE

Vigil waved his arm around inside the opening to the tunnel and fluorescent lights cycled on as they had in the garage. He leaned over the hole. Looked down at what there was to see.

Which wasn't much.

And that was a good thing.

No water to wade through, for instance. No mold. It smelled dry. Moisture would be a sign of shoddy construction. He wasn't phobic when it came to enclosed spaces, but he wasn't looking to die in a tunnel-collapse, either. He needn't have worried; the floor, the walls, and the ceiling were immaculate. Smooth. No cracks. Whatever the former gangster's faults, the man knew concrete.

He rose to his feet and closed the hatch. "Let's get outta here."

CHAPTER
SIXTY-TWO

The blue LED blinked off again. Leonard put down the AR-15 and went to bed.

CHAPTER
SIXTY-THREE

It would've been easier to walk to the car along the farm roads. But why get lazy now? The locals were quick to call the Sheriff on late-night loiterers. Vigil had seen that for himself. And if they crossed paths with one of the cotton farmers they'd beaten up at the Diamondback yesterday—buzzed on their way home from the bar, maybe with a few of their buddies—what good could come of that? (Aside from the exercise.) So they backtracked. Found where the fence had been cut and sidled into the brush.

The light breeze out of the west had picked up a little, and now they were walking into it. A warm, dry wind. Whisking through the sage like an angry wraith, masking the sound of their progress. They moved single-file, Vigil in the lead. He held branches for Mira so they didn't slap her in the face. Pointed out sharp-tipped yucca leaves and cactus needles and loose stones.

They made it back to the dried clay tableau of pawed predator and hoofed prey. Vigil froze. Slowly crouching, he raised a fist, and Mira knelt down behind him to present a smaller target. Muffling their footfalls hadn't been the only favor the wind had gifted them. There was something in the air.

He sniffed, but it was gone. Only the expected amalgam of wood and leaf and dirt remained. Closing his eyes, he tried again; imagined himself as a forked-tongue viper capable of tasting the night, or a hungry polar bear that could pinpoint a seal sunning on sea ice a mile away. This time he detected the faintest hint of an all-too familiar odor. An odor that didn't belong:

Cigarette smoke.

No ifs, ands, or <u>butts</u> about it.

Vigil smiled to himself. Not in response to the C-minus pun, but in anticipation of the thing he was put on this earth to do.

"THAT STUPID, ARROGANT SON OF A SEAMSTRESS," Mira hissed, louder than ideal. She was *incensed*—hell hath no fury—and God wouldn't have the stomach to fuck-around-and-find-out after seeing the look on her face.

"Grabasso sent his crew to ambush us," he said.

"No duh, Dick Tracy."

He barely heard the snide rebuke, implications flitting through his mind like bad poker hands dealt from the bottom of the deck:

(A)—Grabasso got cold feet. Maybe the ex-gangster was prepared to go through with Mira's scheme, but only as a last resort. First, he wanted to give his goons a shot.

(B)—Grabasso was never sold on Mira's plan in the first place. Vigil would need to find another way to deliver retribution.

(C)—Grabasso knew Mira was conning him. Which meant Elise was already dead.

Vigil locked eyes with her, looking for tells. "You think he turned on you?"

"No. He's hedging. God forbid a female formulates a better strategy than what he could come up with—misogynist midget that he is."

"Wouldn't he have warned you if that was his play?"

"I don't know. He's never been what you'd call predictable. But I do know Grabasso still needs me."

"You sure about that?"

Mira shrugged. "I've yet to hand over his new passport or other bonafides. Originally, that was our deal. The final arrangement before he'd call his guy off Elise."

"'*Originally?*'—so he reneged?"

"He moved the goalposts. Now he wants me to help with the exchange. He's dealing with Russians—no wonder."

"So he's not laundering the bitcoin, he's selling it for hard currency?"

"That's what he made it sound like."

"Where?"

"Georgia. The country, not the state."

"And why am I only hearing about this now?"

"Because none of that matters. He'll be dead soon."

But it *did* matter. It mattered, because the withheld plans put Mira in another country with Grabasso, flush with a shit-ton of cash. Plus, now that Vigil was aware of this added wrinkle, it gave him an idea for tomorrow night's hit he wouldn't have otherwise considered (whether he'd tell Mira about it beforehand, was a different question).

"Why Georgia?"

"Because Georgia doesn't extradite? Beyond that, no clue. I got the impression he's still hashing out the details."

They were still crouching on the hard-packed clay. Vigil examined the hoof print, and the massive clawed track superimposed on top of it. He wondered, briefly, if he was as oblivious as that bison had been. Concluded: *Nope. Because the bison wouldn't have thought to ask.*

Mira said, "Here's an intriguing possibility: What if Grabasso didn't send his crew to kill you? What if—"

"He's banking I'll kill them."

"Exactly. After all, the greedy fuck must've promised them a cut. This way?—more money in his pocket, and fewer loose ends."

"Well then he'll wake up happy in the morning. Because I don't like loose ends either."

MIRA SAID, "HOW DO YOU WANNA DO THIS?"

He knew she was more than capable of planning an ambush of an ambush, and that she was only deferring to him to prove she had nothing to do with the goon's arrival. Talk was cheap, but he appreciated the gesture.

Vigil took a moment before answering and thought it through. All three of Grabasso's crew were brain-dead byproducts of natural selection gone awry. He knew that for a fact. And he was pretty sure they were also cowards. It was hard for him to predict how a coward would approach a deadly encounter; the smart move usually required more balls than the coward had at their disposal. But this time it was easy. Given the rural location, where the Prius was parked, the distance to the road, the ample cover, and how narrow the dirt track was, the most cowardly way to execute the ambush happened to coincide with the smart way.

He said, "One of them will stay behind the wheel of the Navigator, just out of sight between us and the road. The other two will flank the Prius on opposite sides of the track— in the woods, but closer to the Lincoln, so they don't shoot each other in the crossfire. They'll stay hidden until we're inside the car. Then the driver blinds us with his high beams and it rains bullets."

Mira was quiet for a moment as she visualized his rundown. Then she said, "Yeah, that's how I'd do it. Except—with me sitting right next to you—how would they ensure I didn't get shot?"

"Begs the question, doesn't it."

Her knees clicked as she stood to full height. "Believe me, when I touch base with Grabasso, that's the first thing I'll ask. Right now, I can't go there. Because that would mean . . ." she trailed off, chin askew, eyes darkened with the unimaginable. "Like I said, I can't go there."

"That was cold of me." But he didn't apologize. He wasn't sorry. He was relieved she'd responded with fear for her daughter's life. No hesitation. Because if she had hesitated? Well, he could picture a way Grabasso's goons might avoid killing Mira with a stray round: Maybe they paused a beat before firing?—gave her a chance to do the deed for them, proving her loyalty to their boss in the process.

She said, "I have to assume this is about greed, and that he's intentionally sending his crew to get slaughtered."

Vigil nodded. "The good news is, even if that's not his goal, he'll play it off that way when you confront him about it. And as long as he thinks you're buying his explanation, we can still use the tunnel to gain entry tomorrow night."

"Fingers crossed."

He said, "Grabasso ordered you to send these chumps to Carlin, right? I wanna know their names."

"Why?"

"They're ex-gangsters. They killed people that didn't deserve to die. When this is all over, the families of their victims also get a cut of Grabasso's loot."

Mira humored him: "Bruno Nash—formerly Bruno Colosimo—he's the youngest. Thirty-five or thereabouts. The biggest of the three, too. Looks like a gorilla wearing a human costume for Halloween.

"Then there's Anthony Twitty. Anthony Bianca, before he entered the program. He's fifty-eight I believe. Good with numbers. Bad with women.

"And finally, Vinny Scaramouche. Their captain. Grabasso's oldest friend and most trusted associate. Age seventy-six. Car thief and wheel man. His new name is Vinny Swain, but everyone calls him 'Vin.'"

When she was finished he said, "WITSEC's reputation takes a hit tonight."

"How so?"

"Bruno, Anthony, and Vin will be the first ever casualties while under the protection of the U.S. Marshals."

Mira shook her head. "That statistic only applies to participants who follow our guidelines. Which they most certainly did not."

He was tempted to say, *"Thanks to you,"* but Vigil still hoped she might switch divisions at the end of all this, and he didn't want her digging in her heels. He shrugged, said, "Well, first thing's, first . . . " Then he found a sturdy twig and they used it to sketch out a crude plan of attack on the dried clay.

CHAPTER
SIXTY-FOUR

Vigil kept the thirty-aught-six Winchester and the attached Athlon Optics scope, and left the night vision binoculars with Mira. He ninja'd south toward FM-608, conveying the rifle muzzle down with a support-side carry to keep it from snagging on vegetation. The holstered Sig P220 Legion didn't slow him down either; he could feel its weight beneath his waistband and found the pistol's bulk comforting. Always good to have a backup. *Two is one, one is none.* He might've been a minimalist when it came to housing and travel, but in armed conflict, 'less is more' was wishful thinking.

Even so, it hadn't stopped him and Mira from debating the merits of killing the goons barehanded. Grabasso's compound was little more than a mile away, and Vigil's initial concern was, if shots were fired, 'The Lion' would hear them. But as Mira pointed out, even if neither of them discharged their weapons, at least one of their targets probably would. It wasn't like the movies; people fight back when you're strangling them to death. "Besides," she'd argued, "Grabasso's *expecting* a gun battle. Nothing would spook him more than silence." And she was right. They were playing a confidence game, with Grabasso as their mark. To win such a contest, it was imperative your opening moves didn't upset the opponent's expectations. You played the long game, lulling them into complacency with predictable tactics until it was time to deliver the final, fatal—and crucially—*unanticipated* blow. Therefore, they decided to stick with the most efficient way of dispensing with these chuckle-fucks: Firearms.

Vigil emerged from the woods near the intersection with FM-107. He couldn't see the little farmhouse, but the glow from the yard light was visible, as was the harsh glare of Grabasso's stadium lights further east. "I'm to the first farm road," he spoke into the microphone of the comm unit. Then he set out at an easy jog on the smooth asphalt. They hadn't heard or seen a single vehicle all night, and so given the circumstances, he figured expediency outweighed the small risk of bumping into a local this far out in the country. From the earpiece he heard Mira whisper, "Copy that. Still crawling into position."

After halving the distance to the intersection, he slowed down. Two man-made structures had captured his attention. A tall sign mounted to a narrow steel post, not more than a yard from either road—almost certainly a stop sign—and a shorter one, set back a half dozen yards or so, attached to two wooden posts.

They were just signs. Not people.

Man-made, not men.

Even so, something about them prompted Vigil to approach with caution. Some kind of irregularity, triggering an instinct for self preservation. He imagined it was the same instinct that caused a buck or bull elk to stare directly at a motionless hunter, even when the threat was downwind and therefore invisible to the animal unless it moved. An ancient instinct passed down from a common ancestor. Older than language. Wiser, and much harder to ignore than a voice in your head or a chiding angel perched on your shoulder.

He walked closer. Then, still twenty yards away from the signs, he stopped cold. Scrutinized them like he was lost in a foreign country, and they were the only things written in English. Then he spotted it: The solar panel. The camera body. The transmitter. Attached to the rear of the short *No Hunting* sign with bailing wire and putty. That's how Grabasso had known where to send his goons: There'd be another camera hidden closer to the interstate, which had captured the Prius shortly after Mira took the exit. Because they'd never made it to this camera, and because Grabasso undoubtedly knew about the dirt track and the little clearing, locating them had been a simple process of elimination. Mystery solved.

Vigil made sure to stay well out of frame as he cut the angle from FM-608 onto FM-107, giving the No Hunting sign and its makeshift surveillance setup a wide berth. Disabling the device would only alert Grabasso that he was wise to it. And if Mira had been mistaken about him sending his crew to get slaughtered, the ex-gangster could warn them of his approach.

"On FM-107. All clear. Heading your way."

"I'm in position," Mira replied, her words now barely audible in his earpiece. "Two lying prone in the woods . . . guns drawn . . . on either side of the path . . . Just like we drew it up."

He realized her pauses coincided with lulls in the breeze, so she wouldn't be heard. "Hold tight," he said. Vigil jogged north until he was close enough to the dirt track that stealth became the priority and then slowed to a brisk stride.

His heart rate was elevated but nowhere near maxed out. Underneath the black clothing, his skin was damp with a thin layer of sweat. His muscles were warm. His breathing, steady. No tunnel vision, no ringing in the ears, no butter-flies in the gut. He was alert, but calm. Every sense was heightened, and every biological system was in perfect working order.

He removed the Model 70 from his shoulder and carried it in front of him in the ready position. Strode quickly along the final few yards of asphalt before the dirt track, then slowed way down as he eased onto the loose dirt littered with busted flint. He kneeled and could just make out the wide, deep tread pattern of the Lincoln, and the skinnier, shallower tire marks left by the Prius.

Now it was a proper stalk. Not the first that had gone down on this land. He advanced slowly, one tender step at a time, resting his boot delicately on the dirt in front of him before gradually shifting his weight to the forward leg. Like a Shaolin monk walking on rice paper. Like a big cat closing in on a kill.

Keeping the element of surprise was the tricky bit. The moon had dipped below the horizon and the dirt track was barely distinguishable from the surrounding brush, a slate line smeared on a dark canvas. Spotting the Lincoln Navi-gator—without tripping over a root or kicking a loose stone —was no easy task. The vehicle's Darth Vader paint job and tinted windows were the perfect camouflage.

His gut told him to stop and he did, closing his eyes and counting to two hundred to coax whatever light he could into dilated pupils. When he opened his lids, the rear end of the Navigator had materialized out of the gloom; a smooth-edged 3D shadow against the calligraphy of tree trunks and the charcoal smudges of sage and wintergrass. He could probably Hail Mary a rock and hit the hood from this distance. But why would he? He had the Winchester.

Vigil raised the rifle and rolled his support shoulder forward to create a groove of muscle between his right pec and deltoid, into which he pulled the butt of the rifle, trapping it there, steady and secure against the coming recoil.

With so little light, he couldn't see into the SUV, so he centered the cross hairs in the upper left quadrant of the tinted back glass, level with where he pictured the driver's head would be on the other side. He bent his knees a little to ensure the trajectory of the supersonic round leaving the Model 70's barrel would be reasonably flat; somewhere on the other side of the Lincoln and Vinny Scaramouche's head was Mira.

"Ready?" he whispered into the microphone of the comm unit.

"Ready," came her reply in the earpiece.

"Hit it."

Which came first? The opening salvo from the horn? or the initial pulse of the Toyota's headlights when Mira pressed the "panic" button on the Prius' key fob? Hard to tell. Both distractions erupted into the night damn near concurrently. And the effect on Grabasso's crew must've been like a flash-bang grenade. Though Vigil couldn't know this for certain because he was zoned in on his target and applying slow, steady pressure to the trigger.

Before the second *honk* sounded, the big gun went *boom!* and the back glass shattered and Vin's think-meat biohazarded all over the interior like explosive diarrhea, shit-for-brains that he was.

A short distance from the clearing, the two remaining goons jumped to their feet and sprinted away from the sound of the rifle blast. Deeper into the woods. Toward Mira. It wasn't quite *blind* panic, because the Prius' strobing headlights illuminated their progress at ten-yard intervals like lightning in a horror movie: *Honk / flash . . . Honk / flash—bang!-bang!—thud. Honk / flash—bang!-bang!—thud.* Two shots, per, from Mira's Glock; two new souls bound for hell.

Scratch that. One new soul. The next volley from the Prius' California idiot detector showed the big guy—Bruno Colosimo—had scrambled to his feet. He'd been wearing a vest.

Bruno squeezed off three shots in Mira's direction, almost certainly too blinded by the headlights to see her, but aided by the afterimage of her muzzle flash and the crude triangulation afforded by two working ears. Too close for comfort if you were on the receiving end.

"Shit! Almost hit me," she confirmed in his earpiece.

Vigil glassed for him through the scope, but there was only darkness. The sonic assault from the Prius had ceased—*good*—along with the lame light show—*bad*. Mira must've rolled on the key fob after Bruno fired at her.

"Turn the lights back on!"

"Negative. Dropped the fob. Can't find it."

"Copy that. Stay down. I'm returning fire."

Vigil took a knee and imagined what he'd do in Bruno's situation. The way he saw it, Colosimo—outnumbered and outgunned—had three options:

1. Hunker down in the woods and hope they couldn't find him.
2. Outrun them to Grabasso's compound.
3. Make it back to the Navigator and take his chances driving out.

(1) Unlikely . . . (2) not on your best day . . . (3) when hell freezes over and the devil takes up ice fishing.

Bruno went with the third option. Vigil still couldn't see him, but he heard the man's heavy footfalls thundering in his direction on the path. He returned the rifle to the sling, drew the heavy Sig, and sprinted toward the Navigator, the only real shelter between them.

Bruno had a head start.

Vigil was faster.

Neither man could aim for shit at a full sprint, but that didn't stop Colosimo from trying. He was thirty yards from the hood when he fired three times at Vigil, never breaking stride. The shots didn't find their mark, and Vigil knew better than to try. Therefore, he reached the SUV a full second-and-a-half sooner, and when Bruno squeezed off two more rounds, they pinged harmlessly off sheet metal.

Because Vigil had to duck behind the rear bumper of the Lincoln, however, the shots had their desired effect: Buying Bruno just enough time to dive in front of the hood. Vigil heard the man land, kevlar and metal jangling off hard-packed earth and rock; the rustle of nylon on denim as he scrambled to his feet and ducked behind the driver-side wheel well.

Now it was a game of whack-a-mole. Who would show their head first?

Vigil had a big advantage. Unlike Bruno, he wasn't trying to gain access to the getaway vehicle. There was nowhere he needed to be. He could stay crouched behind the luxury SUV and simply wait. All night if he had to . . . and of course, he *didn't* have to.

Because he had Mira on Colosimo's unprotected side to flush him out.

If it came to that.

But it didn't.

Because Bruno Colosimo wasn't so dumb after all.

THERE WAS A METALLIC *clink* FROM THE OPPOSITE end of the Navigator. A familiar sound, but one he hadn't heard for a long, long while.

He found himself counting—reflexively—zero input at all from the executive functioning centers in his prefrontal cortex. Or more accurately, counting down: *Five, four, three*—the way a boxer slips a jab and fires a left hook, or a wrestler sprawls when his opponent attempts a double-leg; it seemed instinctual, but wasn't. The counting was a trained skill. Drilled into him over hundreds, if not thousands, of repetitions.

If he'd have completed his countdown, then it was a false alarm. Nothing to worry about.

But Vigil didn't complete his countdown.

Because—before he made it to *two*—he heard another sound he recognized. A second sound he also hadn't heard in many years. Similar to the first sound, the second sound was likewise metallic in nature. Unlike the first sound, however, the second sound contained a *thunking, clattering* element, which the first sound lacked: A noise not unlike a hand grenade would produce—bouncing and rolling over hard clay beneath the undercarriage of a large SUV—because that's exactly what it was.

If this were a movie, he'd scoop up the live ordnance like a baseball shortstop and sidearm it down the path. Cinematic, but stupid. The NATO mandated spec on time-to-detonate was anywhere between 4.5 and 5.5 seconds. Sometimes, grenades made it off the assembly line out-of-spec. Quality control was a challenge. Instead, Vigil launched himself vertically from the lunge position, up and back and onto the roof of the Navigator a millisecond before the grenade exploded.

For an instant, night became day. The blast bounced the Navigator on its suspension, but fortunately, Made In America still meant something, and no shrapnel got through. The fuel tank was another matter. Vigil smelled gas and rolled off the side of the roof and hit the ground running—

literally in hot pursuit behind Bruno as a fireball erupted at his heels in a tremendous *whoosh* of heat and flame.

The former mob muscle was intent on the clearing where the Prius was parked; the Lincoln wasn't going anywhere. That was for damn sure. It was a crematorium.

Bruno had a pretty good lead on him. He'd wisely run like hell after tossing the grenade. No way was Vigil going to catch him before he made it to the Prius, where Colosimo would have cover, and Vigil would still be exposed.

Mira had the keys, though—*what if Bruno has another grenade?* He couldn't risk it. "Stay down!" he yelled into the comm unit.

Vigil slid to a stop, took a wide Isosceles stance for accuracy, and fired the big Sig at the back of Bruno's skull three times in rapid succession.

All three shots missed their target. Because that's what happens in real life. Colosimo was most of a football field away and Vigil's heart was hammering in his chest like Thor in a cave-in.

He holstered the Sig and shouldered the rifle. Lined up the reticles center-of-mass on the zigging and zagging ex-gangster; the 30-06 didn't give a rat's ass about his vest. Vigil pulled the trigger and the big gun went *boom!* and—

Bruno kept on trucking.

Because in real life, scopes have to be recalibrated after you smash them beneath two hundred and fifty pounds of man.

He cursed, then heard Mira in his earpiece: "Duck—it's my turn." Vigil kissed the dirt. A double *crack!* issued forth from the barrel of her Glock, concomitant orange globes belching forth in the wake of two bullets traveling at roughly 1,000 feet-per-second—a full two hundred feet per second slower than they would've traveled from a longer barreled Glock (a Glock 19, say) because she carried the more concealable 43. Even so, the diminished velocity made no difference as the hollow point rounds rapidly decelerated on the other side of Bruno's forehead. Blood geysered from both of the goon's earholes and then he face-planted, dead before he hit the ground.

CHAPTER
SIXTY-FIVE

The last day of his life, Justin Lackey thought about death.

The animated gif of Prosser's brains volcano-ing from the base of his skull hadn't let up, not even in sleep, and when he'd crawled out of bed that morning at 10:35, hungover, as tired as he'd ever been in his life, he finally realized how absolutely *absurd*—how pointless, fickle, and cruel the world could be. Hell, maybe death was the only thing about it that made any sense.

Of course, a defeated man *would* think that way.

He staggered to the kitchen and poked around in the cabinets until he found the jar of pods and a mug for the Keurig. Let the beagle outside while the coffee brewed. Then he went and sat in the rocking chair on the back porch and squinted against the glare reflecting off Lake Turner. He'd never been to Grainger's cabin before, but he'd trawled the dam for catfish plenty of times. Caught some lunkers, too. A couple of them so big, he'd wondered what they'd been eating.

A more thoughtful, sober man might've noticed the empty buckets and bags of cement in the shed.

The coffee was doin' a whole lotta nuthin' for his

headache. He tossed the cold dregs over the railing and searched inside for ibuprofen. Didn't find any. Said fuck it and came out with a cooler full of beer from the fridge. He sat down in the rocker and gave Betsy a pat on the head; it wasn't even noon yet, but she never judged. She licked his hand and went back to snoring.

A more self aware man would realize that's *why* he was so alone—precisely because he wouldn't allow anyone in his life who might hold him accountable.

Ironically, Justin wished he was at work. A first. There, at least, he could distract himself with banter and bullshit from the other wind jockeys. Get his hands dirty. Attend to the very real demands of the job and role-play that he had a purpose. It was too quiet here. Too isolated. One of five cabins on the west side of the lake, and the only property overlooking the cove. Here, all he could do was sit and drink and stew in dark thoughts. No shortage of those.

Of course there were an equal number of (if not uplifting) *productive* considerations he could've pondered to distract himself from the throbbing in his head. But doing so would take effort, and like all addicts, Justin preferred the path of least resistance—self-inflicted pain, in particular; the ready-made excuse always in his back pocket for why he hadn't lived up to his potential.

He stared at the lake for a while and almost convinced himself he was some kind of a country boy intellectual. He probably looked pretty damn rugged. Sittin' there in the shade of the awning in a plaid shirt, all introspective and shit. Maybe he'd whip out a pen and a legal pad and Cormac-McCarthy some neo-noir masterpiece nobody would suspect he had in him.

Bitch, please.

Four beers in, he started picking at old scabs he knew would bleed; they'd bleed profusely because he never let them heal; the same tired questions, answered with the same ol' lies: *"This is just who I am."* / *"Anyone who's been through what I've been through would want to numb the pain, too."*

He'd told the insurance company investigators about getting kicked off the baseball team in high school—punishment for introducing his coach's niece to tequila at junior prom. But what he'd neglected to tell them was how Coach Womack had molested him, starting his freshman year. Or how, prior to giving up on the Marine Corps, he and three other degenerates had sodomized a black kid from Alabama in the barracks one night. Or how, after marrying the stripper, he'd gotten drunk and nearly beaten his three-month-old son to death for crying too much.

Gut wrenching trauma to have endured, and terrible acts to have committed—no doubt. But worse yet? In Justin's mind, these were airtight fuckin' alibis for why he couldn't devote the rest of his life to becoming something greater than his past—growing into someone so valuable to the world that all that shit was a footnote no one ever bothered to read, himself included.

Midway through beer number eight, Will Prosser and his dead eyes crashed the pity party: *You should just kill yourself. I could use some company.*

Maybe I will, Justin mused.

He was genuinely surprised Grainger's crew hadn't killed him. More certain every swig of Lone Star lager, they would.

And soon.

But then again, why hadn't they pulled him outside yesterday? Shot him behind his shit-box trailer execution style, like the fuckin' ex-gangster wops they were? Instead, they'd brought him here to, quote: *". . . lie low for a while."* Hell, they'd let him take Betsy along and bought him a few cases of beer, to boot. Not to mention, his Bronco was parked out front. He could hightail it outta here if he wanted to. All of which implied he wouldn't be taking a dirt nap anytime soon.

But then he reconsidered his situation. Poked at it from that paranoid state of mind between merely shitfaced and blackout drunk. He was witness to a murder. Fact. Even though he hadn't said squat to the sheriff, the big guy (had he *really* been an insurance investigator?) lulled him into saying a lot more than he should've. Maybe him and his pretty partner had encouraged Baker to keep the case open? Or maybe farmer Schnell didn't feel like taking the fall for Grainger? Or maybe someone had seen Grainger's Ford King Ranch driving away from Schnell's and LG was now a suspect? And if he was a suspect, then the evil sonofabitch couldn't risk letting Justin flip. Better for LG if he disappeared.

And don't forget the rumors! Prosser's corpse cackled.

How could he?

A competitor who'd bragged he would underbid LG on the wind farm project ended up entombed in the foundation of a tower, rumor had it. Rumor had it Grainger Fargo-ed a sidepiece's husband headfirst into his wood chipper—kicking and screaming—and let his Dobermans devour the bloody mulch.

Justin's phone buzzed in his pocket and he almost pissed himself. It was his buddy Nelson with the PTSD:

> Oh shit! Hear about Oswald Schnell? Where the hell are you, anyway?

Justin hadn't heard, but a quick search on his phone brought up the article in the Sweetwater Reporter, published a half hour before:

NOLAN COUNTY COTTON CROPPER BUYS THE FARM IN CHILLING MURDER-SUICIDE

Apparently Schnell had heard the rumors, too.

And ol' farmer Schnell? He was a way harder man than Lackey ever was. Lost his leg to a harvester blade and was back out in the fields six weeks later, providing for his family, sending money to his boy in college, and standing by his sick wife while the cancer chewed her up. If *that* ol' bird feared what LG's crew would do to him, Justin wanted no part of it.

By the time the cooler was empty, he'd accepted his fate. Too drunk to talk himself out of it, too soused to be afraid, he plotted the ultimate ending to his tragic life. Because if there's one thing a lush loves, it's the grand gesture—the final 'fuck you!' to the world that says: *See? See what I was capable of? I just never tried.*

Of course, ninety-nine times out of a hundred, the grand gesture gets postponed. Put off until 'someday.' No different than every other grandiose turnaround the addict brags he's right on the cusp of making . . . *Tomorrow—just lemme get right / hit this pipe / snort this line / slam this drink.*

But not this time.

This time was different.

And I'm takin' LG down with me.

HE WAITED TO LEAVE UNTIL WELL AFTER DARK AND thanked the good Lord above that Grainger's crew hadn't come for him yet.

Jed Burke was the lone man working the control center that night, and Justin figured he could lay on some bullshit about forgetting his phone in the equipment shed: *"Nah, man, it couldn't wait until tomorrow. Booty call. You know how it is."*

Then again, Burke was married, so maybe he wouldn't empathize with his cover story like Justin assumed—or maybe he was tired of fuckin' his old lady, and he'd ask if Justin's hookup had a discrete friend. Either way, didn't matter, because Justin didn't bother. It's not like he needed a safety harness. Tonight he could make do with the stuff he kept in his Bronco: a DeWalt cordless drill with a hole saw bit, a box cutter, a tire iron, and fifty feet of yellow nylon ski rope.

He drove on dirt roads due east from the lake, toward the 11b tower line. Any tower would do, but 11b's towers were the furthest from town; the nearest house was at least ten miles away. He knew these roads better than Garmin, but he still took his time. He was three sheets to the wind in a hurricane. Barely conscious, he'd drunk so much beer. Nothing new and nothing to worry about. As long as he went slow. It wasn't like Nolan County posted deputies out here in the back of beyond to do sobriety checks.

When he got to the access road he stopped and took out his phone and launched the SCADA mobile app. Optimized for small touchscreens, the app wasn't as powerful as the version that ran on laptops, but it did everything he needed it to. He thumbed through the menus and found the option for applying the brakes. Typed in "11b-002" in the tower identifier input field, and then made sure to choose the "Blade #3" option under the "Level Blade?" heading. This told the braking module to stop rotation when the third of three blades was parallel to the ground. He drove into the field, parked at the base of the second tower, and waited for the spinning to cease.

He topped off Betsy's food and water dishes and sat them on the floorboard. Rolled down the windows a little and gave the ol' gal one last belly rub. Then he left her there on the passenger seat. She'd be fine until morning. After that, one of the other wind jockeys would adopt her. Nelson, most likely.

Justin gathered his tools. Tucked the cordless drill under his waistband like a gangbanger's *pistola*, and wore the coiled ski rope around his neck like the fakest and gaudiest of gold chains. The box cutter and the hole saw he stowed in a pants pocket along with his phone. The tire iron, he'd have to hold in his hand, but he'd manage.

At the tower access door he silently mouthed the twisted mnemonic device—*one-eight-seven-to-hell*—as he punched in the security code one last time: 1-8-7-2-4-3-1-1. "Literally," he mumbled behind a stupid grin. He didn't bother initialing the safety checklist, and didn't padlock the emergency shut-off, either. Sure, Burke would eventually notice the service disruption and attempt a remote override, thus releasing the brake and causing 11b-002 to spin again—but only if the onsite tech (who'd initiated the braking signal from the app) confirmed that it was safe to do so (which Justin obviously wouldn't do). Back in the control room, Burke would shrug and create a ticket: *"Probable computer glitch"* or some-such, then return to surfing r/preppers on Reddit.

Justin started the climb. Having to grip the tire iron in one hand made it cumbersome, but by the time he reached the first platform he'd more or less mastered the technique. Large hands helped; he pinched the crowbar-shaped tool against his palm with his thumb, and used his fingers like meat hooks to grasp the rungs. Not that his progress was easy. He'd been up and down ladders just like this one thousands of times—hundreds of thousands. Never drunk, though. Hungover? That went without saying. But never wrecked like he was tonight.

By the second platform he was sweating. The coil of rope was chafing at his neck and he wanted to throw up. He caught his breath and made some adjustments. Switched the tire iron to his left hand to keep his right from cramping. Cinched his belt tighter to keep the drill from wriggling loose and falling down his pant leg. *That's better.* He climbed the final two stages without passing out, painting the walls, or dropping tools, and by the time he got to the staging platform, he was slightly more sober.

He opened the small hatch and scrambled up the last few rungs into the nacelle. It was oppressively hot in the confined space, warmed by the friction of many recently moving parts. The air smelled of scorched hydraulic fluid, warm paint, and plastic fumes. Justin rested a few beats and then made his way past the gearbox and the main shaft into the hub, which the blades attached to.

What people unfamiliar with wind turbine blades didn't realize was that they were hollow, which allowed workers to crawl inside them for inspections and maintenance. Not an every day kinda thing, but fairly routine, and nobody's idea of a good time. On the outside, the fiberglass blades were as smooth as the hood of a C6 Corvette, but on the inside, they were rougher than cat tongue. Which was why Justin pawned blade jobs off on someone with less seniority whenever possible. Tonight he'd just have to suck it up.

At first he crab-walked, and then, as the walls sloped in around him and there was less room to maneuver, he shimmied on his back. Slow going with the bulky rope turtleneck. And though he was nowhere near as soused as he was before the climb, lying flat induced the spins. Miraculously, he made it to the midpoint of the blade without puking.

Justin set the tire iron down beside his legs and removed the DeWalt from his waistband. Attached the hole saw, tightening it with the chuck. He turned his head and closed his eyes and held his breath to avoid the abrasive dust, then placed the cutting edge against the unfinished fiberglass overhead and started drilling.

It wasn't a big hole. But it didn't need to be. He uncoiled the rope and secured one end to the tire iron with a rolling hitch knot. The opposite end, he laced through the hole he'd just cut, threading enough rope through to grab from outside.

Back in the nacelle, he patted his pants pocket nervously to make sure the box cutter or his phone hadn't slipped out. Reassured, he walked to the short ladder that led up to the roof. Placed his foot on the bottom rung and froze.

Am I really going through with this?

Justin didn't have to strain too long for the answer; he pictured all the terrible things Grainger's goons might do to him before letting him die. Bruno Nash in particular, who had thick scars on his knuckles, no doubt from beating people to death. He imagined the horror of suffocating inside a cement truck. Or being shoved into a wood chipper. *And what if it's not head first like the cuck husband? But feet first, and the damn thing jams halfway? Nope to the hell no.* Justin would rather take the easy way out, even in death. He filled his lungs with a deep breath of resignation and climbed outside.

In all his years as a wind jockey, he'd never been up top at night and the novelty of it caught him off guard. The red aircraft warning light blinking like the goddamned eye of Sauron, for starters. It was mounted to a stalk at the rear of the nacelle, so at least he wouldn't have to look into it while completing his tasks. The stars were also a surprise. After his eyes recovered, he realized he'd never seen so many— sparkling like busted windshield glass on a black felt head-liner (*that*, he had seen, before he'd perfected the art of driving under the influence). Also unexpected: The meth-ed out butterflies swarming in his gut. He'd lost any fear of heights ages ago, cleansed through countless exposures. But without the harness? With no way to clip-in to the safety anchors? Different ballgame. Now the risk of falling was very real. The terror, tangible. It felt like someone was sneaking up behind him with long arms and bad intentions, and Justin had to fight the sensation just to make his legs work. The wind didn't help. It was really whipping this high up. Fifteen to twenty miles per hour, sustained. His heart was beating so fast it practically vibrated, and his shallow, rapid breaths resembled a midget inflating an air mattress.

The hub was shaped like the nose cone of an intercontinental missile, and roughly the same size. Justin baby-stepped his way to it, sticking to the center of the platform. Between each blade there was 120° of separation. Blade #1 jutted skyward from the hub at a 150° angle to the ground, while blade #2 pointed down at a 30° angle. Extending plank-like from the hub, was blade #3. Justin's sole and final aim.

To reach it, however, he'd have to maneuver himself off the flat roof of the nacelle, and onto the slippery curved shell of the hub. Then it was an asshole-puckering, six foot descent to where blade #3 bolted on. Not a great distance, but without a harness and cable tethering him to the nacelle, it was easier to slip forward and fall, than it was to slide sideways to the relative safety of the turbine blade.

One step at a time.

Justin eased down onto the hub. Sat on his butt and pointed his toes the direction he wanted to go.

Here goes nothin' . . .

If he'd missed any cling-ons during his last wipe they were diamonds now, and Justin managed the controlled skid without creating any new skid marks.

He rose to his feet. The turbine blade stretched out before him into the void, flexing and undulating in rhythm to the breeze. Nothing that large was actually rigid. Not even skyscrapers constructed of steel and concrete, and certainly not a mechanism molded from fiberglass. In fact, the "blade" was shaped more like a gigantic wing, with curved surfaces engineered to catch the wind and create lift. Even so, its sheer scale rendered the convex bends more or less level, providing ample purchase for someone brave enough to take a stroll.

Justin wasn't brave, but he still had just enough liquid courage flowing through his veins to keep going. He raised his arms out to his side like a tightrope walker and proceeded gingerly to the hole he'd cut at the midpoint of the blade. There, he paused. Suddenly doubting whether he could pull off the most audacious part of his plan. Afraid—that if he kept going—he might stumble off the edge and fail the world's highest sobriety test.

And then what? Die for nothing?

Justin barely recognized this inner voice, so long suppressed. But knew he must answer its call. For once in his miserable life, he would man-up and finish something. He took another step. And another. Until there were arguably no more steps to take. The blade was still wide enough, but this far out its geometry was no longer conducive to walking.

He reached in his pants pocket and came out with the box cutter. Thumbed out its razor-sharp edge and pressed it against his left palm. Then, he cut.

Deep.

Way more than skin-deep.

Almost to the bone.

Which produced the desired effect:

Blood, and lots of it.

Almost too much.

So much blood, Justin realized he'd better get to work right away or risk losing consciousness. He got down on his knees and prepared to write his suicide note. A much better note than the one Schnell left. More concise, by necessity. And a note many more people would read. That was for damn sure. This note would go viral. No question. Which mattered to Justin, because the most important thing about his last words, was that they were true.

He used his right hand like a paint brush, and his left like a palette, scissoring his way back toward the hub on his knees and toes after smearing each letter on the slick canvas of the blade.

He realized there was only enough room if he used initials. And he was very mindful about his choice of verb. It was a slogan, not a short story; a bumper sticker, not a brochure. Short and sweet and better for it. Justin was confident the message wouldn't be misinterpreted. Especially given the context.

Only one thing left to do.

He stood and walked back to the little hole with the ski rope snaking out of it, careful not to step on his grim graffiti. He pulled the remaining length of rope up and through the hole—all of it—save for the end still tied off to the tire iron. With the bitter end, he fashioned a noose, and then placed it over his head. Snugged it tight around his neck, but not so tight that he couldn't breathe and passed out. He still needed to use his phone.

The SCADA app remained in the foreground, but now there was a pop-up dialogue:

> Remote brake-release requested.
> Please <u>Approve</u> or <u>Deny</u>.

Justin pressed Approve. Another pop-up appeared:

```
WARNING: Approving this request may put on-
site personnel in danger.

Are you sure you wish to approve this
request?
```

<u>Yes</u>, I understand the risks and wish to
approve.

<u>No</u>, leave the brake engaged.

    Justin pressed Yes. There was a thunk as the hydraulic brakes released their grip on the main shaft, and the turbine blade pushed against his feet.

    The wind blew.

    The world tilted.

    Justin jumped.

CHAPTER
SIXTY-SIX

"We should get rid of the bodies," Vigil said.

"Vultures?"

He nodded. Inevitably, someone would discover the crime scene. But with vultures circling overhead, it would happen a lot sooner. Vultures were a problem.

"What do you have in mind?"

He shrugged, said, "Might as well burn them."

They started with Colosimo because he was the heaviest. Vigil walked backward, gripping him under the armpits, while Mira took the brute's ankles and wheelbarrow-ed ahead in lockstep. The blaze was too hot to approach without protection; they dropped him a few dozen yards from the burning wreck and then retrieved Bianca from the woods.

Mira said, "How do we get close enough to toss them in the fire? Let it cool down some?"

"Better if there's nothing left but teeth," he said.

Vigil hoisted Bianca's doughy corpse off the ground and slung it over his shoulder. Then he closed his eyes and sprinted toward the inferno, relying on the intensifying heat to gauge the distance. When the sweat on his brow threatened to boil, he adjusted the load, lifting the dead weight until it draped overhead, protecting his face and torso like a shield. Now he was so close it felt as if his clothes might ignite; Vigil stopped on a dime and launched Bianca toward his waiting hell. Legs thrusting and arms piston-ing to full extension, brute force adding to the momentum already gained. He directed his full strength into the toss—quads, glutes, hamstrings, and calves firing in perfect harmony along with every other muscle in his two hundred and fifty pound frame. Like a strongman heaving a keg.

Physics 101: *Bodies in motion tend to stay in motion.* Anthony Bianca's body certainly did. His lifeless mass left Vigil's hands like a Steph Curry three-pointer and sailed into the center of the firestorm.

Short a couple eyelashes, Vigil was already backpedaling. He returned to Colosimo's significantly larger carcass and stood over it for a moment, psyching himself up for the much more difficult athletic display necessary to catapult a far heavier human.

Mira must've read the doubt in his face, said, "I've got a better idea: Why don't we put him on the hood of the Prius, buckle-in, build up some speed, and then slam on the brakes?"

More elementary physics: The kinetic energy of an object in motion is equal to one half its mass times the square of its velocity—and a moving vehicle had a lot more of that. Vigil was embarrassed he hadn't thought of it. "Smart."

Though it didn't work out quite like they pictured it.

Given the angle of the hood, and the anti-lock brakes, Bruno's body didn't so much launch, as slide. It hit the ground a few feet in *front* of the fire. Fortunately, it was traveling at over thirty-five miles an hour upon impact, and the big man bounced the rest of the way into the flames. There was also a brief moment of panic as Mira struggled to shift the unfamiliar rental into reverse, which in Toyota's infinite wisdom had been placed on the dash instead of the center console, where generations of drivers have been trained to reach for it. A few more seconds and the paint job would've bubbled, but she tracked it down in the nick of time and motored them back to the clearing.

Bodies disposed of, they recovered the goon's weapons, emptied them of ammunition, and pitched them into the fire as well. Identifying the remains would require dental records, and he guessed that Mira might've obfuscated those prior to relocating Grabasso's crew to Carlin. Either way, Vigil hoped he'd be long gone by then.

THEY HAD TO WAIT FOR THE BLAZE TO DIE DOWN IN order to skirt the smoldering heap. The dirt track was narrow. The Prius, the polar opposite of an off-road vehicle. They didn't arrive at the hotel until nearly four in the morning.

Other than to compliment one another's execution during the ambush, they said very little on the way back. At one point Mira teased, "Not to be a one-upper, but I dropped two of them compared to your one." He smiled and reminded her that she was the professional. She had obviously been flirting. Such brushes with death often lead to arousal. Some kind of a primal response. Like an evolutionary directive: *Breed now, or forever rest in peace.* Vigil was well versed.

It was late, of course. The adrenaline had dried up and they both were exhausted. Even so, when they got to the elevator, it was clear they were both doing the math:

This could be their last opportunity.

Neither of them was looking for an ongoing entanglement. That was clear. Long-term relationships were wholly incompatible with Vigil's lifestyle, and Mira was obviously aware of how he chose to live. Which, he supposed, was part of the appeal. For some women: A very different guy from the kind they typically paired up with, without the worry of justifying him to their friends or family. They could pretend it never happened. That he never even existed. No judgment. No attachment. No expectations.

When the door closed he only pressed one button.

CHAPTER
SIXTY-SEVEN

W hen the sun rose the next morning, Justin Lackey's grand gesture was there for all to see. And it wasn't long before it went viral. Indeed, by the time Leonard woke in the spare bedroom and checked his phone, gifs of the gory scene—many of them already meme-ified—were all over Instagram and trending on Twitter. Every podcast host, morning shock jock, and YouTube influencer was talking about it. The Paul brothers (with *Round and Round* by Ratt, playing in the background—a popular '80s metal band) predicted the footage would become internet trolls' next Rickroll. Radio personality Horatio O'Connell (whom online haters had dubbed 'the unholy lovechild of Terry Gross and the late Paul Harvey') described the scene thusly, for listeners too squeamish to watch the video:

"The modern equivalent of a crucifixion. A dead man—not hanging, but—*swinging* from the end of a rope like a tetherball made of meat . . . violently whirling, 'round and 'round in profane arcs propelled by the pinwheeling indifference of human ingenuity. Bringing—not salvation, as Jesus offered his flock, but—cruel injustice. A cynical proclamation inflicted on a world still reeling from a pandemic and plagued by war. And yet, perhaps not unexpected from a man called Justin Lackey. After all, it's right there in his name.

"But maybe there's more to the story . . . maybe this tragic final act of a desperate man was actually a bold, last-ditch effort to . . . *restore* justice? You see, Mr. Lackey left a message, written in his own blood, visible after his flailing corpse was finally allowed to rest: LG SHOT WP."

Leonard Grabasso leapt out of bed like a man half his age and called the number Lebedev had given him.

CHAPTER SIXTY-EIGHT

Vigil crawled out of Mira's bed soon after the sun came up. So it was confusing when—now asleep in his own room—he heard her voice urgently calling his name. He glanced at the clock. It said he'd only been sleeping for a few hours.

No way is she ready for another round.

He shrugged, rolled out from under the sheet, and answered the door.

"What is it?"

Mira handed him her phone. On the screen was a video captioned: 'Hang in there all the way to the end—of the video!' He managed about ten seconds. Enough to conclude the man had hung himself in the most hyperbolic way possible.

He handed the phone back. "Lackey?"

"Yeah, but you really have to see the end." She used her finger to advance the video.

He'd assumed the caption was a sick joke and wasn't amused. He plucked the device from her hand, paused the video, and read Justin's suicide note. "Do you have any idea how happy it will make me to kill that piece of shit?"

"I do."

"How does this impact our op?" he asked.

"I don't think it does. Grabasso will want to expedite the exchange with the Russians, but if he doesn't eliminate you first, he'll always be looking over his shoulder."

"He wanted you to call him and touch base beforehand, right?"

"Right."

"Have you?"

"Next on my list," she said. "I've got a FedEx in the lobby. Then I'll call Grabasso. Anything changes, I'll let you know."

Vigil nodded. "I'll call you when I wake up."

CHAPTER
SIXTY-NINE

L eonard's call with Lebedev's Russian contact went smoothly. No threats, no bullshit. All business.

$500,000,000 USD fits on five standard pallets loaded into the trailer of a semi truck. Leonard requested something lighter—ten half-pallets. Even a Soviet-era forklift held together with glasnost and superglue could handle that.

"No problem."

He told the Russian the name of the commercial district in Tbilisi where they would do the exchange. Said he'd give him the exact warehouse and which door to back into, the day of.

"Of course."

It was like the guy handled these kinds of deals every day. The way Putin's war was going, he probably did.

He skipped breakfast and took his phone outside while he walked the property with Irish and Ruskie. Called the Sheriff. Best if he was proactive regarding Lackey's suicide, he thought. He reminded Baker how big his campaign contributions were last election and hinted at how they might grow in the future.

"Yes," he acknowledged, "I know how it must look. But

would it be alright if I came by tomorrow and answered your questions? I've got a lot of important business I need to handle today."

"That'd be fine."

Moron.

He was watching the dogs fight over a dead rabbit they'd chased down when Mira Getty called. Later than expected, but then, she hadn't gotten much sleep last night. He'd heard the gunshots. Smelled the smoke. Unsurprisingly, her call didn't go as smooth as the previous two.

"Good afternoon, Sugar Tits."

"I wish you wouldn't call me that."

"And I wish I had another five hundred million layin' around . . . oh wait—I do. We just have to go get it."

Mira didn't sound impressed, said, "That was some fucking stunt you pulled last night. What the hell were you thinking?"

"I had to know if this bum was as good as you said he was. Seein' as how he found the tunnel, and Vin isn't answering my texts, looks like your assessment was on the money."

"Well you should've given me a heads-up."

"The less you knew, the better. Remember? So Vigil wouldn't sense your betrayal?"

Mira said nothing.

"If it's any consolation, I told my guys not to harm you."

More silence.

"Hello? You there?"

"I'm here," she said.

He heard her sigh. Long and labored. Like maybe she was thinking. Or irritated. Or reluctant to share bad news. Or—knowing Mira—all the above. He said, "Is there a problem?"

"Not anymore. I fixed it."

"What happened?"

"I told you he's smart. So what would a smart person think when he notices your crew isn't shooting at me?"

"He'd wonder if you set him up." Now Leonard understood why she was upset. In his haste—in his greed—he'd jeopardized tonight's trap.

"That's exactly what he thought."

"So how did you put him at ease?"

"I didn't," she said. "I came clean."

"You came clean?" Leonard scoffed. "Good one. But seriously—what'd you tell 'em?"

"I told him you're Lenny 'The Lion' Grabasso, not Leonard Grainger. That I'm really a U.S. Marshal, and you're in Witness Protection. And I explained how you turned me by threatening my daughter. I told him everything."

Irish had torn one of the bunny's legs off and she dropped it on Leonard's shoe, staining the leather with slobber and blood. He kicked at her but she was too fast for him.

"This isn't funny, Mira. And I've never known you to have a sense of humor."

"I'm not joking."

"Why in the fuck would do that, you stupid cunt? You realize Elise is as good as dead now, right?"

"Calm down. I said I fixed it."

"It doesn't sound like you fixed it. It sounds like you fucked things up beyond all repair."

"Quite the opposite," she said. "Because now? Vigil *really* trusts me. He didn't before. Not all the way. Now he sees me as a damsel in distress. Believes he's my last hope of saving Elise."

"Listen, Princess, and listen good: *I'm your last hope of saving Elise. I'm your only hope.*"

"I know that. Which is why I preyed on Vigil's hero complex and convinced him you wouldn't honor our deal—not exactly a stretch, given your history. And so tonight, instead of asking you for the key to your bitcoin wallet, he'll tell you to disable the deadman's switch. You'll laugh in his face; he'll move to persuade you. Then I shoot him in the back, just like we planned. Nothing else changes."

At first, Leonard wanted to call her something even worse than cunt, but he couldn't think of anything and Mira didn't speak Italian. Then the clever ruthlessness of her ruse sank in, and the more he considered it, the more his rage morphed into an entirely different emotion. Suddenly he found himself grinning like Joe Biden on an escalator. *This bitch is devious! Definitely wettin' her beak—with or without a blowjob.*

"There is one change," he said.

"What's that?"

"As soon as he's dead we're headin' to the airport."

"Lackey?"

"Goddamned right, Lackey. The punk. It'd be a miracle if all the news coverage didn't embolden a farmer to tattle on me."

Mira said, "Can you get Raymond to help with the body? Vigil must weigh like two-fifty. Neither of us are strong enough to move him."

"Sure. He'll be tickled pink. I caught him jacking-off to the security footage of you on the back deck."

"Thanks for sharing. Sick fuck. Just make sure to stash a tarp so he doesn't get blood everywhere."

"Will do."

"Midnight," Mira said, and ended the call.

Leonard backtracked until he found the mangled rabbit's foot. He put it in his pocket. For good luck.

CHAPTER
SEVENTY

Vigil ordered pizza and had it delivered to Mira's room. She'd asked him if he would prefer steak—her treat—but he declined. After their meal at Perini Ranch the other night, any entrée that rode shotgun in a styrofoam box would surely disappoint. That, and steak had a "last meal" kind of vibe he'd rather not entertain.

They ate in relative silence, still groggy from their naps. Hungry, too, since they hadn't eaten all day (not to mention the calorie deficit they created last night beneath the sheets). Mira put cable news on the television, the volume turned down so it was easy to ignore. Vigil, meanwhile, pondered the contradictory advice preached by his father on the topic of planning.

A favorite doctrine was, "No plan survives contact with the enemy." An insight attributed to well-known generals such as Dwight D. Eisenhower and Colin Powell, who (depending on whom you asked) cribbed it from The Duke of Wellington, Napoleon Bonaparte, or the great warrior sage, Sun Tzu. Vigil believed in giving credit where credit was due, and he suspected the quote had actually originated in the 1800s with Moltke the Elder, a Prussian field marshal. As for who said it best? That would be none other than Iron Mike Tyson: "Everyone has a plan until they get punched in the mouth."

Other times his father would espouse the opposite view: "If you fail to plan, you plan to fail." A quote Brits liked to attribute to Winston Churchill. ~~Winners~~, *ahem*—Americans, to Benjamin Franklin.

As a boy, the apparent inconsistency drove him nuts. As a man, Vigil appreciated that the paradox resulting from these two stances was perhaps the clearest indication of an underlying truth, and that wisdom was knowing when and where to apply each view.

For many, if not most of the dangers he'd dealt with in life, he'd taken Tyson's words to heart. Relying on his gut and figuring shit out on the fly; overwhelming his foes with balls-out bravado and unrelenting violence. But this time, he'd embrace the way of the general. Leverage Mira's feminine wiles and defeat Grabasso by flawlessly executing a superior plan.

Which didn't mean that there wouldn't be violence. On the contrary.

Cunning only gets you so far in life.

When they finished the pizza, they spent the next three hours rehearsing. Because another thing Dad used to preach was, "Don't practice until you get it right. Practice until you can't get it wrong." Often reinforced with: "Repetition is the mother of all skill." Wisdom which had no counterexample, and words both Mira and Vigil had benefited from throughout their lives. Therefore, they visualized their plan dozens of times, reviewing each stage again and again and again: The approach through the tunnel and bursting into Grabasso's safe room, the interrogation and the disabling of the deadman's switch—all of it—every last detail to the bloody end.

THEY GEARED-UP AT 11:00 AND WERE ON THE ROAD by 11:30. At ten 'til midnight, they were parked in front of the garage at the farmhouse. So what if they'd blocked in Grabasso's Range Rover? Wasn't like he'd need it.

Vigil said, "You have a picture of Elise I can look at?"

She selected a headshot from a gallery of favorites on her iPhone. He studied her face. She was beautiful, like her mother, and the resemblance was striking. Same green eyes. Same dark hair. Same dry-brush-dusting of faint freckles on her cheekbones. He nodded and returned the phone. Mira looked lovingly at her daughter then put it away.

They got out and walked around back to the already busted rear door, then made their way into the garage. They hadn't bothered replacing the empty plastic bins or the rug which had camouflaged the opening to the tunnel, and so the hatch was right there, beckoning to them.

"Ladies first," he said, and then followed her down the ladder.

Motion-activated lights blinked on as they had topside, illuminating the passage. Cold, practical, blue-tinged fluorescent tubes like you'd find in the hallway of a mental hospital, or a public high school, or some other institutional building where creative minds were destroyed. They drew their weapons. Mira carried her petite Glock 43, and Vigil stuck with the hefty 10mm Sig. They gave each other a once-over and then set off toward Grabasso's compound.

They strode through the smooth-walled cement corridor, neither fast nor slow. Pistols at the ready, reasonably confident they wouldn't need them until they'd emerged into The Lion's safe room. They didn't talk. There was no need. Every aspect of the operation had been choreographed, visualized, and rehearsed. Dozens of times.

Vigil paid attention to his breathing. Ensured it was deep and slow. Figured Mira was likewise managing her biology. Adrenaline was flowing, that was for damn sure. As evidenced by the tingling in his forearms and fingers, and the slight buzz in his ears, like a hornet's nest hidden inside a hollow tree. Whether the fight-or-flight chemical was inducing tunnel vision, Vigil couldn't say; they were in a tunnel.

And soon, they were to the end of it.

The subterranean passage terminated at a sturdy steel stairwell. Six steps, treads perforated for traction, leading up to a wooden hatch flush with the ceiling. At the foot of the stairs was an electric scooter to expedite an escape; Grabasso had seemingly thought of everything.

They slowed down the last few yards and tiptoed up the stairs, purely out of habit. After all, there was no need for stealth.

Grabasso knew they were coming.

CHAPTER
SEVENTY-ONE

Hell, Leonard knew, *that Vigil knew*, that he knew they were coming.

All thanks to Mira—same as he'd learned about Vigil's pathetic ploy to protect her precious Elise, and the same way he knew what the dumb brute *didn't*:

That Mira had betrayed him—that he wasn't getting out of here alive.

He'd spent the afternoon preparing. Booking flights and reserving hotel rooms, using the name printed on the new passport Mira would soon hand over. He'd also prepped the safe room. The rolled-up tarp was stowed beneath his desk, ready to go. The Persian rug was peeled back from the escape hatch so it didn't get damaged, or in any way hinder his guests' dramatic entry. The vault door was cracked open so Raymond could slip in and dispose of Vigil's body when the time came; the wood chipper topped-off with gasoline and staged next to the vegetable garden.

Fifteen minutes after midnight, Leonard sensed Mira and Vigil on the stairs below the hatch, their furtive approach reverberating through the foundation as they crept up from the tunnel floor. His heart was banging away in his chest, but not so fast he feared a coronary. His life story was a true crime epic. Pure gold for the lucky writer who got to tell it someday. Fate wouldn't dare ruin the ending with such anti-climactic bullshit. Thinking of a good title, then fantasizing about the Netflix series necessary to cover such a long career as a criminal, Leonard leaned back in his chair and actually managed to relax.

CHAPTER
SEVENTY-TWO

Vigil crowded in tight against Mira at the top of the stairs, hunched over with one hand on his pistol, and the other hand on the hatch. She nodded *ready*, and he mouthed a silent countdown: *One . . . two . . . three!*

He shot-putt-ed the trapdoor with almost as much force as he'd launched Anthony Bianca last night, and it flew into the safe room like a barn door caught in a tornado. An aggressive maneuver, even for him. He wanted Grabasso out of his comfort zone.

"The Lion" yelped like a startled Chihuahua as they burst into his basement den. He leapt to his feet, knocking over his office chair and nearly tripping over its wheeled base as he shrunk away from their charge.

They fanned out, weapons raised. Vigil went left, Mira sidestepped to the right. Two lethal vertices aiming at an unarmed third in no kind of a love triangle.

Mira reverted to her training, yelling cop-like commands. "Get on the floor! Hands on your head!"

Grabasso composed himself, slowly raising his hands in mock surrender, smirk on his face as if he was anticipating the punchline of an inside joke.

"I said get down!"

His eyes narrowed as he complied, smiling like a talking shark in a kid's cartoon. "Easy, Sugar Tits. My knees ain't what they used to be." He used his desk for support and inched his way down into the prone position, fingers laced behind his head. Former inmates knew the drill.

Vigil stepped to the ex-gangster and patted him down. Satisfied, he took note of the impressive bank of security monitors mounted to the exterior wall. *Time to improvise.* He grabbed a fistful of silk shirt and jerked Grabasso to his feet —and then off his feet—up and over his head in one smooth motion. He walked him around the desk, spindly legs dangling like a marionette. Then Vigil bounced his dome off an LCD panel hard enough to crack it—the screen *and* Grabasso's face. Rat bitch that he was, he squealed in pain, but Vigil wasn't finished. He slammed the ex-gangster's face into a different screen, just in case his nose wasn't crooked enough after the first impact. Confident he'd established the desired rapport, he dropped him back down to his feet, spun him around, and put the fat barrel of the Sig against his temple.

Grabasso's eyes darted inadvertently toward Mira then back to Vigil. He forced a pained smile. "Was that really necessary?" he said.

Vigil replied with a quote from the UFC fighter, 'Game-bred' Jorge Masvidal. "Super necessary."

If the ex-gangster thought this was all for show, he was gravely mistaken.

Because Vigil had no intention of sticking to the script.

Blood trickled down Leonard's throat from his broken nose, threatening to gag him, and he swallowed it before he was forced to cough. Hacking up mucus and gore in the giant's face would only encourage further abuse. Vigil stepped back a long stride, perhaps aware of this disgusting possibility, but kept his gun steady.

"What the fuck is this?"

When they'd gone over the new twist in Mira's scheme earlier today, Leonard hadn't fully appreciated the damage the bum might inflict *prior* to his interrogation. But now there was no going back. If Vigil dished out more punishment, he'd have to endure it for as long as it took to sell this whole charade. If Leonard didn't put up with it—if he said something clever like, *"No need to get handsy, we all know why we're here"*—then the wanna-be vigilante might not believe, *that he believed,* that Mira was ultimately going to save his wrinkled ass. And if that happened, Leonard would have a real clusterfuck on his hands. One he could deal with, because of course he had a backup plan (The Lion *always* had a backup plan). But he preferred to stick with Mira's much simpler, much more devious ploy.

Vigil said, "You're going to die soon. There's no changing that. But what you need to ask yourself is, how long are you willing to suffer beforehand?"

Leonard swallowed more blood, thought: *Good. We're gettin' to the part where Mira puts a bullet in your back.*

"I'm going to ask you a question. Answer me promptly—*truthfully*—and I'll make it quick. But if you hem and haw? Or worse—lie? Then at least twenty-two agonizingly long and extremely painful minutes will pass before I let you die—one minute each for the nineteen victims on your Wikipedia page, plus three more for Prosser, Schnell, and Lackey. And trust me, you'll end up answering the question, regardless. Because I can be *very* persuasive."

Vigil was beaming ear-to-ear as he said this, and Leonard didn't like it. The big guy seemed *too* confident. And more than a little unhinged. He glanced nervously at Mira. He was still in character, but the fear in his eyes was legit. He noticed something disconcerting in Getty's eyes, too—repulsion maybe, at just how psychotic her fuck-boy 'hero' sounded while threatening him with torture.

"What do you want?" he said, playing dumb, pretending like she hadn't already told him what Vigil would ask.

"I discovered your crypto mining operation," he said. "Gotta hand it to you—pretty damn clever. Very profitable with all that free electricity you stole.

"But profitable enough to kill Will Prosser? I wasn't sure. So I did a little research. Performed some back-of-the-napkin math. By my calculation? You mined around $2.5 billion worth of bitcoin. *Plenty* of motivation to murder someone over . . . *even for me.*"

Something churned in Leonard's stomach. It could have been all the blood he'd ingested, but it felt more like a warning. Mira hadn't budged from her initial position. She was standing a few feet away from Vigil, inline with his shoulder.

Therefore, in no position to sneak up behind the brute just yet. Worse, she was chewing at the inside of her lip, a nervous tic he'd witnessed on many occasions.

"Now, I live a fairly humble existence," Vigil continued. "Always have. Nobody's idea of materialistic. That said, never in my wildest dreams did I imagine I'd stumble across *yacht* money. And let's be honest, it's easy to embrace the simple life when obscene wealth isn't even on the table. But now— thanks to you—it's within reach."

Mira was throwing the bum more side-eye than Brad Pitt in a gay bar. This didn't sound like a man motivated by heroism; it sounded more like a man motivated by money. Leonard would know.

"According to the crypto geeks on the internet, all I need is the private key to your bitcoin wallet, and we walk outta here richer than a Bond villain. So . . . what's the password?"

Not: *"How do you disable the deadman's switch?"* like Mira had assured him. Vigil must've gone rogue. The churning in Leonard's gut intensified—an entire colony of eels throwing an orgy in his small intestine. But he didn't panic.

Not yet.

He'd been in situations every bit as tense in the mafia. And this one remained salvageable. Obviously, Vigil had abandoned the script; the look on Mira's face all but confirmed it. But what wasn't clear, was whether he'd conned her?—or merely failed to mention that $2.5 billy in bitcoin mattered more to him than Elise's life?

It was the 'we' that gave Leonard pause: " . . . _we_ walk outta here richer than a Bond Villian." Not: *"_I_ walk outta here . . ."* This was either Vigil's way of buying time—of stringing her along so Mira didn't shoot him—or, the 'we' was sincere, in which case Mira had been hustling Leonard all along. The former mob underboss prayed to a God who owed him no favors, that it was the former.

Then he told the bum to go fuck himself.

Vigil shook his head, frowning solemnly, like a father saddened by a wayward son. The Lion braced himself for what was sure to be an epic dose of punishment—the only way to know where Mira stood.

"Kneel down, old man."

Leonard kneeled.

Vigil holstered his pistol and closed the gap, said, "This is gonna sting a little."

Before he could react, the giant's enormous hand clamped down on the side of Leonard's face, palming his head like a basketball. Then his thumb, rough with calluses, dug into his eye socket and massaged the sensitive orb in tight, excruciating circles. The pain was orgasmic in its intensity. He writhed and thrashed and flailed. Used both hands to try and pry away his bear-like paw, but it was no use. Vigil's grip was a vice. All Leonard could do was weep, and in between sobs, beg his tormentor for mercy. Finally, moments before The Lion swore he would pass out from the pain, Vigil relented.

"Just so you know, that was a warm-up. It only gets worse from here. But if you tell me the password, the pain stops. It just . . . goes away. So let me ask you again: What's your private key?"

The fact that Mira hadn't intervened already was damning. How could a mother sacrifice her own child for a payday? Even a cold-hearted criminal like Leonard found it hard to believe. *If I die, Elise dies—she knows that.* He wondered if she didn't have the angle . . . if Vigil had kept an eye on her while gouging his? This was probably just the desperation talking, but hope was all Leonard had left. He rocked back and sat down on his bony ass, kicked his legs out to scoot himself toward the wall, and put a few extra feet between him and the bum. He figured he could take one more round of agony before he tapped.

"Go. Fuck. Ya-muther," he said with his last ounce of balls.

Once more, Vigil shook his head, eyes full of sorrow. And once more, he closed the gap. But this time, Mira could slip in behind without him noticing.

The question was, would she?

Vigil took a knee and pinched his broken nose between fingers so strong they might as well've been pliers. He jerked left. He jerked right. He jammed up. He yanked down. Leonard hurt so bad it was surreal—like he *was* the pain, hallucinating a body. "Please!" he begged. Vigil ignored him, working his snout like a gearshift. Right before he lost consciousness, Mira showed her hand.

"Christ, Vigil! This isn't how we rehearsed it. *First* he disables the deadman's switch, *then* we take his bitcoin. Remember? Look at him—he's about to stroke out."

Hearing her betrayal was even worse than the torture. How could he have been so stupid? How could she? The only silver lining was that Mira's objection prompted the bum to let go of his nose. A temporary reprieve as it turned out. Minuscule and fleeting.

Vigil shrugged. Went to work on Leonard's eye again. A bit more pressure than last time. Faster laps around the cornea. "Change of plans," he quipped. "Roll with it."

"*Yooouuuuu-fuuuuuuuuck-innnnnnggggg-cuuuuunt!*" The Lion roared. "He's going to kill me! My heart! Oh shit, my heart! *Please—*"

Bang!

The shot was thunderous in the small room. Glass and sparks from the bullseye-ed security monitor rained down like warm hail, scenting the air with noxious fumes from melted plastic and rare-earth metals mined by slaves in the Congo. To Leonard, it smelled like hope.

Vigil stood up and spun around. "Dammit, Mira. I'm not

gonna kill him yet. He's faking. Watch . . . " He reached for The Lion's nose again.

Leonard couldn't take anymore. "Okay! Okay! I'll tell you the password." It was the last thing he wanted to do, but he had to buy more time, and he couldn't handle more torment. Not without a breather.

"I'm listening."

"There's a book on my desk. Next to the keyboard."

Vigil found it. Read the title, *"A Princess of Mars,* by Edgar Rice Burroughs. That the one?"

"Yeah. Open it to the third chapter."

"Chapter three. 'My Advent on Mars.'"

"That's the one. The password is the entire third paragraph. Word for word. Except when you type it in, you'll replace every space with a dash, and every lowercase 'l' with a capital 'L'. Same thing for all the lowercase *g's*—make them all capitals."

"Good," Vigil said. "But I'll need to verify it."

Leonard told him the software he used to access his crypto wallet and got him logged-in. Vigil used his pistol as a paperweight to keep the moldering paperback open to the correct page. Maybe he could type, maybe not, but for this tedious task the bum hunted-and-pecked each character into the password field. Mira was gnawing at the inside of her cheek like it was ten-year-old jerky, no doubt anxious and wondering whether she'd placed the right bet. *You bet wrong, bitch. But you can still win back Elise's life if you play your cards right.* Her Glock was still aimed at his head. Leonard needed her to pivot and point the weapon at the man she truly ought to fear.

With Vigil distracted at his computer, he made his move.

Tapping into his inner Al Pacino, Leonard contorted his battered face into an expression of plaintive despair and nodded toward the bum. Mira's pistol veered in his direction

369

ever so slightly, but in the end she kept it pointed at The Lion.

"Bingo." Vigil said. "Or should I say, *Yacht-zee.*" He whistled. "Damn, that's a lot of zeroes."

If he transferred the bitcoin to a different wallet, then Leonard might as well force Mira to suicide him. There'd be no point in surviving. As soon as Lebedev learned that he'd bungled the deal, the old school Bratva boss would send his hitmen, as promised. And those evil fucks would make Vigil's abuse feel like a night at the Bunny Ranch.

"Do you really think he'll share the bitcoin with you, Mira? Are you that fuckin' stupid? He played you. Just like you played me. Don't forget: I die, Elise dies—for nothin'. He's keeping it all for himself, I promise you. A criminal recognizes his own kind."

"Shut up, Grabasso."

There was an urgency in his voice that hadn't been there before. Mira must've heard it, too. Her aim wavered a little in Vigil's direction.

"The second he makes the transfer, he's done with you, Mira. If he really wanted to disable the deadman's switch, he'd have stuck to your plan and forced me to do it first-thing. Shoot him! Before it's too late. I swear on my father's grave I'll honor our arrangement. Elise lives *and* I'll give you half."

Vigil just shook his head and chuckled. Used the keyboard to type something. The login and password to his bank account, presumably.

The balls on this guy. Leonard could see what the bum couldn't: A seed of doubt had taken root in Mira's heart. All he had to do was water it.

She said, "We can handle the bank transfers later. I need to know my daughter's safe. Do what you have to do."

Vigil kept typing. "Just give me a second. Almost done."

"See! He's fuckin' you. Elise will die and you won't get shit. Come on, Getty. Please. I'll take my guy off Elise and give you seventy-five percent of the take."

Mira adjusted her aim. Now the gun wasn't pointed at Leonard. Now, it was pointing at the bum.

Vigil was oblivious. The cocky sonofabitch was pointing and clicking and mashing the keys like James Patterson on Adderall.

"Eighty percent," Mira said.

"Deal!"

She pulled the trigger and shot Vigil in the back.

THE BIG MAN JERKED AS THE BULLET HIT HIM between the shoulder blades. He gasped, clutching his chest, and attempted to spin around to confront his killer. But Vigil only made it halfway. His legs buckled and he collapsed, first to his knees, and then timbering forward as he succumbed to his wound.

The best part was, Leonard got to see the look on his face before he died. All the testosterone-fueled bravado and puffed-out-chest pride—sucked right out of him—replaced with wide-eyed shock and disbelief and the doubled-over gut punch of Mira's ultimate betrayal. He'd have preferred to witness it through both eyes. And without the blurred vision from the broken nose and tears. But beggars couldn't be choosers. "I told you, Mira. Dumb muscle. Always their downfall."

Mira said nothing.

He scrambled to his feet, hobbled over to the fallen giant, and kicked him as hard as he could in the ribs. "*Shit!*" Even dead, the big guy was built different. Felt like soccer-kicking a felled tree. Leonard added a bruised foot to his list of ailments.

Blood was wicking into the bum's denim shirt in a rapidly expanding puddle. "Hurry, let's get on him the tarp." He was a heavy SOB alright, but they managed before making too much of a mess. "Raymond! Take your hand off your prick and get in here."

The brilliant, blushing house-tard stepped through the open vault door, but didn't make eye contact with Mira. And sure enough, he sported a monumental waste of wood for a man too meek to fuck an actual flesh-and-blood female.

"Drag him outside and fertilize the garden."

Raymond wasn't as formidable as Vigil (and constitutionally incapable of harming a living soul), but the 6-foot, 2-inch autistic savant was stupid strong. He nodded sheepishly and bent to the task.

Leonard fetched his suitcase, an icepack, and some eye drops and rejoined Mira in the safe room. "Mariana's pitching a fit upstairs. Dumb bitch called 911. We'll take the tunnel."

As they were about to make their descent through the escape hatch, Leonard heard something. "Wait," he said. "Listen . . . "

From the backyard came a terrible and unmistakable grinding squeal.

The sound a dead body makes going through a wood chipper.

CHAPTER
SEVENTY-FOUR

H is head throbbed, his eye burned, and his broken nose made it difficult to breathe. Yet, Leonard smiled. He was officially in the wind.

They hopped on the electric scooter and zoomed to the farmhouse. Mira hugged his waist for balance, and he was pretty sure he felt her convulse once or twice in a failed attempt to hold back tears. He wasn't surprised. She had a soft spot for the bum. And who could blame her? Vigil had been a fuckin' specimen. A beast of a man. Descended from Vikings, if Leonard had to guess. It was a good thing his Roman ancestors never encountered Norseman in battle—*to the victors, go the spoils;* those pale fucks would've spread their seed all the way to Sicily (though he wouldn't have minded being a little taller).

They paused below the hatch under the farmhouse and listened until they heard a pair of sirens scream past on the road toward his compound. When they emerged from the tunnel Mira pushed the button for the garage door opener. Her Prius blocked them in.

"Move that thing outta the way."

"Negative," Mira said. "I'm returning it to the airport."

"Bitch, do you not see this Range Rover? I'm not ridin' in that fabric-upholstered econobox."

"I'm a federal employee. Abandoning a rental vehicle with my name on the lease, a mile away from three dead bodies, isn't conducive to keeping my job."

"Do you have any idea how much eighty percent of $500 million dollars is? You ain't gonna need a job no more."

"And then what? Live in hiding the rest of my life? Never see my daughter again? Unlike you, I'm not a monster."

"Okay, Saint Mira. Fuck wettin' your beak for savin' my ass, then. I'll keep all the filthy lucre." Which was what was going to happen, anyway, he thought. *'Cause you ain't gonna be alive to spend it.*

IT WAS A THREE-AND-A-HALF HOUR DRIVE TO Dallas, but it took them four on account of Leonard's geriatric bladder. Other than to convey details concerning the cash drop, they spoke very little. He wanted to beat Mira senseless for daring to cross him, and he was sure the feeling was mutual.

Their flight didn't leave until late that evening, so he got his nose bandaged at an urgent care near the airport. As for his eye, the doctor said there was no permanent damage and his vision would likely improve in the coming weeks.

They spent the rest of the day in the Qatar Airways lounge, located in Terminal D inside a section of DFW dubbed The Club. Leonard wasn't impressed. Beat the food court or the boarding area, but not by much. Formica tables, faux leather recliners, and stale food on hot plates beneath plastic lids. He'd seen nicer amenities in the lobby of a Best Western.

Mira worked on her laptop in one of the cubicles. Leonard

checked on her periodically for status updates. Last night's letdown aside, he'd been very lucky to have Getty as a resource. She got shit done:

A scanner to detect transponders hidden in the bundles of $100s? *Check.*

Specialists to sample random bills to spot counterfeits? *Check.*

A security detail to guard the exchange? *Check.*

Thanks to her unique skill sets (and his unlimited budget for bribes), key logistics were quickly coming together. Leonard had already lined up the forklift driver who would unload the pallets of currency, as well as a scale to weigh the cash. All that remained was how to get the money from the warehouse to his new home in the Caucasus mountains. Easier said than done, because the Russians might decide to stick around after the exchange and hijack his score en route.

Mira didn't seem too worried. "I'm on it."

An hour later, she had a workaround. The cash would be mixed with legitimate consumer goods before it ever left the warehouse, and then loaded into five different shipping containers. The shipping containers would be hauled by truck to the port in Batumi, tagged with RFID chips upon arrival, and then placed onto a ship bound for Athens. There, the containers would be unloaded with thousands of others, and moved to the freight yard. Finally, a Greek freight forwarder would ship the right containers back to Poti (the other major seaport in Georgia), where Leonard could arrange for delivery at his leisure. As long as the Russians didn't have access to the Bills of Lading, they'd have no way of knowing which shipment, let alone which containers his loot had been stored in. Crude, but it would get the job done.

They boarded at 10:15 PM. First class, of course, because Leonard could afford it. With the layover in Doha, they had twenty-four hours of travel ahead of them, and Mira took full advantage. By the time they passed through Georgian immigration, she had most of the pieces in place.

So it came to pass that a mere two days after landing in his new country of residence, Leonidas Galani—aka Leonard Grainger, aka Lenny The Lion Grabasso, aka LG—stood with Mira Getty next to dock door 19 in a warehouse located in Ponichala, a dreary industrial district south of Tbilisi. He was anxious to seal the deal with his Russian buyers. And she was no doubt eager for him to cancel the contract on Elise.

Only one of them would leave happy.

CHAPTER
SEVENTY-FIVE

I t was very quiet. The exchange was scheduled for midnight, and unlike in the U.S., twenty-four-hour facilities were uncommon in Georgia. Many of the surrounding buildings were falling down or abandoned. There were rats in the walls. There were rats in attendance.

His Russian contact, Anton Krylov, showed up to the meet on time wearing a black suit. He was joined by an entourage of three men. They wore black *Spetsnaz*-style fatigues accessorized with ski masks, body armor, and AKS-74U assault rifles.

Leonard's security was ten men armed with ancient AK-47s. They were lined up beside the forklift operator a short distance away from the dock door. Dressed in threadbare Soviet-era camo, they looked shabby compared to Krylov's crew. They also wore ski masks, but he didn't need to see their faces to know the Russians made them nervous. Which was fair, given Vladimir Putin's recent incursions into bordering countries and previously ceded lands.

The atmosphere was tense. There were few pleasantries exchanged. Mostly grunts and nods and kilometer-long stares. Everyone was here to do business. Leonard's cash would arrive soon, Krylov explained. The truck had been delayed briefly. The Lion was annoyed, but hid it well enough. There was nothing to be gained by berating the man, and much to lose.

After ten minutes of standing around with their thumbs up their asses, however, the silence became awkward. Leonard noticed Krylov's guards ogling Getty and used it as an excuse to fill the dead air. "This is my . . . partner. Her name is—"

"Never fucking mind what my name is," Mira finished.

"My bad," he said. "I keep forgettin' she prefers Sugar Tits."

Krylov laughed along with his men. Mira rolled her eyes but said nothing, no doubt appreciating the value in tamping down the tension.

Encouraged, Leonard offered more small talk. "When the truck gets here, we'll unload the pallets, scan for bugs, and make sure it ain't light. Everything checks out, I give you my private key. You verify it's good, and never again our paths shall cross."

Krylov nodded at his phone. "I will call driver."

He spoke in Russian, but Leonard didn't need a translator. The *where-the-fuck-are-you* tone sufficed.

Krylov held up two fingers. "Almost here."

Moments later they heard the telltale rumble of a big diesel engine, lining up to back in. Leonard pressed a button on the wall and the aluminum door rattled open. Krylov leaned out and gave the driver a thumbs-up. A bald man with a beer gut hopped out of the cab holding bolt cutters and walked to the rear of the trailer. He cut the metal pin, levered open the latch, and swung the doors out wide, securing them to the sides of the trailer with small hooks on a length of chain. Leonard was comforted by the sight of shrink-wrapped stacks of cash on pallets and relieved there wasn't a team of heavily armed Russian soldiers also in tow. The driver returned to the cab and finished backing in. The trailer bumped the dock, the air brakes hissed, and the forklift operator got to work.

Ten minutes later, the pallets were all on the warehouse floor in a neat line. Mira nodded to a member of the security team and he used a device about the size of a TV remote to wand for transmitters.

"Clean."

One of the guards wheeled out a portable industrial scale. Since they were in Europe, the math was easy and the numbers were round. All U.S. paper currency weighs one gram per bill; five hundred million USD in $100 bills weighs 5,000 kilograms. Therefore, each of the ten pallets should hold 500 kilograms worth of currency. Mira recorded the weights. After zeroing the scale at eighteen kilograms (the standard weight of a wooden pallet), all ten came in at the expected 500 kilos, give or take.

Next, three women dressed in gray slacks and white blouses sampled the individual bundles to ensure they weren't laced with lesser notes. This was necessary because, indeed, *all* U.S. paper currency weighs the same, no matter the denomination. They also checked for counterfeits. It wasn't feasible to examine all the money, but by inspecting a dozen or so bundles selected at random from each pallet, one could be reasonably confident that neighboring bills were also legit.

When the women were finished they nodded an okay to Mira.

"Our money is good," Krylov said. "Now you give password."

To save time, Leonard had already copied and pasted the passage from the ebook version of the Edgar Rice Burroughs classic, and made the necessary substitutions in a separate text file on his iPhone. He wanted the handoff to go as smoothly as possible. Mira had shown him how to use AirDrop if Krylov had an iOS device, or how he could text the private key if—like the Russian military—he relied on inferior technology. He switched on bluetooth and found Krylov's iPhone in the AirDrop menu and clicked the icon. A pinging noise sounded to commemorate the successful transfer.

"Now we access wallet."

Leonard nodded nervously even though he'd checked his balance on the ride over from the hotel, and all $2.5 billion worth of bitcoin was accounted for. In fact, he'd been checking obsessively since boarding the flight in Texas.

Krylov's nimble fingers poked at his screen as he opened the text file with Leonard's private key. He selected it, copied it to the clipboard, and then launched the wallet app. He was a much younger man than Leonard, and therefore far more adept at operating a smartphone.

Leonard held his breath.

Krylov frowned. Then the Russian repeated the same sequence of pokes and swipes before emphatically tapping the screen one last time. He looked up from his phone. Expression blank. "There is problem."

"What problem?" Leonard said, his voice straining up an octave.

"Password is no good."

"Really?" Leonard said, legitimately perplexed.

"You are old man. Old eyes. Maybe you type mistake."

"I must've. Lemme double check." Droplets of sweat appeared on his forehead as he pulled up the text file and examined it word for word, letter by letter, one painstaking symbol at a time. All the dashes and Ls and Gs had been substituted accurately. Of course they had—he'd also been copying and pasting in the password every time he'd checked the balance. "You must be doin' something wrong on your end." Leonard held out his hand, said, "Mind if I have a look?"

Krylov looked at him as if he'd volunteered to babysit his preteen daughter. "Come," he said, motioning for Leonard to stand beside him.

Leonard approached the man tentatively, afraid to make any sudden movements.

Krylov repeated the exact steps that had already failed.

"Lemme try on my phone," Leonard said, thinking: *How could this be happening?*

He selected the private key from the file.

Copied it to the clipboard.

Pasted it into the field under his login in the crypto wallet app.

Login failed. The password you entered is incorrect.

"Deal is off." Krylov stepped away from Leonard and signaled to his trio of *Spetsnaz* comrades. They raised their weapons.

Pop!-pop!-pop!—three shots in rapid succession—*pop!*— and then a fourth . . . all of which The Lion heard because he wasn't the target.

Not yet.

CHAPTER SEVENTY-SIX

"For Ukraine," Vigil said.

The triple-tap—head shots, because of their body armor—had eliminated the guards, while the fourth bullet tore through the chest of the Russian in the black suit. Everyone was so fixated on the unfolding password drama, they hadn't noticed him emerging from the shadows. Well, everyone except Mira and the men she recruited for the security detail. They *had* noticed Vigil's stealthy approach. But then, they'd been expecting him.

Leonard "The Lion" Grabasso? Not so much.

"We'll take it from here," Mira said. "Help yourselves on the way out." The local contractors each pocketed a stack of bills worth $10,000 en route to the exit. Not bad for a few minutes of unskilled labor. Most of them hadn't even shot a gun before.

Leonard was splatter-painted with blood and brains from the fallen Russians but he didn't even notice. He was gaping at Vigil who now stood a few feet away holding a pistol.

"But I *saw* her kill you."

"No," Mira said. "You saw what we wanted you to see."

"And what you didn't see was no accident," Vigil added.

Leonard shook his head, like maybe he was clearing the cobwebs after a concussion. "But I watched—"

"*Shhh*," Mira interrupted. "We'll break it down for you. I want you to grasp just how badly you got played."

Leonard shifted his weight to one leg and crossed his arms, grinning like an idiot—like he couldn't wait to deliver the punchline of a crass joke he'd filed away for just such an occasion.

"You knew I'd do anything to keep my daughter safe," she said. "And so when I 'admitted' to coming clean to Vigil, I knew you'd buy my explanation. You've gotten so used to threatening her life to get what you want from me, you assumed my last minute 'betrayal' of a mere 'bum' meant that I'd come to my senses and accepted you as her only possible savior. You still needed my help, after all. So you agreed to go through with the plan, confident in your ultimate trump card."

Vigil picked up where she left off. "Now you might be wondering, *if this was all about saving Elise, why didn't he stick to the script and torture me until I disabled the deadman's switch?*

"Simple: Because when I agreed to help Mira, I'd already decided that merely killing you wasn't good enough. That not only Prosser's family, but *all* your victims' loved ones should be compensated—that they'd finally receive the small measure of justice you denied them with your plea deals, and your extortion, and your bribes. So then the challenge became, how to save Elise *and* put your ill-gotten gains to good use?"

"But as you well know," Mira said, "crypto currency can be traced. And as I pointed out to Vigil, we could no more distribute the bitcoin to victims' families, than you could spend it without getting caught."

"Lucky for us, you found a buyer who could pay cash. But then we had a different problem: If I forced you to disable the deadman's switch, and Mira failed to shoot me in the back like she'd promised, then obviously you'd have known we screwed you. And while it would've been easy enough to persuade you to go through with the deal, we were worried you might fuck it up somehow—maybe tip off the Russians, hoping to collect at least some of the cash.

Mira said, "I know what you're thinking: *But why did Vigil pretend to break bad? Couldn't he have forced me to disable the dead-man's switch, and then have Mira fake the shot so I wouldn't see the deception?*

"Maybe. But if we did it that way, then I'd have had no incentive to keep helping you, beyond whatever money you tried to bribe me with. You might've gotten suspicious—maybe fired a few shots of your own into Vigil's back just to make sure he was really dead."

"So to really sell you," Vigil said, "I made it look like I'd conned her, too. That way, Mira's shot looked like revenge, and you believed you still had leverage over her. Hell, you probably do even now—but we'll get to that—I don't wanna skip any highlights. Mira, tell him about the squibs."

"There's a company out of Pittsburg called Squib FX. They make air powered devices that simulate gunshot impacts. 'Blood squibs' as they're referred to by stunt coordinators in Hollywood, but the U.S. Marshals also use them in training exercises. I had them overnight a rig for Vigil. When he clutched his chest, a small pressure pad taped to his sternum activated the device. The round I put into your security monitor was live, but that was just to prime you. The shot I fired at him was a blank."

"Speaking of those security monitors," Vigil interjected, "the two I smashed with your head? Those weren't random. I targeted the screens displaying footage from the back deck and the yard so you wouldn't be able to see what really happened when Raymond got me to the wood chipper.

"It wasn't pretty. I let him drag me all the way out there. He fired it up and when he leaned down to hoist me over his shoulder, I opened my eyes and introduced myself. Poor guy. Passed out cold. Naturally, I caught him and eased him down so he didn't hurt himself, but one of your dogs wasn't havin' it. He lunged for my throat. I sidestepped. He landed in the chute and Kibbles 'n Bits came out the other end. I felt pretty bad about it, but the female dog seemed grateful—licked my hand—like she was happy to be rid of the male dog."

If Leonard was upset about his Doberman's demise, his face didn't register it. The smirk remained.

Mira said, "Remember arguing with me about having to ride in the rented Prius? That was the plan all along. Because Vigil *also* needed to get to the airport. And he needed to get there faster than we did. As luck would have it, a 2021 Land Rover Defender is much faster than a Prius. Vigil, why don't you tell Leonard why you had to hustle to the airport."

"Not only did I need to fly here to this beautiful country," he said, "I had to take care of a little business in the northeast, ASAP. Boston, in particular. You know—the major metropolitan area across the river from Cambridge, where Harvard University is located? Elise goes to school there. Mira tells me she'll graduate in a year. Double major. She's doing well.

"You know who's *not* doing so well? The hitman you hired to keep tabs on her. He drowned. Someone may have thrown him off a bridge." Vigil paused a moment to let this sink in.

Grabasso's smirk melted faster than gelato.

"Anything you'd like to add, Mira?"

"Just one thing," she said, striding to the ex-gangster until they were nose-to-bandaged-nose. "Call me Sugar Tits one more time, you piece of shit. Do it. I fucking dare you."

Grabasso said nothing.

"Do it! Call me Sugar Tits. See what happens."

"*Ssshhhhuuugar Tiii—*"

Mira head-butted him right in his broken nose. Grabasso howled in pain. She wasn't done—swept his legs out from under him and pummeled him with kicks until Vigil picked her up and pulled her away.

"You threatened to live-stream my daughter's rape, you sick fuck!"

Vigil didn't blame her. All those years she'd spent cowering under his thumb . . . all the rage she'd been forced to suppress—it had to go somewhere.

"Alright, alright. I'm done. Put me down."

He told Grabasso to get up. It took him a while after Mira's beating, but he managed to stand. "How does it feel, knowing that—for the first time in your undeservedly long life—someone held you accountable for the evil you've done?"

Grabasso's eyes lit up (his good eye, anyway) and a malignant sneer slowly spread across his swollen face. Then he opened his mouth to spew a final, remorseless quip:

Vigil shot him in the head.

"Don't care."

CHAPTER
SEVENTY-SEVEN

They loaded Grabasso's body into the semi trailer along with Krylov and his dead guards.

"Be right back."

Vigil took a stack of bills and went to speak with the driver. He found him conscious, and not exactly thrilled to see the guy who'd strangled him to sleep and then taped him to the steering wheel. The $10k helped convince him that no, Vigil wasn't going to kill him now, and yes, it would be a good idea to drive this load to a busy distributor, drop the trailer, and then disappear for a while—before Vigil changed his mind.

When he came back inside, Mira was busy repackaging the cash into smaller boxes. It was a lot of work, and very tedious, but together they got it done in a couple hours. The result was five large stacks of boxes to be intermingled with other freight and shipped back to the States. Plus a smaller sixth, totaling $20 million in cash, which was a generous payment for such a run-down building.

"Never thought I'd own a warehouse," Mira said. "If only for a couple weeks."

They agreed Elise would put her International Finance

education to good use this summer, doling out the money to victims' families as discretely as possible. Mira offered to set aside whatever Vigil thought was fair for all that he'd done, but he declined.

"It was never about the money."

"Of course not," Mira said. "It's just . . . I can never thank you enough."

He considered broaching the topic of a transfer again. Out of Witness Protection, to something with fewer ethical compromises. But if it wasn't her idea, it wouldn't mean as much. He said, "Speaking of money I won't spend—would you like to know what I changed the password to?"

"I guess. I mean, if the Feds weren't already watching the wallet, it's only a matter of time. But then again, if you only transferred small amounts . . . not too frequently . . . *Hmmm.* You might get away with it. And the way technology changes —who knows? Sounds like a rainy day fund at the very least."

Vigil nodded. "For you too. And Elise."

"Well, are you going to give me the password?"

"*Password,*" Vigil said. "All lowercase."

Mira rolled her eyes. "For a bitcoin wallet worth billions? You're unbelievable. You know that, right?"

"That's what you keep telling me."

"I'd like to tell you one more time," she said behind a salacious grin.

"Just *one* more?" he teased.

Mira had booked them a room at the Ambassadori. Five stars. A first for Vigil, and a fitting end to a week of firsts: First time overseas, first time in a government database, first time playing dead.

The hotel was a short walk from Freedom Square in the cultural heart of Tbilisi, and before their bodies became too predictable they toured the city together for a day. They visited the sulfur baths and the Sameba Cathedral. Ate

Khachapuri, a boat-shaped bread dish topped with eggs, cheese, and butter. It was a nice change of pace for Vigil, who usually kept himself company. But neither of them were under any illusion that their brief affair would continue stateside.

They spent one more night together. Mira would stay behind in Tbilisi for another week to manage the shipments, and Vigil was flying back to the U.S. in the morning. They made the most of it.

When he woke she'd already left for the warehouse. There was a note taped to the bathroom mirror:

I'm no good at goodbyes. But please know, I am forever grateful.

~ Mira

P.S. As promised, your father's journals . . .

↓

On the counter was a USB stick. Now he'd have to purchase a computer. Another first. He found an electronics store on the way to the airport and bought a cheap laptop.

Ticket counters were still a thing, which didn't seem weird because he'd never booked a flight before, online or otherwise. The agent told him what was available. Returning to Texas so soon after the trouble in Carlin seemed like a bad idea, but more than that, Vigil had never been keen on retracing his steps. He decided to fly to Los Angeles. New York was the other option, but it was still cold this time of year and he wanted some time alone in the wilderness.

Usually when he had a lot of time to kill he read a paperback. Thrillers or crime novels or the odd western, typically.

This time it was nonfiction. When he inserted the thumb drive, a long list of files with an extension of .pdf was displayed. Each filename was prefixed with a date stamp, and so a quick glance confirmed Mira's earlier estimate; the drive contained thirteen-plus years of his dad's writing.

It was much more than a simple diary. It was the story of a young father, and a manifesto of a hard man . . . an instruction manual detailing how to survive a societal collapse (among other things). He was tempted to skip to the most recent entries, but resisted the urge. Vigil didn't like jumping to conclusions, and he rarely did.

The only break he took from reading was to check the status of Joe Rogan's new club. The flight attendant helped him connect to the internet and he googled the homepage for the Comedy Mothership in Austin, Texas. There had been a few delays and the grand opening wasn't until the first week in March, which was still over a month away. Maybe he'd attend. Maybe not. After he'd reached a certain point in his father's journals, Vigil was no longer in the mood for comedy.

If you enjoyed this *Nate Vigil Thriller*,
PLEASE CLICK HERE TO LEAVE A REVIEW
Written reviews help the most, but star ratings are just as welcome. It really helps spread the word. Thanks!

AN EXCLUSIVE OFFER FOR FINISHERS

You've made it to THE END, but don't worry, there's more Nate Vigil waiting for you on my website:

https://conor.black

The novella: *Vigil, A Nate Vigil, Vigilante Thriller,* is my thanks for the honor of having you as a reader. I know there's a lot of books you could've read, and you chose mine. It means a lot to me. Truly.

Keep Reading My Friend,

Conor Black

Dedicated to my sweet Eve. Always and forever.

CREDITS AND ACKNOWLEDGMENTS

I'm grateful for the feedback and encouragement from Don & Claudia Whitsitt, and for being the family I never had. I love you both so much.

A big thanks to Jason Hook, the "King of Northwoods Noir," for all your helpful suggestions during the writing process.

Motivation comes in many forms; I'd like to thank Michael Steven Gregory for throwing some fuel on the fire, and for building a wonderful community of writers and friends—a.k.a. The Southern California Writers' Conference. [https://writersconference.com]

Thanks to Ryan Hunter and Laura Perkins for [redacted].

ABOUT THE AUTHOR

 **CONOR BLACK** is the author of the *Nate Vigil Thrillers*. For readers who enjoy lone wolf heroes, cunning conspiracies, and artful violence.

Bad people do bad things in his books—but unlike your boss, or degenerate billionaires who always seem to get away with it in the real world—his protagonists deliver justice to them by THE END, no matter how high the cost.

Conor lives near the ocean in Southern California with his beautiful partner in crime, Sweet Eve, and his soft, yet savage cat, Picasso.

Made in United States
Orlando, FL
23 April 2024

46100323R00238